Class No. _____ F _____ Acc No. C 59249

Author: FRANCOME, J. Loc: _____ 5 APR 199

-2 APR 1996

LEABHARLANN
CHONDAE AN CHABHAIN

1. This book may be kept three weeks. It is to be returned on / before the last date stamped below.
2. A fine of 20p will be charged for every week or part of week a book is overdue.

John Francome

STONE COLD
•
STUD POKER

John Francome

STONE COLD

●

STUD POKER

CHANCELLOR
PRESS

Stone Cold first published in Great Britain in 1990
by Headline Book Publishing Plc.

Stud Poker first published in Great Britain in 1991
by Headline Book Publishing Plc.

This collected volume first published in 1992
by Chancellor Press
an imprint of
Reed International Books Limited
Michelin House
81 Fulham Road
London SW3 6RB

Published by arrangement with Headline Book Publishing Plc.

ISBN 1 85152 212 3

Printed in Great Britain by the Bath Press.

Contents

STONE COLD

Acknowledgement

The author would particularly like to thank Terence Blacker for his invaluable help in the preparation of his manuscript.

Chapter 1

The air-conditioning in the large blue Mercedes had been pumping out cold air for forty-five minutes, but the sweat was still trickling down the two rolls of fat on the driver's neck. The smell in the car – essence of Harry Short, mingling with stale cigar smoke – was none too sweet but Harry didn't mind. He was a good three stones overweight, it was the hottest summer on record and he was just about to become the most successful racehorse trainer in Britain. If that wasn't an excuse for generating a bit of your own heat, what was?

Harry shifted his bulk in the seat of the car and smiled, an unnerving sight. Just over six foot tall with straight brown hair cut brutally short at the sides, he looked like a bouncer who somewhere along the line had got lucky, which is what he was. There was a high colour to his cheeks, suggesting a man with a temper straining at the leash like an angry Rottweiler. Sometimes the leash snapped. Right now the thought of his horse Pendero getting beaten this afternoon made him grip the large steering wheel so tightly he could feel the moisture squeezing from his palms. It had been a year, a year of planning. If it all went wrong, he really didn't know what he would do. Some act of mindless violence probably.

He loosened the collar of his shirt where a water-line of sweat was visible.

'Can't happen,' he muttered. 'Cannot happen.'

He pressed a fat finger at the car radio and the sound of strings filled the car. Mantovani, he loved it. Sweet, soft and easy – everything Harry Short was not.

There were two ways to win the flat trainers championship, Harry reflected. One was to be born into a rich racing family, like the two chinless wallies above him in the current winners table, Edward Denton and Ian Gardem. Harry winced at the mere thought of them. Without inherited wealth, those two couldn't have held down a job mucking out, let alone training expensive horses. Their success had been assured the moment their mothers had lain back and thought of England. No way was Harry Short hung up on class – he just hated any bastard that went to public school.

Then there was the other way to the top, Harry's way. He had been born into a poor family in Doncaster. Everything he knew about horses he had learnt from the gypsies who camped south of the racecourse. He understood horses – or, rather, they understood him and his none too subtle methods. Briefly he had wanted to be a jockey but, as little Harry became big Harry, the dream receded.

He worked the clubs for a while, on the security side, but racing was what mattered to him. Thanks to a spot of friendly pressure – Harry didn't like to think of it as blackmail – he landed a job as assistant to a trainer with an unfortunate fondness for curb-crawling on Saturday nights and, within a couple of years, he had seen more of the underbelly of racing than the Dentons and Gardems would see in a lifetime. When his boss was obliged to retire after someone thoughtlessly exposed him to the press, Harry Short took over the yard.

Today, ten years later, Harry was a name to be reckoned with. He wasn't liked by those who ran racing, or by other trainers. He wasn't much liked by his owners either; he treated them with careless contempt. But he did get winners when it mattered.

Like at 3.30 this afternoon at Ascot with a four-year-old called Pendero.

Harry smiled. It was the sweetest deal you could imagine. Pendero had run four times this season and his form, which read 4–3–5–2, was enough for the handicapper to give him nine stone for the race at Ascot. But then, on this occasion, the handicapper was himself working under a handicap. He didn't know, for example, that Pendero's best distance was a mile and a half. All he knew was that the horse was better than average over a mile. He didn't know either that last time our jockey had been warned that if he was seen doing anything more strenuous than breathing during the race he would get a good hiding. He didn't know that, just to make sure, his trainer had put an extra stone of lead in his weight cloth to anchor him.

The Kings' Food Handicap, Ascot, was hardly the richest race in the calendar, being worth a mere £20,000 to the winner, but for Harry Short it mattered more than a classic. It would give him what he needed to crack the magic circle of fashionable trainers; a blue-chip owner rather than the fly-by-night builders, nightclub owners and footballers that he mostly dealt with at present. A moneyed lord would do it but an Arab was even better. It gave you credibility, class – suddenly everybody would want to know him.

Harry had set his sights on Ibn Fayoud al Hassan, which translated as Son of Fayoud of the House of Hassan. His English friends called him Ibn or Ib for short. The house in question happened to be royal. In Arab terms that meant rich, too, which was more than could be said for most of the British variety.

It was rumoured in the business that young Ibn Fayoud was in a spot of financial bother. He was something of a playboy, very different from his famous wealthy father. According to Harry Short's sources, he owed a cool £600,000 to Reg Butler Ltd, a chain of bookmakers much respected by gamblers on account of the risk of quite serious injury to the person if you didn't respect them.

Jack Butler now ran the firm. He was thirty-six and not an unreasonable man; he knew you didn't go around breaking the legs of rich Arabs who owed you a bit of cash – at least not if the Arab in question had a daddy for whom the honour of the family was more important than a mere six-figure gambling debt. On the other hand, the Butler family honour mattered too. Once the word spread that Jack was owed six hundred big ones by someone who was still walking around in perfectly good health, his reputation would take no end of a hammering. So one of Jack's men had a quiet word with Ibn Fayoud to the effect that, if he didn't see his way to clearing the debt plus interest by the end of the season, Mr Butler would have no alternative but to take his problem to the Sheikh.

It was at the Newmarket Craven meeting that Ibn Fayoud, now desperate, was approached by an unlikely benefactor in the form of Harry Short. He had heard of Ibn Fayoud's little problem and he had a solution. In three months' time he would give the young Arab a stone cold certainty to clear his debts in one. All he would expect in return was that Ibn Fayoud should move his nine horses, currently being trained by Ian Denton, to Harry's yard. Ibn Fayoud had agreed.

Harry had booked a good apprentice to ease Pendero's task. With the seven-pound claim reducing his weight, the horse couldn't lose. The apprentice could even make a cock up and still win. Harry chuckled. Cock up? It was hardly the right phrase when his apprentice was one Kelly Connor.

The day started badly for Kelly. She'd had to ride out three lots before setting off for Ascot in her rusty Saab. Then she had a puncture on the way to the races. By the time she reached the weighing room, Harry Short was steaming like a pressure cooker.

'Walked the course yet?' he snapped by way of introduction. This was their first meeting.

Heads turned in the weighing room. Harry Short's rages were legendary and this one was warming up nicely.

'My car – '

'I'm not interested in your fucking car.'

Kelly sighed. 'I'm here,' she said, her smile sweet, her tone razor-sharp and so quiet that only Harry could hear. 'I know the course. If the horse is good enough, I'll win. Nothing else matters. All right . . . sir?'

Harry was taken aback. He wasn't used to backchat, not from female apprentices anyway. He flushed a deeper red. 'Get yourself ready then,' he growled and strode out of the weighing room.

It had taken five years for Kelly Connor to reach this moment, five years of hardship and dedication, five years of trying to make the world ignore the fact that she was bright, intelligent, goodlooking and female. Racing, she discovered, had no time for looks in a jockey; it distrusted brains. Her appearance – dark, slim, pale-skinned – which, in any other profession, would have been an advantage, was for her a liability.

Ever since she left school, she had worked for Bill Templeman, who kept a small string of horses but had a big reputation as a trainer. Bill and his wife Annie had been impressed by the way Kelly rode from the day she'd arrived on their doorstep. They had expected competence – after all, she was Frank Connor's daughter – but Kelly had something more; judgement yoked with an iron determination to win at all costs. There was a touch of class to her.

Bill had given her as many rides as he could but, with only twenty horses in his yard, the chances were limited. It had been Kelly who had pushed her career forward by ringing other trainers, riding work for as many people as she could, picking up whatever spare rides were going. Soon she had established a reputation as one of the most professional apprentices riding, and great value for her seven pounds. All she needed now was the opportunity to do well for one of the big stables. Then she would be on her way. The call from Harry Short asking her to ride Pendero at Ascot was what she'd been waiting for.

She had hesitated briefly. Short had a reputation as a ruthless womanizer – there had been talk of stable girls in his yard being the subject of his hefty, unpleasant attentions – and she was not naive enough to think that she was the only good apprentice available. So why her?

'Just get to the course in time for us to walk it,' he had ordered.

Kelly dismissed Short from her mind as she pulled on her silk breeches and changed into the orange and black colours of Pendero's owner Colonel Twyford. She had more important matters to think about.

In a small, tidy flat in Newmarket, Frank Connor sat in front of his television, occasionally glancing at his watch. Kelly's race was in forty-five minutes' time. It was unlike her not to ring him from the racecourse as soon as she arrived. Both of them had become used to his ritual, which had nothing to do with advice – Kelly was beyond needing help of that kind from her father – but was simply a ritual. 'Good luck, girl.' 'Thanks, Da.' It set them both up for the afternoon.

Normally Frank would have dismissed any worries about Kelly from his mind. An important spare ride, a notoriously difficult trainer for whom she had never ridden before; it was hardly surprising that she had forgotten to phone. After all, nobody knew the pressures of racing better than Frank Connor; Irish champion jockey at nineteen, winner in one season of both the George VI, the Gold Cup and the Irish National at twenty-three, and then at twenty-nine washed-up, just another has-been with a dodgy past. He knew all about the ups and downs, the winners and the losers. Most of all, the losers.

Frank Connor hated memories – there were no trophies in his flat, the only framed racing photographs were of Kelly – but recently the past had been stalking him like a hungry wolf. Not the winners, the laughs in the weighing room, the champagne, the congratulations, but the other side; clipped instructions over the phone, secret meetings, the look of bewilderment on trainers' and owners' faces, the jeers of the punters who knew, almost by instinct, that Frank boy, yesterday's folk hero, was now Connor, just another bent jock on the skids.

Once they got their claws into you, there was no escape. Frank had started drinking – not champagne in the Members' Bar now, but whisky on the morning of the race. The whirlpool of corruption and failure dragged him down faster with every season. There were scandals, rumours; he lost the best job in Irish racing, that of stable jockey to Tim Collins. Soon the only spare rides he was offered were dodgy jumpers, non-triers; the only trainers who used him were those who hadn't heard that Frank Connor was finished.

'Stop it,' Connor whispered to himself, trying to concentrate on the television, which was showing the race before Kelly's. That was the thing about the past. It wouldn't let you go. Even when you thought you'd shaken it – a new chapter, a new generation, a new future – it played itself again and again.

He opened a can of alcohol-free lager and thought of the day when he'd lost it all. Driving to Naas with his wife Mary to ride a novice that would surely bury him, the past caught up with him on a bend in the road outside Cork. Maybe it was the booze racing through his veins, or the worry, or simply fear. Whatever the cause, the result was the same. Connor's car had left the road at seventy miles an hour; he had hardly hit the brakes before it piled into a tree. He had regained consciousness twenty-four hours later and, when they had told him, he wished that he hadn't. Mary, one of the few people in Ireland who had trusted him, was dead. Killed, and by what? Racing? Corruption? No. Frank knew there was only one answer; Mary had been killed by her own husband.

His life had changed that day. He had quit racing and had never touched another drop of alcohol. In an attempt to escape the past, he had brought his daughter Kelly to England and settled in Newmarket where he worked part time in a garage. He had never spoken of the past to Kelly and had never encouraged her passion for horses. He had done everything in his power to stop her working in a yard after she had left school but racing was the only thing that interested her.

In spite of himself, Frank had willed her to succeed. He gave her advice on race-riding and, more importantly, warned her of the pitfalls and temptations ahead of her. But not only was Kelly a good little rider, she was wise, cooler by far than he had been at her age. It began to look as if she might just make it as long she, too, could escape the past.

The telephone rang and Frank leapt across the room.

'Kelly,' he said happily. 'I was worried that – '

'Have you spoken to her?'

It was the voice that, over the past week, he had come to dread.

Frank hesitated. 'You'll be finding out soon, sure enough.'

'Connor, we mean business. We've asked you for one little favour. One little item of parental influence.'

'You've . . . you've got nothing to worry about.'

'Good. Because all you had to do was explain very gently to your little girl not to try too hard this afternoon. We really hope you've done what you were told.'

'Have you finished?' Connor gripped the receiver with anger. 'I have a race to watch.'

'Oh, we're watching too, don't worry. It's going to be just like the old days. Watching a Connor pulling the back teeth out of a good thing.'

Frank Connor slammed down the receiver. In the background, the television commentator was reading out the runners and riders for the 3.30 at Ascot.

Just like the old days. The past was back. The past was now. But this time he was ready for it.

Kelly Connor had weighed out and was trying not to think of her father as she stood, waiting for Harry Short to collect the saddle. Although wining on Pendero was all that mattered now, it bothered her that she had been unable to ring Newmarket. Her father had been quiet and preoccupied over the last few days; Kelly had sensed that he had something to tell her but for some reason was holding back. Perhaps if Pendero won it would cheer him up.

The assistant to the Clerk of the Scales approached her. 'Call for you, Connor,' he said, nodding in the direction of a telephone in the corner. Kelly smiled with relief.

'I'll keep an eye on your saddle.' Damien Gould, one of the older jockeys Kelly seemed to meet every time she went racing, stood beside her. 'If Fat Harry turns up I'll give you a shout.'

'Thanks, Damien,' said Kelly. 'I won't be a minute.' She gave him the saddle and hurried across to the telephone.

'Hi,' she said eagerly.

'Hello.' The cool, laconic voice was not that of her father. 'This is Giles Williams, Associated Press. Do you have a moment?'

'A moment?' Kelly tried to conceal her impatience. 'I'm about to ride in a race.'

'Sorry,' said Williams dismissively. 'I'm not much of a racing man myself. I work on the magazine. Now,' the man ignored Kelly's attempt to interrupt him, 'I don't want to do the interview right this minute but I was hoping to set up a meeting when I could come down and see you at work for a sort of "Day in the Life of a Leading Woman Apprentice" piece.'

'I can't think of that – '

'Hopes, ambitions, boy friends, what you have for breakfast – human interest stuff. Anyway, I'll call you at your Mr Templeman's tomorrow morning, if I may. I think it could do you a bit of good, don't you?'

'All right. Tomorrow morning. Listen, I must go now. I – '

'Are you going to win?' Williams' voice was deceptively casual.

'Hope so.' Kelly hung up. Quickly she tried to phone her father but his line was engaged. She returned to where Damien was standing.

'Would you believe it? Some bloody journalist wanting an interview.'

Damien smiled with a hint of envy. It had been years since he was asked for a press interview. 'Lucky old you,' he said.

At that moment, Harry Short bustled into the weighing room to collect the saddle. Kelly was grateful that he hadn't seen her talking on the telephone. No doubt that would have been cue for another public exhibition of bad temper.

'Thanks, Damien,' she said quietly.

Gould watched her as she listened to Harry Short's instructions. Pretty little thing, she was. Too pretty for this game. For a moment, he felt bad about the task in hand, but then he thought of the money. Five grand to make sure a girl apprentice didn't win. It was going to be so easy, it was almost criminal.

Would she win? Kelly pondered the journalist's question as she walked out to the paddock. The previous night, she had looked at the form and concluded that, even with her seven-pound claim, Pendero would be lucky to run into a place. Yet Harry, for all his bluster, was a shrewd trainer and his confidence was infectious. You're only as good as your last race, they said, but Kelly knew that this particular race mattered more than most. If she won a good, televised handicap at Ascot, the offers would start coming in. On the other hand, ride a bad race and nobody would want to know.

As if reading her thoughts, Damien Gould winked at her as they made their way through the crowd around the paddock. 'Good luck, sexy,' he muttered. Kelly smiled.

Pendero looked magnificent. A strongly built grey, he was bred to be a sprinter but by some genetic queue-jumping had inherited his great-grandfather's stamina.

He had been weak as a two-year-old but last season had won a couple of good races over a mile. Yet this year, nothing.

Harry introduced her to the horse's owner Colonel Twyford, a red-faced old enthusiast who looked as if his heart would give out with too much excitement.

'He's straightforward,' said Harry, speaking to her with a quiet authority which Kelly found strange after his behaviour in the weighing room. 'Just settle him halfway down the field and aim to hit the front at the furlong marker. He stays well and he's got plenty of speed, so make sure you don't get into trouble.'

The sun was warm on Kelly's back and her confidence was growing with every stride as she cantered down to the start. Pendero was class; he didn't pull but took a nice hold of the bridle and had a long, easy stride that seemed to eat up the ground. For the first time, she understood what it was like to ride a real racehorse. Used to pushing tired, scraggy second-raters round the likes of Wolverhampton and Leicester, she now knew what she had been missing. It was like a pub pianist being let loose on a Steinway grand.

When she reached the start, Kelly let Pendero stop blowing before getting the girths checked and then made her way behind the stalls as the starter called out the jockeys' names and the handlers began to load them up. Pendero was drawn between Damien's horse Come Tomorrow and a big black horse ridden by Paul Clark which was known to be difficult to load up and normally entered the stalls last.

'Where you going?' Damien called across as they waited in the stalls.

Kelly pulled down her goggles. 'Halfway,' she shouted, and at that moment Clark's horse barged into the stalls and head-butted the front gate. Clark whipped the hood off its head and, within two seconds, the starter had pulled the lever and they were off.

Kelly caught hold of Pendero's mane as he sprang forward and was immediately into his stride. Once her body had adjusted to the new pace, she let go and settled him into the middle of the field as planned.

The ground was riding on the fast side and, as the field raced down the hill and picked up speed, Kelly found that she was only just able to hold her position. Even in this company, the race would not be run at such speed to the finish, so Kelly settled Pendero and waited for the pace to slow down. They had taken the bend at the bottom of the hill and were facing the uphill run to the finish that would sort the field out when Kelly felt Pendero hit his stride and begin to feel comfortable. He seemed to prefer galloping uphill and as they reached the final bend, she moved easily up into fifth place.

She took a quick look round. Nothing was going as well as Pendero. All she had to do was steer him and they'd be certain to win. She was imagining the post-race TV interview when the horse directly in front of her began to tire. There was room enough to move up on his inside but she was going so well that cheekiness of that sort was a needless risk. It was as she pulled to go round on the outside that it happened. Suddenly a horse appeared from nowhere and knocked her off balance towards the rails. Pendero briefly lost momentum but, in the time it took him to find his feet, the gap on the rails had disappeared. Kelly suddenly found herself tightly boxed in behind a horse going backwards.

She looked across at the jockey who stayed tight on her outside. It was Damien.

'You're going nowhere, sexy,' he said, almost conversationally. 'You're staying with me.'

In the stands, Harry Short gripped his binoculars with rage. 'She's losing her place,' he hissed through his teeth. 'The bitch has got herself boxed in.' Nearby, a pale, good-looking young Arab looked away from the race as if his last best hope had just died. On the rails, a bookmaker smiled.

One hundred miles away, Frank Connor groaned as he sat in front of the television. 'Oh, jeez, Kelly,' he said. 'They've done you now.'

The horse in front of Pendero was losing ground so quickly that, short of standing up in the irons and pulling Come Tomorrow's back teeth out, Damien Gould had no alternative but to go on, leaving Kelly behind him but now lengths off the leader. Those few immobilizing seconds would be enough to earn him his money. He kicked on. Maybe his horse would run into a place.

Behind Damien, Kelly Connor despairingly pulled Pendero from the rails and into Come Tomorrow's slipstream. The horse had lost his stride and, with less than a furlong and a half to go, the two leaders were battling it out some six lengths adrift of her. Briefly, like a distant echo, Kelly heard the voices which had haunted her ever since she had started riding in races. No strength, these women jockeys, no battle in them, no bottle. She changed her grip on the reins and, once again, Pendero was running. As Kelly passed Come Tomorrow, she knew she was riding for nothing now but her own pride.

Pendero felt as if he was giving his all but, a furlong from home, Kelly picked up her whip and gave him one good crack behind the saddle to make certain. The response was immediate. The early pace began to tell on the leading horses and, as Pendero lengthened his stride, they lost their rhythm, began to come back to him. There was just a slight chance. No strength, no battle, no bottle. With a hundred yards to run Kelly gave him one more crack, and then rode him out with hands and heels as the final uphill run took its toll on the leaders. Fifty yards from the post she passed them and won going away by a length and a half.

'She did it!' Frank Connor danced around the flat in Newmarket, laughing, tears in his eyes. The television was showing replays of the race's final stages; each time it looked as if Pendero could not possibly win and each time, in relentless slow-motion, she did. The commentator's words, 'Superbly ridden race . . . look at the way she kept him balanced. . .a tremendously promising apprentice', filtered through to Frank. Today it was all worth it, the pain of the past, the hardships; he only wished Mary were alive to see this moment. It was the best day of his life, better than any of his own big winners.

There was a ring at the door. With a joyful whoop, Frank bounded across the room. Maybe it was a neighbour, come to congratulate him. Or the milkman collecting payment. Or Jehovah's Witnesses. He didn't care, he'd tell them all about his brilliant daughter. Beaming with pride, he opened the door.

Two men stood before him, their hands hanging loose at their side. They wore heavy combat jackets and dark glasses. One of them placed a large booted foot in the door before Frank could slam it. They pushed their way in, bolting the door behind them.

'So,' said the larger of the two men. 'We hear congratulations are in order. Mind you, we're not surprised. That's why we stayed close at hand to help you celebrate.'

Frank backed towards the wall, his eyes darting from one to the other. He knew why they were here and he knew he had no chance of escape, but he didn't intend to go down without a fight.

The smaller of the two men yanked the telephone lead from the wall and with a weary sigh pulled a baseball bat from inside his combat jacket.

'You're a loser, Connor.' The man looked down at the weapon in his hand almost regretfully. 'You were a loser as a jockey. Then you lost your wife. Now you've landed your daughter right in it.'

As the man spoke, Frank lashed out at him with his right fist but missed as his target moved sharply to the side. The weight of his body kept Frank moving forward as another baseball bat crashed into his skull.

Pendero's lad could hardly speak for excitement as he led Kelly and his charge through the crowd at Ascot on their way to the winners' enclosure. He'd quite forgotten that he had been among those who had assumed his guv'nor had taken leave of his senses when he booked a girl apprentice for the ride. 'Brilliant,' he gasped, looking back at her as he scurried along with one hand on the reins.

'I couldn't have done it without him,' Kelly beamed. She was thinking of her father and the call that she would shortly be making to him.

Ahead, she saw Damien Gould glance round at her as Come Tomorrow was led away to be unsaddled. For a moment, Kelly held his stare with undisguised hostility.

'You ain't won nothing yet, sweetheart,' he said quietly.

Kelly looked away. There was something in the confidence of that leathery, taciturn face which, even in her moment of triumph, nagged at her like a distant alarm bell.

Chapter
2

'You nearly cocked that one up, didn't you?' Harry Short stood with his binoculars hanging round his neck in front of him as he reached out to pat Pendero. Apart from a dangerously high flush on his face and beads of perspiration on his brow, Harry showed little emotion as, amidst cheers from the crowd and shouted questions from a gaggle of pressmen, Kelly dismounted in the winners' enclosure.

'Someone didn't want us to win, that was all,' she said bending down to undo the circingle. It had been too much to expect gratitude or congratulations from him. Her father had often told her never to expect anything from a pig but a grunt, and she smiled to herself as she thought of it.

'In this game, darling,' said Harry with the first hint of a smile, 'No one wants you to win anything. Ever. Don't forget to weigh in.'

Kelly took off the saddle, gave Pendero a final pat and, half answering requests for her first reactions from the press, skipped down the steps into the weighing room. In spite of her apparent coolness, her mind raced with thoughts of the future. She knew that one race would hardly change her career overnight but it had been a spectacular win and it had been on TV. It was a breakthrough, the first significant rung on the ladder to the top.

She stepped on to the scales and called out her number to the Clerk at the desk, who looked up to check her weight. He was in his fifties, a typical racing functionary with horn-rimmed glasses and black hair slicked down with a military parting. There was something absurdly fussy about the way he looked at the scales, then down at the book in front of him, and then back at the scales. Kelly smiled.

'You're five pounds light,' he said.

At first Kelly thought he was joking, but Clerks of the Scales were not known for their sense of humour. She turned quickly round to look at the face of the huge black scales. She had weighed out at eight stone seven; now she was a shade under eight stone two. As the nightmare engulfed her, she felt sick to her stomach.

'It's not possible,' she said quietly. 'I put the lead in myself.'

'Stay on the scales, please,' said the Clerk. 'Mr Morley.' He called over a steward who was standing nearby. 'The winner's five pounds light.'

Nick Morley, one of the new generation of stewards, walked quickly over to the scales, his expression intent, to confirm what the Clerk had just said. Then he walked off to get a message announced over the tannoy system.

Word of what had happened spread from the weighing room well before the announcement was made. Kelly stood, pale and drawn, as Morley returned to her.

'The stewards will see you in five minutes,' he told her. 'You'd better give me your saddle and weight cloth.'

'*Objection to the winner by the Clerk of the Scales*,' droned the public address system as if announcing the late arrival of a train.

'Bitch!' Harry Short burst into the weighing room like a tidal wave. Nick Morley quickly moved between him and Kelly. 'Who was the bastard who paid you to do that?' screamed the Yorkshireman.

In a low, shaky voice, Kelly said, 'It wasn't me. I don't know how it happened.'

And then she remembered who'd looked after her saddle and the look on Damien's face as they walked in.

'You're bent,' Short was yelling, his eyes bulging in their sockets. 'I'll see you never get another ride.'

Morley pushed him back, more firmly this time. 'Any more of that, Short, and you'll be in front of the stewards too.'

Outside the weighing room, journalists were straining to hear what was being said. 'D'you have any comment, Harry?' one called out.

Short looked at Kelly with hatred in his eyes.

'You bet I do,' he said.

Jack Butler was chatting to a fellow bookmaker when the announcement came through. *Objection to the winner of* – coolly he held up a finger like a man trying to catch the weather forecast on a distant radio – *Please hold your tickets*. And then someone rushed up to the two men with the full story.

'Oh dear,' said Jack. 'I'd better check where that leaves us.' There could only be one result from this inquiry. He cuffed his friend on the shoulder. 'See you later,' he said.

As he pushed his way through the crowd, racegoers nudged one another and nodded in his direction. One or two of the more daring said, 'Wotcher, Jack!' or 'Got any tips, Jack?' as he brushed past them. But he ignored them. Pillocks. These were the sort of people who stood behind him making idiot faces and waving as he talked to camera. Just because he appeared in their living room, the familiar TV bookie, they seemed to think they owned a part of him. Nobody owned Jack Butler.

On the other hand, Jack Butler owned a few nobodies – indeed a few some-bodies, now that he had Ibn Fayoud in his pocket.

He looked at his watch. If he skipped off before the next race, he'd have a couple of hours with an ex-girl friend who lived nearby before driving back home. Time for a spot of the auld lang syne. He had earned it this afternoon.

As he made his way back to his pitch on the rails Jack felt good, but not as good as he had anticipated. The look on that girl's face as she was pulling up after the post was troubling him. Ecstatic, over the bloody moon, and, to be fair, she deserved to be pleased with herself – she had ridden a blinder. Five pounds would have made no difference to the result. He just wished he hadn't seen her face. It was like offering a child the biggest and best ice cream in the world and then knock-ing it out of her hand as she was about to taste it.

An odd, unfamiliar feeling nagged at him. What the hell was it? Guilt?

Conscience? Jack shook his head as if insulted by the very thought. She was young, good-looking, talented; Kelly Connor would survive this. He thought of the stewards' inquiry, the scandal, the avenging fury of Harry Short. Maybe she wouldn't survive it. It wasn't his problem, was it? Suddenly he wanted to be away from the racecourse. Upstairs with Linzi, that would fix it.

Twenty minutes later, after Pendero had been officially placed last, Jack gave an older man who worked for him a large manila envelope filled with £20 notes. 'Jim, get this to Gould. I have some urgent business to see to.'

Kelly had never attended a stewards' inquiry, but she had heard all about them from her father. The stories he told made them seem absurd occasions, a line-up of bowler-hatted old buffers most of whom knew more about pig-sticking in the Punjab than riding a finish on a tired three-year-old. As she walked into the stewards' room at Ascot, she saw that, in this at least, racing had changed little since her father's day. The atmosphere was as tense as that of a courtroom. Only Kelly had no one to defend her.

Colonel John Beamish, the senior steward, looked at Kelly with some distaste before turning to Nick Morley, the acting steward.

'Mr Morley, perhaps you'd get proceedings under way.'

'Yes, sir.' Nick Morley took a step forward. 'The facts are straightforward.' He spoke with a clipped formality but Kelly sensed a note of regret in his voice. 'The horse Pendero was given nine stone by the handicapper and its jockey Kelly Connor claims seven pounds. She weighed out correctly at eight stone seven. On weighing in, having won the race, however, she was found to be eight stone two pounds.'

Kelly looked at Colonel Beamish. 'The reason –'

'You'll get your chance in a moment,' the colonel said briskly. 'Please be quiet.'

'Listen to your elders and betters' was the implication. It was like being back at school.

'I looked at the weight cloth, of course.' Nick Morley reached down behind his chair and produced Kelly's saddle and weight cloth. 'There's nothing wrong with it. None of the lead could possibly have fallen out on its own and as both the Clerk of the Scales and Miss Connor are certain that she went out at the correct weight, I can only conclude that lead was removed expressly and on purpose.'

The steward on Beamish's left roused himself. 'Of course jockeys do lose weight during a race.'

The colonel allowed the full fatuousness of this remark to sink in before chuckling humourlessly. 'If Billy Bunter was riding round the Grand National,' he said, 'The loss of five pounds might be understandable. But Connor,' he glanced at Kelly's trim form as if assessing a yearling, 'Is hardly likely to lose that much over a mile and a half, I would think.'

There was another silence before Beamish said testily, 'Well, Connor? What do you have to say for yourself?'

Kelly was grateful that a full five minutes had elapsed since the moment when she looked at the scales and realized that she had been cheated out of the race. Sitting alone, she had been assailed by feelings of bewilderment and disappointment. As she thought of her father's reaction, her eyes briefly filled with tears. But now she felt only a cold, implacable anger towards Damien Gould and whoever else had destroyed her ambitions and possibly the one career that she cared about.

'I have only this to say.' Kelly spoke with quiet dignity. 'I wanted to win this race more than any other I've ridden in. Nothing would persuade me to lose a race. I'm innocent.'

'None of which explains why you were five pounds light.'

'I believe I have an explanation for that.' The three stewards looked at her intently. In the silence, the sound of the stenographer's pencil could be heard. 'After I weighed out, I was waiting for Mr Short to collect the saddle and I was called to the phone. I gave the saddle to another jockey for what must have been a minute or so. I can only think – '

'A phone call?' Beamish interrupted. 'You're just about to ride in a race at Ascot and you're wandering off to chat on the phone?'

'I thought it was my father. He likes to wish me luck. But –' Kelly faltered, sensing that her story was beginning to sound absurd '– it was only a journalist wanting an interview.'

'A journalist.' Colonel Beamish made a note on the pad in front of him. 'I see.'

'So what you're saying,' – Nick Morley took up the questioning – 'Is that you were called deliberately to the telephone and, while you were away, the lead was removed from your weight cloth.'

'Yes, sir.'

'And who was this journalist? Someone we can talk to?'

'Someone called Giles Williams. Associated Press. I hadn't heard of him.'

'Williams?' Colonel Beamish looked at his fellow stewards. 'Nor have we,' he said.

'And the jockey?' Of those questioning her, only Nick Morley seemed interested in her version of events.

'That,' said Kelly quietly, 'was Damien Gould.' And then, as it suddenly came to her, she added, 'If it wasn't him, it was the trainer.'

Harry Short rarely gave interviews to press or television. Even in moments of triumph, after one of his horses had won a race, he gave the wrong impression. Red-faced, inarticulate, arrogant, he couldn't even be described as a rough diamond. Harry Short was merely rough.

But today, for the first time in his life, he needed the press. He wanted all the publicity he could get. Nobody did that to him and got away with it.

'So, Harry,' the smooth-faced television interviewer looked warily at the angry trainer, 'It would be fair to say you're a disappointed man at this moment.'

'Bloody right,' said Short. 'Wouldn't you be if you'd just been cheated?'

'There's an inquiry going on as we speak so perhaps we should be careful – '

'Careful?' Short's eyes flashed with anger. 'I'll be as careful as she was to make certain she lost me that race.'

'You're referring to – '

'I'll say it now, I don't care who knows it.' Harry Short turned to the camera,

ignoring the interviewer's attempts to interrupt him. 'I gave Kelly Connor her big
chance today and she's fitted me up. I don't know why or who's paid her but only
one person could remove five pounds from that weight cloth. It was her.'

'Turning to the race itself – '

'I curse myself for putting her on Pendero. Never trust a Connor, that's what
they used to say when her father was riding. And she's a definite chip off the old
crooked block. She's finished in this game.' Harry Short stabbed the air with an
angry forefinger, spitting as he spoke. 'Finished, got that?'

'And now,' the interviewer said hastily, 'While we're waiting for the outcome
of the stewards' inquiry, let's catch up on the results from elsewhere.'

Still scowling, Short stormed off.

The interviewer listened to his producer on the headphones. 'Yes, of course it
was slanderous, but don't worry, we're not talking about Jeffrey Archer. She's only
a bloody apprentice, for God's sake.'

'It's a lie, sir.'

Damien Gould knew all about stewards' inquiries, he'd been up before them
more times than he could remember, and he knew Colonel Beamish. Stand to attention, stare ahead like a private on parade, throw in a few 'sirs' and you were halfway
there. 'I don't know why she would want to say that about me.'

He sounded so plausible and looked so innocent that for a moment Kelly felt
that maybe she'd been wrong about him.

'But did you look after her saddle?' The colonel allowed his impatience with
this inquiry to show.

'Of course, sir. She got a telephone call and she asked me to look after her
saddle.' As soon as the words were out, Kelly knew she'd been right.

'I never – ' she interjected.

'You've said your bit, Connor,' Colonel Beamish snapped without looking at
her. 'Go on, Gould.'

'Anyway, as we're not allowed to leave our saddles unattended, I agreed to keep
an eye on it for her. And that's all I did.'

Nick Morley leant over to Colonel Beamish and whispered something in his ear.

'Yes, all right,' the colonel nodded. 'Step forward, Connor. You've heard Gould's
testimony. Have you anything to add to it?'

Kelly said, 'If Damien Gould was so keen to help me, I'd like to know why he
boxed me in two furlongs from home and tried to stop me making my challenge.
Why wasn't he trying to win the race himself?'

'Gould?'

'I don't know what she's talking about, sir.'

'And then after the race,' Kelly continued, 'Why did he say "you ain't won nothing yet, sweetheart".'

'Gould?'

'That's not true, sir.'

Colonel Beamish made another note on the pad in front of him. 'It all sounds
rather flimsy to me, Connor,' he said wearily. He turned to Gould once more. 'Do
you have any further comments on what Connor has had to say for herself?'

'I do, sir, but I shall keep them to myself if I may. After all,' he looked at Kelly and smiled coldly, 'There are ladies present.'

'Thank you, Gould, you may go.'

After Gould had left the inquiry, Harry Short was called in to give his own abusive detail of events. Kelly stood beside the stipendiary steward trying to hold back her tears. When Harry had finished, Colonel Beamish asked the other stewards if they had further questions. They shook their heads. Harry was dismissed but Kelly was told to wait outside while they made their decision.

Barely one minute later she was called back in, and while she was being given the inevitable news that Pendero had been disqualified and placed last, Nick Morley was relaying the same information to the public.

'We will of course be referring the matter to the Jockey Club.'

Colonel Beamish's last words to Kelly were too much and as she turned and opened the door to leave, she quietly began to cry.

Another day's racing at Ascot was over, but the Members' Bar was still noisy and crowded. Winning owners, surrounded by friends, family and hangers-on, relived their moment of victory over bottles of champagne, forgetting the countless times when they had driven home in silence after another expensive and disappointing day. This moment was what they owned racehorses for; they drank to the jockey, the trainer, the lad, all of whom were making their way home at the end of another working day.

Racing journalists who had filed their copy hung around the bar, moving from group to group, accepting free drinks, picking up gossip. The talk was of a highly promising two-year-old owned by a shipping magnate that had trotted up on its first public appearance and was now ante-post favourite for next season's Two Thousand Guineas, of the breathtakingly close finish to the big race of the day, and, of course, the astonishing business of Harry Short's girl apprentice who had lost her race in the weighing room. Poor old Harry. You'd think he'd know better than to trust a Connor. Just like her father, that girl. Brilliant, but bent.

Yet the noisiest party in the Members' Bar was not being held by a winner and was avoided by journalists. For Ibn Fayoud, to go racing without treating a few friends to champagne at the end of the day was unthinkable. Here the conversation rarely touched on racing (although Serena, who said she had once been girl friend to a member of the royal family, claimed to have had a seriously successful gamble on the colt), it was about London, parties, who had spent the night with whom.

Ibn Fayoud, who took his pleasure quietly, observed his friends with a smile on his face. He liked to take them to the racecourse because they protected him from the tiresome racing people – trainers, bloodstock agents, advisers to his father – who would try to impress him with their knowledge of and interest in his horses. Since the age of thirteen, Ibn Fayoud had taken what he wanted from life. His teens and early twenties were a riot of sexual and narcotic excess. Now he was like a little rich boy in a toy shop. He went out, he partied, he took his friends racing, but he was bored. Nothing mattered to him. Or almost nothing.

'Ib, God you're so silent down there.' The blonde publicist for a high-profile

London nightclub leant towards him, flashing an expanse of tanned cleavage. 'What evil plans are you hatching now?'

Ibn Fayoud fixed her with his dark eyes and smiled. 'I'll show you later.'

The fact was that, although Ibn Fayoud had stopped feeling anything in about 1983, he was now assailed by something approaching concern. That bloody horse, that bloody fat trainer, that bloody little girl. Between them they had ensured that his debt to Reg Butler, Turf Accountants, topped the million mark. Pounds. (Fayoud was almost certain it was pounds.) If Butler jerked his lead, there was no way he could pay it off without speaking to his father.

Now that *was* a problem. Sheikh al Hassan did not share his son's view of Western life as a fun-palace built for his own diversion. The Sheikh believed that, if you had money, you should behave responsibly; he actually had religious objections to some of his son's wilder stunts. His threat to send Ibn Fayoud back to Qatar where he would have to work as Minister of something or other, was not an empty one. Jack Butler had the power to have everything he enjoyed – women, parties, horses, Ascot – taken away from him if he so wished.

Ibn Fayoud shuddered. Then he stopped thinking about it. He was good at not thinking about unpleasant things.

Outside, in the deserted members' enclosure, a tall man in a suit and a bowler hat walked with a young girl, deep in conversation.

'Hope you don't mind talking out here,' Nick Morley was saying to Kelly Connor as they wandered slowly down towards the race-track. 'The weighing room lacks privacy.'

'No, that's fine,' Kelly said. 'I prefer to be outside. I was beginning to feel like a prisoner in there.'

Nick Morley smiled. 'I'm sorry about the inquiry. The colonel is not the gentlest of inquisitors.'

'Particularly with women apprentices.'

'He belongs to the old school. I spoke to him later about it.'

Kelly glanced at the steward in some surprise. After the formality of the inquiry, his friendliness was welcome.

'You know that Gould was lying in there, don't you?' she said.

'Among the stewards, Damien is hardly renowned as a reliable witness. I don't think he's told the unvarnished truth to an inquiry in his life.' Nick leant on the rails and looked across the course. 'That's off the record, by the way.'

For the first time, Kelly looked at him as a man rather than as a Jockey Club steward. He wasn't unattractive. He was in his thirties, tall, strongly built, with straight, sandy hair and a squarish chin. Although it occurred to her that he might be using the sympathetic approach to break her down, he seemed uneasy with the role that had been thrust upon him.

'Hadn't you better tell me what happens now?' she asked.

'I've been instructed to take more statements, make a report of what happened and then file it to Portman Square advising as to whether you should appear before a formal hearing of the Jockey Club. In the meantime, you're not suspended.'

Kelly sighed. 'I suppose I should be pleased.'

'It could be worse. Oh, and you're not to talk to the press.'

'Unlike Harry Short?' There had been much talk in the weighing room of Short's comments to the press.

'Short's a bad man to cross,' said Nick. 'Try to ignore his remarks.'

'Even when he insults my father?' For the first time, the anger and hurt Kelly was feeling flashed in her eyes. 'I want to find out who was behind all this.' She started walking back to the weighing room.

'Kelly.' She turned, surprised that a steward should use her first name. Nick was still standing by the rails. He looked serious. 'Keep yourself to yourself for a while. Don't play the detective. Let us do the investigating, OK? I'll be in touch.'

It was only when she had returned to the weighing room and was dialling her father's number that the significance of Morley's remark filtered through. *Don't play the detective.* That could only mean that he believed her story.

There was a continuous low tone at the end of the line. Kelly tried again without success.

'Bloody phones.' She slammed down the receiver, collected her racing gear and headed home. It really wasn't her day.

Frank Connor's flat looked like a hurricane had swept through it. Tables had been overturned, the contents of drawers strewn about. The screen of the television had been shattered and there were gaps on the mantelpiece where he'd kept his few items of value; a silver cigarette case, a silver frame round the photograph of his wife, a set of antique china plates.

None of this Kelly saw when, with a growing sense of dread, she pushed open the unlocked front door and stepped into the flat. For a moment she was transfixed by the full horror of her father's body lying on the carpet, his head covered in blood and bone splinters showing through his temple.

'Dad!' she cried, stumbling across the room. She crouched beside the still figure, afraid even to touch it. Frank Connor's eyes stared unseeing out of a face contorted with pain. 'Oh my God, Dad.'

Chapter
3

In racing, as in life, rumour breeds on rumour. Within days of Frank Connor's death, the word on racetracks and stable yards throughout the country, repeated and embroidered upon in the bars of Newmarket and Lambourn, was that the ex-jockey had paid the price for falling into crooked company. Nobody knew the details – maybe it was a gambling ring, or doping, or drugs – but everybody knew the truth about Connor. As a jockey, he had sold his soul to the devil; as a civvy, he had continued to work in some capacity for his corrupt paymasters. Somewhere along the line he had crossed, maybe double-crossed, them. He had been on the run, hiding out in Newmarket, but they had found him out, warned him off, stopped him once and for all.

Frank Connor, small-time failed hood, deceased. Frank Connor, victim of just another gangland killing. The winners, the glory days, were all but forgotten.

Almost lost in this swelling symphony of gossip and hearsay, a sad minor theme in counterpoint, was the story of his only daughter Kelly. Tragic, really. A talented enough rider, strong, balanced, with the knack of getting the best out of a horse, but caught in the same gin-trap of corruption as her father. Harry Short was no angel but when Harry pointed the finger, you had to take note. If he said he'd been stitched up by an apprentice with dodgy connections, then that was the way it was. All right, so she hadn't actually been suspended, so Morley of the Jockey Club had gone on record as saying no specific guilt in the matter had been proven but, in this game, there was no smoke without fire. It all added up; sad, but true.

Initial police investigation did nothing to still the rumours. The Newmarket constabulary reported that there was no evidence that the killing involved anything as melodramatic as gang revenge. It was the considered opinion of their officers that the deceased was the unfortunate victim of a break-in which had gone wrong. There had been several robberies in the Newmarket area, thieves working on the sound assumption that racing people liked to keep a spot of ready cash under the floorboards and out of the grasp of Her Majesty's Inspector of Taxes. How were the thieves to know that Frank Connor didn't have two pennies to rub together? This incident had all the hallmarks of a robbery – the flat had been torn apart, several items were missing and it had taken place on a Saturday afternoon when many people in the industry were at the racecourse. It was unfortunate for Mr Connor that he had been at home when the break-in occurred. Police issued descriptions of three men, already suspected of robbery with violence in the East

Anglia district and now wanted for questioning in connection with the murder of Frank Connor.

Racing's rumour-mongers knew better. Yet again, the police had got it wrong.

Kelly Connor was in too great a state of shock to listen to the grapevine. All that she knew was that the most important person in her life, the man who had brought her up since she was eight, a gentle, wounded, wise man, was now gone. There was no hate in her heart, not yet, only pain and bewilderment.

During the time that Kelly had been working for Bill Templeman she'd become firm friends with his wife Annie. Just as Annie had confided in her when her marriage to Bill had been going through a shaky time, so Kelly had revealed her anxieties and ambitions. It was to Annie that Kelly turned for help now.

'Christ, whatever's the matter with you?' had been her first words when Kelly appeared through the back door. Before she had a chance to say any more, Kelly burst into tears and flung her arms round her, sobbing uncontrollably.

While Annie hugged her tightly, Kelly blurted out an account of what had happened. When the worst was over, Annie made her drink a large mug of sweet tea. She stayed up with her talking about anything and everything until they were both exhausted, and then she took Kelly upstairs and put her to bed.

For the first few difficult days Kelly stayed with the Templemans. Annie fielded the inevitable calls from the more ghoulish members of the press who smelt a story and were prepared to lie, cheat and bribe to get at it. She protected her from the news that several of her husband's owners had rung him to request that, whatever happened, he did not put the apprentice Connor on their horses in future. Smoke, fire, rumour – Bill Templeman's oft-repeated support for his protégée could do nothing against them.

For the two days before her father's body was released for burial, Kelly spoke little, spending many hours in her room, thinking of the past. The race at Ascot was all but forgotten and, in her grief, she gave little thought to her career beyond the conviction that, at this moment, any plan to live by riding seemed an absurdity. If a life with horses had led her father to his death, she would earn her money elsewhere. Perhaps her schoolfriends had been right – being a jockey was no job for an intelligent, good-looking girl.

After Frank Connor's body was released by the police, the autopsy having confirmed that he had been killed by three blows to the cranium with a blunt instrument or instruments, Kelly found the old determination and resolve slowly returning to her. She politely rejected Annie's suggestion that her father should be buried near Newmarket, insisting that she would fly home with the body and see it interred in Adare, County Limerick, where he had been raised and lived during the years before it all went wrong. Annie offered to come along.

'No,' said Kelly. 'I want to do this by myself.'

'I just wish I could help.'

Kelly looked at Annie's lightly freckled face and smiled for the first time in days. 'You can,' she said, giving Annie her keys. 'You can keep the cat fed.'

Annie returned Kelly's smile and the two women hugged each other. 'I hope it goes all right,' she said.

It was a wise decision. A funeral in England would have attracted gossips, journalists and rubber-necking members of the public. The ceremony in Adare was simple and affecting. The small village church was packed with people, many of whom had known Frank since he rode his first winners at local point-to-points. To his friends in this neighbourhood, rumour meant nothing, particularly if it originated from across the Irish Sea. All they knew was that Frank Connor was a fine, kind man who rode horses like a young god and who had been unlucky.

'Ashes to ashes.' The ringing tones of Father O'Brien could be heard in the town square as Frank Connor's body was laid to rest. 'Dust to dust.' Kelly stood alone at the foot of the grave, slightly apart from the rest of the congregation. 'Dust to dust.' These last few days had been as near to a living hell as she hoped she would ever suffer. She had gone to sleep crying and had awoken with tears in her eyes. Part of her had died with him.

She looked up from the coffin, across the wild green fields of County Limerick. Her father had not died in vain. She had come through.

'The Sheikh is waiting for you upstairs.' A tall black American held open the door of Sheikh al Hassan's London house in Eaton Square, scanning the street with apparent casualness.

'Thanks, Tom.' Nick Morley stepped into the house, noting with approval that Sheikh al Hassan's security arrangements were as subtly impregnable as ever. An ex-SAS man himself, Nick could appreciate the lengths to which the Arab potentate went to avoid kidnappers, assassins and political enemies. A few yards down the street, a man was washing a Daimler, eyeing anyone who approached the front door. Upstairs, he happened to know, another member of the Sheikh's entourage would be seated before a bank of television monitors covering all approaches to the house. Tom, whose euphemistic title was 'Butler', was a fully trained security guard, as were most of the staff of twenty who ran the household. Here, even the pantry maid included marksmanship and kung-fu among her job qualifications.

'Mr Brompton-Smiley is with him, sir.'

Nick nodded. Of course, he would be. Simon Brompton-Smiley, international racing manager to the Al Hassan family, one of the most assiduously courted men in British racing and, in Nick's private view, a slimy, worthless creep. Admittedly Nick was biased, having known him since they were both at Harrow. Then little Simey was a pitiful creature – pale, ingratiating, the school sneak. These days, Nick tried to treat him with respect; after all, as the Sheikh's bloodstock adviser, he had to work with Brompton-Smiley, but it was not easy. Where the world saw a self-assured, pin-striped little man with greased hair Nick saw a jumped-up schoolboy, a sneak made good.

'Simon, how are you?'

'Nick.' Brompton-Smiley greeted him at the top of the stairs. 'Good of you to be so prompt. The Sheikh has a dinner, so perhaps we could sort this out within the half-hour.'

Nick smiled coldly. 'Suits me.'

The two men made their way into a large drawing room hung in perfect taste with eighteenth-century sporting pictures. With its Chippendale furniture, and a well-known Stubbs over a blazing log fire, the room suggested the lifestyle of one of the great landowners of the past, a Lord Derby or a Duke of Norfolk. Nick knew several Arab owners, but only Sheikh al Hassan seemed so effortlessly at home with Western culture.

The Sheikh sat on a sofa by the fire, a small, neat man in a dark suit, sipping iced mineral water and reading *The Times*. He welcomed Nick with a natural, gracious authority. Brompton-Smiley poured them both a mineral water as the Sheikh discussed the plans for a yearling Nick had bought for him the previous week at the Kentucky sales. No one listening to their casual conversation would have guessed that the colt in question had cost the Sheikh just short of three and a half million dollars.

'The problem we need to talk about,' Sheikh al Hassan said, as the two men settled into their chairs, 'is unfortunately a human rather than an equestrian one, namely – ' he frowned at the thought '–my son. You probably know that he's in something of a mess.'

'Mess, sir?' It was unwise, Nick knew, to give the impression that everyone in racing knew about Ibn Fayoud's debts which, naturally enough, they did. 'I hadn't heard.'

The Sheikh smiled. 'Of course not,' he said. 'Simon can probably fill you in on the details later but the fact of the matter is that my son's well-developed appreciation for the good life has recently got rather out of hand.' He sipped thoughtfully at his mineral water. 'Now, much as I believe that the young should be allowed to make their own mistakes – and after all my son is, on paper at least, an adult – his financial situation is such that I can no longer stand aside. Like any family, we have our name to consider.'

Nick nodded. It was one of the Sheikh's favourite tricks to talk as if the Hassan dynasty, which was worth several billion dollars, was not that different from any other family – his, for example, or even Tom's downstairs. It was only the scale of their opportunities and difficulties which set them apart.

'A month ago,' the Sheikh continued, 'I was obliged to tell him that, unless he made a fresh start, there would be the most serious consequences – for him, of course, but also for me. Since then, I have been informed by an impeccable source' – Brompton-Smiley pursed his lips self-importantly – 'That my son's gambling debts have, if anything, increased. More seriously, he appears to be obligated to a particular bookmaker, Mr . . . ?'

'Butler,' said Brompton-Smiley.

'Jack Butler?' Nick winced. 'That's not good. He's tough.'

'Tougher than my son, I fear. Very reluctantly, I have to consider sending him back to Qatar for a course in home economics.' The Sheikh smiled wanly. 'An open-ended course.'

'What about his horses, sir?' So far, nothing Nick had heard surprised him. Ibn Fayoud was a nuisance, an embarrassment. British racing could do without him.

'His horses I shall sell unless Simon advises me to hold on to any of them. On the whole, they seem to have as disastrous a track record as their owner.' The two Englishmen laughed dutifully. 'Of course, none of that concerns you.'

'I'm sorry to hear about all this, sir.' Nick glanced over to Brompton-Smiley, whose expression suggested that worse was yet to come.

The Sheikh shrugged. 'Family life,' he said wearily. 'I can see no way to avoid stories in the press. Already the gossip columns are talking of a rift between my son and myself. When he is sent back to Qatar, there will doubtless be something of a fuss, particularly in the racing press. And that's why I've asked you here.' He glanced at his watch. 'I'll make this brief. Because of the probable scandal, I feel inclined to move my principal racing interests from the United Kingdom to France.'

'France, sir?' Nick tried to sound as calm as he could while his mind was racing at the implications of the Sheikh's remark. 'I would have thought that any family problem would be well known there.'

'The prize money is better and they don't have bookmakers,' said Sheikh al Hassan more firmly. 'I find I have something of an aversion to bookmakers.'

'The Sheikh and I have been looking into the economics,' Simon Brompton-Smiley added. 'It makes sense both on the training and – ' at this point he was unable to keep the smile off his face '– the bloodstock side.'

'That,' Nick said weakly, 'would be a major decision.'

'Not that major.' In Sheikh al Hassan's world, steps were taken in a brisk, businesslike way. It wasn't that he lacked sympathy for the hundreds of people whose livelihoods were affected by the change, simply that he didn't think of them. Life was too full of first-hand problems to worry about side effects.

'On the bloodstock side alone, we have some hundred or so animals,' Nick said quietly.

'We'd move them,' said Brompton-Smiley with the smugness of a man who, as international racing manager, would be unaffected by such a radical move. At a stroke, a handful of large trainers with whom the Sheikh kept his horses would find their yards devastated. He owned up to forty per cent of the horses with some of them and replacement owners of his calibre didn't just fall off trees. The face of British breeding and racing would be changed, and Nick would lose his principal source of income.

'Naturally,' the Sheikh said, 'We hope that you will continue to buy and sell on our behalf, but from France.'

'I'm very grateful, sir,' Nick smiled palely, 'But, as a member of the Jockey Club, I have my duties here.'

'You'll just have to make a choice.' Brompton-Smiley made no effort to hide his pleasure.

The Sheikh stared at him with piercing eyes and the international racing manager shrunk back into his chair. He had gone too far.

'Any choice that Nick may or may not have to make,' said the Sheikh, 'will be in a month's time and not before. He should think it over, the decision need not be hurried. And, of course, my son may find a way out of his difficulties so that the move will be unnecessary, although personally I doubt it.' The Sheikh got to his feet, the cue for Nick to leave. 'Let's all think about this, shall we? We'll talk soon.'

Simon Brompton-Smiley showed Nick out. 'Don't fall for the old options open line,' he said on the doorstep. 'The Sheikh has made up his mind, I'm afraid.'

'We'll see,' said Nick, turning on his heel and marching briskly down Eaton Place, past a man washing his car.

It was good to be riding again. An early morning mist shrouded Newmarket Heath as the first lot from Bill Templeman's yard made its way to the gallops. It was cold, with the first hint of autumn in the air, and a sullen silence hung over the string. Later, after breakfast, when a watery sun showed through the mist and the larks chattered high in the sky, the lads riding out would talk and laugh, but for now they sat hunched and silent, sleeping in. If one of the horses jigged about or bucked, it could expect a sharp dig in the ribs and a curse from its bleary-eyed jockey.

Kelly was gradually getting back to normal. Yes, it was good to be riding out again.

She had flown in from Dublin the previous evening and, despite Bill's offer of a few days' compassionate leave, she had insisted on working. The following Saturday, a promising two-year-old called Diamond Dealer was due to make his first appearance on a racecourse at Kempton. Kelly had ridden him in most of his work and, since she would be riding him on Saturday, it was important to see how he went today. Bill, a man of few words at the best of times, had agreed, but only with considerable reluctance. Kelly had put it down to embarrassment over her father's death.

There had been a time when Kelly had dreaded riding out. The life of a stable lad was harsh and full of frustrations and, even in small yards, newcomers were treated with leery suspicion until they proved themselves. For a teenage lad, this was a relatively simple process; during his first week, he would be dumped in the yard's water trough after second lot. If he reacted to this initiation ceremony with loud good humour, he was in, one of the lads. If he cried or complained to the head lad, he could expect no mercy.

For girls, it was different. You didn't chuck girls in water troughs. Their initiation ceremony was more subtle.

Before Kelly had arrived, there had been only one girl working in the yard, a wiry, ginger-haired teenager called Bonny, who was tougher, louder and could pack a harder punch than most of the lads. For this reason, she fitted in easily and was treated with a certain wary respect. The fact that she was known to be meeting the much-feared head lad in the horsebox after evening feeds may have helped her position too.

Kelly was different. She was well spoken, quiet and her good looks noticeably raised the sexual tension in the Templeman yard. Worse than all this, she rode neatly and well, and was riding work for the boss within a couple of weeks of arriving. All this hadn't done much for her popularity.

One by one, the older lads tried it on. Bullying, nagging, threatening. Come to the pictures, Kelly. Come and watch a video round at my place. You need a friend in this yard, Kelly, a protector. One by one, Kelly turned them down. She was there to ride horses, not extend her sexual experience. She wasn't interested.

At first it was just names. Fridge. Prick-teaser. Dyke. Kelly ignored them. Then they would tell her insultingly filthy jokes. She laughed at them. Even when one of the lads marched around the yard holding a pair of black knickers, claiming that he had broken into the Fridge, Kelly smiled and went about her work.

At one point, she considered giving up racing altogether. The persecution, the loneliness in the yard were getting worse by the day. She had decided not to speak to Bill or Annie about it – that would only make her position worse. After the knicker incident, she had confided in her father and he had simply smiled and said, 'Sure, you'll just have to show them what you're made of. They'll respect you if you fight back.'

So she had. Dennis was the worst of them. Now in his late thirties, he had all the anger and resentment of a man who has been offered the chance of success and has failed to take it. Dennis rode light, was strong and looked good. A few seasons ago, Bill had started giving him the odd ride in apprentice races. But for some reason, the poise and balance that he showed riding work at home deserted him on the racecourse. He rode two winners and that was it. These days, he was given the occasional no-hope spare ride by the guv'nor but, by now, even Dennis understood. He was just another might-have-been on the way to being a has-been.

Dennis resented promise, particularly in the younger lads. He teased them, tried to show them up on the gallops. Behind his cheery, grinning façade, he hated Kelly with a passion.

She had been at the yard two months when Bill had asked her to ride work with Dennis on a couple of four-year-olds. At one point, the gallop went out of Bill's sight before coming round a hill and back into view. Kelly was a neck up on Dennis when she heard a clicking noise from him. Quite coolly, he took his right hand off his reins and held it firmly between her legs. Kelly cursed him and tried to wriggle away but they were riding at racing speed and it was impossible to escape without the risk of damaging her horse. For what seeme an eternity, Dennis held her in a humiliatingly intimate grip. 'Nice,' she heard him say. 'You like it too, don't you?' Sick with anger, Kelly remembered her father's advice. Fight back. She steadied her horse slightly, cupped her left hand under Dennis's foot and, with a swift, businesslike movement, tipped him out of the saddle.

Bill was furious when Kelly pulled up alone and rushed off to catch the loose horse. Shortly afterwards, Dennis came into view, limping, followed by Bill leading the horse.

'What happened to you?' he stormed. Dennis glanced up at Kelly, hate in his eyes. Her look told him all he needed to know; shop me, buster, and I'll shop you. 'He stumbled, guv'nor,' he muttered. 'One moment he was going fine, the next I was on the floor.'

Word of the incident spread through the stable. The new girl had dropped Dennis. He'd tried it on and ended up on his backside. It was the joke of the week. Nobody really liked Dennis, although some of the younger lads were afraid of him. To Kelly's relief and surprise, she was accepted at last. Her initiation ceremony had been completed with honours.

'He'll go close on Saturday.' Kelly patted Diamond Dealer, after pulling up. 'With my claim.' The horse had worked well, getting a previous winner well off the bridle over the last furlong.

Bill nodded. 'We'll talk about that over breakfast,' he said, turning to walk back to his car.

It was not unusual for Bill to ask Kelly to take breakfast between first and second lots, and normally it was an occasion she enjoyed. Conversation with Bill was limited as he stayed absorbed in the morning's racing papers, but Annie more than compensated with a never-ending supply of local gossip. She was also a great cook.

On this occasion, though, something was wrong. The two of them talked to Kelly about the funeral in Ireland, but when she switched the conversation to racing matters they became evasive and Kelly noticed odd glances passing between them.

'So,' she said brightly at one point. 'How do you think Diamond Dealer will run on Saturday? He went well this morning.'

There was silence. Annie looked significantly at her husband, urging him to speak.

'Was it something I said?' Kelly smiled.

Bill frowned. 'The horse runs,' he said quietly. 'But I'm afraid you're not riding.'

It was as if Kelly had been slapped in the face. Diamond Dealer was her ride. He went better for her than anyone else. It was unthinkable that Bill, her greatest supporter in the past, should book someone else to ride him.

'May I know why?'

'Lady Dereham has insisted.'

The owner had jocked her off? It made no sense to Kelly. 'But I've ridden winners for her. It's crazy.'

'She's not alone, I'm afraid, Kelly,' said Annie gently. 'We've been getting calls all week. It's a serious problem.'

'Not because of Ascot, surely?'

Bill nodded. 'Harry Short is a very powerful man. He's been running something of a character assassination campaign on you. Apparently an extremely large bet on Pendero came unstuck. You were too busy dealing with your father's funeral to notice, but the racing papers gave you a real hammering.'

Kelly looked at Bill in amazement 'But you don't believe I'd do that, do you?'

'Of course not,' said Bill impatiently. 'But I'm not an owner. I'm sure it will blow over in time.' He sounded unconvinced. 'Until then you'll have to sit tight. Can you ride out second lot?'

'Of course I can.' Kelly felt a knot of anger in her stomach. 'I'm not finished yet. Who am I on?'

'Shine On.'

Kelly smiled. It was lucky for her that the yard's star three-year-old was owned by Bill himself, who had bred him. There was one ride she could still depend on.

After she had left to tack up, Annie looked across the table at her husband.

'You should have told her,' she said.

Bill rubbed his eyes. 'I will.' Unusually for a trainer, he hated confrontations, awkward scenes. 'One thing at a time.'

'Forget it.' Annie folded her *Racing Post* briskly. 'I'll talk to her after second lot.'

Later that morning, as she returned her saddle and bridle to the tack room, Kelly found herself reflecting on what had been said over breakfast. The Templemans were honest people, rarely influenced by the racecourse gossip which dictated who was in and who was out at any particular time. There were certain yards where a stable jockey going through a difficult patch could expect no mercy, the best rides would suddenly start going outside, but the Templemans were not like that. Never having been fashionable themselves, they didn't give a damn for the ebb and flow of public opinion. Loyalty, judgement was what mattered to them.

And yet, there was something about Bill's manner this morning which had alarmed Kelly. She was used to his silent moods, which she put down to the pressures of his job, but she had never known him so evasive and ill at ease. In fact, the yard itself was not the same since her return from Ireland. It was as if the lads were party to an embarrassing secret, a conspiracy of silence which excluded her. Maybe it was the Ascot race, or the death of her father, but that would be surprising. Apart from Dennis, whose loathing she now took for granted, they liked her here and, even if they thought she had ridden a bad race the previous day, they would express their views with open good humour.

As Kelly made her way to her car, Annie emerged from the house and walked towards her. 'How about a coffee and a sticky bun in the town?' Annie was ten years older than Kelly and a couple of inches taller. She was also quite a bit fatter due to a passion for anything with sugar in it.

'Let's make it three sticky buns,' Kelly said gloomily. 'After all, I don't have to watch my weight any more now I'm being jocked off.'

'Don't be like that,' said Annie, climbing into Kelly's Saab.

On their way into Newmarket, the two women talked about the horses in the yard. Shine On had been impressive in his work and Bill planned to run him at York and then maybe a big race abroad.

'Sounds like bad news for me,' said Kelly. On the international circuit, she would be unable to claim her seven pounds and most trainers would opt for the experience of one of the top jockeys.

'Depends how you ride him at York.'

Annie suggested a tea-house frequented by shoppers and visitors rather than racing people and, as if to confirm Kelly's suspicion that this was to be more than a casual chat, picked a corner table away from the other customers.

'So,' she said, stirring her coffee. 'Ireland was all right, the funeral?'

Kelly nodded. 'It was as Dad would have wished. I'm glad I took him home.'

'And now?' Annie asked casually.

'Now I pick up the pieces. Ride out. Resume my career. Back to normal except I'm going to look for another flat. I can't bear to be in the old one any more. I keep seeing Dad's body lying on the floor.' There was something about Kelly's tone of voice that betrayed her.

'That's not all, is it?' asked Annie.

Kelly shook her head. 'I can't let it go,' she said with quiet determination. 'Someone murdered Dad. That wasn't a botched break-in. I've got to find out who killed him.' Raking over painful memories, she frowned. 'There was something on his mind the day before he died. I'm sure it was something to do with my race at Ascot. He was so desperate that I should win it.'

'Your dad wanted you to win everything.'

'I know.' Kelly smiled thinking of her father's enthusiasm.

'Kelly.' There was a new seriousness to Annie. 'You were right. Something is going on. We've been getting calls – not just from owners worried about your riding their horses but anonymous calls. Threats. They want us to throw you out, sack you.'

Kelly sat bolt upright. 'I don't believe it!' she said. 'Why should anyone want to do that?'

'I think you're right. I think there is a connection between Pendero's race at Ascot and your father's death. Someone somewhere has been playing for very high stakes and they don't want you spoiling the game.'

Kelly could feel her temper begin to rise. 'I told the police it was no ordinary break-in,' she said angrily. 'I'm not going to be scared off by – '

'Look, you'll get going again. The rides will come. But you'll just have to take things quietly. Forget these people.'

'And if not?'

Annie sighed. 'If not, I've overestimated your good sense.'

Kelly agreed, not wanting to prolong the argument, and changed the subject.

After the two women had parted, Kelly drove back to her flat. The events of the morning had made her weary. On her return from Ireland, it had seemed so simple; resume riding and make a few calls to people who could help her. Now she was faced by a choice; on the one hand, her future career; on the other, the memory of her father. She wanted to be a jockey more than anything else, but she knew which she'd choose.

She cursed as she entered the flat. It was warm as if she had left the central heating on by mistake. There were two messages on her answering machine. Kelly picked up a pen in the hope that she would be taking down details of spare rides.

'This is Giles Williams.' Kelly recognized the voice of the journalist who had spoken to her before the fateful race at Ascot. The man sounded drunk. 'I'd quite like to talk to you. Soon. Don't call me. I'll be in touch.' There was a click, followed by a tone.

She didn't recognize the voice of the second caller. 'Hello, Connor. There's a message in the oven to tell you to mind your own business.'

Kelly walked quickly to the kitchen. Nothing appeared to have been moved but the oven was turned full on. That was why the flat was warm. She could hear the sound of her heart beating as, like someone in a dream, she opened the oven door – and then reeled back, gagging, her legs weak beneath her. Looking out of the oven with white unseeing eyes was the corpse of her cat.

Chapter

4

They might have been lovers. In a small French restaurant off Sloane Square, the couple sat at a corner table, their faces lit by candlelight. They talked in low voices, pausing when the waiter put food before them, as if whatever they had to say could not be shared, even by a discreet French boy with an imperfect grasp of English. The understated beauty of her face was framed by the dark curls of her shoulder-length hair – looks which attracted covert glances from other men in the restaurant. But there was something tense about the girl, almost haunted. She smiled little and listened intently whenever the man, sober-suited and authoritative, spoke. He seemed to be a reassuring, comforting presence. An observer would guess that their conversation was troubled, intimate. Maybe he was married. Maybe she was pregnant. Maybe they were just lovers.

But the conversation between Kelly Connor and Nick Morley was not of matters of the heart, but of life, death and horses.

The call from Nick that afternoon had been well timed. Kelly was still upset and dazed by the events of her first day back at work. He had news of the investigation, he said. They needed to talk. Portman Square? she had asked, and he had laughed almost boyishly. He thought she deserved better than that after all her troubles. How about Au Père de Nico at eight thirty? 'Where on earth is that?' she inquired. He gave her directions and she agreed to meet him there. Maybe it would do her good.

All her troubles. What did Nick Morley know of her troubles? A race lost, a father murdered, a career on the skids – they were no more than the opening scenes of a nightmare which was engulfing her. Alone in the flat, she had shuddered with something approaching fear. What would her father have done under these circumstances? With heaving stomach, Kelly had gone to the kitchen, tipped the burnt remains of her cat into a plastic bag and took it downstairs to bury it in the garden. She was a Connor. They – whoever they were – had underestimated her if they thought she could be cowed into submission by threats and violence. It was at that moment that she had resolved to tell Nick Morley everything that had happened to her.

'Who knows about this?' he asked when Kelly haltingly told him of the latest threat to her.

'I've taken the tape to the police, of course, and told them about my cat, but that's all. I just thought that the Jockey Club should know too. The Templemans have had a few anonymous calls as well.'

'Will you tell them?'

Kelly shook her head. 'No, I've got hardly anything to ride as it is. If they knew I was under that sort of pressure, they'd stop giving me rides altogether. I have to sort it out myself.'

'You're tougher than you look.' Nick smiled. 'I can see why you were less overjoyed by my news than I had anticipated.'

'Of course I'm glad that the investigation has come up with nothing incriminating against me, but it's no surprise. In a way I wish you had pursued it.'

'What?' Nick was used to the tunnel-visioned stubbornness of jockeys but it was difficult to square this cast-iron inner confidence with the slight features of the young girl sitting across the table from him. 'You actually wanted to be hauled up in front of the stewards in Portman Square?'

'Yes, I did,' said Kelly, surprised that he hadn't grasped what she'd been saying. She spoke with a new intensity. 'Someone needed to stop Pendero winning at all costs. Gould tried it on during the race. Then there was the lead missing from a perfectly sound weight cloth. Then my father was killed, there were threats against me, the Templemans. The last thing I want is for the case to be closed. An accident. A misunderstanding. What's that going to do to my reputation if Harry Short's accusing me of everything short of genocide?'

'Everyone knows that Short's a loud mouth. Ride a couple of winners.' Nick sipped at his glass of white wine. 'Ascot will soon be forgotten, believe me.'

'Either that or I'll be dead.'

Nick shook his head and tried to lighten the conversation. 'You're only in danger if you go around screaming "murder!" every time your father's name is mentioned.'

Kelly looked away. Don't show it, she was thinking. Don't show the pain, the loss, the anger. Why was it everyone seemed to go for the easy way out? If there was a boat to rock, she'd bloody well rock it. In spite of herself, tears welled in her eyes.

'I'm sorry,' Nick muttered. 'That was insensitive. I just . . .' He hesitated. 'I suppose I just don't want to see you hurt.'

Kelly looked at him. 'You're very kind,' she said, and then added, 'For a steward.'

'I wasn't talking as a steward,' he said softly.

There was silence at the table. Not for the first time, Kelly felt an unmistakable tug of attraction towards him. She had always sworn that her private life would take second place to her career until she had established herself, that she would never become involved with anyone remotely connected with racing, and fortunately temptation had rarely come her way. But despite her preoccupation with everything else, something about the man sitting opposite made her resolutions waver.

'Isn't this a touch irregular?' she said. 'Steward enjoying candlelit dinner with apprentice? What would Harry Short say?'

'Somehow,' Nick smiled, 'I can't see Harry spending a night out at Au Père de Nico. Maybe it is a little unusual.' He paused. 'But then so are you.'

Kelly looked away quickly. The thing she needed least in the world at this moment was to fall in love with a steward. In a deliberately uncouth way, she drank back the rest of her wine. 'I bet you say that to all the jockeys.'

The next morning, Kelly heard from her father. There, among the junk mail and bills delivered while she had been riding out first lot, was an envelope written in a careful, neat hand. It contained a note from Dermot Kinane, an ex-jockey who had been a close friend of the family in Ireland. Puzzled, for Dermot had never been a great correspondent, Kelly read;

> Dear Kelly,
>   I hope you are well, and that you had a good journey home.
>   There was something I didn't tell you at your father's funeral because it seemed the wrong time, but two days after he died, I received a letter from him. It said that he had a big problem he didn't want to bother me with, but that if anything happened to him, I was to pass on this envelope to you. He said it was very important.
>   My thoughts are with you at this painful time, Kelly. Please remember that, if you ever need any help, your old friend Dermot is always here.
>   The Lord be with you.
>
> Your loving Dermot

Attached to the letter was a small blue envelope, marked 'KELLY CONNOR'. In the corner, as if added as an afterthought, were the words 'Very Confidential'. Sitting alone at her kitchen table, Kelly read the last words ever written by her father.

> My Darling Girl,
>   I only hope that you will never have to read this letter – not because my life is worth anything to me but because it breaks my heart to think of you alone in a world which I have found to be so harsh and unforgiving.
>   I'm writing this on the morning of your ride at Ascot on Pendero. I hope and pray that you will win – God willing, you will because you have all the ability in the world – but I have discovered over the past few days that there are people prepared to go to great lengths to stop you. I'm told it's nothing personal (it's never anything personal in racing – a fellow who had just put me through the wing at Naas visited me in hospital to tell me it was nothing personal), but the end result is the same. A horse which should win, doesn't.
>   During the week there had been a number of calls to the flat. If it was you who answered the telephone, they hung up but when you were away riding they spoke to me. They told me that, if Pendero won at Ascot, you were finished as a jockey. Come second, third, last and things would go your way from then on. We have friends in high places, they said. There were also threats to me personally – which didn't worry me. I've been threatened before and doubtless will be again!

Kelly felt the tears fill her eyes as she heard her father's voice speaking through the words on the page.

So why didn't I tell you? God forgive me, I nearly did. The first time's always easy. It's just a race, after all – if you're any good, you can wave your arms about while pulling a horse's back teeth out and keep yourself out of the stewards' room. Why not keep in with the people who really run racing, the villains? I know the argument well because I was once convinced by it. But then they come back. It's another race, the stakes are higher and this time you're being watched more closely by the authorities. Too late you realize that there's no going back. They've got you. In this war, there's no neutral territory. You're either with the enemy or you're not. I went over to the enemy and destroyed my life and that of your dear mother, God rest her soul. On the day she died, I vowed that whatever happened, I would keep you away from them. I hoped you would stay away from racing but it was in your blood. As soon as I saw you riding, I knew you'd make it – so long as they didn't get to you.

So I lied to them. I told them I'd squared it with you. They wanted to talk to you direct, but I said that would frighten you off. Trust me, I said and they did.

This morning I heard from them again. They were double-checking everything was still in order. They threatened me once more, only this time they sounded much more serious. It occurred to me that this was not some two-bit gambling ring. This was big. They have powerful contacts, I know. I feared for you, my darling girl. I began to have doubts as to whether I had been right not to tell you what was going on.

The coward in me hopes that Pendero gets beaten in an honest race this afternoon. But if he wins, it's possible that something may happen to me. If it does, I hope and pray that they will stop there and leave you alone, at least for the time being.

The purpose of this letter is to explain what happened. I did what I thought was right for the most precious thing in the world to me. Remember, always do your best, don't let them hook you, however tempting the bait. Remember what happened to me because I was weak. Do it for your future, for the Connor name, for me.

I love you,

Dad

When Kelly had finished reading, she just sat and cried, a horrible empty feeling inside her. She didn't know if the tears were for herself or her father. After a while she got up and walked slowly from the kitchen into the bedroom. She pulled from under the bed a box containing photographs and cuttings from happier days. Frank Connor jumping the last on his way to a win in the Gold Cup. Frank Connor grinning, mudspattered, in the winners' enclosure. Frank Connor, profiled in the *Irish Times*, relaxing at home with his wife Mary and his five-year-old daughter Kelly.

The Connor name. There was a new coldness in Kelly's heart. Deep in thought, she put her father's letter at the bottom of the box and pushed it back under the bed. It was time for second lot.

*   *   *

'Change of plan,' Peter, the head lad, shouted out to Kelly as she crossed the yard with her tack. 'You're to ride Shine On for a spot of work.'

'Work?' Kelly expressed surprise. 'I thought he was having an easy day, today.'

Peter nodded in the direction of the Templemans' house, where a silver Lamborghini was parked. 'Apparently we have someone to impress.'

Kelly shrugged. It was unlike Bill to change his training plans for anyone.

Ten minutes later, the question in her mind was answered. As she brought Shine On out of his box, Bill and Annie approached from across the yard. With them was a tall, dark-skinned man in an expensive suit that looked oddly out of place among the wheelbarrows and pitchforks of a small stable.

'Hold him there for a second, Kelly,' said Bill. Kelly noticed that, while the trainer and his wife were looking proudly at their horse, the stranger appeared to be more interested in her.

'Please introduce me,' he said quietly.

'Of course.' Bill concealed his disappointment that the man had failed to comment on the appearance of the pride of the yard. 'Kelly Connor. This is Fayoud al Hassan.'

The man walked forward and fixed Kelly with his dark eyes. His handshake was like a caress.

Kelly nodded with a brisk, businesslike 'How do you do, sir.'

'Mr Hassan is Shine On's new owner,' said Bill.

Kelly's eyes widened. She felt like swearing but instead said, 'You're a very lucky man, Mr Hassan, he's a lovely horse.' He was also the one good horse Kelly had been certain to ride – while Bill owned him.

But not even the news that the most promising horse in the yard had been sold to Ibn Fayoud, nor the rumour that the rest of the young Arab's horses would also be coming to the yard, could distract Kelly from thoughts of her father's letter. In the string, taking Shine On for a showpiece half-speed over five furlongs, riding home, her mind was on the implications of his message.

Racecourse rumour, as reported by Annie, had it that there had been a big gamble on Pendero, that a professional gambler stood to gain a fortune if he won. It was now obvious that the horse was a stayer and yet Harry Short's stable jockey had recently ridden him as if his best distance was six furlongs, holding him up for a late run. Although Pendero had finished strongly at Ascot, that was because it had been a truly run race and the leaders had finished tired. Over a mile, the only sensible way to ride Pendero was to use his stamina, not hold him up. Short had been saving him for the Ascot race. Kelly was sure of it.

Then why did he put her up at Ascot rather than one of the top jockeys? Her seven-pound claim was one possible reason; another was that, with an apprentice riding him, Pendero's odds in the market would lengthen. Then Kelly remembered Short's behaviour after the race. He had fastened on to the fact that she was a Connor, played on memories of her father's reputation for throwing races. It was a cheap shot but an effective one. Racing people believed in bloodlines. Even if she were finally cleared by Nick Morley's investigation, she would remain guilty by association in the eyes of many racecourse insiders. In other words, when the race was lost in the weighing room, she was an obvious scapegoat. Was it possible that Short was part of the conspiracy, that he stood to gain from his own horse being beaten?

It seemed unlikely. Before the race he had been tense, after it his fury had seemed spontaneous and genuine. A crook and a bastard Short might be, but it would be surprising if he were that good an actor. His deviousness and dishonesty were in the front window for all to see. Yet whatever went on in that race, Kelly was certain that Short was a part of it. She would have to speak to him. She didn't relish the prospect.

Assuming that Short had been playing it straight, then there remained the question of who stood to lose if Pendero won. That there was a conspiracy Kelly had no doubt. Unfortunately she only knew two bit-part players in the plot. The chance of Damien Gould helping her seemed unlikely in the extreme, unless she could apply pressure on him. Someone somewhere must know what skeletons he had hidden in his locker. The idea of employing a spot of judicious blackmail did not appeal to her but what was the alternative? There was little point in appealing to his better nature when he clearly didn't have one.

A more likely lead was Giles Williams, the journalist. It had been no coincidence that she had been called to the phone in the weighing room. She doubted if Williams were a major player – even on the telephone, he sounded a loser – but at least he might tell her who had put him up to it. That would be a start.

Trust no one, her father had said. But there was little chance of discovering who had killed him without help. Kelly decided that she had to talk to Annie, even if there was a risk that she would tell her husband. Bill would have a fit if he knew his apprentice was turning supersleuth. She also had to tell Nick. He had made her promise to keep him in touch with developments. Being part of the racing establishment, he could be helpful to her, and he had seemed to understand why she needed to pursue this, and it wouldn't be that painful to see him again. Far from it. Kelly smiled.

'Thinking of your next winner?' one of the lads interrupted her reverie as the string turned back to the stable.

'Something like that,' said Kelly, and then returned to her thoughts. Her first job would be to show the letter to the police.

Success as a jockey is not just a question of riding winners. Sometimes you have to be able to handle the phone as well as you handle horses. No one in racing is above ringing round for spare rides; one great jump jockey was nicknamed 'Ting-a-Ling' because of his speed and skill in contacting trainers whose jockeys were injured or couldn't do the weight or were simply out of favour. Kelly understood this and played the game as well as anyone. When it really mattered, Kelly could give great phone.

But this afternoon she wasn't looking for spare rides. She had been to see the inspector in charge of her father's murder case. He hadn't held out much hope, although he had agreed that the letter seemed to disprove the theory about a break-in that had gone wrong.

Kelly had driven straight home and embarked on her own investigation. First of all, she rang round her contacts in journalism. Unsurprisingly, none of them had heard of Giles Williams, which was clearly a false name, and Kelly's description of his telephone manner – a slurred, gin-sodden voice with a wheedling insincere tone to it – covered half of what used to be known as Fleet Street.

It was finally Bob Morrow, one of the older racing correspondents on the *Daily Telegraph*, who came up with a lead.

'That's not his name,' he said. 'And he's not really a journo, more a jumped-up PR man. Now – ' There was a noisy inhalation of smoke, followed by a hacking cough '– what the hell was his name?'

'How d'you know it's "Giles Williams"?'

'There used to be a Giles Williams column in the *Life* many years ago. Gossip, jokes, social titbits. This man goes racing every day. He gambles, swears a lot, drinks too much, falls over.'

'So he *is* a journalist.'

Morrow laughed, bringing on another attack of smoker's cough. 'Now, now,' he said, when he had recovered. 'We're not all like that. No, the man gave up writing years ago. There was some sort of scandal.'

'What does he do now?'

'Professional hanger-on. Part-time stringer. Full-time piss-artist. He sells the odd bonk 'n' tell story to the tabloids – Page Three Girl in Raunchy Romps with Royal Romeo, that sort of thing. He's just your basic, traditional smut-peddler really. Tell you what, I'll ask around and ring you back.'

Kelly thanked him.

'Any tips?'

'Yes, Bob,' she said. 'Cut down to twenty a day.'

'Where's that running then?' With a wheezy laugh, the journalist hung up.

Harry Short, Damien Gould. Kelly was tapping the pad in front of her, considering which of these unlikely leads to follow up, when the phone rang. It was Bill.

'Tomorrow evening, at Kempton. Boardwalk runs in the seller. All right?'

'You mean I'm riding him?' Kelly was unable to conceal her surprise. Ascot was barely a week past and all the indications had been that her rehabilitation as a jockey would be a matter of weeks not days.

'Why, did you have other plans?' Bill snapped. 'You'll just have to cancel him, won't you?'

'No, it's just, after last week, I thought that – '

'Don't be bloody stupid. I do have one or two owners who do what they're told. You've got eight stone three with the claim. I think he'll win. I'll see you in the morning.' He hung up.

It hadn't been difficult for Bill to accede to his wife's nagging to give the girl a break. Maybe he was biased, but as far as he was concerned, she was the best claimer in the country.

Kelly put the phone down and skipped around the room. It was the best she'd felt since Ascot. Bill had come up trumps. Abrupt, unsmiling, laconic, he'd kept the faith. She grabbed the copy of *Racing Post* that was on the table. Boardwalk was no flying machine, a big clumsy four-year-old who had yet to win a race, but none of the opposition had any form. Best of all, one of them – a horse with a line of duck's eggs beside its inappropriate name of Dead Lucky – was being ridden by Damien Gould. She'd get a chance to talk to him about Ascot.

The sound of the telephone crashed into her thoughts. A wheezing cough at the other end of the line told Kelly that it was Bob Morrow.

'Quentin St John Broom-Parker. A man as phony as his name. That's your Giles Williams.'

'Have you got a number?'

'No, but you'll find him in the bar at the nearest race meeting to London. Big fellow with a Jimmy Edwards tash and a red face, swaying slightly as he bores all around him with a pack of lies about his past. When there's no racing nearby, you'll find him in the Garrick Club.'

Kelly glanced at the racing paper she was holding. 'It's only Pontefract today,' she said. 'If I come down to London now, do you reckon he'll be at the Garrick?'

'He'll have been there since lunchtime like as not. Phone and see. If he is there, by the time you arrive he'll be nice and mellow.'

'Bob, you're a brick,' said Kelly. 'I owe you one.'

Another attack of coughing forced Kelly to hold the receiver away from her ear.

'I'm too old for it now, but thanks for the thought,' Morrow eventually managed. 'By the way, you have to be a member to get in the Garrick.

Kelly grinned to herself. 'Crap,' she said.

The gentleman who answered the phone at the Garrick confirmed that Broom-Parker was indeed there. So Kelly changed to go, but before leaving for London, she wrote a brief letter to Dermot Kinane.

My dear Dermot,

I've just got your letter and Dad's note to me. It meant a lot and I'm very grateful you sent it on to me.

Thanks for your kind offer of help. I'm beginning to put my life together again now and I'm concentrating on my riding to help me get through.

I hope to come to Ireland at the end of the season and I will, of course, come and see you. I miss you and all my friends there.

All my love,
Kelly

Dear Dermot. Always the thoughtful, worried one. There was no need to get him involved in this.

With her thoughts on another, simpler life back in the old country, Kelly put the letter in an envelope, picked up her coat and left for London.

Bennett had been doorman at the Garrick Club for twenty-three years and had developed a way with unpleasantness. Sometimes tourists wandered in off Longacre and looked about the hall of this famous British institution before he ushered them out. Or members imbibed a little too enthusiastically and had to be helped into a taxi. More often, they simply died; the after-dinner heart attack while slumbering in one of the club's deep leather chairs was a popular way of moving on to the great gentleman's club in the sky. There were low points, of course. First they let journalists in, then literary agents; it would be women members next.

Bennett was thankful that retirement was only two years away. These days, everything was changing, even the Garrick Club.

Then a young woman – dark, quite a looker if you liked that sort of thing but a
bit too full of herself for Bennett's liking – walked into the club and announced
that she was the dinner guest of Sir Robin Day, he could only treat her to his coldly disapproving smile and direct her to the ladies' bar. It was the sort of thing that
happened these days. How was he to know that she was up to some sort of mis-
chief?

Kelly walked up the steps into the hall of the Garrick towards the wide staircase which led up to the bar, then hesitated. In front of an open fireplace in the
hall, a couple of large leather armchairs were occupied by two men in dark suits.
One was reading a newspaper, the other was fast asleep, a rumbling snore like a
low-flying aircraft emanating from him. He had a prominent handlebar moustache
and a high colour to his cheeks. Choosing a chair with its back to the front door
and Bennett's look-out post, Kelly sat herself down.

It took a moment for the full enormity of what was happening to filter through
to the brandy-drenched consciousness of the member reading *The Times*. Then he
lowered his paper with the look of man whose most precious shrine is being des-
ecrated before his eyes. 'This part of the club is for members only, he said in a
voice of strangulated distaste. 'It's not open to – '

'Women?' Kelly smiled. 'Don't worry, I won't be here long.'

At the sound of a female voice, the eyes of the other man snapped open. 'Good
God,' he said.

'No, Kelly Connor. Giles Williams, I believe. Or do you prefer the name Quentin
St John Broom-Parker?'

Kelly stood up, walked slowly towards Broom-Parker and knelt before his chair
like a child about to be told a fireside story. As Broom-Parker attempted to strug-
gle to his feet, she leant forward and tweaked both ends of his moustache.

'I *say*,' the *Times* reader stood up and dithered while Kelly took a firmer hold
of Broom-Parker's bristling moustache.

'Be quiet,' she said over her shoulder.

Muttering, 'Where's Bennett, for God's sake?' the man hurried off.

Kelly pulled Broom-Parker's face towards hers and looked deeply into his
loser's eyes. His breath stank of drink. 'Listen,' she said. 'We've spoken on the
telephone, remember?'

The colour had now left Quentin Broom-Parker's face. To nod would have been
too painful, but he closed his eyes in confirmation.

'I lost the race because of you.' Kelly tugged at the moustache. 'That doesn't
matter now. But someone was murdered the same day and that does matter. I think
the same people were involved. Follow me?'

A knot of dark-suited Garrick members had gathered in the hall and were muttering anxiously. Who was this madwoman? Broom-Parker's mistress? He always
was a game old dog. Doesn't look so clever now, though.

Broom-Parker's eyes swivelled beseechingly towards his friends. Kelly tugged
again.

'Follow me?'

A blink of the eyes.

'Now I need to know who paid you or blackmailed you to call me in the weighing room.'

'Right, young lady.' Bennett stood behind her. 'Leave go of this gentleman or I will have no alternative but to use force on you.'

'Throw me out,' said Kelly without taking her eyes off Broom-Parker, 'And the whiskers come too. This won't take more than a moment.' Bennett hesitated. Nothing in his many years' service had prepared him for this sort of situation.

'I need to know,' repeated Kelly.

'I can't tell you,' squirmed Broom-Parker painfully. 'It's more than my life's worth.'

Kelly stared at the pathetic figure for a moment and then let him go. 'Ok, I'm going straight to the police.'

With that, Kelly got up, brushed past Bennett and walked calmly out. The fact that she'd already told the police didn't matter. She'd just have to think of something else.

Margaret Stanhope worshipped her employer, Jack Butler. She knew that there were murky corners to his business affairs, that for a suave good-looking man, he had one or two unfortunate characteristics, like a ferocious temper. And, of course, she knew that Jack's private life was something of a carnival. She knew all that because, as Jack's private assistant, she organized him; his TV appearances, his meetings with London's shadier characters, his payments for some mucky chore or other, his alibis to the wife (who could blame him, married to that bimbo?), his hotel rooms.

Not that she minded Jack playing around because she knew that one day he would be hers. She may have been three years older than he was, pushing forty and not quite as pert as the sort of girl he favoured at this precise moment, but one day Jack would grow up, look for a real woman to take care of him, and there she'd be, waiting and ready.

Telephone cupped under his left ear, Jack leant back in his chair, put his feet on the desk, almost kicking his assistant as he did it, and said, 'Well, that's *very* inconvenient.' He winked at Margaret as the person at the other end of the line spluttered some apology or other.

Yes, she was ready. Sometimes a wink kept her in fantasies for weeks. Once or twice, Jack had casually goosed her as she reached for a file. She had nearly melted away on the spot.

He hung up and stared out of the window, over the roofs of Victoria.

'Right,' he said finally. 'I need to see Ibn Fayoud again. Tell Johnny and Den I have another job for them. And it looks like I'm going to have to attend to that jockey girl.'

'Attend, Jack?' Margaret Stanhope smiled. 'D'you mean – '

'I mean attend,' Jack snapped. 'I want you to do some research on her. Maybe she's not so perfect. Talk to the usual contacts. Find out if she's ever thrown a race. Past boy friends who could use a bit of spare cash. Any relevant details from her private life. You know the sort of thing.'

'Filth.'

'Too right, darling.' Jack was dialling another number. He glanced up, as if surprised she was still there. 'Well, get on with it then.'

Margaret stood up, blushing.

'Yes, Jack,' she said.

Chapter 5

An evening meeting on a Tuesday at Kempton is not one of racing's most glamorous occasions. There are horses, trainers, lads, jockeys, bookmakers and gamblers but the good-hearted enthusiast, the average racegoer, is hardly in evidence. Sometimes it's like a West End performance with all the regulars in place, but no audience.

Kelly Connor didn't care. She was back in the weighing room again after the nightmare of Ascot. She had much on her mind. To her surprise Broom-Parker had phoned shortly after she'd returned home, pleading with her not to mention his name to the police. He had arranged to meet her after racing in the White Lion at Feltham. But her first, most immediate priority was to win again, to show racing's sceptics that she was not a loser, nor bent, but simply a good, strong apprentice on her way to the top. A week had passed without the offer of one single outside ride; she badly needed a winner.

The one and a half mile John Sturgeon Selling Plate, the second to last race of the evening, was hardly the stuff of headlines. Between them the eight runners had won three races; they were racing's cannon fodder. Some of them would be put over hurdles next season, perhaps one might be sold to Barbados or Abu Dhabi in the forlorn hope that they could win something there, but most of them were racing in the shadow of the knacker's yard.

Boardwalk was not a joy to ride, Kelly reflected as the horse made its lumbering way down to the start. Genuine enough, he pulled your arms out for half the race until you asked him to quicken, when you found there was nothing in the tank. It was only because he belonged to a good-hearted owner, Mrs Prentice, the wife of a local solicitor, that Bill had persevered with him. Maybe one day, Boardwalk would pick up a bad race – like the John Sturgeon Selling Plate at Kempton. Even if he did win, the owner would buy him in after the race, so that Boardwalk would have paid back a small fraction of his training costs. And Mrs Prentice's idea of a gamble was £10 each way. Tonight was not about money, but about winning, fun, maybe a passing mention in the morning's racing press.

The market, if the desultory interest shown in the Silver Ring could be described as such, had made Boardwalk second favourite to a horse called Bite the Bullet. Also in the betting was Dead Lucky, whose jockey was Damien Gould.

'All right, sexy?' Kelly had shouted out to Gould as she cantered past him, almost brushing his boot, on the way to post. Gould, his face expressionless as a mask, had pretended not to hear. He hadn't expected to see the girl on a racecourse so soon after Ascot. She was riding with a score to settle. That was good.

Bill's instructions to her had been simple. Keep in touch with the leaders, aim to hit the front a furlong out, stay out of trouble. It was that last remark that echoed in Kelly's mind as Boardwalk was loaded into the stalls. The last thing she needed was to be up in front of the stewards again. Forget Ascot, she told herself, ride your race, but stay out of trouble.

Although Boardwalk was drawn on the inside, Kelly hoped to get a good enough break to be able to settle third or fourth. Within seconds of the stalls going up, she realized that this would be a problem. Boardwalk bounded along with more enthusiasm than grace at the head of the second group while two horses, including the favourite, made the running some three lengths clear of her.

Two and a half furlongs from home, Kelly couldn't believe it, she was still riding with a double handful. But she knew Boardwalk well enough not to be fooled. He was one-paced and, even at this lowly level, there were likely to be one or two horses behind her with a touch of finishing speed. Ahead of her, Bite the Bullet's jockey was hard at work while the horse on his outside was clearly beaten. Someone was half a length behind her on her outside but Kelly sensed that she had more in hand than he did. She glanced back to see Damien Gould. This time he wasn't smiling.

In any other race, at any other time, Kelly would have acted instinctively and eased Boardwalk away from the rails so as to take the leader in the final furlong. But seeing Damien made her lose concentration and before she knew what was happening she found herself boxed in yet again. Dead Lucky was struggling to stay in touch, but he was still there nonetheless, and if she just pushed her way out, Damien could easily make a show of snatching up.

For vital seconds, Kelly hesitated. Then she saw that Bite the Bullet, now under heavy pressure, was drifting away from the rails. The gap had barely begun to appear before Kelly was driving Boardwalk through, but he seemed to take for ever to pick up speed. Bite the Bullet continued to drift left-handed as the winning post raced towards them. Kelly was pushing and kicking for all she was worth, with her stick working in her left hand. She'd already hit Boardwalk twice and in desperation gave him a couple more, but it was like living one of those nightmares where you can never quite reach what you're trying to catch.

The two of them flashed by the post. There would be a photograph, but she knew that she had failed to get up.

With despair in her heart, she pulled up, cursing herself. She knew that she should have won and so would everyone else. She glanced across at Damien who shook his head with eloquent disgust, as if to say, 'Women jockeys!'

Of course, they all knew. The lad who led her in, the irate punter who looked up at her with contempt and muttered, 'You're useless', Bill, who made little effort to conceal his anger as she unsaddled Boardwalk. Only the owner was excluded from the common knowledge at Kempton that day; that her horse had been wrestled into second place by an apprentice who couldn't anticipate the obvious. Mrs Prentice fussed about Boardwalk and congratulated its jockey. Kelly smiled politely and went to weigh in.

The last hour of the meeting passed in a haze of disappointment. Kelly had no more rides on whom she could expunge the memory of that first race. She hated losing at the best of times but this was the worst. A misjudged race, a wrong decision, a bad run – they happened to everyone. Kelly tried to put the self-doubt from her mind. There was nobody more certain to lose a race than a jockey with no self-confidence. Gloomily, she remembered the smirk on Gould's face, the surprise and disappointment on Annie's. It was almost more painful than being labelled a cheat. She could imagine the gossip in the bar. Sad about that Kelly Connor. Nice little rider, but no good when the chips are down.

'Hey, come on, it's only a seller at Kempton.'

Cy McCray was a tough little American jockey who had settled in Britain and was now retained by the Ian Gardem stable. Unlike many of the top jockeys, he found time to talk to Kelly without giving her the immediate impression that he wanted to sleep with her, although if his reputation was only half true then he did. As Kelly walked thoughtfully towards the car park after the last race, Cy joined her.

'A race is a race, Cy,' she said. 'I blew it.'

'Hey, bollocks, y'hear?' There was something endearing about the way McCray adapted English slang into his American accent. 'Happens to us all. You'll show 'em on your next ride.'

'Yes, I suppose so,' Kelly muttered, wondering when that next ride would be. Bill's loyalty to his apprentice had been ill rewarded this evening and no trainer could afford to be sentimental. She glanced up to see a familiar trim figure strolling languidly out of the entrance to the Members' Enclosure. It was Ibn Fayoud. With a shudder, Kelly remembered their last meeting, his handshake.

'Cy, do me favour,' she said quietly. 'Keep walking with me to my car. I have an owner to avoid.'

'I know the feeling.' McCray smiled, looking in Ibn Fayoud's direction. 'Old Ib, eh? You don't fancy joining his harem.'

'Nope.'

'It's the first time I've seen him without all his hangers-on,' Cy commented. 'I guess he must be here just to see his favourite apprentice.'

Ibn Fayoud had stopped by a Jaguar XJS. The window on the driver's side was lowered to reveal the unmistakable face of Jack Butler.

'On the other hand, maybe not,' said Kelly, watching as the two men conversed. She had never met Jack Butler but she had seen him racing, and on television of course. In spite of herself, she had to admit that he had a sort of rough charm.

'Talk about the odd couple,' Cy McCray was saying. 'I thought those two were enemies.'

'Really?' Kelly half listened as Ibn Fayoud climbed into the passenger seat. The Jaguar pulled out towards where she was standing with Cy McCray.

'Someone was saying Ib owes Butler a million-odd quid. I wouldn't fancy owing him two bob.'

The car approached them and Kelly could see the two men talking animatedly.

'They seem quite friendly now,' she said.

At that moment, Ibn Fayoud looked across at her. As she nodded politely, he looked away. It was as if she didn't exist.

'Looks like you're off the hook there,' said Cy McCray.

Kelly got in her car and headed east towards Feltham. She'd arranged to meet Broom-Parker at nine thirty. As she reached the outskirts of the town she stopped to ask the way, and then discovered that the traffic on the road past the White Lion was being diverted because of an accident. Kelly parked in a side street and walked.

It must have been quite a crash. As she approached, she could see three blue lights flashing in the gathering gloom. A group of spectators had gathered like vultures on the pavement. Kelly made her way through the crowd, vaguely aware of the chatter of people whose dull lives had briefly been made more exciting by another's misfortune. It was when she heard the phrase 'Hit-and-run job' that she glanced into the road.

Behind a police car, which was parked across the road to stop the traffic, an ambulance man was crouching over a body. There was something familiar about the checked suit, lit up by the flashing blue light. She walked into the road.

'Back, please.' A policeman held out his arms as if heading off a loose horse. 'There's nothing you can do for him, dear. He's had it.'

For a moment, she caught a glimpse of the victim's face. It had been bloodied and battered by the impact of the car but, curiously, its handlebar moustache looked as trim and correct in death as it had in life. Turning away, Kelly saw some loose change in the gutter where the car had made contact with its target. There was also a piece of paper.

Kelly picked it up. It was a betting-slip, marked 'REG BUTLER, Turf Accountants'.

Her instinct was to drive – to get in the car, go home, and be safe – resume the life of an apprentice who wanted to be champion jockey. But, with a growing sense of foreboding, she knew she couldn't do that. Broom-Parker had played no more than a small part in the plot to make sure Pendero was beaten, she was certain of that. He was too much of a loser to have been anything more than a hired hand. For reasons of guilt, greed of fear, he had agreed to talk to her. And now he was dead. Pawn, stool pigeon, nobody – it made no difference to these people. To be worth two murders in eight days, Ascot had to be more than a mere gambling scam. Turning away would be playing the game their way. She remembered the words in her father's letter; *Don't let them hook you, however tempting the bait.* Right now the bait was not money or easy winners, just the chance to earn a living by riding horses in races without fearing for her life. But the information she already had marked her out as a target. The men who had killed her father and now Broom-Parker could presumably have something similar planned for her. She'd better tell the police in Newmarket and also Nick Morley and his Jockey Club security people.

Kelly asked the policeman what had happened. Apparently the man whose body was now on its way to the city mortuary was drunk. According to the barman in the White Lion, he had been putting away double scotches when he received a telephone call at the bar. Unsteadily, he had made his way out of the door, on to the street – and under the speeding wheels of a hit-and-run driver. The sports car had hardly braked. It had seemed to slow down briefly after the impact, as if the driver was considering whether to stop or not, and then had accelerated off into the night. Kids, probably – joy-riding was a popular pastime among the city's bored teenagers. Our redfaced friend, said the policeman, chose the wrong time in the wrong town to go for a drunken walkabout in the road.

Wearily, Kelly made her way back to her car, drove to the nearest hotel and booked a room. She would not be going home tonight.

She rang the Templemans' number. They would still be driving home, so she could leave a message on the answering machine. That would make it easier.

'This is Kelly here,' she said, trying to make her voice sound as calm and normal as possible. 'I'm still in London. I have to go up north tomorrow on a family matter. It's a bit too complicated to explain right now but it's really unavoidable so I won't be able to ride out tomorrow. I'll be back for Thursday, though. Hope that's all right. 'Bye.'

She hung up. If there was one person she hated lying to, it was Bill. He was one of the few genuinely honest men in racing. He would curse when he heard the message, even though tomorrow the string would be doing road work and she was not needed. Annie would be suspicious about that 'family matter'. She would worry that Kelly was becoming involved in the sleazy aftermath of her father's death.

Kelly switched on the television and stared blankly at the screen as some mindless cops and robbers show unfolded. At the back of her mind, it occurred to her how different real crime was from the glamorous violence portrayed on the screen. Reality wasn't the wailing siren, the squealing tyres of the cop car, the cry of 'Police, freeze!' in the night; reality was the quiet desperation and nauseous fear of ordinary lives caught up, often unwillingly, in a web of deception, greed and violence. Pointless and destructive.

She sighed and turned the television off. Going up north tomorrow. At least that part was true.

Visitors to Harry Short's yard in Blaworth, which was situated some five miles from the maisonette in Doncaster where he was born, were often taken aback, shocked even, by what they found. Despite the size of the stables and the fact that he belonged to the world of flat-racing where appearances count for something, Short had made no compromises. The yard was squalid and run down, the lads slouched about the place resentfully, the tack was old and dirty with repair patches showing on almost every item of leather. The only things that looked good were the horses, whose coats shone under their shabby exercise sheets. At the end of the day, Kelly thought to herself, I suppose it's them that matter.

It was said that Harry Short's great strength was that he had never tried to imitate smarter trainers, that he played by his rules, was his own man, but even this was flattering him. The idea of smartening up had simply never occurred to him; the appearance of his training establishment was how all yards should look. In fact, for all he knew – which wasn't much, since he never visited other trainers – this was how they did look. The only difference was that he trained more winners than most of them did.

First lot was making its way lazily along a path some fifty yards from the road where Kelly had parked her car. She was not the first person to wonder about the secret of Harry Short's success. If anyone else ran a yard of sixty flat-race horses like he did, they would have been out of business years ago. Yet he just went from strength to strength.

It was true that his horses tended to have brief careers. The idea of giving a backward horse time, of not over-racing his less tough charges, of giving the vet the benefit of the doubt when he said a leg was liable to break down on hard ground – these were alien concepts to Harry Short. Horses were there to earn their living, or rather his living. If they didn't run fast enough, or weren't tough enough, then there were always others. They were the means of producing cash, no more and no less.

As Kelly stood watching the string, her hands sunk deep into her windcheater pockets, Harry Short's Mercedes made its way along the gallops between the path and the road. He glanced towards Kelly and slowed down for a moment before speeding onwards. He didn't like people watching his horses work from the road but this was only a woman, probably some jumped-up point-to-point type looking for training tips. Kelly glanced at her car clock. It was time to make her entrance.

'That's very strange.' A woman in her fifties, with a scarf holding a shock of grey hair, stood on the doorstep of Harry Short's house. 'He never mentioned visitors.'

'Well, isn't that odd?' Kelly shook her head. 'It was definitely today. Come up to ride Pendero second lot, he said. I hope he hasn't forgotten – I've driven all the way from Newmarket. Never mind, I'll wait for him in the car.'

'By, you will not,' said the woman, opening the front door. 'You'll come in here and have a cup of tea till his lordship gets back. It's typical of him to forget to tell me he's entertaining. Follow me, love, don't mind the mess in the hall.'

Kelly picked her way through saddles, blankets, old copies of *Sporting Life*, reflecting that Short's domestic arrangements made his yard looked positively pristine.

She was on her second cup of tea when Harry blundered into the house like some evil giant out of a fairy story. He had actually slumped down at the breakfast table before he became aware of Kelly's presence. When he did, his eyes narrowed and for a moment Kelly thought he was going to bound across the room and hit her.

'What the bloody hell are you doing here?' he said in a dangerous, quiet voice. No one entered Harry Short's house without an invitation and to find Kelly Connor of all people sitting across the breakfast table was like a practical joke in very poor taste. Kelly sat in silence and smiled. An odd rumbling sound emanated from Short before, looking towards the door, he snapped, 'Betty!'

'It's not your wife's fault,' said Kelly quickly. 'I lied to her to get in because I needed to talk to you about your big gamble at Ascot.' Harry got up as if to throw her out. Kelly went on, 'I've discovered some things which might interest you.'

In spite of himself, Harry was curious and he sat down again. It must be important for her to have driven all the way up north and bluff her way into his house. He glanced up at her almost respectfully as he poured himself some tea. If she had the nerve, the sheer bloody brass neck, to do that, then maybe he'd give her a few minutes.

Betty put a plate of fried eggs and bacon in front of the trainer. 'Was there something else?'

'Yes.' He shot a warning glance at Kelly, but then said mildly, 'Any chance of another pot of tea, love?'

After the woman had left, he muttered, 'She isn't my wife. She just comes mornings.' Angrily, as if he blamed them for his loneliness, he set about his fried egg and bacon. Then he looked up sharply and, revealing more of the contents of his mouth than Kelly wished to see, said, 'Well, get on with it then.'

'Here's what we both know.' Kelly sipped at her tea. She had been right about Short; the way to get him to listen was to treat him as if he were a human being, which he clearly wasn't. But she had to be careful. With this man, an earthquake was never far away. 'Pendero was a stone-cold certainty for the race at Ascot,' she said. 'You had run him over races short of his best distance. Maybe you hadn't tried too hard in them.'

'Say that to anyone else,' Short muttered without looking up from his fried egg, 'And I'll see you in court.'

'What you did with him before Ascot is your business. Pendero was off the day I was riding him, that's what matters. Why did you book me, by the way?'

'Fuck knows.'

Kelly waited.

'I'd seen you ride. We needed the seven-pound claim.' Short looked up angrily as he remembered the events of that day. 'We all make mistakes,' he snapped, 'What's done's done. If you're here because I said certain things about you after the race, you can sod off back south right now.'

'I'm not here for an apology,' Kelly said quietly. Ignoring a dismissive grunt from Short, she continued, 'Since that race, two people have died violent, nasty deaths. I believe those murders had something to do with the race I rode for you.'

Harry Short shrugged. Life, death, it happened, even in racing.

'One of them was my father.'

'Aye, well.' Short was about to say something about Frank Connor, but thought better of it. 'Aye, well, sorry,' he said. 'The reason I put you up was I heard you were good and . . . straight.'

'I am,' said Kelly. 'I didn't lose you that race.'

'So what happened to the weight?'

'You tell me.'

There was a clatter of cutlery as Short reacted. 'What the fuck are you talking about?' he exploded, spraying small bits of bacon across the table.

'You took the saddle. It would have been easy for you to lose five pounds' worth of lead as you saddled up. Then blame me after the race.' Kelly was unable to keep the bitterness out of her voice. 'After all, I'm just another crooked Connor.'

'You're mad. That's not my way. I wanted to win that race. I was done.'

'There's another possibility.' Kelly told him about the call to the weighing room, her father's letter, the death of Broom-Parker. By the time she had finished, Short was sitting back, the greasy remains of his breakfast in front of him. He lit up a cigarette and looked at Kelly thoughtfully. 'If it wasn't me who wanted Pendero to lose that race,' she concluded, 'And it wasn't you, who was it?'

Short shrugged. 'There was a bet. Quite a big bet.'

'Yours?'

'Look, Connor.' The trainer sat up in his chair and looked about the table as if searching for something to throw at her. 'I'm not used to some bloody apprentice waltzing into my house and asking me about my private affairs – '

'So who else was involved?'

'You should know.' A sulky bitterness had entered Short's voice. 'He's just moved all his horses to Bill Templeman, hasn't he? Bloody Arab bastard.' Short stabbed out his cigarette in the bacon fat on his plate.

'Ibn Fayoud?' Kelly was unable to conceal her surprise. 'What does – '

'Work it out for yourself.' Harry Short stood up. 'I've told you too much already.' He looked at her appraisingly as if, for the first time, it had occurred to him that Kelly Connor was not just another apprentice, but a woman. 'Can't think why,' he added with a telltale catch in his voice.

'I'd better be going,' said Kelly warily, standing up herself and backing away from the trainer.

'Maybe I can tell you more a bit later. Second lot won't take long.'

'Got to get back, Mr Short.'

'Perhaps you'd like to ride a bit of work for me.' The leer was now unmistakable.

'I thought you were never going to let me near any of your horses again.' Kelly made her way through the hall towards the front door.

Short chuckled randily. 'Who's talking about horses?' he called out as she walked quickly towards her car. Kelly waved as she pulled away in her car, and gave a little sigh of relief. Harry Short moving into seductive mode was not an attractive sight.

'Nothing, Jack.'

Margaret Stanhope hated to disappoint her boss. It almost broke her heart when she saw that darting look of irritation cross his face as she brought him bad news. It didn't happen often – when it came to personally assisting, she had few equals – but, when it did, she felt ridiculously guilty. Her point in life was to solve Jack Butler's problems; when they persisted, she felt worse than he did about it.

'What d'you mean *nothing*?'

Margaret shrugged miserably.

'What is she, some kind of nun or something?' Jack Butler was almost ugly when he was angry; it was a side of him that the many thousands of women who watched racing only to catch a glimpse of him never saw. 'She's Irish, isn't she? She's a jockey, she's a looker. There must be something from her past.'

'I've asked around. She had a relationship with a local solicitor a couple of years ago. He's straight as a die. Since then, she's kept herself to herself.'

Jack thought back to Ascot. 'Seems a bit of a waste,' he said. 'What about on the racetrack? Anything there?'

'Just Pendero, nothing else.'

The bookmaker looked at her pityingly. 'I know about that,' he said.

'Maybe,' Margaret faltered. 'Maybe we could . . . fix something up.'

Jack laughed and shook his head. 'You're a wicked old cow sometimes, you really are.'

Uncertain whether to be flattered or insulted, Margaret smiled primly. 'Let me know what you want me to do,' she said.

Bill Templeman was a man of few words. He could talk horses, he could give instructions to a jockey but the confidential fireside chat was not his style. Kelly liked the man but dreaded those rare occasions when their conversations lasted for more than a couple of sentences. When he asked to see her in his study, a few days after her return from Blaworth, she feared the worst.

'Family all right?' he asked, riffling through the papers on his desk.

Kelly remembered the lie that she had had to tell to take a day off work. 'Not too bad,' she said. 'Under the circumstances.'

'Nothing new on your father's death?'

'No, not yet. But I think that – '

'It's not your job to think.' Bill's voice betrayed genuine anger. 'We're still getting calls here about you, anonymous calls. Whoever it is says you're still nosing about in business which doesn't concern you.'

'My father's death concerns – '

'Listen, Kelly, I know you're still upset about your father's death, but if you want to play detective, you'd better give up riding and join the police. You've already lost me one race because you're still hung up on that business at Ascot. If it were up to me, I'd jock you off for the rest of the season. Maybe next year, you'll be a jockey again.'

'I'm sorry.' Kelly hung her head at this unusually long speech. He was right. None of this had anything to do with the Templeman yard. It was run on a shoestring at the best of times and Kelly was merely adding to his problems. But something nagged at her about what he had just said. 'How do you mean "if it were up to me"?'

'You seem to have an admirer in Ibn Fayoud al Hassan. He's instructed me to give you the ride on Shine On at York next week. In fact, he wants you to ride all his horses.'

Kelly smiled and sighed with relief. 'Thank you,' she said.

'Don't thank me, thank him. He likes the way you ride him. Bloody fool.'

Kelly knew Bill well enough to be certain that no one, least of all a new owner, would dictate to him which jockey to put up. In spite of this show of gruff disapproval, he was giving her one last chance.

'Don't screw it up this time,' he said, turning back to his correspondence and entry forms. 'Remember you're a jockey.'

Kelly was down to ride a two-year-old called Billy Liar for second lot. He was one of Ibn Fayoud's colts and apparently bone idle. This morning was the first time he was to be given a serious piece of work before running later in the week.

Within moments of climbing on board, Kelly could see why Billy Liar had won few friends at the yard. He was oddly sluggish and lazy, more like a leery veteran than a horse that had never seen a racecourse. Dennis, who was down to ride work with her on another two-year-old smiled with open hostility as they made their way up to the gallops.

'You've met your match there, darling,' he said as Kelly pushed and shoved the colt along, tying to keep him from stopping altogether.

'Really?' Kelly was used to Dennis's sarcasm and had come to pity his jealousy of her. 'What makes you think that?'

'He's a lazy bastard, that's why. He needs a strong pair of legs on him.' He winked across at her. 'Not that I've personally got anything against your legs.'

Kelly laughed and muttered an expletive which Dennis pretended not to hear. She'd show him.

And she'd show Bill. To people in racing, there was nothing more suspect than a professional who allowed outside concerns to impinge on the real world – the world of racing. Outside was dangerous, complicated; outside contaminated the already difficult business of getting horses to win races. To be a true professional, you had to live in a closed world. It's not your job to think. Remember you're a jockey.

From the moment the two horses jumped off to work, Kelly knew she was in trouble. While Dennis was well on the bridle, she was having to work hard to keep Billy Liar up to the pace. After a couple of furlongs, Dennis let out a notch on his reins and moved half a length up on her. Kelly gave her horse a slap down the shoulder; it grunted but failed to quicken.

'This horse is wrong,' she called out. 'I'm going to pull up.'

Dennis turned round and shook his head. 'Legs,' he shouted. 'Told you.'

For a moment, Kelly felt a flare of anger within her. They were out of sight of the guv'nor, so she yelled at Billy Liar and cracked him one behind the saddle. The horse made another noise, more a groan than a grunt this time, and, as his stride faltered, Kelly knew that she had made a serious mistake.

A split second later, the earth was hurtling towards her.

Chapter
6

Sheikh al Hassan had a lot on his mind. The price of oil was tumbling again, one of his most reliable brokers on Wall Street had just been arrested for insider dealing, the acquisition of a highly prestigious London hotel had been held up by a query as to who actually owned it and, back home, one of his sisters had just committed suicide, causing a tremor of scandal throughout the country. The death under somewhat dubious circumstances of a racehorse belonging to his son was frankly the least of his problems.

He looked through the smoked window of his Rolls-Royce and sighed. The traffic on Piccadilly was a great leveller. Salesman making deliveries, out-of-towners visiting a show, executives on their way to a board meeting which would decide the fate of thousands of employees; they all moved at West End speed – that is, not at all. Sheikh al Hassan smiled wearily. In this benighted country, simple solutions – banning traffic, arresting illegal parkers, giving the wealthy and powerful a police escort through the streets – were apparently too complex for its befuddled government.

'There is, I believe, a serious risk of a scandal, sir.'

The Sheikh turned back to Simon Brompton- Smiley. It was bad enough sitting in the London traffic without having to listen to the mumblings of his international racing manager. Mistakenly, he had agreed to let Brompton-Smiley travel with him in the Rolls and discuss the matter of some urgency he had been whining about for the last two days. Now the meeting, which should have taken ten minutes, was being dragged out to three-quarters of an hour. The temptation to open the door and to apply a dark shiny shoe to the seat of the man's pinstriped suit was almost irresistible. If he had been born in Australia or Lithuania or even Manchester, Sheikh al Hassan could have ejected his minion on to the street in the sure knowledge that it would be put down to robust good humour. As it was, he was obliged to behave with decorum.

'I'm so sorry, Simon,' he said, smiling. 'I think I lost the drift of what you were saying.'

'It's your son, sir,' said Brompton-Smiley. 'He has now moved his horses to a small yard in Newmarket run by Bill Templeman. As you know, they were with Ian Gardem.'

'I fail to see a problem there. Maybe he was trying to save some money at last.'

'He then invested in another horse.'

'Ah.' The Sheikh rubbed his eyes. The last thing he needed right now was more bad news about his son.

'A rather expensive horse called Shine On.'

'How much?' Sheikh al Hassan asked the unfamiliar question with some distaste.

'I don't know,' said Brompton-Smiley. 'It was a private sale from Templeman himself but it's got to be six figures.'

'I thought he was broke.'

'Precisely, sir. Then, two days ago, one of his two-year-olds collapsed during a gallop. I've heard, unofficially,' Brompton-Smiley was proud of his network of contacts and could never resist reminding his employer of them, 'very unofficially, that the post-mortem shows that he was got at.'

'Was anyone hurt?'

'Not really. The girl who lost that race at Ascot was riding him. Broken collarbone, that's all.'

At last, the Rolls had broken free of Piccadilly's log-jam and was making its way at something approaching normal speed towards Knightsbridge.

'What exactly are you saying?' Sheikh al Hassan's mind had returned to the important meeting before him.

'Something's going on, sir, and I'm very much afraid that your son is involved. The sooner you make the announcement that you're moving your horses away from Britain the better.'

'I'll need to speak to Morley.'

'I'll arrange that, sir,' said Brompton-Smiley.

The Sheikh's car pulled up outside the hotel where his meeting was to take place. For a moment, he considered letting Brompton-Smiley use the Rolls to get home, but then he thought better of it. There were taxis.

A deputation of dark-suited, middle-aged men appeared at the hotel entrance, smiling like grannies at a railway station. The Sheikh spoke quietly to his chauffeur, then stepped forward to acknowledge them with a courteous inclination of the head.

Standing by the Rolls, Simon Brompton-Smiley turned towards the chauffeur and said something clipped and military. When the man shook his head, he looked at his watch as if yet another important appointment awaited him, and strutted off. There were taxis.

It took a fall at thirty-five miles an hour, a night in Addenbrooke's Hospital in Cambridge, and a broken collarbone to remind Kelly of the life she was missing as a professional jockey. The doctors had told her to take it easy. According to their records, she had not lost consciousness, but she had been badly shaken up. She wouldn't be fit enough to ride for at least a week, but she was able to organize the move to a new flat which Annie had found for her, situated just behind the saddler's shop. It wasn't as nice as the one she'd shared with her father but at least it was cheap. Annie and one of the lads in the yard helped to move what furniture she had. After that she settled down to rest properly. Three days after the accident she agreed to let Nick take her out to dinner.

'Ouch.' Morley winced as Kelly appeared at her front door, her shoulder strapped up, a graze down the side of her face and two blackened eyes. She still managed to look wonderful.

Kelly smiled. 'You should see the other feller,' she said, easing herself gently into the passenger seat of his Aston Martin.

'And you're telling me you weren't concussed?' Morley looked at her with genuine concern.

'No, I'm telling the doctor I wasn't concussed. I have an important ride next Saturday.'

Nick nodded. Under safety regulations, no jockey was allowed to ride in a race within one week of being concussed. If Kelly's fall had happened on a racecourse, she would have been sidelined as a matter of course. It had been fortunate that, by the time a doctor saw her, she showed no signs of having lost consciousness.

'I suppose I'm meant to turn a deaf ear to that.' He grinned and looked across to her as he changed gear.

'It was only a small knock. I'll be fine.' Nick was frowning. 'All right?'

He shrugged. 'Just don't go about saying you had a bang on the head. You're not short of enemies already. You want to be careful what you say.'

Kelly half laughed. 'Funny, that,' she said. 'How I seem to trust you.'

Nick smiled grimly. 'I mean it about the enemies. You'll have heard from your boss that the two-year-old you were riding had been got at.'

'No.' Kelly couldn't help sounding shocked. She stared straight ahead. 'No, he didn't tell me that.'

'A post-mortem showed that the horse had traces of Imobolin in its blood. It's what they call Elephant Juice. It's basically a very powerful anaesthetic. The tiniest amount will knock out an elephant. Hence the name. There was a case some time ago where a vet accidentally injected himself with some. He was dead before he could get back to his car for the antidote.'

'How do you know all this?' Kelly's mind was racing. If the horse had been doped, it could only mean that someone in Bill's yard had been involved. If that was the case, who was the target, the horse or her?

'I heard from the equine laboratory in Newmarket. Officially Templeman should tell me himself, but he hasn't. At least, not yet.' They took a left turn and picked up speed. 'Imobolin doesn't even need to be injected,' Nick went on. 'If you mix the stuff with an absorption agent like DMSO and rub it into the skin it would get into the system within half an hour. Wetting the underneath of the saddle with it would have been more than enough to kill the horse. It was due to run in a couple of days, wasn't it?'

Kelly nodded. 'Nottingham.'

'Were you going to ride him?'

'I'm meant to be riding all Ibn Fayoud's horses.'

'Well, it's a good thing it happened at home and not at the racecourse. Otherwise you might have been much more badly hurt.'

'Tell you what.' Kelly made an unconvincing attempt at cheerfulness. 'Why don't we talk about something other than racing?'

It was an uneasy evening. Nick took her to a small restaurant a few miles outside Cambridge, where they both tried to behave as if nothing untoward had happened. He joked that the other diners were looking at him like a wife-batterer. She found herself talking about her father – the way he had brought her up alone, how he had tried to dissuade her from a racing career. And, of course, he had been right. If she had done as he had suggested, become a doctor maybe, or a teacher, he would be alive today and she would be living a normal life.

Nick listened intently. Kelly no longer thought of him as a steward, a central player in the racing game, but as someone who seemed to understand her better than anyone ever had, apart from her father. It was good to talk to a man with whom she felt comfortable.

Nick looked surprised when she told him this. 'So there's no . . .' For a moment he looked embarrassed. 'You haven't got a boyfriend, then?'

'No, thank goodness. Life's tricky enough without that. And you?'

Nick looked away, trying to attract the waiter's attention. 'I married young,' he said. 'It was a mistake. She was a lovely girl and we're still good friends, but we just couldn't live together. These days I value my freelance status. The eligible bachelor.' Kelly thought she detected a trace of bitterness in his voice.

'Playing the field?'

'Hardly. Concentrating on my career. Looking after Sheikh al Hassan's blood-stock interests. The Jockey Club. It keeps me busy.'

'D'you know his son?' Kelly asked suddenly.

'I've met him. He's not exactly on my circuit.'

'Is he bent?'

'What, gay, you mean?' Nick raised his eyebrows.

'No, not that way. I mean corrupt.'

'No. I'd say he was weak rather than corrupt.'

'I believe he was involved in the Pendero business,' Kelly told him and then went on to fill in the details – Broom-Parker, seeing Ibn Fayoud with Jack Butler in the car park at Kempton racecourse, her conversation with Harry Short. She told him exactly what she had told the police.

'Ibn Fayoud and Butler,' he said eventually. 'They're an unlikely pair.'

There was something subdued about the evening after that, as if the full signif-icance of the events of the past few days was oppressing both of them.

They drove back to Newmarket in virtual silence. Nick spoke quietly as he pulled up outside her flat. 'Call me if you hear anything else.' Troubled, distract-ed, he looked into Kelly's eyes. Her bruised face gave her a new look of vulnera-bility. In an almost fatherly way, he placed a hand on her good shoulder and kissed her gently on the lips, like a promise. 'And, for God's sake, take care.' For a moment, he held her more closely.

'Ouch,' said Kelly.

Nick quickly apologized. 'Look, I know that one shouldn't mix business with pleasure, but if I asked you again, would you come out with me?'

Kelly returned his kiss and held it for a fraction longer than she should have. 'Of course.'

The next morning the post brought a letter that was as brief and to the point as it was surprising.

Dear Miss Connor,

I was most distressed to hear of your fall. I hope that you are now well enough to accept the attached invitation to a charity ball on the first evening of the York meeting. I am taking a party of racing people, some of whom you will surely know.

Please confirm that you are able to make it to my personal assistant.

Yours,

Ibn Fayoud

Attached to the note was an ornate invitation to the Marquess of Flaxton's Charity Black and White Ball and a ticket of entry. Kelly shook her head incredulously; Ibn Fayoud had taken her acceptance for granted. Presumably few people said 'No' to him. Well, Kelly reflected as she dialled the Templemans' number angrily, there was a first time for everything.

'You're going to *what*?' Annie's voice all but went off the chromatic scale when Kelly told her that she was turning down Ibn Fayoud's invitation.

'I'm not at my best at parties. My mind will be on the big race. Anyway, I'm not certain that I like him. He's far too smooth for me.'

'Kelly, you don't seem to understand. One of the reasons Shine On is running at York is to give Ibn Fayoud the chance to take a table at the ball. He wants to show you off. He wants to show *us* off, for Christ sake.'

'You mean you're in his party too?'

'Of course. Although I must admit we were obliged to fork out for the tickets – a mere hundred quid each. What we do for our owners.'

'I don't know.' Suddenly Kelly's objections seemed priggish and defensive. 'I look a sight at the moment, what with my eyes.'

'It's a black and white party. You'll be a wow. Anyway you needn't stay long. Treat it as an education. How often d'you get the chance to watch the mindlessly rich eat and drink themselves into a stupor on behalf of Ethiopia?'

Kelly laughed.

'This is your boss's wife speaking,' Annie continued. 'Accept Ibn Fayoud's invitation. That's an order.'

Margaret Stanhope put down the telephone, stood up, smoothed her tight skirt down and knocked on the door next to her desk. A voice from within muttered, 'Yeah'.

'Newsflash, Jack,' she said, putting her head round the door. 'Our little fish has nibbled the bait.'

Jack Butler puffed on his cigar. 'Brilliant,' he said. 'Maybe she'll get a nibble herself – from the big fish.'

'Maybe.' Margaret smiled at her boss. 'If she's lucky.'

Henry, the Marquess of Flaxton had known hard times. At Eton, he had been fag to a charmless older boy who had wasted no time in introducing Henry to the joys of homosexuality. Today his seducer was a respected Tory backbencher while Henry – in this as in all other matters of pleasure, a broad-minded man – had retained a part-time interest in members of his own sex. But Eton, in those first terms, was tough, frightening. Maybe Henry would have ended up warped and perverse but his unofficial education among the elite certainly helped him along the way.

Then there was the Isle of Wight. For an ordinary Joe, two years spent in the open prison at Parkhurst was no big deal but for Henry, to be starved of decent food, a regular intake of recreational drugs and all but the most basic of sexual activity was deprivation on a grand scale. He was not often given to anger, which required more energy than he had to spare, but two years without life's bounty, all for a small matter of dealing drugs to his friends, seemed little short of scandalous. Of course, since his release, he had made up for lost time, becoming quite a wheel in the charity game, but those two years had stayed with him. The people, the routine, the boredom; frankly, he had been to hell and back.

Balls. That was how he became rehabilitated. Charity parties. Society auctions. It seemed that these days his friends needed an excuse to blow the family money on their own pleasure; it had to be in a good cause. Thanks to his efforts – or rather the efforts of a couple of socially mobile former PR girls who worked for him – several fortunes were directed, with maximum publicity, into the coffers of the needy.

It was brilliant. World starvation was halted in its tracks, Henry became a hero of the gossip columns, and everybody had one hell of a good time. These days, nobody cared what high-grade powder he put up his nose, whom he spent the night with. Henry was all right, a good sort. His heart was in the right place.

The Black and White Ball was going to be a winner. There would be a thousand people there, dressed with varying degrees of elegance in black and white. Some would come in racing silks, or T-shirts with amusing messages, or in clown outfits. Henry had decided on the black-and-white minstrel look – rather apt, he thought, since most of the money would be going to Africa. He had heard that Camilla Welmsley would be all in white, something fluffy and revealing, but with black lipstick. Never was there a less likely vestal virgin. Henry thought that he would probably have Camilla tonight, or maybe Tavic, the black society sculptor everyone was talking about or, hey, maybe both. It was going to be that sort of party.

Ibn Fayoud entered the great black and white marquee. It was decorated with thousands of black balloons, white roses, black bottles of champagne on white tablecloths. He accepted a glass from a black waiter and a kiss from a white puffball who turned out to be Camilla Welmsley. A glance at the assembled guests told him what he already knew – that no one looked quite as good as he did. In the dark mourning robes left to him by his grandfather, he was as exotic as Valentino, as dangerous as a black prince of the desert.

One of Henry's PR girls, almost wearing a cutaway schoolgirl outfit, showed him his table. Ibn Fayoud looked at the place settings, noting that the few racing contacts he had been obliged to invite had sensibly been distributed among the more amusing people who had come up from London. God knows what Tavic would find to say to dear, homely Annie Templeman, or what his favourite ex-girl friend, Mina Beresford, had done to deserve the lugubrious Bill Templeman as a neighbour. Ibn Fayoud sipped his champagne thoughtfully. Doubtless Jack Butler and Kelly Connor would discover subjects of common interest.

Annie Templeman had been at the black and white ball for five minutes, and it was five minutes too long. Although she caught sight of a few racing friends, she felt ill at ease among the social butterflies that trilled and chattered all around her. Above all, she felt guilty that she had persuaded Bill, who looked as happy as a man with a toothache, to make an appearance. He had never been a party-goer and it had been against his better judgement that they agreed to join Ibn Fayoud's party. Good owner relations, Annie had argued. The party had seemed like fun to her then. Bill now shot a baleful glance in her direction. 'Two hundred sodding pounds,' he mouthed.

Kelly was late. She'd managed to flood the carburettor on her car. For a moment she stood uncertainly at the entrance to the marquee, the simplicity of her dark long dress in elegant contrast to the exotic fancy-dress all around her. She smiled at the black and white minstrel who approached her.

'Well,' said the Marquess of Flaxton with an appreciative leer made grotesque by his make-up. 'Who's the lucky man you're with?'

Kelly decided to ignore the implication that she could only be someone's girl friend. 'I'm here by myself,' she said. 'I'm with the Ibn Fayoud party.'

'Ah yes.' Henry looked at her more closely, mistaking the dark rings round her eyes for signs of late nights and fast living. 'You would be.'

He took Kelly by the arm to where a man in dark robes was in earnest conversation with a girl in a skimpy black T-shirt with 'BIMBO POWER' scrawled in white across her chest.

'Kelly!' Ibn Fayoud turned away from the girl, smiled warmly and held out his arms as if greeting an old friend. Kelly managed to turn her head in time for his kiss to miss its target on her lips. 'I'm so happy you could make it, my *favourite* jockey.'

Leaning away slightly as Ibn Fayoud enveloped her in his gowns and aftershave, Kelly found herself looking at a smiling Annie. She crossed her eyes and made a face.

There was something different about Kelly that night. She could see it in the covert glances of the London girls, some of whom had been planning how to look at the Belvoir dance for the past month. She could sense it in the way men talked to her, the sideways glances of strangers. As if, by wearing the simplest of dresses, pale make-up and no jewellery, she had trumped them all.

It was a pity, she thought, that her mind was on Shine On's big test tomorrow afternoon. It was a shame, too, that, because she had unstrapped it for the evening, her shoulder was already aching. Then she looked around at the men on offer, braying nightclub fools mostly, and decided that, even without racing commitments and pain, she would be planning to leave early. This was not her sort of party.

She was nodding politely on the fringes of a group listening to their host talking about himself when she heard a familiar voice behind her.

'So it's true what they say about you and Ibn Fayoud.'

Cy McCray pecked her on the cheek. 'Don't worry,' he said. 'Your secret's safe with me.'

'Duty,' she said with a smile, and lowered her voice. 'Personally, I'd be happier watching television back in the hotel.'

'Hey, tell me about it. Can I give you a lift back there?'

'Cy, you're a gentleman,' said Kelly. 'But I'll be going back with the Templemans. Just as soon as I can.'

'Not before I have a slow dance with you, I hope.'

'Do you think you're tall enough for that?'

'No, but your cleavage looks a great place to rest my head,' he grinned. 'Then you can tell me the truth about Ibn and Butler.'

'I plan to avoid them tonight.'

Cy looked surprised. 'You haven't seen the seating plan then? You've been drawn next to Jack Butler.'

Kelly winced. 'Oh great. That's all I need. Dinner with a bookmaker.'

She should never have come. She would be stuck with a man who, she was now convinced, was in some way involved in the Pendero case. The last thing she wanted, the day before she rode Shine On, was to be drawn back into the past. There were questions she needed to ask Butler, but not yet, not now and not here.

'You look after yourself, y'hear,' McCray was saying. 'You know what Jack's like with the ladies.'

That was the worst of it. In spite of herself, Kelly felt a quickening of the heart, that she was going to sit next to Jack Butler – bookmaker, bastard, crook – and she couldn't wait.

'Thanks, Cy,' she said quietly.

Kelly had expected that Jack Butler would live up to the image she had painted of him in her mind. A wide boy on the make, a rake of the Silver Ring – vulgar, randy, pleased with himself. But he wasn't like that at all, in fact. He appeared almost shy among the other party-goers, a little boy let loose in the big playground, nervously looking about him. As Ibn Fayoud's guests took their seats for dinner, he introduced himself to Kelly with edgy formality. This was not the Romeo she had expected.

'Kelly Connor?' It was almost a mutter. 'I'm your dinner partner. Jack Butler.'

Kelly shook Jack's hand and felt a shiver of excitement run through her body as they touched. His manner was polite but his handshake held an unmistakable invitation. He was taller than she expected and wore a well-cut dinner jacket that contrasted with the eccentric fancy-dress of some of the other diners. She was about to say something when he turned away to introduce himself to the girl on his right.

A goofy individual in a Batman cape distracted her attention by falling into the seat to her left, spilling some champagne in the process. 'I'm Johnny Prescott.'

Kelly smiled politely as the man tried to focus his eyes on her.

Prescott shook his head slowly. 'God, you're lovely,' he said. 'Haven't we met at Tokyo Joe's?'

'I don't think so.' Kelly was annoyed with herself for feeling a pang of jealousy that Jack Butler was now deep in conversation with the girl on his right. A waiter brought smoked salmon. Kelly turned back to the partner on her left. 'Tell me all about yourself, Johnny,' she said with an interested, dinner-party smile.

It took Prescott a good ten minutes to describe the full pointlessness of his life as a stockbroker and man-about-town before the combined effects of drink and sustaining a conversation took their toll and he declined into a glazed, sullen silence.

Jack Butler's conversation with the girl on his right seemed to have dried up too. 'Dear, oh dear,' he said, almost to himself. 'I think I've enjoyed myself more after the housewife's choice has just won the Grand National.'

Kelly laughed. 'So why did you come?'

'I like to do a bit for charity now and then.' When Kelly raised a sceptical eyebrow, he added, 'Even bookmakers have hearts, you know.'

'It's hardly your image.'

Jack shrugged. 'Journos,' he said. 'What do they know?'

'And presumably you didn't want to disappoint Ibn Fayoud.'

Jack Butler glanced across the table to their host who was listening with rapt attention to a woman dressed as a schoolgirl. 'He bets with me now and then, nothing special. Tell me, why are you here? You don't look the charity ball type.'

He was looking at her now, not with the leer of a natural lecher, nor with the beady eye of a professional digging for information, but with polite, sympathetic curiosity. Jack Butler was not at all what she'd expected.

'Ibn Fayoud is an owner,' she explained.

'But he doesn't own you.'

Kelly smiled. 'These days jockeys have to be diplomats.' As she spoke, Jack moved his hand gently on to hers and asked for the salt. Again she felt the same shiver down her back like an electric current.

Eating smoked salmon while talking to Johnny Prescott had seemed to last a lifetime. The two subsequent courses, passed in conversation with Jack Butler, took no time at all. He kept Kelly amused with a string of stories about his life as a bookmaker, and then surprised her with his knowledge concerning the world's fifteen million refugees. Kelly found herself fascinated by him.

'You'll be doing a runner on me in a minute, won't you?' he said. 'You're not here at all. You're at York racecourse already. I doubt you'll even stay for the dancing.'

'I'm here all right.' Kelly smiled. 'Just one dance.'

'Great,' Butler seemed genuinely pleased. 'I'm getting myself a cognac from the bar. What d'you fancy?' He stood up.

'A port please,' she said.

Across the room, amid a throng of guests, Jack Butler was given two drinks by a nun. 'Half will be enough,' she said quietly. 'All of it and we'll be laughing.'

Jack looked uneasy. 'I don't know,' he said. 'I'm not sure about this. She's not like I expected.'

'I'm sure we could find another volunteer.' The nun's eyes were cold, glittering. 'Our little friend appears to have plenty of admirers.'

Jack thought of the job in hand.

'Leave it to me,' he said reluctantly, and made his way back to Kelly.

Across the table from Kelly, Annie and Bill were engaged in a silent battle of wills. Chin set in a parody of male stubbornness, Bill was attempting to convey to his wife his urgent need to get away from this madness and return to the house where they were staying. With equal determination, Annie was making it clear by chatting away happily to Ibn Fayoud and his schoolgirl friend that it would be rude to leave before the dancing had been under way for half an hour or so.

To Kelly, watching them as she sipped her port, it was clear who was going to win. On training matters, Annie deferred to her husband; on everything else, she had the last word.

'We'd better have that dance,' she said to Jack Butler. 'I get the feeling that my boss and his wife will be out of here before long. They're driving me home.'

'You don't have to go with them.'

'Yes, I do. I'm riding tomorrow.'

'The dedicated professional.' Jack made the remark without a hint of sarcasm, taking the glass out of Kelly's hand and getting to his feet. 'Maybe we could meet when you're not riding the next day.' He held out his arm in a surprisingly old-fashioned gesture.

Not a chance, thought Kelly, and then found herself saying, 'That would be lovely.'

Normally, at charity functions run by Henry, the Marquess of Flaxton, the music was loud and contemporary. Tonight, in a rare moment of good judgement, he had hired a big band whose music would not drive his older guests out into the night. When Jack and Kelly joined the dancers, they were playing a waltz.

'How are you feeling?' Jack said quietly as they danced.

'Good,' said Kelly.

And she did feel good. Was it because the man who held her in his arms was a confident and easy dancer? Or that she had drunk one glass too many? Her anxieties, her tension, her thoughts about racing tomorrow had never seemed so distant. She felt light-headed, idiotically, illogically happy. The music stopped, but she stayed in Jack's arms. The next dance was a foxtrot, but they continued to dance slowly.

It must have been several dances later that she noticed Annie standing on the edge of the dance floor. It seemed to Kelly that she was trying to catch her eye for some reason. Eventually, between dances, she came over.

'We're off,' she said in a voice which seemed oddly distant. 'Are you coming?'

Kelly found it hilariously difficult to concentrate. 'I think . . .' she said. 'I think I'll get a lift with Cy McCray, if you don't mind. He's staying in the same hotel.'

Annie looked concerned. There was something about the way Kelly was speaking that seemed unlike her. And she was normally keen to get an early night before a race. 'Are you sure?' she asked.

'Absolutely. I'll be home soon. Drive carefully.'

After Annie had left, Kelly realized that she hadn't asked Cy for a lift home. She certainly wasn't going to drive herself home. For all she knew, he might have gone already. 'Got to find Cy,' she murmured. Suddenly the idea of tearing herself away from Jack's warm, firm body, even for a minute, seemed heartbreaking. She looked across the dance floor and for a moment lost her balance. The band, dressed all in white, seemed miles away. The dancers were no longer people but there was something hostile, dangerous about them. Kelly swallowed hard, and closed her eyes. She felt cold and slightly sick. Behind her, she heard a voice. Snapping open her eyes, she realized that everyone was staring at her, everyone was talking about her, everyone knew that she was about to –

'You all right, Kelly?'

With staring, dilated eyes, Kelly looked up at the man who held her. His gentleness was fake, she knew that now, his face distorted as she looked at him. Jack Butler, the wolf; there was no escaping him. 'Let me go, let me go,' she whispered, discovering her helplessness too late. 'What have you done to me? What have you given me?'

'Is something the matter with her?'

It was a nun, who now stood beside Jack. Both of them looked at her with apparent concern but Kelly knew with utter certainty that they were together in this.

'I think she's had a spot too much to drink,' said the nun. 'I'll just take her to the ladies'.' She took Kelly by the arm; terrified, Kelly allowed herself to be led away like a little girl. The world was staring at her. She looked back at Jack in wordless supplication. As the nun passed Kelly's table, she knocked the remains of a glass of port on to the ground.

Kelly's scream echoed silently within her as, like something out of a distant dream, the band played on.

She must have lost consciousness. For a moment Kelly thought that she had been buried alive. Afraid to move, she became aware that she was in a strange room, in a bed. Her black dress, her underclothes were hung over a chair. Was it morning? Where was she? Had she had a fall? Was she meant to be racing somewhere? She tried to sit up but a wave of nausea engulfed her and, with a sob, she fell back on her pillow.

The door opened, slowly at first. She could see the figure of a man in the shadows. Jack Butler. He looked down at her, like a surgeon before an operation. She could see his mouth moving but the words were strange, alien. 'Worry . . . don't worry . . . all right . . . all right?' He took off his jacket. Was he going to cover her up? She was so cold now. Her shoulder ached. Slowly, he undid his bow tie, pulled it off. He was unbuttoning his shirt.

Kelly looked away and drifted off once more into a hallucinogenic nightmare.

Behind the mirror was a nun with a camera. Breathing heavily, she occasionally brushed the sweat from her eyes as she photographed the scene in the next room.

'Oh, Jack,' whispered Margaret Stanhope to the whirr and the click of the camera. 'Oh Jack, you bastard.'

Chapter 7

An early morning mist hung over York racecourse, gift-wrapping it for the fine autumn day's racing that lay ahead. In the stables, the horses on whom thousands of pounds would be won and lost that afternoon stirred as their lads unlocked their boxes, brought them their feed. Kevin Briley, whose favourite horse Shine On was to run in the big handicap, talked to his charge as he mucked him out. He told him how much of his pay he had saved up for today, how he would personally kick him all the way back to Newmarket if he didn't win, how he was a big beautiful bastard that couldn't fucking lose, could he? Shine On, who knew Kevin well, concentrated on his breakfast.

Damien Gould walked briskly from his BMW towards the stables. Three rides he had today, for three different trainers, and not one of them had a squeak. To make it worse, the Connor bitch was on a fancied runner in the big race. The idea of her succeeding annoyed him. She was everything he wasn't. Young, charming, talented; she was also more resilient than he had anticipated. She must be screwing either Bill Templeman or that Arab bastard. Probably both. That would be a good rumour to start. He could maybe wind her up a bit if he had the chance. A thin smile, like a scar, spread across his face. Perhaps today was going to be all right after all.

At the York Hotel, a phone rang in Room 3012. It was Kelly Connor's early morning call. After two minutes, it stopped ringing.

Roddy Chalmers lifted his head from a table at Flaxton Hall, tried unsuccessfully to focus on his surroundings, and belched. His brain, never an over-active organ even on those rare moments when it wasn't pickled in alcohol, grappled with the fact that he appeared to be in some sort of tent before triumphantly reaching the conclusion that he was at a party. That was it, Henry's charity ball. Christ, it had been one hell of a thrash, an absolute bloody classic.

Roddy shifted his eighteen-stone frame and looked about him. Although it was light outside the tent, music was still blaring from a disco in the corner and Henry was dancing about the floor, ashen-faced and wide-eyed. When Roddy had last been conscious _ about an hour ago, maybe two – he had seen Henry playing hunt the little white worm with a straw and a hand mirror. Snort, dance, bonk, snort some more – bloody good value, old Henry. Right now he was groping Joanna who had taken her top off, as she always did on these occasions. You could tell how a party was going by the number of items of Jo-Jo's clothing scattered about the dance floor.

There was a glass in front of Roddy which he drained. It was time for kip. Thank God he was staying with Henry. He thought he could just about make it up the stairs. At the third attempt, he managed to stand up. He staggered out of the marquee in search of his bedroom.

It was a dream.

Kelly was in a large room she had never seen before, lying alone, naked under a sheet. She felt heavy-lidded and drowsy, as if she had been asleep for a week. Through the heavy curtains, a shaft of sunlight cut through the gloom. It revealed, at the foot of the bed, a fat man taking off his trousers and mumbling to himself. As she stirred, the man seemed to become aware of her presence. 'Well,' he said, trying to focus on her. 'Well, well.' A drunken grin spread across his flushed, porcine features. Kelly pulled the sheet to her. As she moved, her body ached as if she had been in a fight.

It wasn't a dream.

'Girl in my bed,' the man was muttering incredulously. 'Got a girl in my bed.'

Kelly could see her clothes in the corner across the room, but she needed to get to them without being jumped by this barrel of lard. She said nervously, 'Would you mind . . .'

The man held up a finger, as if he had remembered something very important. 'Better freshen up,' he said, wheeling round and staggering into a bathroom next door. Kelly heard a tap running. She leapt out of bed, shut the bathroom door, ramming a chair under the door handle. Trying to ignore the buzzing in her head, which was like a badly-tuned radio, she scrambled into her clothes.

Seconds later, there was an elephantine thud from the bathroom as the man tried the door. 'Cheeky,' he was chuckling drunkenly. 'Saucy little minx.' There was another thud. Kelly made her escape.

What the hell had happened? As she hurried down a long corridor, her mind groped backwards over the events of the previous night. She remembered dinner, then dancing with Jack Butler, Annie saying something to her, a nun taking her by the arm. After that, there was a series of horrific, shaming cameos that could only have come from the unconscious.

Downstairs, it was like a battlefield in which the only victors were excess and decadence. Champagne bottles were strewn about the floor. In the hall, a woman gloomily collecting dirty plates and ashtrays looked up as Kelly appeared. She had seen it all before – last night's high spirits turned to this morning's hangover, last night's gay blades to green-faced ghosts, last night's belles of the ball to tousled tarts with smudged lipstick and laddered tights. Kelly paused and looked about her.

'Where are the coats?' she asked the woman.

The maid smiled. By the look of this young girl in black, she'd have some explaining to do to someone. Serve her right.

'Cloakroom's over there,' she said, pointing. Kelly found her coat without too much difficulty.

'What's the time?' Kelly asked.

Time you knew better, young lady. That was what she wanted to say. 'Ten past seven,' she muttered.

Thank God. Kelly walked quickly through the marquee where her host Henry was dancing with a girl dressed only in black knickers.

Shivering in the morning chill, Kelly got into her car and started the engine. Bill expected her to be at York racecourse to ride out at eight – if she put her foot down, she could just about make it. Her head was clearing now but she still felt strange, drowsy. If it hadn't been for her fat friend, she would have overslept.

Something odd had happened to her last night. She must have passed out, but then she had drunk so little. It was just possible that the painkillers she had taken for her shoulder had reacted with the alcohol, but it seemed unlikely.

She was back at the hotel by 7.45. As the man at reception gave her the key to her room with a knowing look, Kelly reflected that she hadn't felt so guilty since her teenage party days. Her head pounding, she took the stairs to the second floor two at a time. The phone was ringing as she entered the room.

It was Annie.

'Thank God,' she said, when Kelly picked up the phone. 'I thought something had happened to you. Where have you been? Or shouldn't I ask?'

Briefly it occurred to Kelly that it would be sensible to lie. Apprentices do not wake up in strange beds the night before an important ride and then tell all to the boss's wife. But Annie was a friend.

'I'll explain later,' she said. 'Why didn't you bring me home like you promised?'

'Bloody hell,' Annie said loudly. 'You must have been in a bad way. I tried to drag you away but you were too engrossed in the Butler man to pay any attention.'

'*What?* I can't remember – '

'I'm sure you can't,' Annie said sarcastically. 'If I were you I'd get down to the racecourse pronto.'

'Annie. I must speak to you about this.' Kelly thought fast. 'Could we meet downstairs later, after I come back from the course?'

'Come on, Kelly, for God's sake. You're meant to be thinking about your big ride not a married man.' Annie sighed. 'All right,' she said reluctantly. 'Can't have our star apprentice worried on the day of a race, can we? I'll see you at ten.' She hung up.

A married man? Kelly held her head. Right now she needed about a million cups of coffee.

If she had any doubts that Shine On was good enough to win that afternoon, they were dispelled by the way he felt during his early-morning pipe-opener. The way he worked upsides her other ride, Spooked, showed that Bill had trained him to perfection. Today was Shine On's day, given a bit of luck and a decent run.

And a jockey who felt more alive than dead. The exertion and fresh air had done nothing to ease the pain Kelly felt in her head, the weakness in her muscles. Shine On took no hold at all, yet she had difficulty in pulling him up.

After the gallop, Bill was his usual communicative self. He looked the two horses over, then glanced up at Kelly. 'What's the matter with you? You looked like a wet rag coming up there.'

Kelly felt her face turn red with embarrassment. Bill missed nothing. 'I feel fine,' she bluffed. She always said she felt fine when asked, no matter what state she was in.

Bill looked as if he had something else to say. 'Just pretend he's Jack Butler or something,' he muttered loudly.

Kelly felt sick. It must have looked bad last night for Bill to say anything. Worse, his remark had been heard by Dennis, who was riding Spooked. By this afternoon, the events of last night, or Dennis's lurid version of them, would be common knowledge on the racing gossip circuit.

'Jack Butler, eh?' Dennis winked unpleasantly as they walked back to the stables. 'You little raver, you.'

The low murmur of conversation in the hotel's sun lounge was like the crashing of waves to Kelly as she entered to see Annie at a corner table. It was true, as Annie had said, that now was hardly the time to talk about dances, drugs and Jack Butler but it was important for Kelly to talk to her. Something strange had happened last night, she was sure of that. As far as Annie was concerned, Kelly had drunk too much, slept with Jack Butler and put her rides on Shine On and Spooked at risk. Trainer's wife, best friend – either way, she had to be told the truth.

'This had better be convincing,' she said frostily after they had ordered coffees.

'If our friendship means anything,' Kelly said, 'You're going to have to believe me.'

She described the events of the evening slowly, as if afraid that one word out of place would make Annie more sceptical than ever. Yes, she had spent a lot of time with Jack Butler and, yes, she had found him interesting, attractive even. She would have danced with him anyway. But it was the events after dinner that defied explanation.

'I can't remember anything clearly after that first dance,' she said. 'Maybe I heard you when you told me you were going home, but I was miles away. It was as if I couldn't act on my own behalf. I was suddenly . . .' The memory of how she felt made Kelly feel sick once more. 'Helpless.'

'Or legless.'

'I swear I had had one bucks fizz and half a glass of port. It wasn't like drunkenness anyway.'

'So it was the painkillers. You should have known better.'

Kelly shook her head and winced. It was like running razors through the brain. 'I don't think so,' she said. 'I took two pills that evening – they've never affected me like that before.'

'So what are you saying?' Annie sipped her coffee thoughtfully. 'That you were drugged? Who by? And why?'

'I think I'd better tell you about what happened after you left,' Kelly said quietly. Haltingly, she spoke about her sudden irrational terror on the dance floor, the nun leading her away, how she found herself in a bedroom with Jack Butler. Tears filled her eyes as she described seeing him looking down on her.

'Did anything happen?'

Kelly shook her head. 'I'm not sure,' she said. 'It was all hazy. I remember him getting into bed with me. Then I must have lost consciousness.'

Annie smiled humourlessly. 'Something happened,' she said. 'I rather doubt if Jack Butler would climb into bed with you to keep warm.'

The two women sat in silence for a moment. 'D'you believe me?' Kelly asked.

'Even if it's true and not some sort of dream, what can you do about it?'

'But why?' Kelly's question came out as a loud protest. A couple of middle-aged women at a nearby table turned to look at her disapprovingly. 'Why should he do that?'

Annie shrugged. 'The usual reason. What else?'

'Pendero.'

Annie struck her forehead in exasperation. 'For God's sake, Kelly. You're becoming obsessed by – '

'Listen.' Kelly lowered her voice. 'The big gamble on Pendero was by Ibn Fayoud – Harry Short told me that. The person who stood to gain most from Pendero losing the race was Jack Butler. After the race, Ibn Fayoud moves all his horses to Bill and suddenly he's big buddies with Butler. Why?'

'Racing's a small world.'

'And was it just coincidence that I get invited to the Flaxton dance, that I'm seated next to him? There's something going on, I'm sure of it.'

Annie sighed wearily. 'It sounds a little elaborate as an excuse for getting yourself laid,' she said half-jokingly. 'And at the moment, one of your villains, Ibn Fayoud, is your best owner. Bill's been told to enter his horses in several races abroad, with you riding.'

'Why abroad?'

'I suppose he has ambitions to be a great international racing owner like his dad. Or more likely it's a good excuse for a party abroad.'

Kelly shook her head gloomily. 'Everything seems to be going wrong at the moment.'

Annie drained her coffee and stood up. 'Here's what you do,' she said briskly. 'You ride horses. You mind your own business. You stay clear of Jack Butler – that's for certain. And you don't drink port.'

'You're right.'

'And you can do something for me.' For the first time Annie smiled with genuine warmth.

'What's that?'

'Win on Shine On.'

Kelly nodded. The razors leapt in her brain. 'Piece of cake,' she said weakly.

Later, much later, Kelly was to reflect on how lucky she had been that day. There was the fat man who had woken her up, Annie who had at least made her feel slightly better, and then Cy McCray and his diet pills.

She had just walked the course and was making her way to the weighing room before the first race when she heard the familiar Bronx accent behind her.

'How ya doin', sweetheart?'

Kelly turned and gave McCray a wan smile. 'Ok,' she said.

Cy looked at her more closely. 'Jeez,' he said. 'You look like shit.'

'Thanks, Cy. I feel better already.'

'What's the problem?'

For a moment, Kelly considered telling him about the dance, but then she thought better of it. 'I had a hard night,' she said. 'I think something disagreed with my painkillers. I feel terrible.'

'You mean I might win this afternoon? With Shine On being ridden by a hospital case, my horse could have a chance.'

Kelly didn't laugh.

'Hey.' Cy reached inside his jacket pocket and took out a phial of pills. 'I wouldn't do this for anybody else, but take these,' he shook out three yellow capsules, 'And you'll be OK. They're great for tiredness, flu, hangovers.'

'What are they?'

'Diet pills.' He winked. 'On three of those, you'll be flying.

Trust no one. Kelly remembered her father's word. Cy was riding against her this afternoon. It was a risk, and she'd already made one monumental error of character judgement.

She decided she couldn't be so wrong twice in as many days. 'Thanks. I'll take them.'

'Their only disadvantage is that you can't take the painkillers with them. You'll be in agony but you'll feel so good you won't care.'

'As long as they get me past the post.'

'In second place.'

'First,' said Kelly. She glanced at her watch. Spooked was running in the second race. It was time to get changed. As she walked to the weighing room, she gulped down the three pills.

Two hours later, Kelly sat on the scales, reflecting that Cy had been right. Her collarbone felt as if it were about to burst through her skin but her head had cleared and she felt strong.

'Thank you.' She alighted from the scales.

She'd just ridden Spooked like her old self and the horse had run above himself, finishing third in a field of twenty. In the enclosure afterwards, Bill Templeman had grunted in a way that suggested satisfaction with her. Standing behind him, Annie had shaken her head as if disbelieving the race Kelly had ridden after the excesses of the previous night.

Thank God for Cy and his pills. If she'd cocked up a second race, Bill would have jocked her off Shine On, whatever Ibn Fayoud said.

Cy emerged carrying a saddle, ready to weigh out for the next race. He winked conspiratorially at Kelly.

'They say they're dope-testing jockeys of the first three,' he muttered out of the side of his mouth.

Kelly laughed. 'They're not addictive are they, those things?'

'Not if you keep taking them,' said McCray. 'Catch ya later.'

Bob Collins didn't like it when the past came knocking at his door. It was ten years since he came north, married a young Indian model called Raksha and went straight. Now he lived in a neat semi-detached on the outskirts of Bradford with his wife and three lovely kids, earning a comfortable, respectable living doing weddings, portraits, the odd news pic for the local paper. It was a long way from Brewer Street.

Not that he had regrets. If it weren't for his days at the mucky end of the trade, he would never have earned enough to buy a house and he wouldn't have met Raksha who had been doing a bit of topless work to supplement her salary as a nurse. He had learnt his craft the hard way; after you had shot an Ibizan beach orgy sequence in a studio in Soho on a cold January morning with a load of complaining bimbos and a gay black man coked out of his brains, any other gig was a breeze.

The only time that he wished he hadn't been quite so deeply involved in the skin trade was when the past came to visit. Like two days ago. Margaret Stanhope. A posh secretarial voice on the phone.

'Who?'

'Margaret Stanhope.' A pause, a sigh. 'Maggie.'

Oh my Gawd. Maggie. Mad Maggie. Do-anything-if-the-cash-is-right Maggie. Quite a little cracker in her day, she must have been in her late thirties now. God knows what kind of seedy cinematic productions she was involved in these days.

'Hullo, Maggie.' Bob had dropped his voice so that Raksha in the next room wouldn't hear. She didn't like the past any more than he did. 'What are you up to then?'

'I'm a bit like you, Bob,' she said. 'I've gone legit.' She gave him a brief, sanitized account of her life as Margaret.

'And now you want something from me.' Bob knew that, whether she called herself Mad Maggie or Margaret Stanhope, friendship came at a price.

'Just a little favour,' she said. She gave him the details, sparing him time, place, names.

Bob leant against the wall and rubbed his eyes wearily. 'And that's what you call legit, is it?' he said.

'Bob.'

He knew that tone of voice. This was one dangerous bitch if you crossed her. So he agreed to give her the camera, show her how to use it; he'd make sure the family were out the afternoon she came round to get the film developed.

At least, looking on the bright side, he didn't have to take the shots himself. 'No, I want to do that,' she had said. Mad Maggie. She always was a weird one.

Now she was here and it was just like old times; in the darkroom with Maggie, working on filthy pictures. With the other girls, it had been simple; morning, darling, a quick strip, a bit of pout, grunt and groan under the studio lights, then off they went to the next job. Mad Maggie was different. She liked to stick around, see the results, maybe enjoy some off-camera larks in the back office. Not that there was the slightest danger of Bob getting into that these days, thank you very much. At least not on his home ground.

'Not bad.' Bob took the first contact sheet from the developing fluid and hung it up. 'You did a good job here, Maggie. Apart from a spot of camera shake.'

'It's Margaret,' she said, pushing him aside. 'Never mind the photographic quality. Can you see the faces?'

Bob Collins looked at the contact sheet through a magnifying glass.

'Hope you're not going to try and sell these,' he said. 'She looks as if she's asleep and he doesn't seem to be having much fun either.'

The second contact sheet was ready. Margaret inspected it and asked for a number of prints to be made.

As he worked, Harry muttered, 'If I didn't know better, I'd say that was your Mr Butler on the bed there.'

Margaret was examining the prints, absorbed. Now as she looked up at Bob Collins, the smile left her face. 'One word of this and I tell your local rags where you learnt your craft.'

Harry shrugged. 'My mistake,' he said. 'Must be a Jack Butler look alike.'

'Let me have an extra copy of these ones.' Margaret gave the photographer three prints in which her boss's face was clearly visible. The show had been set up for the little jockey but maybe, at some time in the future, Mrs Butler would be interested.

Two birds with one stone. Margaret Stanhope smiled.

Driving back to Leeds, Margaret tuned her car radio to the commentary from the York races. Personally, she couldn't stand horses but these days Jack's interests were her interests. After all, she was his personal assistant.

'Shine On has drifted slightly in the betting,' the commentator was saying. *'He's now 4–1 third favourite behind the Irish challenger Breakdancer and The Guppy.'*

Drifted. Margaret laughed softly. The punters had probably caught a glimpse of Shine On's jockey. You wouldn't want to lay the family heirloom on a horse ridden by a zombie, would you? In fact, it was amazing the Connor girl could even find her way to the racecourse the way she must be feeling today.

'. . . while there's a slight question mark over Shine On's ability to stay this distance and of course it's a big test for his rider Kelly Connor, who's having her first ride in a listed race. Kelly, of course, is the daughter of the great Irish jockey Frank Connor who died so tragically last month. They're all in now . . .'

Frankly Margaret couldn't give a toss. She'd feel a little sorry for the little girl if she blacked out in the race and fell under all those hooves. After all, it hadn't really been her fault that she became mixed up in Jack's business affairs. A bit nosey, that was all, and Margaret understood what it was like to be nosey.

The commentator was reeling off horses' names like an auctioneer, mentioning Shine On only occasionally. Bringing up the rear. Backmarker. Making no impression . . . Silly sport it was. Making horses run faster than they wanted to. And they always let you down when you least expected it. The things she had heard Jack say after a favourite that he had carefully arranged to get well stuffed, as he put it, promptly went and won. Secretly Margaret thought he'd be better out of the racing business. Show business, boxing, snooker – that was where the money was. She'd tell him that when they were together at last. Maybe over dinner one night.

'. . . as they pass the three-furlong marker, it's still The Guppy, who's made every yard of the running, behind him a group of horses led by the grey Prince Charming, Cy McCray has yet to move on Breakdancer, Shine On has an awful lot still to do . . .'

Jack would be going all pale and intense now. Margaret smiled affectionately. She had seen him surrounded by people shouting and screaming, 'Go on, my son', not one of them down to lose or win as much as Jack, and he'd just stand there like a beautiful, pale statue. Involuntarily, Margaret thought of Jack's muscular body last night. She hardly heard the growing excitement in the commentator's voice.

'. . . *into the last furlong, and The Guppy looks beaten, Breakdancer takes up the running with Prince Charming on the stands side – it looks to be between these two – but now Shine On's absolutely flying on the outside, a terrific challenge, the three locked together, Breakdancer and Shine On stride for stride, at the line it's very close but I think it's Shine On who gets it on the nod. There'll be a photograph but there's not much doubt about the winner. Shine On ridden with breathtaking confidence by the young apprentice Kelly Connor who got up in the last stride to –*'

'She didn't look so breathtakingly confident last night, darling,' Margaret Stanhope said to the radio set. 'She was more like something out of *The Night of the Living Dead.*'

Switching to a music channel, Margaret wondered how Jack would be feeling right now. Pleased that his little doll had won? Surprised that she had the energy? Pissed off? Personally, she thought it was fair enough if Connor had a small moment of glory before Jack, armed with the material in the briefcase beside her, hauled her in and finished her little investigation for good and all.

'Yeah,' Margaret muttered. 'Good for Kelly, that's what I say.'

After all, the higher she was riding, the further she had to fall.

Within Kelly's body there was a war going on. Her collarbone was ambushing her with surprise guerrilla raids of searing pain while her head was screaming revenge for the ordeals it had undergone during the past twelve hours. Don't do drugs, Kelly. Nix those narcotics. She felt like a government health warning, but the sheer pleasure of having won her first big race made up for it all. If only her father had been there to see it.

Wincing, she eased on her coat, picked up her bag and saddle and walked slowly out of the weighing room. Ibn Fayoud would be celebrating in the bar and Annie had urged her to join them, but there was only one place Kelly wanted to be – home, in her bed, lying there reliving today's race.

It was the last time she was going to take diet pills before a race, that was for sure. They had made her feel so confident that, from the moment Shine On had jumped off, she had been utterly convinced that she would win. Even when she passed the two-furlong pole, some five lengths off the leaders, she knew she had them; but if the post had come ten yards earlier, she would never have got up. Those pills were lethal.

'How d'you ride on these things?' she had asked Cy as, pulling up, he shook her hand in congratulation. 'Doesn't your judgement go?'

'Sure.' He smiled across at her. 'I wouldn't dream of taking them before a race.'

Kelly's head was swimming as she left the racecourse. She hardly had the energy to acknowledge the odd 'Well done, Kelly' she heard as she walked slowly towards the car park. She would be mad to drive home tonight, she decided. She would book in for another night at the hotel and leave in the early morning.

She glanced at the winners' enclosure. It had been a great moment. A tremendous reception. Ibn Fayoud and his blonde of the day; Annie, hardly able to conceal her astonishment at the way Kelly had been able to ride after the events of the previous night; Bill himself, flushed and more inarticulate than ever. 'Never do that to me again, Kelly,' he had muttered. 'My heart couldn't stand the strain.' It was as near to a compliment as he could manage.

'Two winners in twenty-four hours, eh sexy?'

The unmistakable tones of Damien Gould interrupted her thoughts as Kelly was putting her bag and saddle into the boot of her car.

She turned to see him standing ten yards away.

'Just the one, Damien,' she said quietly. 'One more than you, I think.'

'No, surely.' Damien scratched his head, frowning. 'There was that Shine On this afternoon then . . . what was it?'

Kelly knew what was coming. All afternoon she had been waiting for evidence of the racing rumour-machine at work. Even a loser like Dennis would know how to get word around. There was an angry throbbing in her head as she walked slowly towards him.

'Or maybe . . .' Damien assumed a smug little smile. 'Maybe it wasn't you who rode the winner but – yes, that's it, the winner rode you.'

Kelly found her breath was coming thick and fast. There was a tight knot of anger in her stomach. Damien paused to savour the moment as fully as possible.

'Go on, Damien.' Kelly's voice was almost a whisper. At another time and in another place, it could have been almost seductive. 'Say it.'

'You *know*, sexy.' Damien was truculent now, leering. 'Your boy friend Jack –'

The blow from Kelly's right fist brought blood spurting from his nose and sent a searing pain up her arm which she refused to show on her face.

'Bitch,' he hissed, trying to staunch the blood which flowed from his left nostril.

'Yes, and you're just a chippy little has-been.'

Booking into the hotel for another night, Kelly was told that someone had been trying to call her. Nick Morley – it must have been. Although he had declined to leave a name, he must have hoped to catch her before she returned south. She smiled. After the madness of the last twenty-four hours, he'd be a welcome relief.

'Oh, and Miss Connor,' the receptionist called out as she made for the stairs, 'There was a delivery for you this afternoon.' The woman disappeared into a back office and returned with a bunch of ten red roses. She looked surprised when Kelly seemed reluctant to take them.

With a sense of foreboding, she read the note attached to one of the stems. It read, 'We'll be paying out a fortune on Shine On but you were brilliant. Congratulations. Thinking of you. Love, Jack.'

Kelly groaned. She tore the note off and gave the roses back to the receptionist.

'Keep them,' she said with a grim smile. 'I'm allergic to roses. They make me sick.'

After last night, she never wanted to see him again. Maybe, briefly, he had awakened in her a craving for the wild, the dangerous, the forbidden, but whatever had happened later had cured her of that. More than ever she needed to talk to Nick.

Anyway who needed danger if you were a jockey?

Jack Butler stared morosely at the large white television in his modern penthouse flat in the centre of Leeds. Nothing could lift his mood – not the fact that his supplier had managed to get his hands on a pirate video of the new Schwarzenegger, nor the really quite healthy profit he had made on the afternoon's racing at York, nor even the fat Havana cigar to which he had treated himself.

It wasn't despair. Jack had no time for the dark night of the soul. It wasn't the sort of long-term depression that had settled on him when his wife persuaded him to take her on holiday to Marbella. But it was bad all the same. At this particular moment, Jack didn't like himself, and popularity among people that mattered – and who mattered more than himself? – was very important to him.

'Shit,' he said, pressing the remote control, plunging Arnold into darkness mid-massacre.

He stood up, wandered over to the cocktail bar in the corner and poured himself another cognac. He stood by the large window, looking down on the lights of Leeds. Normally he enjoyed staying over at the firm's northern hospitality suite which was situated above their offices – bloody hell, he had treated a few girls to his own style of hospitality there enough times – but tonight it was all wrong. He didn't feel like company, however blonde, young or willing. For a moment, he almost wished he were at home, but then he shook his head as if to rid himself of the thought. Home, with Charmaine and her hurt, resentful eyes, her domestic conversation, her irritating attempts to keep their marriage alive.

'Jesus.' Jack shuddered. He felt bad, but not that bad.

Kelly Connor had probably received the flowers by now. He had spent ages trying to get the words right on his note but somehow it all came out wrong. He was genuinely delighted that, in spite of last night, she had won the big race. But what exactly do you say to that special someone whom you drugged to get into bed? It wasn't the sort of situation the etiquette books catered for.

He picked up the phone. He'd call her. Not to apologize – that would be asking for explanations he wasn't able to give right now – but to see that she was all right. Frankly, it had amazed him that she had been able to ride at all that afternoon, given how wasted she was the previous night, but then she was quite a determined little thing. Too determined for her own good really, which was why he had had to agree to last night in the first place.

Her line was engaged. Jack put down the receiver. Perhaps that was a good thing. He didn't know what was the matter with him.

The phone rang. He picked it up with a quiet 'Yeah?'

'I have something to show you.' It was the last person in the world he wanted to talk to, apart from Charmaine.

'Not now, Margaret.'

'I really think you should see these. After all the trouble we've taken.'

Jack sighed. He couldn't stand Margaret when she was in one of her perky moods. Normally, he'd slap her down but, right now, he didn't have the energy. 'I'll give you five minutes,' he said wearily.

There was something unfamiliar about Margaret Stanhope as, moments later, she entered her employer's hospitality suite, brushing past him, a triumphant smile on her face. She threw the black leather briefcase on to the sofa and said briskly, 'Gin and It for me, please, Jack.' It was almost as if she were in charge.

Setting it all up so beautifully, manipulating Jack and the girl into the most compromising of positions had done her self-confidence a power of good. She looked at Jack now as, sulkily, he fetched her a drink. A fine figure of a man, even finer without his clothes – Margaret had no complaints there – but not quite as strong as he made out. It was like a trick, a game she had played. Strip Jack Naked. Now that she had stripped Jack naked, she felt stronger. This was one game she was going to win.

'About last night.' Jack handed her a drink.

Margaret held up a hand, her eyes twinkling with amusement. 'About last night, you need have no worries.' She picked up the briefcase. 'No one need know about your first-night nerves.'

Butler looked at her coldly. He hadn't anticipated this change in Margaret. It made him feel even worse than before. 'Cut the crap and show me the pics,' he said. 'I'm not in the mood.'

Margaret laughed lightly. 'When *are* you in the mood, Jack?' She pulled out two contact sheets from the briefcase. 'Only kidding, love,' she added with unwelcome intimacy.

Sighing, Jack glanced at the first sheet. He and Kelly had only been together five minutes but the photographs brought back the full nightmarish shame of it all. She had stared at him wide-eyed, unseeing, and any desire that he might have felt had died in that instant. He may have the morals of an alley cat but raping a semi-comatose girl was beyond him. She was so out of it that it would have been like making it with a corpse.

Butler threw the sheet on the sofa. He was paler than Margaret had ever seen him. 'They make me feel sick,' he murmured.

'Of course, we need to get rid of the shots that look obviously posed.' Margaret pored over the sheet as if they were wedding photographs. 'But these two here look very natural. Almost as if you were – '

'Keep a couple, destroy the rest. And all the negatives, OK?'

'Anything you say, Jack.' Margaret closed the briefcase with a click, like someone who has just completed a sale. She sighed thoughtfully. 'If only you'd let her finish her drink before dancing with her. That was Ecstasy crossed with smack. Good stuff, too. The whole glass and she'd have been climbing the walls – just how you like – '

Jack walked quickly over to the door. He held it open. 'Get the fuck out of here,' he muttered.

Margaret shrugged and sauntered through the door. She smiled at Jack. He would be better in the morning. Then he would realize what a good girl she had been, how she had helped him. It had been difficult, of course, but the experience would bring them closer together. After all, what other personal assistant would have done what she had?

Jack Butler closed the door, turned and leant against it, as if afraid that she might suddenly return with more horrors. He covered his face with his hands and groaned.

Chapter 8

A vixen barked in the woods behind Dermot Kinane's cottage, breaking the early evening silence with its plaintive cry of love and need. Kelly Connor sat on an old garden bench in Dermot's orchard thinking of her father and the past. They had always spent a few weeks every year in Ireland, relaxing and visiting old friends. When she had been a child, those holidays had seemed magical, a time when everyday concerns were put in perspective by the rhythm of village life. At church, at the pub, or sitting by Dermot's roaring peat fire, she would catch a glimpse of her father as he once was, before his life turned sour – expansive, smiling, good-humoured.

Now, without him, she was back, taking stock of her life.

She had loved both her parents. Her mother had filled her early childhood with wonderful memories of picnics and riding ponies and of a stream of smiling school-friends who were always made welcome, but it was her father to whom she'd felt closest. Somehow he'd always been much more sensitive to her feelings. He could judge her mood almost before she was aware of it herself. After her mother had died, and despite his own grief, he'd done everything possible to help her forget. They had little money to spend once he'd given up riding altogether but they shared love in abundance. Kelly smiled as she thought of his early attempts at cooking and the hours he'd spent coaching and encouraging her while she'd practised riding a finish on the back of the sofa.

The racing world was more fickle than any other she knew of. After Shine On had won at York, the papers had sung her praises. Kelly, our most promising apprentice. Connor turns tragedy into triumph. Will Kelly Connor be the first woman champion jockey? The phone at the flat rang constantly. Spare rides. Requests for interviews. Old friends who had forgotten her during the hard times. During the subsequent week, she had ridden three winners, only one of whom was for Bill Templeman. There was talk in the racing press of her being retained by one of the country's top trainers for next season, but that was the first she'd heard about it.

At York, she had ridden no better than she had ever ridden before. It was a bigger race, she was on a better horse, maybe she had ridden with more coolness than usual thanks to the emergency prescription of Dr Cy McCray. But what racing could give after one good day, it could take away after a bad one. Nothing had changed. Now, there were two days on which the only race meetings were in the north; Kelly had asked Bill for time off and he had agreed.

It was as if events had conspired to make her forget Ascot, Pendero, the fact that

the most important person in her world had been clubbed to death because he wanted to save her from the fate that he had suffered. Kelly was ambitious; there was
almost nothing she wanted more than to ride winners, to be next year's champion
apprentice, to make it. She had the ability and now she had had the break. Her
moment had come.

Almost nothing. She knew what the sensible course of action was. Make racing
the reason for your existence, your religion, forget the outside world. All that happened out there – love, life, death, murder even – they could wait until the day you
hung up your saddle and retired rich, successful, envied.

Almost. Her father would have had words with her about that. The idea that she
should risk her future by dwelling in the past, raking over the cooling embers of
his life in order to discover who killed him and why would have enraged him.
Even now, she felt his silent reproval from the grave. Don't let them hook you.
Don't get involved in corruption even if it's on the side of the angels. Do your best
at the work you've chosen. Ride winners.

'Just listen to her, will you?' Dermot Kinane appeared out of the gloom and sat
beside Kelly. She had been so caught up in her memories that she hadn't heard
him approaching. He nodded in the direction of the woods from where, every few
seconds, the thin cry of the vixen could be heard. 'It's like she's laughing at us.'

Kelly smiled. 'She's calling for her mate.'

Dermot Kinane took a tin of tobacco from the pocket of his old tweed coat and
rolled a cigarette.

'Last week that little bitch broke into my hen house. Ten bantams she killed.'
The flare of the match lit up his thin, craggy face. 'She's reminding us who's boss.'

'She won't be so noisy when the hounds come. The hunting season starts soon,
doesn't it?'

Kinane nodded. Now in his sixties, he still rode out with the Black and Tans, as
wild and fearless as ever. He had broken more bones in his body riding horses than
anyone she knew, yet he lived for his hunting. He'd probably die for it in the end.

'Makes no difference,' he said. 'She'll be back. Or if they get her, one of her
cubs will be back. We can chase her across fields, lock away our birds every night,
protect them with wire and all sorts of nonsense but, when we're dead and gone,
a fox will still be coming back. She'll have the last word because she had nature
on her side.'

Kelly laughed softly. 'You make it sound like a war,' she said.

'Not at all, not at all. It's a game. The day after she came I put up another roll
of chicken wire.'

For a moment, they sat in silence, Kinane puffing at his cigarette, the pungent
smell of cheap, strong tobacco wafting across to Kelly.

'What should I do, Dermot?' she said eventually. 'What should I do about Dad?'

Kinane looked at her tenderly. 'It wasn't thieves, was it, that killed him?' he
said.

'No.' Kelly shook her head. 'He had been told to stop me winning at Ascot. He
didn't.'

'Poor old Frank. Always was the pig-headed one.'

'I've found out who wanted Pendero not to win. There was a big gamble on him.

A bookmaker paid Damien Gould to take some lead from my weight cloth while a journalist distracted me.'

'You know this, or are you guessing?'

'I found the journalist but the day he was going to talk to me he was killed by a hit-and-run driver. Gould virtually admitted it the other day.'

'So someone tried to stop you. It happens all the time. How d'you know it had anything to do with Frank's death?'

'The letter. Then, as soon as I started asking questions, they tried to stop me. There were threatening calls to the Templemans and – ' Kelly decided to spare Kinane details of the death of her cat – 'to me. They were prepared to kill the journalist Broom-Parker rather than let him talk to me. And I think they tried to drug me the night before I rode Shine On at York.'

'Why? What do they care if you ride winners?'

Kelly stared out into the darkness. 'That's what I don't understand. Shine On's owner was the man who had the big gamble on Pendero, and Jack Butler, the bookie, was the one who slipped me the drug. They're up to something, but I don't know what. It doesn't make sense.'

Kinane stared at Kelly in the evening gloom. He had known her since she was a baby. Even then, she had been wilful, determined. Today her soft, dark features concealed a tough obstinacy. That was why she was making the grade as a jockey. And that was why she was allowing herself to become sucked into a whirlpool of corruption which could destroy her career, or worse.

'Does the term "conspiracy theory" mean anything to you?' he asked softly.

Kelly looked surprised. 'You mean, as in "it wasn't a lone lunatic who killed Kennedy but the Mafia working in collusion with the Russians who had a deal with the FBI" – that kind of conspiracy?'

'Precisely. Look at a crime closely enough and everything becomes significant. Accidents, coincidences, ordinary, everyday events are all part of a great plot and – '

'Thanks, Dermot,' Kelly interrupted. 'You don't have to explain. You think I'm inventing all this, seeing shadows behind every door, right?'

The fox was barking more closely now. Kinane stood up. 'Let's go and look at that henhouse. I can do without losing any more bantams.'

They walked in silence to a gate at the end of the orchard and into a farmyard. Beyond some stables, there was a chicken run. Kinane opened the door.

'Eejits,' he said quietly, as he looked at the bantams roosting on a low perch. 'Mrs Charlie's at their front door and they still don't get out of her reach.' One by one, he put the drowsy birds on to the top perch.

'Sure, you're as bad as your father,' he said, as he worked. 'You can't leave well alone.' A black bantam squawked in surprise as he picked her up. 'As it happens, I believe you. I'm sure the people who murdered your father are up to something.' He turned to Kelly. 'But so what? People are always up to something. They're like that vixen. There's nothing you can do about it.'

'Listen, Dermot, there's a reason for everything. The reason that vixen killed your bantams is because it's nature. Maybe she wasn't even hungry but it's in her to kill. I want to know the reason why someone killed Dad.'

'That's what the authorities are there to find out. The best way you can repay your debt to your father is to be a success as a jockey.' Gently, he lifted the last bantam to the top perch.

'So you won't help me?'

'Me?' Kinane looked round as he closed the henhouse door behind him, bolting it twice. 'What could I do?'

'You know everyone in racing. You could ask around about Jack Butler, Ibn Fayoud, Dad's dodgy contacts from his riding days. No one would be suspicious of you.'

Dermot Kinane took Kelly's arm as they walked back towards his cottage. 'D'you know what I think? It's not racing at all. I'll bet you it goes outside the business.'

They walked on in silence. 'Here's what I'll do,' Kinane said eventually. 'I'll talk to some friends of mine if you promise to tell what you know to the Jockey Club. Officially.'

'I've already done that. I've told them everything that I've told the police, but nothing's happening.'

Kinane stopped and looked at her, a deep seriousness in his eyes. 'Well, give them time.

'And promise me it's no more Kelly Connor, private detective, all right?'

Kelly nodded. 'Promise,' she said.

Reg Butler sat beside a roaring gas log fire, smoking a fat cigar and wondering when he was going to be able to retire, relax, play golf, take in the odd West End show like other successful men of seventy-two. The dreams of his youth, when he was a tough, small-time bookie around the dog tracks of London, had long since come true. He had his luxury mock-Tudor mansion in Purley, his holiday home in Tenerife. He had a young wife who, although she was thirty years his junior, loved him dearly or, at any rate, behaved as if she did. He had a bank balance that a senior merchant banker would not be ashamed of. He had a son, running the family business for him.

He sucked greedily on the cigar, like a heart patient needing oxygen. Ah, that Jack. What a problem he was. A chip off the old block he was not. Bright, yes. Motivated, yes. But tough? Dream on. Young Jack thought he was hard, thought that having a few blondes and getting a few legs broken made you a man, but underneath it all he was soft, a little boy. If Jack had had to protect his pitch at Dagenham and White City in the days when men were men, he wouldn't have survived until the third race.

Not for the first time, Reg Butler tried to analyse what was wrong with his son and the way he ran the business. First of all, he appeared on television like he was some kind of game-show berk, not a businessman. Reg didn't like that. Bookmakers had no place in front of the cameras. Then he wanted to stay with the horses. He just would not diversify, that boy. And what was the point of ambition if it was limited? If Reg Butler hadn't looked beyond the horizon, he'd still be a one-pitch loser down the dogs. He'd had it too easy, Jack. That's what Reg had told his mother, God rest her soul, and he'd been right.

Soft. That was Jack. Soft-centred. He had two fundamental weak spots. One was situated behind his fly-buttons; greed was good in Reg's book, but sexual greed was dangerous when it interfered with business. The other was in his heart. That was the problem, Reg smiled grimly. His son had a heart, the stupid, randy little bastard, and what good were brains and charm if you had a heart?

Butler stubbed out his cigar in an ashtray and reached for a telephone on the table beside him.

'Jack?'

'Hello, Dad.'

The voice was weary, as if this was the fourth time he'd been called by his father that evening. Which it was.

'You set it up yet?'

'I told you. I'm just putting the finishing touches on. The Arab's cutting up rough.'

'Pull him in then. He owes us a fucking million quid, don't he? Squeeze the bastard.'

'Leave it to me, Dad.'

Leave it to him. Reg Butler felt a tightening in his chest. Leave it to Jacko. That would be the day.

'What about the girl?'

A pause. 'She's a problem. I think we'll send someone else to Tokyo. Someone like McCray. She's trouble, that one.'

See? Heart. And probably fly-buttons too.

'Send her, Jack. She's better in than out.'

'Dad, I've told you. Don't worry about Kelly Connor. She's in.'

'You've spoken to her? She agreed?'

'Not exactly. But she'll do what she's told. We've got her.'

Reg Butler hung up. The boy was talking riddles. In? Got her? What half-arsed plot was that berk hatching now? Don't worry, he'd said. Some fucking chance.

It wasn't meant to happen. Kelly had called Nick Morley from Ireland and had arranged to visit Jockey Club headquarters in Portman Square when she returned. It was to be a formal, confidential statement, she had said. Nick had seemed concerned and had agreed at once to convene the security subcommittee. After the meeting, she would drive back to Newmarket. It was never meant to become complicated.

Kelly felt quite calm as she entered the large committee room. Before her, across a large mahogany table, where three stewards, two of whom she knew. To Nick's left sat Colonel Beamish who was looking as sceptical and impatient as he had in the stewards' room at Ascot, and Lord Chester, a wealthy landowner who had ridden as an amateur until recently. At the end of the table, a middle-aged woman stenographer sat impassively with her notebook in front of her.

It was a more sympathetic hearing than Ascot. Nick introduced her to the panel and explained the background to her visit. He was so candid that, for a moment, Kelly expected him to reveal that they had had dinner together, but with the slightest hint of a cautionary glance in her direction, he merely referred to 'A follow-up meeting away from the office'.

Carefully, soberly, Kelly told them everything she knew. It was like a confession, a purging, except that her only sin had been an over-zealous curiosity, a need to discover who killed her father. It was easier than she had anticipated. The three men listened to her without interrupting. Every name she mentioned was noted down, not only by the stenographer, but by Beamish. Short. Ibn Fayoud. Broom-Parker. Gould. Butler. Kelly held only one detail back. Although convinced that she had been drugged before the race at York, she had little chance of persuading three Jockey Club stewards that she had not been drunk, out of her depth, hysterical, and she didn't want Nick to know either. The rest of her story was too important to take the risk.

When she finished, Nick had a few muttered words with his colleagues before asking her one or two questions, mostly concerning times, places and names. If the events outlined by Kelly came as a shock or a surprise, he concealed it in his calm measured tones. He might have been asking her about the traffic on the way in from the airport. It was almost as if he and his committee dealt with murder and corruption every day of the week.

'We shall, of course, look into these allegations,' Nick concluded, winding up the hearing. 'It would be helpful to know if you wish to be kept in touch with developments.'

'Yes, of course I do,' Kelly said quietly.

Colonel Beamish gave a wintry smile. 'Naturally, if there are legal proceedings, you may be required to testify as a witness here, or even in a court of law.'

'I understand.'

'Thank you for bringing this to our attention, Miss Connor,' Nick said, standing up. 'I'll show you out.'

It was as he escorted her through the hall that he quietly suggested a drink after work. Kelly agreed. She had made up her mind to put the past behind her. Now would be a good time to start. She wanted to talk about something other than death and danger. Racing perhaps, or even life.

Nick didn't send any shivers through her the way Jack Butler had but after he'd kissed her softly goodbye and she was walking through Portman Square, she found herself looking forward to seeing him later.

He took her to a club in Camden Town, a dark cellar where a jazz quintet played hypnotic Chicago blues and where the pale faces of London's night people were lit by candles as they drank, smoked and laughed. Some of them looked as if they had only just risen from their beds, as if this was breakfast time to them; others had the look of people who hadn't slept for a week.

Kelly was glad of the anonymous atmosphere. She was still in the dark coat and dress she had selected for the Jockey Club hearing and Nick was in pinstripes. A spotlight on them in this company and they would feel like tax inspectors. But it was a good place to unwind; the chance of either of them being recognized was remote.

Kelly smiled at him. His hair was tousled, his tie at half-mast.

'How d'you know this place?' she asked. 'It hardly seems your style.'

'I love this music. Sometimes I come here by myself, just to relax, think things over. They know me here.'

'By yourself?' Kelly narrowed her eyes with mock suspicion. 'The eligible bachelor on the pull?'

Nick didn't smile. 'I rather think my pulling days are done. And anyway,' he nodded in the direction of the dance floor where a young girl in a T-shirt and torn jeans was entwined in the arms of a dreadlocked Rastafarian, 'I'm not quite the type for the regulars here.'

There was something sad about him, Kelly realized. It was as if there were no place where he quite belonged. On the racecourse, in Portman Square, he was treated with the wary politeness reserved for outsiders. Here he was a punter, a champagne Charlie, dossing with the underclass. Briefly, he reminded Kelly of her father. Once Frank Connor had left the certainties of life in County Limerick, he always seemed like an actor who had wandered into the wrong play. Frank Connor and Nick Morley, they were both uneasy with their surroundings, out of context.

'I brought my wife here once,' Nick said suddenly. 'We lasted half an hour. She said a black man had made an obscene suggestion to her outside the ladies' loo.' He smiled as Kelly burst out laughing. 'She was easily shocked, my wife.'

'Bet she loved it really.'

'No.' Nick frowned and looked at his glass. 'Her niceness wasn't just on the surface. She was nice all through. One hundred per cent nice. That was probably why I married her. Everybody liked Sarah. My parents thought my marriage was the first sensible thing I'd ever done. But she turned out to be too nice for me.' He raised a glass to Kelly. 'Down with niceness,' he said.

A waitress brought them a bottle of champagne. 'With the manager's compliments,' she said. Nick looked across the room to where a fat man in jeans stood by the bar and ticked the side of his forehead like a taxi driver acknowledging a tip. The man gave a portly little bow and smiled.

'I knew him in the army,' he said simply. 'We've kept in touch.'

Kelly sensed a strange vulnerability in this man. She asked him about his parents, how he became involved in racing.

'My father's a lawyer,' he began, sipping at his champagne, adding quietly, 'In fact, he's a judge. Very successful. My mother,' he smiled wryly, 'Is a successful lawyer's wife.'

'They must be proud of you.'

Nick shook his head. 'They expected me to be a lawyer too. Join Daddy's chambers. So I went into the army. Looking back on it, I realize it was some sort of act of rebellion. Then, just to make it worse, I went into the SAS. Ireland. Antiterrorist stuff. Intelligence.' He smiled distantly. 'Father hated it.'

'Why did you leave?'

'I got married. Sarah disliked the idea of being an army wife. The only other thing I knew about was racing so I went into bloodstock.'

'And the rest is history.' Kelly smiled. It was reassuring to hear of another life that had gone wrong, to be reminded that, however successful a person might seem, things weren't always easy. Nick reached across the table, took her hand and held it for a moment. He looked into her eyes, and she knew she was lost. It wasn't exactly love, but it was close enough to love not to matter.

'Stay with me tonight,' he said.

'I've got to work in the morning.' Kelly cursed her job, thinking how nice it would be to have someone she trusted holding her.

'Leave early.'

'I'll see,' she said. But she'd already made up her mind.

The flat in Pimlico was much as Kelly had expected. Spacious, tidy, decorated with old-fashioned, bachelor good taste. 'Night cap?' Nick asked as they walked into the drawing room. He fetched some chilled white wine from the fridge.

They stood in the middle of the room, chinked glasses and kissed.

'Shall we take our drinks to the bedroom?' she said softly.

Nick smiled and took her hand.

It surprised Kelly how much she wanted him. She wasn't drunk. She wasn't like some of her friends who needed sex like they needed food and drink. It had been almost a year since she had found herself alone with a man in a bedroom, voluntarily, at least. It had been a tearful last time with Jonathan, her boyfriend of the time – but casual sex had never been among her hobbies. She watched him as he switched on the light by the bed and drew the curtains. No, it wasn't love. Reassurance, warmth, sanity after the craziness and sadness of the past few weeks.

Nick stood by the bed, smiling, sipping his wine.

'This is mad,' she smiled. She reached behind her neck and undid the clasp. Her dress fell obediently to the floor around her ankles. Standing semi-naked in the bedroom of a Jockey Club steward. Yes, it was mad.

'More,' said Nick with some difficulty.

Kelly hooked her thumbs in the tops of her pants. 'Turn the light off,' she said.

He was a good lover, slow, gentle, aware of Kelly's needs almost before she was aware of them herself. Once, feeling herself slipping away dangerously into another land, a land of sweet warmth, desire and sensation, she opened her eyes to see him watching her and, for a moment, Kelly felt uneasy, almost manipulated. But then he whispered, 'All right?' and touched her again. She closed her eyes, bit her lip and nodded.

Yes, she was all right.

Afterwards, they slept. At three or four in the morning the telephone beside the bed rang shrilly. Nick picked up the receiver and listened for a moment, before muttering 'Wrong number' and hanging up. He turned to Kelly, smiled and kissed her softly, and then with renewed desire.

Kelly laughed softly. 'Thank you, wrong number,' she whispered.

It should have been a new beginning, a clean slate but, as she rode out the following morning, her head clouded from lack of sleep, Kelly knew that life was never that easy. A rest in Ireland, a confession before the Jockey Club, possibly a new relationship – it all should have signified a break with the past, particularly the recent, unhappy past, but history can't be discarded like an old coat.

As soon as first lot pulled out that morning, she sensed that something had changed. The lads were as cheerful as ever but guarded, like the possessors of unwelcome news. Then there were the riding arrangements; she was on a four-year-old called Captive Audience. Dennis was riding Shine On. Today was to be his last serious gallop before Tokyo.

'He's a lovely little ride, that one,' Dennis called out to her as they rode along in the string. 'Doesn't pull too hard. You can place him just where you want him.'

Kelly looked at him. Now she knew she was in for an unpleasant surprise. It was never good news when Dennis was happy.

'I know,' she said. 'I've ridden him before.'

'By heck,' Dennis slapped Shine On's neck. 'This one's been going well. I reckon he'll win in Tokyo.'

It was true that Shine On looked magnificent. He had lost a bit of weight after the race at York but now seemed stronger, harder.

'Are you riding him work?' Kelly was unable to resist asking the question.

Dennis frowned, as if he weren't sure quite what was happening that morning. 'No,' he said. 'I don't think I am.'

The string was walking round in a circle at the end of the gallops when Bill's Audi drew up. A small figure was seated beside the trainer and it was only when the two men got out of the car and walked briskly towards them that Kelly saw that it was Cy McCray.

'Oh yes,' said Dennis, enjoying every moment. 'Now I remember who's riding Shine On. It's Cy. D'you know him? Good jockey.'

Bill and Cy were now standing a few yards from the string. The trainer called Dennis over. Jauntily, he slipped off Shine On's back and gave Cy a leg up. 'Let's have Captive Audience over here then.' Bill's voice gave nothing away but Kelly noticed that he avoided looking at her as he gave them their orders.

'Thanks, Cy.' Kelly looked straight ahead as they cantered down to the start of the gallop.

'Hey, Kelly, I'm sorry, all right?' The American sounded sincere. 'Bill called me a couple of days ago. What could I say?'

They pulled up at the end of the gallop.

'Are you riding him in Tokyo?'

Cy shrugged. 'Guess so.' He busied himself adjusting his leathers. He glanced up. 'It's a tough break, Kelly. I'm sorry it had to be me. If I'd said no, he'd have booked somebody else.'

Kelly tried to smile gamely. 'That's racing,' she said. 'Ready when you are.' Cy nodded.

Bill's orders had been for Captive Audience to lead Shine On at racing speed over six furlongs, then for them both to stride out for home over the last two furlongs.

That's racing. Kelly jumped Captive Audience off smartly, glancing back to check that Shine On was with her. Cy had him handily tucked in a couple of lengths behind her. How many times had she heard the phrase that she had just used so easily. Get robbed of a race in the weighing room, smash your shoulder up in a gallop – that's racing. The wind whistled in her face bringing tears to her eyes. Captive Audience was going easily but Kelly knew that behind her, Cy would be swinging off Shine On, who was in a different class to her horse. Ride a big winner, hit the headlines – that's racing. The six-furlong pole approached and Kelly heard Shine On moving closer to her. His head was nodding beside her left boot. Lose a ride to one of your best friends, on the horse people had said you rode better than anyone else – that too was racing. Shine On was upsides her now. She saw Cy change his grip on the reins; Shine On effortlessly moved into overdrive and, in a matter of yards, was well clear of her. Captive Audience was tiring. She rode him out over the last furlong and finished some six lengths behind Shine On. Yes, that was racing.

'Nice horse, isn't he?' she said to Cy as they pulled up.

'Sure is.' Cy nodded. 'He's a fucking flying machine.'

Bill was not one for lengthy explanations. Standing in the middle of the yard, he called Kelly over after first lot had returned.

'Captive Audience runs at Sandown on Saturday in the lads' race,' he said.

'Right,' said Kelly. She could see Dennis watching them from one of the stables behind Bill. 'And Cy rides Shine On in Tokyo,' she said as casually as she could manage.

Bill looked embarrassed. 'Sorry, I've been meaning to tell you. Owner's orders.'

'I thought Ibn Fayoud liked the way I rode.'

'He did.' Bill looked down. 'It appears that he's changed his mind.'

'And you?'

'You know what I'd prefer but the man's got nine horses with me now.'

Behind him, Dennis smirked. He might not ride winners these days, but just now and then all the disappointment of his life in racing was forgotten for one sweet moment. She had it coming to her, that girl.

'Come and have breakfast.' Bill felt like a weight had been taken from him now that he'd told her. 'Cy's in the house.'

Kelly smiled politely. Just this once, she would risk being considered a bad loser. 'No thanks,' she said. 'I have a couple of things to do.'

It was nine thirty when Kelly rang Nick's number. As she had anticipated, he was out.

She left a message on his answering machine; 'Nick, I wanted to thank you for last night. For everything you said and for listening and for – ' She paused. 'For everything. I have a busy schedule for the next few days, so I may not be in touch. Perhaps I'll see you racing. Hope so anyway. 'Bye.'

It wasn't perfect, she reflected after she had put down the telephone, but it wasn't bad. Friendly, open, but containing an unspoken message that Nick would hear. Last night was last night; today's different. Let's take this one day at a time.

Kelly sighed and looked at her watch. It was time for second lot.

When in doubt, keep going. That was what her father used to say. Don't look to the right, to the left, or over your shoulder, but concentrate on where you're going. Kelly sat in the jockeys' stand at Sandown and gave a quiet laugh. Where the hell was she going? She was no longer sure, but at least she had a job and was offered rides. That was something. Keep going.

Half an hour previously, Captive Audience had run to the best of his ability in the lads' race, plugging on one-paced up the Sandown hill to take second place.

It had been a rough race and Kelly had been glad that she had elected to be among the leaders throughout. By the sound of it, World War III was breaking out behind her and after the race there had been a stewards' inquiry. The last thing she needed right now was another confrontation with the bowler-hat brigade.

She was offered a spare ride in the last race, a two-year-old trained by Ian Gardem, for whom she had never ridden before. She had time to kill before then. As she looked down from the stand, the horses for the third race, a handicap over six furlongs, were filing out on to the racecourse. Cy McCray was riding one of the joint favourites and, somewhat to her surprise, Harry Short had retained Damien Gould to ride Heraldic, a three-year-old with negligible form.

'What's Harry doing bringing that yoke down to Sandown?' one of the jockeys sitting behind Kelly asked.

'Spare place in the box, I suppose,' his companion muttered. 'He's got a horse running in the big race, hasn't he?'

'It's a right camel, that horse. Pulls like a train. I saw it pissing off with an apprentice on the way down to the start at Chester. He'd done a couple of circuits before they stopped. That's probably why Damien's riding it and not his retained jockey. That's the only type of animal he gets to ride these days.'

The two jockeys laughed. Yes, Kelly reflected, there was something odd about it. Harry Short rarely brought his horses south when they had no chance of winning and, on all known form, Heraldic was outclassed in this race. And why put Gould up? After Pendero's race, the trainer would hardly speak to him. What was Short up to? In spite of her determination to leave the past to look after itself, Kelly found herself speculating as to where the fat trainer fitted in with Jack Butler and Ibn Fayoud.

'There he goes,' one of the jockeys laughed. Even by the standards of Harry's yard, Heraldic was no looker, a great, gangling colt with a head and neck that seemed to have been added to his body as an afterthought. As his lad let him go, he set off towards the start flat out with his mouth open and his nose in the air. For a brief moment, Kelly felt almost sorry for Damien Gould.

'Christ!' Both jockeys were staring horror-struck out on to the course.

Kelly looked up to see Heraldic bolting towards the start with Damien clinging vainly upside down round his neck.

There was a gasp from spectators and a solitary scream as Damien fell towards the fast-moving ground, but instead of lying there he was yanked mercilessly forward as it became obvious that his foot had slipped through the iron and he was hung up. Panicked, the horse dragged Damien along under its flailing legs towards the steeplechase fence, bumping his body like a yo-yo as it went.

'Oh my God.' Kelly covered her face with her hands. It was a jockey's nightmare, being dragged under a horse's feet, held by a leather that won't break. Damien's body appeared to be twisting and writhing like a fish on a line but there was no escape for him. A groundsman ran on to the course waving his arms in a vain attempt to head the horse off but Heraldic was panicking even more now. Maddened by the limp rag doll banging against his legs, he veered to the left.

Kelly could feel her stomach turning. 'Why doesn't the leather break?' she muttered as the horse continued its terrifying charge downhill.

And then suddenly it was all over as Damien's body smashed with a sickening thud into the solid frame of the fence. A stunned silence fell over the racecourse as he lay motionless in the grass while Heraldic galloped on. Kelly's eyes flicked from the body on the ground to the horse, trampling the saddle beneath its unfeeling hoofs. Then she strained her eyes. There was something else. As she realized what it was, she turned and threw up. Damien's left leg was still in the iron.

A sense that what had just happened involved her in some way made her pull herself together and run down on to the course where racecourse attendants were already putting up a screen.

It was no accident, she thought as she ran. It was too much of a coincidence.

She hurried across the course and pushed through a knot of ghoulish spectators who were standing gloomily by the area which had been cordoned off. She walked round the ambulance. The stretcher holding Damien's inert body was just being lifted into it. An ambulanceman held out an arm. 'Sorry, love,' he said. 'We've got to get him to hospital.'

The man pulled himself in after the stretcher, the doors were closed and the ambulance began to move off, its siren wailing mournfully. Kelly headed back towards the stand.

Heraldic had finally pulled himself up at the start. He was being led back by his lad who held the saddle under one arm. Kelly stared at it and the lad hurried on.

Someone touched her arm. 'Cup of tea?'

'No,' she muttered. 'That was no accident.' She turned to walk to the weighing room. She had a horse to ride in the last.

Chapter 9

'So it's another winner for the girl wonder?'

Dermot Kinane liked to bring a ray of sunshine wherever he went. If someone had told him a nuclear bomb was targeted on County Limerick, he'd be delighted that his heating bills would be reduced. But that Sunday morning, Kelly was in no mood for optimism.

'Yes,' she said unenthusiastically. 'It was a nice little horse. Gardem says he'll be offering me more rides.' She held the phone to her ear with her shoulder and sat up in bed, pushing the newspapers on to the floor. Normally, Sunday breakfast time spent reading the papers in bed was one of Kelly's favourite moments, but not today. The news on the radio had seen to that. Damien Gould had died during the night.

'Sure, you'll be first jockey to a big stable within the next couple of seasons,' Kinane was saying. 'What did I always –?'

'You heard about Damien Gould?' Kelly interrupted.

There was a pause. 'Yes,' Dermot said quietly. 'Poor bastard. Horrible thing to happen.'

'It didn't just happen, Dermot. I think it was murder.'

'Ah, Kelly,' he sighed. 'What did we agree when you were over here? No more conspiracy theories, wasn't it?'

'Dermot, I saw the saddle when the lad brought the horse back. At the time I thought something must have been tampered with. It wasn't until later that I realised what it was. I'd seen it but it hadn't sunk in. The irons were much too big. More like hunting irons. But when I went back to have another look they'd been changed. The lad must have done it. It's a terrible thing to say, but I think the lad may have pulled the iron over Damien's foot as he let him go.'

'Jesus.'

'If I'd only realized sooner – '

'Kelly, I know it doesn't look good but for God's sake, leave it be.' Dermot's voice took on a new urgency. 'Tell your friends at the Jockey Club. Leave it to the experts.'

A vision of Colonel Beamish, listening to her with undisguised scepticism, loomed before her.

'Experts?' She laughed bitterly. 'Two days after I tell them about Damien Gould, he's dead. That's where their discreet inquiries have led.' A thought occurred to

Kelly. 'Anyway, what about your part of the deal? Did you find out anything about Ibn Fayoud or Butler?'

'I think Jack Butler's the most likely of the two. They say he's a hard bastard, like his dad. There's rumours that he's involved in some sort of organized crime caper outside racing, but it's difficult to find out more. He doesn't like gossip, our Jack. Those who gossip about him tend to meet with nasty accidents.'

'Like Damien Gould.'

'Could be. There was one other thing. Before your time, during the sixties, there were finance restrictions in the UK. It was made very difficult for businessmen to ship money abroad.'

'You think Butler was involved?'

'Not so far as I know. It was the method used for smuggling that interested me. Bloodstock, mares, stallions, used to travel abroad loaded up with notes. For some reason, the Customs inspectors never suspected horses as smugglers.'

'You mean Ibn Fayoud might be entering his horses abroad as part of some sort of smuggling operation?'

'It's a thought. He needs the money. The word is that Ibn Fayoud's in Jack Butler's pocket. So you watch yourself in Tokyo.'

Kelly smiled wryly. 'That's one thing I don't have to worry about,' she said. 'I've been jocked off. Cy McCray's riding Shine On.'

'Why's that?' Dermot sounded almost as angry as Kelly had felt when she'd heard the news.

'It's the owner's decision.'

'Bastard.' Then his voice lifted. 'Oh well, maybe it's for the best.'

After she had put down the phone, Kelly sat deep in thought. It was almost as if someone were keeping her away from trouble. There was no other explanation for Ibn Fayoud's insisting that she shouldn't ride Shine On.

Maybe Dermot was right. She should leave it to the Jockey Club, suggest to Nick that he take a closer look at Harry's yard for a start. He seemed to be up to his fat neck in this.

There were some aspects of her job that Margaret Stanhope really did not like, and spending every other Sunday in bed with Reg Butler was one of them. All right, it was at the Sheraton Park and there was champagne and chocolates and the odd item of expensive jewellery, but then there was also Reg Butler.

Margaret looked across at him as he checked his pools in the *News of the World*. He was not one for the romantic niceties, was Reg. Do it, read the papers. Maybe do it again, order up a bit of nosh and champagne. Talk a bit of business. Then it was 'Fuckin' 'ell, is that the time?', back into the vulgar check suit and home to his little wife, who had been told that he had a business meeting in the City. Not that she believed him. She knew her Reg. She was probably delighted that someone else had to submit to his unsavoury needs now and then.

Seventy-two, and getting filthier by the minute, Reg Butler had sex like other men of his age spent Sundays digging their vegetable patch down at the allotment. It got him out of the house, gave him a bit of exercise, kept him young. The only difference between them was that the bloke on the allotment was probably more careful when he prepared the soil, gentler when he started digging.

'Reg?' Margaret Stanhope saw by the watch that never left his wrist that their unromantic interlude would soon be drawing to a close.

'In a minute.' Reg Butler frowned as he read the newspaper. He was on the racing page now. His reading routine was always the same. Pools. Racing. Bonk stories.

'Shame about the Gould feller,' he muttered. 'Nasty accident, that.'

'Reg, it's about Jack.'

'I said,' Reg Butler looked up from his newspaper, 'In a minute.'

Margaret sighed. What she put up with. She couldn't nag because Reg said he got enough of that at home. And she knew she was expendable; one word out of place and he would find another Sunday partner. In fact, it was only because he was chronically mean that she had lasted this long. 'Reg Butler was never a fuckin' punter,' he had once said. 'Never will be.' And, frankly, who else would do this for free? Since the age of seventeen, Margaret had regarded her body as a tradeable commodity; she saw a fortnightly meeting between the sheets with an elderly bookmaker as an investment, a means to an end. It helped, albeit in an unpleasant way, in her campaign to become the next Mrs Jack Butler.

'It's just that he looks like bottling the Tokyo job,' she said quietly.

Reg Butler took a long drag on his cigar and glanced up from his newspaper. 'You what?' he said, expelling a cloud of smoke in her direction.

Margaret stifled a cough. 'He's pulled that little girl jockey off the job. Says he doesn't trust her. She's too nosey.'

'He told me. All the more reason to send her out there, I said. If it goes wrong, she's in the shit with Ibn Fayoud. We can't lose either way.'

'That's what I said to Jack.'

'And?' Margaret was pleased to see that she now had Reg's full attention.

'And he still got Ibn Fayoud to jock her off. Some Yank's riding now.'

'Fuckin' useless, that boy,' Reg said, as if none of this came as a surprise to him. 'I think he likes her.'

'Jesus.'

'But I've got an idea, Reg. A little plan.'

Reg Butler swept the *News of the World* off the bed. This was one evil woman, no doubt about it, but she knew how to do it. These days he liked a woman who knew how to do it.

'Later,' he said, resting his cigar carefully in an ashtray. He stroked Margaret's hair. 'What *is* the problem with that son of mine?'

'He's soft, isn't he?'

Reg Butler took her hand, kissed the palm and pushed it downwards. 'Not like his old dad, eh?'

Margaret smiled professionally. 'No, Reg,' she said. 'Not at all like his old dad.'

Nick Morley had said he'd be visiting the Whetstone Park Stud that Sunday afternoon. There had been talk of meeting for a drink in the evening, but the talk had taken place at five in the morning as Kelly was hurriedly slipping into her clothes and now Nick seemed to have forgotten. There was no answer from his London flat or from his car. The Damien Gould business couldn't wait. On an impulse, Kelly decided to drive to the stud and catch him there.

Charles Caldecott, who owned the Whetstone Park Stud, was an odd character whom Kelly had met a couple of times and had never really taken to. He had been an unsuccessful amateur jockey some fifteen years ago and had then been assistant to a leading jump trainer in Lambourn. He had been a flop there too because, after a couple of years, he had left amidst rumours of misconduct. Some said Charles had been having an affair with an owner's wife, others that he was involved in some gambling scam. Whatever the reason, no other reputable yard would touch him and for a while Charles drifted about on the fringe of racing. He ran a transport company, sold insurance schemes to jockeys, worked for a dodgy outfit that specialized in horse tonics. Among racing people, Charles Caldecott was something of a joke.

Then he got lucky. His father died. The family money, acquired from mining interests in South Africa, was divided between his brother, a rather dim stockbroker, and Charles. He invested in a stud. To everyone's astonishment – after all, Caldecott's knowledge of bloodstock could be summarized on the back of a postage stamp – it prospered. There were still rumours that the Caldecott business methods were not above suspicion, but he became part of the establishment. His yearlings sold for astonishing sums. The Arabs liked him. Charles had made it.

All the same, it was surprising that Nick dealt with him, Kelly thought to herself as she drove her car down the drive of the Stud. They seemed so different; Caldecott was the epitome of the public school chump that Nick detested.

They were sitting together in the garden, their backs to the gate through which Kelly appeared. For a moment, she hesitated. She hated arriving at places unannounced and, although Charles Caldecott had always been at his most ingratiating when he met her, that had been on social occasions. The two men sat with catalogues in front of them, deep in conversation. Then she remembered Damien. The stirrup. Nick had always said that his Jockey Club duties came before his business. She would take him at his word.

Caldecott saw her first.

'Why, er, Kelly,' he said, standing up. 'What a lovely surprise.'

'I'm sorry to turn up without warning like this,' Kelly said. 'I was told that Mr Morley was here and I just needed a brief word.'

Nick was standing too, smiling, holding the catalogue under his arm. He was pleased to see her. 'Kelly, I'm sorry, I meant to phone you. Whatever are you doing here?'

'There's something you ought to know and it couldn't wait.'

'Of course it couldn't,' Charles Caldecott said heartily.

'I'll get you a cup and saucer and you can join us for tea.' He walked off briskly towards the house.

'Nick, I'm sorry, just turning up unannounced. But I had to talk to you today.'

'That's OK. Charles is the biggest gossip in racing but I don't mind people talking about us,' said Nick, grinning slightly.

'It's not about us. It's about Damien Gould.' She told him what she had seen at Sandown.

He appeared to be only half listening. 'Kelly, it sounds implausible,' he said finally. 'And anyway, what am I meant to do on a Sunday?'

Kelly glanced towards the house. Charles Caldecott was returning, a cup and saucer in his hand.

'You could go and see Harry Short and ask him why Damien was riding his horse,' she said sharply.

'Of course.' Nick looked contrite. 'You're right. I'll ring you later.'

'Now,' said Caldecott. 'Shall I be mother and pour or d'you want me to disappear while you two talk Jockey Club business.'

'That's fine, Charles,' Nick smiled. The colour had returned to his cheeks. 'We've sorted it all out.'

'A steward's work is never done, eh?' Caldecott laughed with hearty insincerity. He turned to Kelly. 'By jove, that was a nice winner you rode for Gardem yesterday. Are you going to be first jockey for him next year?'

Kelly smiled. 'Hardly,' she said.

The three of them talked politely about horses and racing for a few minutes, before Kelly decided it was time to leave. She had done what she could.

'Thank you for the tea,' she said, rising to her feet. The two men stood up and said goodbye.

'Goodness,' she heard Caldecott say as she walked across the lawn towards her car. 'What a little popsy that girl is.'

'I'm sorry I was a bit short with you this afternoon,' Nick said when he rang Kelly later that night. 'It was just that I had other things on my mind. Anyway, I got one of my lads to go up and see Harry Short.'

'And?'

'He's just phoned from the car to say that as far as he could tell Harry had nothing to do with it. He seemed genuinely upset that the boy had been killed. Apparently he'd rung up for the ride. It wasn't Harry who'd booked him. He said he'd been pleased because his own jockey hated the horse.'

'And what about the lad who led the horse up?' Kelly asked.

'He's only been working for Harry for a few weeks. Came from a yard in the south. My lad said he was still suffering from the shock of seeing Gould's leg in the iron.'

'Maybe he never meant Damien to end up dead, but I'm certain he had something to do with it.'

'Well, let's hope we find out. The investigation is still going on.'

'A steward's work is never done,' Kelly quipped.

'Precisely,' said Nick seriously. 'Precisely.'

It was just like old times. Annie and Kelly sat drinking sweet tea in a noisy café in the centre of Newmarket. It had been an uneventful morning, apart from the trainer behaving with more surliness than usual, and Kelly needed to talk to Annie. Catch up on the gossip, she said. Girl talk. She managed to guide the conversation round to Ibn Fayoud. Lightly, she asked Annie why Bill Templeman had booked Cy McCray for Shine On in the Japan Cup.

Annie sighed. 'It's like Bill told you,' she said quietly. 'Ibn Fayoud wanted experience.'

'Listen, Annie, you can't tell lies to old liars.' Kelly sipped her tea. She had been friends with Annie long enough to know when she was holding back on her. 'What really happened?'

'All right.' Annie gave up. 'Ibn Fayoud rang late at night. Eleven thirty. You can imagine Bill's reaction.'

'I'm amazed he answered it even!'

'There was something about Ibn Fayoud's voice, he told me. Something . . .'

'Wired?'

Annie laughed. 'Yes, he was probably on something. But Bill said he seemed frightened. Like a little boy. Almost pleading.'

'So he listened.'

'Right. Ibn Fayoud talked and talked. He seemed to think that the Tokyo race was particularly important. He said that his future plans as an owner were very uncertain at the moment.'

'Meaning?'

'Bill took it to mean that he might have to pull out of the yard or even out of racing altogether.'

'Which still doesn't explain why he dumped the one person who knows how to ride Shine On.' Kelly pushed her cup of tea away from her. None of it made any sense.

'That part of what Bill told you was true. Ibn Fayoud said that the stakes were too high to risk using an apprentice.'

'D'you think McCray had got at him?'

Annie shook her head. 'No,' she said. 'It was Bill who suggested Cy when it was clear that Ibn Fayoud would take his horses away from the yard rather than use you.'

'Nice, isn't it? After the winner I rode for him at York.'

'There's something odd about it.'

Kelly thought for a moment. 'I was really looking forward to the trip, too. Maybe – ' She didn't like play-acting for her friend, pretending that the thought had just occurred to her, but this was important. 'Maybe I could go anyway. As a lad.'

'You'd do that?' Annie looked surprised.

'Of course. It's all experience. And I'd like to see how Shine On goes. Would Bill agree?'

'Why not?' Annie smiled. 'You could keep your old friend Dennis in line. And we've got to pick up a mare that Ibn Fayoud's bought out there. I'll talk to him.'

'Promise?'

'Trust me.'

It was as they left the cafe that Kelly noticed a Lamborghini, bearing the number plate FAY 1, badly parked outside a chemist's shop on the High Street. She told Annie that she had to do some shopping, then doubled back and waited. It was too good an opportunity to miss.

* * *

Ibn Fayoud didn't like mornings and he didn't like country air. Right now, he was overdosing on both. That was why he needed a hit of Valium before he headed back to London, to his bed. Sometimes being a racehorse owner was tough on the nerves.

Ibn Fayoud wasn't a normal user. He needed to come down from a greater height than most. Last night, he must have done about three grams of the white stuff, plus cognac to stop the shakes, plus not going to bed all night, plus having to behave like a serious grown-up with his trainer and make sure his horses were going to the right races in the right countries at the right time, plus a screaming anxiety attack about his father and Butler and the mess his life was in, plus the horrific combined effects of the morning and the country air. Now *that* was stress.

'Are you sure this is right?' The small grey-haired chemist returned from the back of the shop, still bearing Ibn Fayoud's prescription. 'The quantity seems – '

'It's correct,' Ibn Fayoud interrupted through clenched teeth. He fixed the man with his cold black eyes. 'And it's urgent.'

The man went off, muttering to himself. Ibn Fayoud clenched his fists to stop himself trembling. Country bumpkin. Racist. They didn't know what it was like, these people.

'Looks more like a horse prescription to me,' the man said gloomily when he returned with a phial of pills.

Ibn Fayoud, holding out his hand, flashed him a gleaming, insincere smile. 'They're for my wife. And she's not a horse.'

Emerging from the chemist, he winced as the morning sun danced around his brain. He walked quickly towards his car, got in, and fumbled with the bottle of pills. He was just cursing the child lock which his sweating, trembling hands were unable to work when he noticed the girl jockey walking towards his car. Shit. There was no way to avoid her. She was smiling at him. It was instinct – the natural reaction of a predatory male – that made Ibn Fayoud smile back and press down the automatic window beside him.

'Hello there,' he said. His mouth felt dry. His body was screaming for relief.

'Morning, sir.' Kelly Connor gave a polite little bow, glancing at the phial of pills in his hand. 'Everything sorted out with Mr Templeman?'

'Absolutely fine.' The girl was leaning on the car door, her face unnervingly close to his. Within Ibn Fayoud's racked, confused person, there was a moment of conflict. His body, out of sheer force of sexual habit, wanted her; his brain, despite the ravages of the previous night, was sending out warning signals.

'Cy riding the horses everywhere, is he?'

Ibn Fayoud looked uneasy. 'Not at all,' he said. 'I hope you'll be riding for me again soon. Now I must – '

'Me too,' Kelly interrupted with a sweet smile. It was true what they said about Ibn Fayoud. The sweat was pouring down his forehead. The man was a serious user. 'Especially after York,' she added conversationally.

'York?' Ibn Fayoud managed to say. 'That was a social thing. This is business.'

'Oh, I didn't mean the Flaxton dance with Jack Butler.' Kelly was amused to see the Arab flinch at the name. 'I meant York races.'

Ibn Fayoud smiled and glanced at his watch. The pills rattled in his hand.

'Better be going,' he said almost imploringly.

'Are you all right, sir?' Kelly looked at him more closely. 'You don't seem quite yourself.'

'Fine. I'm fine.'

Kelly made no move. 'If you happen to see Mr Butler, you can tell him I'll be going to Tokyo anyway.' Ibn Fayoud half closed his eyes as if someone had turned a knife in his guts. 'I just want to see how things go.'

'Things?' Ibn Fayoud fiddled with the car keys and eventually managed to start the engine.

Kelly stood back. 'Goodbye, sir,' she said, smiling as the Lamborghini drew away. Ibn Fayoud was in control of nothing, least of all himself. The user used. But if he was the puppet, wh was pulling the strings and to what dance?

Jack Butler really didn't like the idea that he had been nobbled and worse than that, nobbled by a girl. On the surface, his routine had changed little; travelling around the country, shaking hands, keeping his staff in order, checking his contacts were behaving themselves, sleeping with his girl friends. But he was more withdrawn, tetchy.

His father was on his back night and day. Do this, do that. However bent, however evil Jack was, it was never bad enough for his father. One spark of decency and Jack was going soft. A hint of humanity and he was a disgrace to the family name. Deep down Jack Butler was a simple man – give him a couple of Jaguars, a regular income pushing the half mill, a half dozen talented sack-artists, preferably blond, and he'd be happy. But Reg wanted more. For Reg, bookmaking was a mere step along the road to riches and power on the grand scale. In a rare moment of fatherly frankness, he had once told Jack of his dreams of floating the company on the stock market, of the Reg Butler (Entertainments) Corporation being a name in the City, of maybe even being Lord Reg one day. For services to industry.

Moodily, Jack stabbed the intercom on his desk. 'Get me General Winstanley,' he said. Services to industry? Services to brutality and corruption, more like. Services to keeping the National Health supplied with patients. Services to giving his only son more grief than any mortal should have to bear.

There was a polite 'beep' from the intercom.

'He's out for a walk at present, Jack. He'll call you when he gets in. Should be a few minutes.'

That was another one. Margaret Stanhope. Jesus, that woman had turned out to be the biggest mistake of his life. All right, so she was an adequate fixer, she helped him cut corners, smoothed out the rougher edges of his life. But these days she was stepping way out of line, coming on like she had something on him, like she was something more than a two-bit secretary. Ever since York.

She knew too much to be fired and she refused to be bought out with money or offers of promotion. All she wanted was to be by his side. What had happened? How come Jack Butler was no longer in charge? How come, all of a sudden, everything was out of control?

Ever since York. That was the worst. Wanting someone, like he wanted Kelly

Connor, was no novelty to Jack – hardly a day passed when it didn't happen to him – but a quick telephone call and a Suzi or a Debra, one of his sexual Samaritans, would be there to make it feel better. This was different. Thanks to Margaret, her box of drugs and her camera, Kelly was beyond his reach probably for ever.

Jack leant back in his chair, put his feet on the desk and stared out of the window. Was that all? The fact that she was unavailable? That she was virtually unique in that she would say no to Jack Butler? He sighed. Hardly. He found that he wanted ed the sort of things girls, his wife even, demanded from him – chat, company, sharing.

Not just need, but affection. It was like discovering an old trick, something he hadn't done for years and had thought was dead – unnerving but not entirely unpleasurable.

Jack Butler had discovered he could still love. Shit. That was all he needed.

The intercom sounded once more.

'General Winstanley for you,' said Margaret.

Jack picked up the phone. 'Put him on.' He rubbed his eyes as if to rid himself of thoughts of Kelly Connor.

'David,' he said with a dangerous, false heartiness. 'How ya doin'? Good.' He interrupted the small talk. 'Then you can do something for me.'

The truth was that General Winstanley did quite a lot for Jack. He told him which of his fellow owners were open to a spot of friendly blackmail, when they had a horse running that stood to lose the firm a lot of money. He put in a good word for him at meetings of the Jockey Club. He landed him invitations to society dances where Jack would normally have been lucky to be collecting coats at the door. Poor old General David Winstanley. His weakness for girls from an escort agency run by an old friend of Jack's had cost him dear over the years.

Mind you, he was never Mr Co-Operative. Even before Jack had given him his instructions he was moaning, silly old bastard.

'Shut up, General,' said Jack, suddenly losing patience. 'It's a simple job. Any of your horses running next week? Well, they are now. I want Marking Time and that three-year-old filly of yours to run at Kempton on Saturday. Of course they're ready to fucking run. Otherwise your trainer wouldn't have entered them. And get him to book Kelly Connor.'

There were sounds of protest from the other end of the telephone.

'Bollocks to the stable jockey. Bollocks to what your poxy trainer wants. You tell them. You're a general, right. Give them their marching orders. Otherwise I'll give you yours. If I don't see their names in the overnight declarations on Friday afternoon, I'll be on the blower to the *News of the World* before you can say "flagellation", right? Right.'

He slammed the phone down and allowed himself a small smile. He liked dealing with army types. They understood orders.

Predictably, Margaret Stanhope found an excuse to interrupt his thoughts within moments of his conversation with the general.

'Just a couple of letters to sign, Jack,' she said lightly. As he glanced over his correspondence, she muttered, 'You'll do anything to help that little jockey, won't you?'

Jack looked up sharply. 'I've told you about listening to my calls. What I do about Tokyo is my business.'

'Your business is my – '

'Close the fucking door behind you.'

The look of hurt astonishment which crossed Margaret's face pleased Jack. He hadn't talked to her like that for ages. It felt good. Maybe everything was going to be all right. This time he would do it himself, without Margaret, without any of her pet goons who could be guaranteed to get it wrong – to maim when they were meant to frighten, to kill when they were meant to maim. Jack sighed. If you wanted something done, you just had to do it yourself. You couldn't get the staff these days.

For Kelly, it was just like it used to be. The early-morning call, then down to the yard to get the horses ready for their big day. She hadn't been a lad for a couple of years now, but she knew the routine. Shine On had to be at the airport by ten. The four o'clock call would give her enough time to make it with ease.

She smiled as she sipped her coffee. It was the one part of the job her father had hated. Getting up early, making time, punctuality. He would doubtless disapprove of what Kelly was doing. Turning down two good, last-minute rides at Kempton in order to be a lad. But she needed to know. She had gone too far towards discovering who killed her father to turn back now.

She set the answering machine, grabbed her bag and locked up the flat. Travelling with Dennis was hardly going to be a delight, but it would be worth it. Tokyo was not just about Shine On winning a big international race and collecting a top breeding mare, she was sure of it.

Minutes later, she was down in the yard, unlocking the feed shed in the morning darkness. She'd agreed with the head lad that there was no need for him to get up extra early, but he'd insisted on leaving Shine On's feed already made up. She walked across the yard to check Shine On. As soon as Dennis arrived, she would bandage him up and they would be on their way by five thirty. She glanced at her watch. It was unusual for Dennis to be late.

It was as she approached Shine On's box that she noticed a torch light in the tack room.

'Dennis?' she said quietly. The light was snuffed out. Kelly walked over quickly to Shine On's box to check that he was unharmed. Switching on the light, she saw that he was fine.

She turned out the light and reaching for a pitchfork crept towards the tack room. It was unlocked and in darkness. When Kelly turned the light on, there was no one to be seen and nothing seemed to have been moved.

From beyond the other end of the yard, she heard the distant whistling of Dennis, getting closer. She turned. Perhaps he would have an explanation.

She was just about to call out when she felt the iron grip of an arm clasped round her throat. Before she could scream a damp rag had been clamped over her mouth, and suddenly there was pain behind her eyes and all was darkness.

The man carried the limp body to where the Saab was parked. Expertly, he tied her hands behind her back, felt inside her pockets and took out a key. He unlocked the boot and, almost tenderly, lifted the body into it.

He looked at her for a moment. She would be out for an hour. He would have to lock the boot but he would leave the key in the ignition. By the time she was discovered, it would be too late for her to catch the plane.

The man paused before closing the boot. Her face looked calm and beautiful as it slept its enforced slumber, the lips slightly parted, the dark curls spilling over a pale cheek. Please God, she'd never discover who had done this to her. She hated him enough already. First drugs and now chloroform. It was no way to start a relationship.

The man closed the boot quietly and put the key into the ignition of the Saab.

He was whispering something, repeating it, like a chant, a mantra, a magic spell to make everything better.

'You always,' he said, swaying slightly in the darkness. 'You always hurt the one you love.'

Chapter 10

Shine On travelled so well it might have been a trip to Yarmouth. He took the long air journey and everything else in his stride like an old police horse. The high-rise stable block next to the racecourse, the lift which took him to and from his quarters with an eerie, high-tech smoothness, the canned music which wafted over the looseboxes from seven in the morning to nine at night, the noisy chatter of the Japanese stable lads – none of it concerned him. He had travelled well, lost not an ounce of weight, and eaten up since his arrival as if he were at home.

'You're a professional, that's what you are.'

Kelly patted Shine On's neck and scratched behind his ears. They had been in Tokyo for two days now and she had seen little of the sights beyond the stable block and the racecourse where the horses exercised. This evening she had agreed to look after him while Dennis explored the back streets of the city in search of Eastern decadence. It was no good telling him that one red-light district was very much like another, that there was little or nothing here that couldn't be found on a quiet night in Greek Street. Dennis had seen the films, read the magazines. The East was the place where young beauties did weird and wonderful things on stage. Bangkok, Hong Kong, Tokyo – to Dennis they were the ultimate in sleaze and kinkiness. As far as he was concerned, if Kelly wanted to turn her virginal little nose up at the idea of a good time, that was her problem.

As it happened, all Kelly could think of was the following day's big race, the one in which she should be riding but wasn't. She drained the automatic trough in Shine On's box and measured in a small amount of fresh water. Of course there would be other races, other class horses to ride but getting jocked off hurt as much as being dumped by a lover. Perhaps, after all, it had been a mistake to travel here as a stable lad. If he won, it could only add to the pain.

A Japanese stable lad walked past Shine On's box and made a clicking sound with his teeth. Kelly wasn't sure whether the greeting was lewd or merely polite, or indeed whether it was intended for her or the horse, so she smiled coolly.

No, she had been right to come. Her suspicion that there was something odd about the trip to Tokyo had been confirmed on the morning of their departure. Someone didn't want her to make the trip, and was determined enough to knock her out with chloroform and then lock her in a car to make certain that she didn't. If it hadn't been for a lad who had come to work early and a go-slow by the handling staff at the airport, they would have succeeded. She couldn't have afforded to buy her own ticket. After rushing down the M11 and round the M25, she had finally caught up with Dennis and Shine On as they waited in the horsebox on the tarmac.

She looked up at the red eye of the stables' camera as it ranged over the loose-boxes. The Japanese left nothing to chance. If a horse was going to be doped, it wouldn't be from within the racecourse stables; twenty-four-hour surveillance protected every one of the runners in the big race tomorrow.

It wasn't a question of doping, almost certainly. There were too many inponderables in an international race for it to be the subject of a major gamble, with or without narcotic assistance. Not only was the form of horses from different countries difficult to equate, but there was the toll of travelling to consider, the vagaries of a foreign racetrack. Shine On was among the favourites but, Kelly was almost sure, the danger was not to him.

She locked the stable door and walked towards the lads' room, deep in thought.

'Wanna game, Kelly-san?' An Australian stable lad, playing cards with three Japanese boys, looked up and smiled at her. He was only eighteen but what he lacked in years he made up for in confidence. Ever since they had met, he had joked and flirted with Kelly, putting on an absurd Nippon accent, as if she were only holding out against his pint-sized Australian charm as a matter of form.

'No thanks, Craig,' she smiled.

'Drink? Take in a club? Tonight's the night, eh?'

'No, Craig, tonight's not the night. Stick with your game. It's all you're likely to win out here.'

'Ah, lighten up, you frigid pommie.' Kelly closed the door to the sound of male laughter. The Japanese lads spoke little English but they could recognize an exchange of small-arms fire in the international battle of the sexes, and they knew which side they were on.

Kelly used the second pass-key she had been given to check the storeroom where all the runners' tack and spare rugs were kept. The locker marked '31. SHINE ON (Brit)' was as tidy and ordered as any of them. Dennis may have been a jerk in his private life but at least he knew his job. She closed the door and locked it.

Why her? Why did someone want to stop her coming to Tokyo? Kelly pressed the button for the lift which would take her to the top floor where her sleeping quarters were. First of all, she had been jocked off Shine On, then locked in her car on the day she was meant to fly out. Why?

By some miracle, the ubiquitous canned music failed to reach the inside of the lift. Kelly leaned against the side with her head back and enjoyed a few seconds without a distant, sanitized version of a Beatles hit.

Her room was at one end of a long corridor and was the ultimate in Japanese economy. Somehow, all the basic requirements of an overnight guest – bed, table, shower, cupboard – had been compressed into a room with as much space as a British Rail toilet. Craig had told her that the men's bedrooms were spacious and airy, but Kelly was not tempted to check his claim at first hand.

She dialled a number. 'Cy?'

'Who's this?'

'This is your stable lad speaking. I was just checking that you were getting an early night.'

Cy laughed. 'I've just had dinner with the Templemans,' he said. 'Trying to make conversation with Bill as he complains about having to eat raw fish would make anyone tired.'

'Cy, don't get me wrong here, but have you time for a nightcap? I need to talk.'

There was a pause from the other end of the telephone. Cy McCray was a charming, straightforward guy but he was a man of the world. When an attractive, single woman rang you in your hotel room and suggested a nightcap, it could only mean one thing.

'Sure,' he said. 'I've got a bottle in my room.'

'I think the hotel bar would be a better idea.'

'You mean,' Cy allowed incredulity to enter his voice, 'nightcap as in drink?'

'Of course.' Kelly laughed. 'What else?'

'Nothing.' He sighed. 'Anyway, I never do it the night before a race.'

'Cy, you're a liar. You'd do it down at the start given half a chance. The Hilton bar in ten minutes, OK?'

'Sure. I'll be there.'

Ibn Fayoud bit his nails as he paced the length of his suite at the Tokyo Hilton and swore. It was eleven o'clock in the evening. He was in an exotic Eastern city. There were girls out there, clubs, interesting local drug cocktails, and he was alone, sober, in a hotel room. It was unnatural.

Ten forty-five, Butler had said, and the shifty son-of-a-bitch was late. Fifteen minutes was nothing to Jack Butler but to Ibn Fayoud, fifteen minutes without laughter, fawning waitresses, the pop of champagne corks, the flash of tanned female flesh, the breathtaking sensation of his brain humming into life under the influence of that sweet white powder – fifteen minutes without all that seemed like an eternity of deprivation.

The phone rang. Ibn Fayoud brought his hand down on the receiver like a man swatting a fly. 'Yes?' Jack's voice sounded drowsy, laconic.

'Everything in order?'

'Of course.'

'Horse all right, is it?'

'Sure. Look, could you make this quick. I have . . . people to see.'

'You're alone there, are you?'

'Of course I'm alone. What d'you think I am? Stupid?'

There was an eloquent silence from the other end of the telephone. 'We're green,' Jack said eventually. 'Go for it.'

'Fine. I'll see you in London.'

Ibn Fayoud hung up, ran a comb through his dark hair, grabbed his wallet and made for the door. At this particular moment, it didn't bother him that tomorrow his fortune would be made or broken, that his partner Jack Butler had seemed weary, almost regretful, now that there was no going back. At this particular moment, only one thing mattered to Ibn Fayoud. At last, it was playtime.

'No.' Cy sat back at a corner table in the Hilton bar and shook his head. 'To me, there's nothing odd about my being booked for tomorrow. I've ridden for Bill before, and I've ridden here before. You know yourself what an advantage it is to have ridden round a course beforehand. It's experience, that's all,' he said sympathetically. 'Your time will come.'

Kelly smiled. She knew McCray well enough to be all but certain that he was not involved with Ibn Fayoud or Butler. Maybe in the past he had tried a little less hard than was strictly ethical on a horse that, once it was down in the handicap, would be the medium of a hefty gamble, perhaps he was on rather more friendly terms with certain bookmakers than professional jockeys were meant to be, but so what? That wasn't corruption. That was racing.

Kelly put her drink down. 'I think,' she dropped her voice, 'I think there's some kind of smuggling ring that Ibn Fayoud's part of.'

'Oh yeah? What about Jack Butler?' Cy was unable to conceal his scepticism. 'I think you might be getting a little paranoid here.'

'Ibn Fayoud owes Jack Butler a fortune. That's why Pendero was stopped at Ascot. From then on, Ibn Fayoud was in his pocket.'

'And how exactly does this involve you and the ride on Shine On?'

Kelly told him of the events at the Templeman stable on the morning of their departure for Tokyo.

'Why?' The American looked confused. 'I still don't see why they wanted to stop you coming out here.'

She shrugged. 'I can't work it out either but I'm certain it's all got something to do with my father's death. Think about it. Broom-Parker. Gould.'

'Who else knows about this?'

'Just an old friend back in Ireland and the Jockey Club. And the police, of course.'

'They believe you?'

'Who knows.'

'And now you think it was these guys who gave you chloroform and locked you in the boot of a car. Sounds more like the Boy Scouts than the international Mafia.'

Kelly sighed. Certainly, it was odd that the attempt to stop her travelling to Tokyo had been so uncharacteristically half-hearted. After all, these were the people who had clubbed her father to death, run down Broom-Parker, engineered the bloody demise of Damien Gould. She remembered the grip round her neck. Firm, determined, professional. He could have killed her, or at least put her out for a long time. Then he could have driven the car to a deserted spot and thrown away the key. But he didn't.

'Of course, it might not have been what I knew that bothered them.' Kelly muttered the words, as if talking to herself.

'Mmm?' The American's eye had been caught by a Japanese girl, sitting by herself at the bar. 'Put me to bed, Kelly,' he said quietly. 'Get me outa here or I'll blow my winnings before I've won.'

'It might have been just to get me out of the way, to save me from something.' Kelly remembered how Jack Butler had looked at her across the table at the Flaxton dance. 'To protect me.'

Cy was raising his glass to the girl, who lowered her eyes in a parody of girlish modesty while crossing her legs. 'Jesus,' he said. 'I think I've seen heaven.'

'Cy?' Kelly touched his arm. She glanced in the direction in which he was staring and sighed. 'Thanks, Cy,' she said. 'You've been a great help.' She stood up, taking him by the arm.

'Maybe,' he said, resisting, 'Maybe I'll just stay down for another nightcap.'

'What about your never-before-a-big-race rule?'

Cy smiled and looked back at the girl who had now abandoned all pretence to innocence and was staring hopefully in his direction.

He looked sheepish. 'I guess that must have been a lie.'

Like racing all around the world, Japanese racing is run on class lines. Racecourses are divided between the heaving populace, the punters, and the enclosures where the sport's aristocrats – owners, administrators, trainers, the established jockeys – can roam in relative space and comfort. At the lowest end of the social scale were stable lads.

Kelly had agreed that, if Bill allowed her to come to Tokyo as a stable lad, she would play the part. There would be no dinners with owners and trainers, no chats with Ibn Fayoud. Like Dennis, she was there to look after Shine On. The fact that, at another time on another continent, she had been his jockey was entirely irrelevant.

Now, as she stood in the ill-appointed section of the stand at Tokyo racecourse reserved for stable lads, she felt apart from the excitement all around her. She wanted Shine On to win – for Bill and Annie, for the horse itself, even for Cy McCray – and yet she was helpless against the feeling of anger at the circumstances which had led to her being in the stand looking down on the crowded racecourse rather than on Shine On's back. There was more than a part of her that dearly wanted him to run badly.

Dennis had insisted on leading the horse up, which had left Kelly free to wander the racecourse while the runners were in the paddock. She had looked at the electric board showing the ever-changing odds on the runners. An American horse Carpetbagger was the firm favourite with three other horses – Shine On, a French filly called My Ninette, and a local horse, Driver – all around the 3–1 mark.

Kelly had tried to get to the paddock but the crowd had been such that she had only been able to catch a glimpse of Shine On before she left for the stand. Despite the noise and the heat, he had seemed remarkably calm, but the French filly was black with sweat. Still, some horses didn't run their best unless they were on their toes.

Looking down from the multi-storey grandstand, Kelly watched the runners filing out on to the racecourse, and then made her move. The horses would parade in front of the stand before turning at the end of the straight and making their way to the stalls on the far side of the course. She had ten minutes before the race started.

Pushing her way through the crowd, she took the down escalator and made her way into the underpass leading to the racecourse stables. It was only a hunch, but she wanted to check Shine On's box while all eyes were on the big race.

'You all right, Kelly-san?' One of the friendlier Japanese lads was walking a horse due to run in the next race round the outer paddock as she hurried past.

'Fine, thanks,' she said.

She held up her pass to the security guard at the entrance to the stables. He eyed her suspiciously before nodding and opening the gate.

Apart from the commentator's voice which had replaced the jangling monotone of canned music, all was silence on the floor where the foreign horses were kept. The lads who were not involved in the Japan Cup would be up in the stands watching it or, like the lad outside, preparing their horses for the next race.

As casually as she was able, Kelly opened the door to the lads' room. The television was turned on, but without the sound, and there was no one watching. On the screen, the runners for the Japan Cup were cantering down to the start. She closed the door and walked past several empty looseboxes to where Shine On was kept. She could feel her pulse quickening as she got closer and told herself not to be ridiculous. All she was going to do was look inside a stable that she had every right to.

She pushed open the door and went in, kicking the sawdust on the floor. Looking for what? Kelly smiled. A large hypodermic syringe? A packet of diamonds? A shopping bag full of heroin? She moved every piece of bedding, but there was nothing. Maybe Cy was right. She was paranoid.

On the other hand, Cy had too much on his mind last night to pay attention to her suspicions. Winning the Japan Cup in the morning. Pulling the girl at the bar. It would have taken a lot more than her conspiracy theories to distract his attention from his own immediate needs and concerns.

Kelly looked at her watch. It was almost time to return to the stand. She'd just take a quick look inside the storeroom. She paused briefly at the large mahogany door. As she reached for her key, she noticed it was ajar. Senses on red alert, she slowly pushed it open – and smiled.

An old man pushing a trolley was muttering to himself. With typical hospitality, the racecourse was giving uniform, emblazoned rugs and beautifully made wooden travelling trunks to the foreign runners so that, as they returned home, they would be walking advertisements for the glories of racing in Tokyo. The man looked up at her in surprise and said something in Japanese.

'Excuse me.' Kelly shrugged apologetically and pretended to be looking for something in Shine On's locker. His new rug and bandages were already neatly placed on top of the trunk which had been hand-painted with Bill's name, round which, in much larger letters arranged in the shape of a horseshoe, were the words JAPAN CUP. Dennis would be thrilled.

The trunk was large enough to hold almost everything needed to travel one horse, and inside, next to the section which had been specially designed to hold a saddle, was an expensively made anti-cast roller. Hand-stitched in leather, with brass buckles, it was about five inches wide and went right round the horse's middle. Something similar to the roll-over bar fitted to rally cars was attached across its top. The idea of it was to prevent the horse from being able to roll right over in its stable and risk getting its legs caught in something.

'Nice,' Kelly said politely.

The old man shrugged and shuffled on with his job.

Kelly had seen enough. She turned and ran back towards the grandstand.

The lads' section was packed by the time she reached the stand and it was only with the help of Craig who, with much unnecessary touching and squeezing, found her a place beside him, that she was able to see anything.

The start was halfway up the straight. Just a short run, and then one complete circuit. A huge roar went up from the crowd as the stalls flew open. All thoughts of wrongdoing and criminality disappeared from Kelly's mind.

When the runners were some distance away, Kelly switched her focus to the enormous TV screen in front of the stands. It was nothing like those she'd seen on occasions in England where the picture looked as if it was being filmed underwater. This one was as clear as the set in her living room.

Kelly picked out the red-white colours of Ibn Fayoud tucked in behind Driver as the runners settled down some ten lengths adrift of the leader.

It had irritated Kelly that Cy hadn't asked her how to ride Shine On. Somehow, if he had it would have made her feel slightly more part of the team, but he'd seemed embarrassed whenever the horse's name was mentioned. Eventually it was a sheepish-looking Bill who had asked her to have a word with the American and she'd done it the evening before at the Hilton. Hold him up and don't hit the front too soon, she'd told him, or he'll think he's won and pull himself up. With the distraction of the girl at the bar, Kelly wondered just how much he'd taken in.

As the field raced past the stands, Kelly stood on tiptoe, holding on to Craig's shoulder, to get a better look.

'Don't worry, he's still there.' Craig put his arm round her waist. Kelly thanked him as she firmly took his hand out of her jeans pocket.

As the field turned away from the stands and Kelly switched her focus back to the screen, the leading horse slowly began to lose his position. His jockey, realizing his chance had gone, eased off the rails to let My Ninette through. The French filly was still pulling hard and quickly opened up a gap of three or four lengths from the others. One furlong later a huge roar went up as the local horse Gyroscope went after her.

Kelly's eyes were fixed on Shine On. Cy waited and waited. Then, as the jockey in front of him made his move on Driver, Cy followed. Slowly but surely, and with neither jockey appearing to move a muscle, the two cruised round the outside of three or four beaten horses and began closing on the leaders. Kelly's eyes darted from the screen to the course and then back again. The French filly was tough as nails and as Gyroscope went to tackle her as they straightened up for home, she laid her ears back and fought like a terrier to stay in front. At the two-furlong pole and with both jockeys going for their lives, the local horse got his head in front. The cheering from the partisan crowd became a deafening roar as they sensed victory.

Driver, his jockey hunched up his neck American-style, whip held upright like a cavalryman with a sword, had now gone in hot pursuit with Shine On still glued to his tail.

'Not yet, Cy,' Kelly whispered, but as she spoke the American pulled his horse out of Driver's slipstream and set sail for home. His electric change of pace made the two horses in front of him look ordinary as he swept past them, with a furlong left to run.

'You've won,' muttered Craig beside her.

A handful of different emotions jostled for Kelly's attention all at once. Pleasure that the horse she loved was going to win, bitterness that she wasn't riding him, sadness for her father, loneliness. She'd barely managed to isolate one of them when she noticed Shine On prick his ears. Driver and My Ninette had shot their bolt but the locals were still cheering Gyroscope who, under the frenzied driving of his jockey, had not yet given in.

'I don't think so,' said Kelly, almost afraid to watch the last few yards of the race. Shine On's concentration seemed to waver as he hit the wall of sound coming from the stands. He changed legs and, too late, Cy went for his whip. As Shine On and Gyroscope flashed past the post, the crowd near the winning post were in no doubt that their favourite had got up on the line. Cy's head dropped as Gyroscope's jockey punched the air. A photograph was announced but the result was a formality.

'Needs blinkers.' Craig shook his head wisely. Like most stable lads, he could ride a great race from the safety of the stands. 'Good try, though.'

Kelly managed a smile as the crowd pushed past her on the way to the winners' enclosure. Second, against an international field, having travelled halfway round the world. It wasn't bad. The English contingent in the crowd would be celebrating, the travelling British journalists would be polishing up the old so-near-yet-so-far clichés, but there were a few who would be more subdued. Bill and Annie, Dennis, even Cy McCray. Above all, Cy. They all knew that Shine On should have won. Kelly hated herself for it, but deep in her heart she was glad Shine On had been beaten. There was still some justice left in the world. She decided not to watch them coming in.

It was hardly a night for celebration, but the plane home left in the morning and Kelly had yet to see more of Japan than Tokyo racecourse. She had wanted to spend the evening having a look round the city with Annie but she was due to play dutiful trainer's wife at a reception given by the Japanese Jockey Club.

Craig had made one last attempt to win her heart. 'Wanna go out, catch a skin show, then mebbe come back to my room and fool around a bit, darling?'

'In a word, Craig, no.'

He'd asked the next girl passing by the same question.

Dennis was still researching bizarre sexual practices of the Orient, and Cy had a date at the Hilton.

'With the love of your life?' Kelly asked as they stood by the paddock shortly after the last race. Cy had given her a subdued account of his ride on Shine On and was clearly in no mood for further post-mortems.

'Right,' he said gloomily. 'With the love of my life. Suki. That's her working name anyway.'

'You don't exactly sound like love's young dream. I thought you had seen heaven.'

'Yeah, yeah.' Cy inhaled deeply on a cigarette. 'I've been to heaven and back. Lost more weight in one night than I would have in a sauna.'

'Where from? Your body or your wallet?'

He shrugged. 'Heaven doesn't come cheap. She wants to be taken out to dinner tonight.'

'Romantic.'

'Expensive.'

Kelly smiled. 'So Cy McCray's in lust with a Japanese hooker. I guess I'll just have to eat alone tonight. So much for friendship.'

Cy shot her a look of embarrassed reproach. 'If it hadn't been for you and your nightcap, I never would have met her.'

'Call me Cupid,' said Kelly. 'I'll see you tomorrow.' As he walked away, she couldn't resist calling after him, 'Hey, Cy, I hope for Suki's sake you don't come as soon as you did on Shine On.' The American put two fingers in the air and kept walking.

Back in her room, the light on Kelly's telephone was flashing. She rang down to reception.

'Two messages for Miss Connor,' the sing-song voice of the receptionist told her. 'Please to ring Mr Morley in London, any time OK. And Ibn Fayoud ring from Tokyo Hilton. He says having party at Club Joey tonight. Can you please go?'

'Club Joey?' Kelly frowned as she noted down the address. 'What's it like?'

There was a pause from the receptionist. 'Smart,' she said. 'Very funky, you know?'

Typical. Kelly smiled grimly to herself as she waited for the international operator to put her through to Nick in London. The man she most wanted to see was on the other side of the world and her only chance of seeing the bright lights of Tokyo was playing bimbo to a playboy cokehead in a funky club, whatever that was.

'Yes.' Nick's voice had an early-morning croak to it.

'Nick, it's Kelly. Sorry to wake you. I just got in.'

'How are you?'

'Fine.' Kelly was going to add that she was missing him but knew that at that moment she was probably just missing company.

'How did he go?'

Kelly took him through the race that afternoon. It was good not to have to fake an enthusiasm she didn't feel. Of all people, with the possible exception of Annie, Nick understood her disappointment.

'What about the other stuff?' he asked. 'Are you still convinced that Ibn Fayoud's up to something?'

'If he is, he's playing it cool. I've just been invited to one of his parties.' Across the thousands of miles, Kelly sensed his disapproval. 'I doubt if I'll go,' she added.

'No,' he said finally. 'I think you should. We've had a whisper that something's going on. From the Drug Squad. Maybe you can find something out, or just make a note of who he's with.'

'Ok. What's been happening at home? Did either of those horses of General Winstanley's win at Kempton?'

'I don't know. I've been busy.' Kelly thought he sounded distracted.

'Are you all right?'

'Yes, it's just that I wish I were there with you.' He seemed embarrassed at what

he'd said and continued quickly, 'Don't go asking questions but listen out for anything he might say. I'll see you at the airport tomorrow evening.'

'The airport?' Kelly was surprised. She would have to take Shine On and the
mare back to the Templemans, so there was no question of his collecting her.

'Yes. I told the police I'd be there. Just in case.'

'Fine.' Perhaps it was the distance between them, but Kelly felt uneasy. The tone
in Nick's voice as he'd spoken that last sentence was brisk, almost military. 'I'll
look forward to seeing you there,' she said.

'Yes.' Nick, ever the Englishman, sounded embarrassed. 'Yes, me too.'

There were few bright lights at the Club Joey. It was a private club, situated in
one of Tokyo's few quiet back streets. Kelly had not been encouraged by the
appraising way the taxi driver had looked at her as he took her fare at the door,
nor by the knowing smile of the doorman who allowed her in almost before she
had mentioned Ibn Fayoud's name. She could sense the pair of them wondering
how much she charged for her services.

She was escorted by a young French waiter across a dark basement, past low
tables where guests, many of them Westerners, sat on cushions. Most had a geisha
girl seated beside them. There was a small dance floor with multi-coloured lights
flashing from a mirrored dome, and a couple were swaying to a disco beat. Beyond
them was a darker section of the club, which seemed less populated.

A fat American looked up and muttered something lewdly appreciative as she
walked by.

'What goes on at the back?' she asked the waiter.

He gave a knowing little smile. 'Private rooms,' he said. 'You maybe see them
later.'

So that was it. A private club with rooms at the back. Very funky. She saw Ibn
Fayoud's party in a corner and was relieved to see that there were more women
than men. If Ibn Fayoud had her marked as his geisha for the night, he had a shock
coming. But it was too late to escape now.

'Miss Connor, you look divine.' Ibn Fayoud extended his arms as he stood up
to greet her. He was wearing silk robes and his dark eyes shone.

'Sir.' Kelly held out a hand for a formal handshake. The Arab took it as if it were
a precious jewel and, gently caressing the fingers, held it to his lips. Briefly, she
remembered the last time they had spoken, the chill morning in Newmarket, the
pinched face and sallow skin of a man coming down from a long and high narcotic journey. From the look of him, he was airborne now, any disappointment at
his horse's defeat that afternoon forgotten.

A waiter brought a small silk cushion and placed it beside Ibn Fayoud as Kelly
was introduced to his other guests. A couple of the men she had seen with him in
England; the rest were instantly recognizable as members of his branch of the international jet set. Heavy jewellery, impeccably cut suits, vacant expressions on their
well-tanned faces. Jet set? Jerk set more like.

'Kelly is the best apprentice in England, the best by far, and she rides all my
horses in England,' Ibn Fayoud was saying, the words tumbling from him as if
his lips could scarcely keep pace with the speed of his thoughts. She shrugged

modestly, noting with some satisfaction that, even in her simple blue silk dress, she had attracted the attention of all male eyes round the table.

'Yes, sir. I'm so good that this afternoon you got someone else to ride for you.'

Ibn Fayoud was in no state to appreciate irony. He laughed loudly. 'My dear Kelly,' he trilled. 'My close friends call me Ib.'

The girls around the table laughed dutifully. In addition to the streak-haired model types without whom no Ibn Fayoud party would be complete, there was a tall black girl with a severe haircut and a dark lace dress that just failed to cover her perfect breasts, and two fragile, young Japanese girls who smiled beautifully and said little.

For a time Kelly sat quietly, trying to look interested as mindless conversation of last night's parties eddied around her, but it was difficult, particulary since the right hand of her host frequently brushed her bare knee. Sitting on the floor, she discovered, posed certain problems of etiquette.

Suddenly, he raised his voice and changed the subject, looking deeply into her eyes. 'Let me tell you all about my guests.' Kelly tuned out as he put names and uncensored biographies to the vacant faces round the table. Only the geisha girls escaped this treatment. 'They're just here for fun, aren't you, girls?' he said. The two girls averted their eyes shyly, like Cy's Hilton Suki had. Girlish modesty seemed to be big in Tokyo.

One of the blonde models stood up, affording the other guests a full view of the length of her tanned thighs.

'Well, I need to go to the girls' room,' she piped. She giggled unsteadily and tapped the side of her nose. 'I need to powder my nose.' She looked across at Kelly. 'D'you want to powder your nose, Kelly?' It was more like a challenge than an invitation.

'I'm all right, thank you,' she said coolly. It had definitely been a mistake to accept Ibn Fayoud's invitation.

'What about you, Ib? Are you – ' the model allowed a sneer, directed at Kelly, to enter her voice '– all right too?'

Ibn Fayoud got to his feet and, placing a confident, proprietorial hand on the girl's right buttock, walked with her in the direction of the back rooms.

'Never says no to a spot of nose-powdering, does Ib.' The man on her right, a blow-dried Italian, winked at Kelly.

'Is that what goes on at the back?'

The man gave her a gleaming smile. 'Everything goes on at the back. Would you like me to show you?'

'No thanks,' Kelly smiled. 'Doesn't he worry about his reputation? He's a member of the Qatar royal family.'

'Precisely. And he's an accredited diplomat. He has diplomatic immunity. He could roll up a fifty pound note and do a line of coke on this table and he wouldn't be arrested.' The man winked. 'But he likes the back room. He says that he can get any girl once she's done half a gram in the back room with him. That's probably why you're here.'

'You reckon?' Kelly had heard enough. She stood up, saying, 'Maybe I will powder my nose, after all.' The men round the table leered knowingly. Good old Ib had done it again.

'Room Thirty,' her Italian neighbour said. 'You'll just be in time for the party.'

Kelly walked swiftly towards the back room. She brushed past a curtain into a dark hall, with rooms on each side. There was a small peephole in each door which, she noticed from one of the rooms that had been left open, could be covered from the inside. Room Thirty was halfway down the hall.

Ibn Fayoud and his friend had not bothered to close the peephole. She remembered the Italian's words. Diplomatic immunity. Ibn Fayoud al Hassan could do anything he wanted. And right now he was. At a glass-topped dressing table he sat crouched over a line of powder, a small ivory tube up his nose. The model knelt at his feet and was attending to his other needs with her mouth.

Kelly was about to leave when she became aware that she was no longer alone.

'You like to watch?' The Italian must have followed her. His mouth was close to her right ear and a hand cupped her breast. 'Want to find another room?' The hand began a slow but determined progress across her stomach.

Kelly grabbed his index finger and, in one fluid movement, whirled round, twisting it painfully. The man gasped and fell to one knee in front of her.

'Not tonight, thanks, Julio,' she said, pushing him backwards on to the floor. The man lay, nursing his finger and looking after her in astonishment as she walked briskly towards the exit.

'Please tell Ibn Fayoud I had a migraine,' she told the doorman, taking her coat. 'I'm sure he'll understand.'

Chapter

11

Even by the standards of a British airport, it had been an unusually long delay. The deep-bellied jet, carrying six horses and their handlers, had landed an hour previously. It had taxied into a bay by the Customs building, cut its engines and now waited in silence to be unloaded.

'Some sort of Customs hold-up, I believe,' a steward with carefully coiffed hair and an unnatural tan had told Kelly. The steward had long since shed his air of courtly politeness. They were on the ground. He was doing Miami tomorrow. His boyfriend would be ready and waiting for him in Putney. Frankly, the last thing he needed was some check-up by the drugs boys.

'Can't we just transfer the horses?' Dennis had seemed distinctly edgy during the flight. Now he was fumbling with a packet of duty-free cigarettes.

'Not until we're given the green light,' said the steward tetchily. 'In the meantime, there's still no smoking, please.'

Dennis sat back in his seat and closed his eyes with a martyred sigh. 'British *fucking* Airways,' he muttered.

'*This is Captain Briggs again.*' The intercom crackled into life as if in reply. '*I apologize for the delay. Our colleagues in Customs wish to make a routine, on-board check-up and are apparently involved in a situation involving an earlier flight.*'

'Bureaucratic bastards,' said Dennis.

'*I'm told that they will be attending to us in a matter of moments.*'

An earlier flight. Kelly found herself wondering whether it was the one taken out of Tokyo by the Templemans and Cy McCray. Bill and Annie had sped off to the airport as soon as they had seen Shine On and Ibn Fayoud's new mare, who had arrived at the racecourse stables the previous night, safely on their way. Kelly had called Cy at seven thirty to check that he had survived his night in heaven. He had, at considerable cost to his wallet. According to Cy, the trip to Tokyo had turned out to be one of his more expensive jaunts; all he had gained was a Tokyo Jockey Club tie and an ornate courtesy suitcase they liked to give visiting jockeys. That, and a few tender memories, Kelly had said. Cy had laughed, wincing at the memory. Tender was right.

'Uh-oh, here come the marines.' The airline steward hurried by them with a tight little smile on his face. As soon as the Drugs Squad people were on board, he would be on his way. Kelly looked out of the window. Ground staff were pushing mobile steps towards the front of the aircraft as a van approached. The driver opened the back door and two men with golden retrievers jumped out. Dennis stared straight ahead like a man who had just been given a death sentence. 'Sniffers,' he whispered.

Four men, including the two with dogs, entered the passenger cabin with a grim, purposeful air. One of the men spoke to the passengers one by one as the sniffer dogs worked their way down each side of the aisle, tails wagging in anticipation.

Dennis gripped the side of his seat as a dog approached. It yelped as it reached his carrier bag.

'Excuse me, sir.' The Customs officer reached down for the bag. He spilt the contents on to a vacant seat. A number of magazines and various plastic sex aids fell out.

'Had a good holiday, did you, sir?'

The man smiled nastily at Dennis who shrugged and muttered, 'Free country, innit?'

The Customs officer turned the bag upside down and unzipped a small pocket underneath it. 'What's this?' he said, pulling out a bag of white powder.

'Oh, Dennis,' Kelly groaned as the Customs man recited his rights.

'Never seen it before in my life,' he said unconvincingly.

After they had completed their search, one of the men escorted Dennis down the steps. The other three stayed on board.

'We'd like to see the horses now, please, miss,' one of them said to Kelly.

She took them through to the back of the aircraft. Shine On and the mare seemed unworried by the delay.

'Quiet, are they?' one of the men asked her as he untied one of the hay nets and began methodically pulling out the hay.

Kelly nodded. 'They're all right.'

The dogs were excitedly wagging their tails, oblivious of the horses. The senior Customs man patted Shine On and felt his rug. He then prodded the new anti-cast roller. He looked significantly at Kelly before pulling a penknife from his pocket. Moving close to Shine On, he cut into the stitching. White powder spilled from it on to the sawdust. One of the sniffer dogs barked ecstatically.

Kelly stood and watched in shock. She cursed herself for being so stupid as she thought back to the old man in the storeroom. 'Of course,' she said. 'It had to be.'

'Yes.' The Customs officer stood up, licked a finger covered in powder and walked slowly towards her. 'It had to be, didn't it?' he said knowingly. 'So what's a nice girl like you doing smuggling high-grade smack into the country, eh?'

She should have been an actress. The show that Margaret Stanhope put on in the arrivals lounge was worthy of the West End. They were her friends, she told the young man with spots who was doing duty on the information desk. Flying in from Tokyo. Her lips quivered, her hand fluttered at her breast. If they didn't arrive she didn't know where she would stay tonight since she had just flown in herself from Scotland. The young man, who had heard about situations like this from the older hands, was soon caught up in the drama. It was more than his job was worth, he said, as he rang through to Customs.

Eventually the word came through. Four passengers from two different flights from Tokyo had been detained in Customs. He gave her the names. Before he could suggest that maybe, since his shift ended in half an hour, he could help her in some way, Margaret had turned on her heel and was on her way. Within moments, a couple of Drugs Squad officers hurried through to the information desk, but it was too late. All they found was a disappointed young man with spots.

Margaret gunned her Golf out of the short-term car park.

So Templeman was delayed in Customs. McCray was nicked. So was the stable lad. In fact, the only bit of good news was that the Kelly woman had been nabbed too.

Jack had done it, the righteous bastard. Pulled the plug on the whole operation. It was time for her to teach him a lesson.

And she knew just where to find him.

It was the longest three hours of Kelly's life. Three hours of questioning in an airless room lit by bright strip-lighting. Three hours in the company of two detectives who, like an alternative comedy double act, took turns at asking her the same questions in different ways. Who had she met in Tokyo? Where had the rugs come from? What was the name of her contact in England? Why did she do it? Money? Love? A ruthless boy friend? She could tell them. They were her friends. If she was a good girl, they'd see her all right when it came to court. Why not save everybody a load of bother and tell the truth? That's what the others were doing. Jim and John took turns to keep up the barrage of questions. Fat, threatening Jim who reeked of aftershave, and soft-voiced, wheedling John. Once, they both left her, doubtless in order to discuss their tactics. The woman police constable had been friendly, almost human, before she too started on the questions.

For a while, Kelly had tried to interest them in the events leading up to the trip to Tokyo, but the policemen made it clear that they were only interested in the truth and not some clever smokescreen. Tokyo was what they were interested in. She told them about the day of the race, the old man with the rugs, the call to Nick Morley.

'Is he here?' she asked. At first, she had assumed that Nick would see that she was released quickly. Out of an obscure sense of loyalty, she had sensed that it would be unwise to bandy his name about.

John glanced at Jim, who said, 'We're the ones asking the questions around here, Miss Connor.'

'But I was the one who tipped him off, for God's sake,' said Kelly with a flash of anger. 'He said he'd meet me at the airport.'

After another few minutes of questioning, both men left her alone once again with the woman police constable. Five minutes later, Nick was at the door.

'Sorry I've been so long,' he said. 'I was helping down the passage. They've charged McCray and Bill, I'm afraid.'

She'd hoped for an embrace or some sign of pleasure from him at seeing her. But he sounded as if he was forcing himself to be polite.

'It's crazy.' For the first time, Kelly was unable to keep a crack of emotion from entering her voice. The two policemen appeared in the doorway behind Nick. 'Tell them about Ibn Fayoud.'

'I have. He's seeing business contacts in Hong Kong. They'll be talking to him when he flies in.'

The smaller of the two policemen stepped forward and said with an ingratiating smile, 'We'll probably be needing you as a witness when your friends come to court. In the meantime, Miss Connor, you're free to go. Thank you for your co-operation.'

Nick smiled and took her bag as they emerged at last into the arrivals hall. He seemed more like his old self. 'Drink?'

'Yes, I'd love one, but not here. I never want to see an airport again in my life.'

'You'd better stay with me. You look too tired to get home and the horses have been collected.'

'What about Dennis?'

'He was released an hour ago. They tested the stuff they found in his bag and discovered it was talcum cut with bleach. Apparently some sex shop had sold it to him as an aphrodisiac. The airport police knew that no one that stupid could be a smuggler and they let him go.'

For the first time in several hours, Kelly laughed.

If anybody could take Jack Butler's mind off his troubles, it was Roseanne. Eighteen, a fresh-faced natural blonde with a perfect face and a flawless body, she had been hired as a teller in the Dagenham shop. One look at her – a look she had returned with interest – had been enough to convince Jack that she was too good to be stuck behind a counter; she had the potential to go places. Like to central office, where she worked in accounts, to clubs where she discovered that, after a few glasses of champagne, she could forget that Jack reminded her of her father, and to his London flat which she visited whenever Jack asked her. Which was quite often these days.

But this afternoon, not even Roseanne could shake him out of it. Her flawless body, now stretched carelessly across the bed, meant nothing to Jack; her perfect face, smiling sympathetically, was almost irritating. Relax, she said, we don't have to do anything. She giggled. 'Sex isn't compulsory, you know. We can just talk.'

'Talk?' Jack muttered. Christ, he felt old. 'Yeah, there's always that.' And what exactly, he reflected grimly, could they talk about? Smuggling maybe? Drugs? How, with one simple call, he had put an end to his father's grandiose plans? Or the future, now that Jack had pulled back at the moment of truth? Maybe they could talk about that.

'You. Me.' Roseanne laid her head on Jack's shoulder and ran her nails gently through the hairs on his chest. 'Us.'

'Mm?' Right now Jack could think only of himself and things he could never tell Roseanne, or any of the other Roseannes. Jack Butler. Formerly as in Jack the Lad. Now as in Jacked It In.

'Doesn't matter,' she was saying. 'This often happens.'

'To men of my age?' He put his hand on hers. He really didn't feel like being touched right now.

'No.' It was a squeak of protest. 'To anyone. You've got a lot on your mind, haven't you? The business. Your marriage.'

Jack glanced down at her. What the fuck had his marriage got to do with this? 'Oh yeah,' he said eventually, with a convincing sigh. 'It gets to you after a while.'

'Love you, Jack, you know that.'

'I love you too, doll.'

For a moment, they lay there on the bed. She was thinking of what her parents would say when she broke it to them that Jack Butler – the Jack Butler – was leaving his wife for her, and he was wondering whether they would keep Kelly Connor in custody. Then the doorbell rang.

Jack closed his eyes wearily. It couldn't be the police, or his father, or his wife, none of whom were aware of the existence of this flat. There was only one person who knew where he would be this afternoon.

The bell rang again, more insistently this time.

He extricated himself from Roseanne, slipped on a silk dressing gown and walked into the next room. 'Yeah,' he said into the intercom.

'Jack. Sorry. It's urgent. Must see you.' Margaret Stanhope's voice lost none of its sharpness over the intercom.

'I'll ring you later. I've got business right now.'

'She can wait.' It was odd how imperious Margaret had become of late. Sometimes she behaved as if he were the hired hand, not her. 'I need five minutes right now,' she said.

Sighing, Jack pressed a button to let her in.

'Sorry, darling,' he said to Roseanne. 'Duty calls.'

'Nanny Margaret?'

He smiled at the nickname Roseanne liked to use. 'Right first time. I'll get rid of her as quick as I can.' He closed the bedroom door.

Margaret was standing outside the front door to the flat when he opened it. She looked at him, standing there in his dressing gown and bare feet, with undisguised disapproval.

'I told you never to – '

'Shut it,' said Margaret, brushing by him and making straight for the cocktail bar in the corner. There was a time when she had fantasized about afternoons spent in this flat with Jack Butler, but not any more. She had grown up. As she poured herself a whisky on the rocks, she nodded in the direction of the bedroom. 'Who is it?'

'Mind your own fucking business.'

'It's your fucking business I'm more concerned about. Can she hear us?'

Jack walked over to a sound stack in the corner and pressed a button. The sound of Jason Donovan, Roseanne's favourite, filled the room. 'No,' he said.

Margaret sat on the sofa and took a swig of whisky. 'Presumably you know that we've been busted,' she said.

'What exactly are you talking about?' Suddenly Jack looked absurd in his silk dressing gown, old even.

'Someone blew the whistle on Tokyo. Templeman, McCray, one of the stable lads and your little friend have been arrested.'

Jack tried a smile. 'Well, none of them can point the finger at us. What about Ibn Fayoud?'

'He's in Hong Kong. They're looking for him.'

'They're not the only ones, I shouldn't wonder. There was half a million quid's worth in that shipment. His contacts are not going to be at all pleased.'

'His contacts? And what about us?'

'Oh, we're clean.' Jack opened a box of cigars on the cocktail bar and lit up. 'I've covered our tracks completely.'

'You know what I think, Jack?' Margaret leant back in the chair and crossed her legs. 'You set it up. You've been unhappy about the way Reg was expanding the business and this was your way of getting out. Jack Butler goes straight. You bottled it.' There was contempt in her voice. 'Because all Jack Butler really wants is to be a little bookmaker who appears on telly and gets to take young girls to bed when the fancy moves him.'

She had to go. Jack looked at the woman who had once made his job so easy and was now making it so impossible. Not just out of this flat, but out of his life.

'Thank you, Margaret,' he said quietly. 'Now would you be so kind as to get the fuck out of here?'

She stood up, ambled over to him and fingered the collar of his dressing gown thoughtfully.

'I've done a lot for you, Jack, over the past few years. I've sold my soul for you. I really don't know what I'd do if you went straight on me. I've outgrown the loyal secretary lark.'

'I've told you. I'll promote you.'

'But I don't want promotion, Jack.' Margaret leant against him. She could smell his body now. 'I don't want money. I want to run the business. Run it my way. Jack and Margaret. You front it with your famous personality and I deal with the mucky bits behind the scenes. It's a simple dream, I know, but I really do want it, Jack.'

'You are one mad bitch,' he said uneasily. 'And what about my father?'

'I can handle Reg,' she said dismissively.

'No.' Butler stepped back. 'I've had enough of the deception, the lies, the cheating.' He shrugged. 'I'm through with our dealing friends. You've got the choice. You can stick with me and go straight or go paddle your own canoe.'

'Deception? Lies? Cheating?' Margaret spat the words out. 'What the fuck d'you call this flat? You want me to tell Charmaine what you get up to?'

'She's too sensible to believe a vicious bitch like you.'

'Unless – ' Margaret walked quickly to the sofa, picked up her bag and reached inside it. 'Unless she saw these.' She threw some photographs on the sofa. 'What do you think?'

Jack looked down at the prints. He recognized them instantly.

'Some racing snaps,' Margaret said. 'A famous young jockey offering a spare ride. Kelly Connor, Jack Butler up.' She looked at one of the prints and smiled coldly. 'Or almost up anyway.'

She gathered up the photographs and put them into her bag which she snapped shut.

'Think about it,' she said, glancing at Jack who stood immobile in the middle of the room. 'Sorry to interrupt.'

Gently, sarcastically, she closed the door as she left.

The Foreign Office exists to avoid unpleasantness, to camouflage the unpleasantness of Us and to neutralize the unpleasantness of Them. As far as Mark Fowler
and his colleagues in the FO's Arab Section were concerned, the Emirate of Qatar
counted as Us, and the events set in motion by the indiscretion of one Ibn Fayoud
al Hassan were no more than a routine exercise in damage limitation.

Yet another indiscretion caused by one Ibn Fayoud. Fowler had been in the job
almost twenty years and was no stranger to the waywardness of certain Arab diplomatic staff – shop-lifting princesses, gun-running naval attachés, the occasional
attempt to smuggle schoolgirls out of the country in a diplomatic bag – they all
ended up on his desk, but Ibn Fayoud's behaviour had tested his patience before.
The man was becoming a monumental pain. It would be good to send him pack-
ing once and for all.

Gatwick and Heathrow were well trained these days. Before some noddy
appeared in front of a press conference to crow triumphantly about another battle
won in the war against the international drug barons, they would put a call through
to Fowler's office just to check that none of the said international drug barons were
in fact friends of HMG. Or friends of friends of HMG. Or even HMG itself.

Within an hour of discovering that certain high-class nags were carrying a few
kilo overweight in the form of heroin, Mark Fowler had been made aware that the
incident had a diplomatic dimension. The horses, and quite possibly their illegal
cargo, belonged to Ibn Fayoud. By some miracle of good fortune – knowing the
man, it would have nothing to do with judgement – Ibn Fayoud was wandering
about the Far East, which would make Fowler's task a good deal easier.

He called an old friend at the Consulate of Qatar to express his concern. The
man promised to talk to Sheikh al Hassan and ring Mark back.

With Ibn Fayoud temporarily in 'Pending', Fowler moved on to his next problem. A member of the Omani diplomatic staff had been caught in the bushes of St
James's Park with a Guardsman. Ye gods and little fishes. Fowler wearily dialled
another number. What a way to earn a living.

Sheikh al Hassan had been having a particularly difficult day when the news of
his son's latest misfortune reached him. If his son had been in his office with him,
the Sheikh might have been tempted to raise his voice, even to direct one of the
weighty ivory ornaments on his desk at the young fool's head. But, fortunately for
him, the boy was away on a business trip. Sheikh al Hassan pressed a button on
his desk and asked his secretary to summon Simon Brompton-Smiley to his office.
The days of Ibn Fayoud's business trips were drawing to a close.

Ten minutes later, the Sheikh's international racing manager was ushered in.

'I'll spare you the details, Simon.' Doubtless, Brompton-Smiley would find out
through his normal contacts the precise details of Ibn Fayoud's indiscretion. At
the moment, something approaching embarrassment constrained the Sheikh from
confiding in him. 'Suffice to say that my son has, over the past few ays, gone too
far.'

'Too far, sir?' Brompton-Smiley looked puzzled.

'Yes. Too far.' Sheikh al Hassan sat back in his chair, rolling his worry beads.

The occasional nonsense with drugs, or money, or women, he could understand, but smuggling – yes, that was certainly going too far. His oldest son had shamed the family name. Sheikh al Hassan felt the deep tiredness of a disappointed parent. He wanted to get rid of this silly, frowning Englishman as soon as possible. He needed to be alone.

'He will be returned home for an indefinite period. I shall take over his racing and breeding interests until the end of the season, at which point I shall sell his horses and move mine to France as we have discussed. This shall be announced in due course but you are to tell no one until I give the word. Merely inform the Jockey Club that the ownership of all my son's horses has been transferred to me.'

'Yes, sir.' Brompton-Smiley nodded thoughtfully. He looked forward to the moment when he could break the news to Nick Morley. 'Would you like the horses with Templeman to be moved to Gardem's yard.'

'No,' the Sheikh said absently. 'Let them stay there for the moment.'

Brompton-Smiley, aware that his audience with his employer was over, stood up. 'I'm very sorry, sir. If there's anything else I can do – '

'No, thank you, Simon,' said Sheikh al Hassan. 'That will be all.'

Alone again, the Sheikh put through a call to the Embassy.

It had all been quite civilized, Mark Fowler reflected when confirmation came through from the Consulate that Ibn Fayoud would be met at Heathrow the following day and put straight on a private jet bound for Doha. Naturally, the Drugs Squad boys would want their pound of flesh and, at some stage, would be allowed to refer to 'An unnamed diplomat who has since been expelled'. At some point, too, over the next few days, the Qatari Consul would be requested to visit the Foreign Office for a cup of tea and a chat which would later be described as a 'formal protest'. It would all take its course in the normal way of things. In the unlikely event of the press taking an interest, it was always sensible to show that the proprieties had been observed in these cases. It was something of an arse-covering exercise, of course. Mark Fowler smiled as he put his report on the Ibn Fayoud incident into the out tray. But then even plump, pinstriped Foreign Office arses needed to be covered sometimes.

Nick Morley believed in the curative powers of strong drink. He gave Kelly an exotic version of a brandy mix which almost lifted the top of her head off. It was just what she needed.

At first, when he had brought her back here from the airport, her anger at what had happened had spilt out in a torrent of words. Nick had put a call through to Gatwick airport and discovered that Bill and Cy McCray were to be detained overnight in the local police station, Bill because they'd found drugs hidden inside the travelling trunk, and McCray because the suitcase he had been given in Tokyo was sealed with yet more heroin.

Now, as the brandy did its work, Kelly needed to know more about what had happened.

'Bill's not involved in this,' she said quietly, cupping the glass in her hands. 'It's the last thing he'd do, however much he needed the money. He was the one who didn't want Ibn Fayoud entering his horses in different races around the world, or trading in foreign mares.'

Nick sat across the room in a deep leather chair, his legs crossed and his tie half undone.

'You and I know that,' he said. 'But try convincing the police. There's just no proof.'

'And how about Cy? It could destroy his career.'

'It might have been worse. What if you had been riding Shine On?'

Kelly shook her head. The brandy cocktail was reacting with her jet lag, making it difficult to think straight.

'If someone didn't want me riding in Tokyo and was even prepared to knock me out to prevent me getting to the airport, they must have known that something was likely to go wrong.'

'It could be. D'you have friends in the drug-dealing community?' Nick smiled questioningly.

'Jack Butler maybe.' Kelly still found it hard to associate the man she had met at York with drugs and violence, but that's how it looked. Perhaps that night was all a figment of her imagination. Nothing seemed certain any more.

'What about Ibn Fayoud himself?' Morley stood up and walked over to the telephone. 'He needed the money desperately enough.'

'No.' Kelly remembered the last time she had seen him, hunched in a back room of the Club Joey, helplessly indulging his favourite habits. A pathetic figure. 'I think he was being used too.'

Nick was dialling a number. 'Indian?' He smiled. 'You must be hungry. They deliver to the door.'

Kelly nodded gratefully. He had his life organized to perfection. Nick Morley, the perfect bachelor. Maybe the perfect husband? She had her doubts. He could be as caring as anyone she'd ever met, but his time in the army had left its mark, or perhaps it was his childhood. There'd been a brief moment at the airport when she'd detected a frightening coldness about him. Now, while they waited for the take-away to arrive, his mind seemed to be not on her but on other matters. Then suddenly he snapped his attention back to their conversation, and she saw it again, a determined, almost fanatical side to him as he went over the evidence with her again and again.

'We're as bad as each other,' she said at one point. 'I'm obsessed with my father's death. You're obsessed with cleaning up racing.' She rubbed her eyes. 'And they'll probably beat us both in the end.'

He looked at her sharply. 'What gives you that idea?'

'There are always more where the Butlers and Ibn Fayouds come from. More plausible villains. More weak-willed playboys. There's a waiting list to get into crime.'

'We can win the battle but they will win the war,' Nick Morley said bitterly, almost to himself. 'You know where I last heard that? Northern Ireland. In the SAS. Every time we dropped a Paddy, discovered an arms cache, took out an IRA hit team, there was some professional wetback who'd come out with it.'

'This isn't quite the same, is it?'

Nick smiled, but his eyes spoke of past horrors committed in the name of winning the battle, or the war, or just winning. 'For me it is,' he said quietly.

He stood up, then knelt before Kelly. He took her chin, lifting her face towards his, and looked into her eyes. The iciness was leaving him now and he sounded almost triumphant. 'Come to bed?'

Kelly shook her head. Somewhere in her body she could feel a guard going up against him. 'I'll stay here,' she said. 'Tonight I need to sleep alone.' She kissed him chastely on the cheek.

He stood up and looked down on her and, for a moment, she felt uneasy, like a spoil of war.

'Of course,' he said, and smiled.

It was twenty-four hours since the Tokyo operation had hit the rocks, twenty-four hours in which Margaret Stanhope had been busy regrouping, planning, making moves to sort out the mess that others, softer and less determined than her, had left behind them. A plume of smoke rose from the cigarette in her hand as she sat in her car, waiting on a side street in Newmarket. She narrowed her eyes. She hadn't had much sleep last night, but then she didn't have time for sleep right now. She was good in a crisis; she acted while others considered their position. By the time the rest of the world caught up with her, it was too late. Margaret Stanhope was in control.

'Come on, little girl.' Margaret inhaled deeply on her cigarette. 'I haven't got all day.' She smoothed the photograph that lay on her lap with a slow caress. There were other shots of Jack, but this was the one she kept with her at all times. She looked at his naked, muscular shoulders, his neat, almost girlish waist, his broad back. He wasn't as tough as he liked to make out. She knew that now, as surely as she knew that she had manoeuvred him into a position where he'd welcome the future that she offered, welcome it with open arms. Margaret clenched her teeth as her body trembled with a passing spasm of desire.

Ambition. Love. The need for security. It was all wrapped up in Jack Butler's perfect frame. It didn't matter that he had proved to be a touch soft at the edges. She liked sensitive men. And she was tough enough for both of them.

The lights in Kelly Connor's flat were still on. Margaret picked up the car phone. She'd call the girl, summon her to meet her destiny.

No. That would be a mistake. Get her on the wrong foot, take her by surprise, that was the way.

Margaret dialled another number. There was no reply from Jack's flat. She tried the number in his car.

'Shit,' she said, as it rang unanswered. She really wanted to talk to Jack right now.

When she rang his home, it was the squeaky voice of his wife that answered.

'Oh hi, Margaret, hold on a minute.' It was one of Charmaine's many affectations that she liked to give the illusion that every call to her had interrupted some astonishingly important task. Like leafing through a magazine. Or arranging an appointment with a hairdresser. Or heaving a large glass of sherry to her cute little lips. ''Fraid he's not here at present. Said he had to go on a trip.'

A trip? What the fuck?

'I'm surprised that you didn't know.' Charmaine gave a nervous laugh.

'Yes, of course. I knew that he had to go on a trip. I thought it was tomorrow. When is he due back? I don't have his diary with me.'

'That's just it.' Charmaine sounded puzzled. 'He said he didn't know. He said it was . . . open-ended.'

'Of course. It would be.'

'Is he all right? He sounded a bit out of sorts on the phone. Like he had something on his mind.'

'I'm sure he's fine, Charmaine. I'll just call our Bradford office. They'll know where he is.'

'Honestly, men. One moment they're . . .'

Margaret held the phone loosely in her hand. She had heard the Charmaine Butler theory of life, love and the universe before. That bastard. Where the hell had he gone? And which of his many bimbos did he have in tow?

'Better run now, Charmaine,' she said lightly, hanging up with a suitably girlish farewell.

Open-ended? She'd give him open-ended when she found him. As slippery as eels, those Butlers.

Glancing up at Kelly Connor's flat where the lights still shone brightly, Margaret reflected on her call to Reg last night.

The old man had been curiously cool when she had told him that Jack had blown the whistle on the Tokyo run. That's a pity, was all he said as if he'd known for ages. She'd added that Jack seemed to have gone cold on the whole idea of expansion. Must be mid-life crisis, he said, as if his son were indulging in some piddling eccentricity rather than putting all her plans – all Reg's plans – in jeopardy. Can you talk? she had asked. Not exactly, Reg muttered, but she hadn't believed him because, when Reg Butler had private business to discuss on the phone, he merely told his wife to fuck off to another room. He was no New Man, was Reg. Sunday, as usual? No, said Reg. That's not convenient. Leave this one with me and I'll get right back to you.

Leave it with him. He must be joking. Margaret hadn't got where she was today by trusting men like Reg Butler, or his shifty son, or anyone else for that matter.

She stubbed out a cigarette as the light in Kelly's window was switched off. Picking up her favourite, slightly dog-eared photograph of her naked employer, she took out of her bag an envelope with two other prints in it and put it on the dashboard.

The girl appeared in jeans and sweater at her front door. She looked good, Margaret thought as she approached; not as cute as the last time she had seen her but not bad considering she had clothes on.

'Kelly Connor?'

The girl turned from fumbling with the lock. 'Yes?' she said warily.

'Jill Turnbull, Reuters. I wonder if I could have a brief word with you.'

Kelly Connor looked pale and distracted. 'It's not a good moment,' she said crisply.

'I know it isn't.' Margaret smiled. 'But, believe me, it would be in your very best interests to give me just two minutes. We could talk in my car over there.'

Kelly looked uncertain.

'It's not about Gatwick,' Margaret added.

There was something about the way the woman threw 'Gatwick' into the conversation that alarmed Kelly. It was the first that she had heard about the press getting hold of the story. 'Two minutes,' she said and walked purposefully towards Margaret's Golf.

'Cigarette?' Margaret was keen not to hurry this. She looked at the Connor girl as she sat uneasily in the passenger seat of the car. Yes, she really was quite appealing; on this occasion, there had been nothing wrong with Jack's taste.

'Thanks, no. How can I help you?'

Margaret lit up, filling the car with smoke. She was going to enjoy this.

'My people have been sent some material about you, Miss Connor,' she said slowly, as if weighing up her words carefully. 'Rather sensitive material, as it happens. Drugs, betting – ' She paused for effect. '– sex. The feeling among my people is that it will make quite a story.'

Kelly looked across sharply. 'I can't think what you're talking about,' she said.

'No, I'm sure you can't. My people, most of whom are rather disgusting middle-aged men, seem a lot more interested in the more intimate side of the story than anything else. You see,' Margaret pursed her lips as if embarrassed by the task she had to perform, 'We know all about you and Jack Butler.'

'What?' Kelly gave a nervous laugh. 'I've only met the man once.'

'Well, once would certainly seem to be enough for you. Under the circumstances.'

The woman's confidence unnerved Kelly. 'What circumstances?'

Margaret reached for the envelope on the dashboard and, with a reluctant shrug, passed it across. Kelly opened it slowly, took one look at the top photograph and gave a little gasp of disbelief. She covered it with her hands and sat with her eyes closed for a moment.

'They're fakes,' she said eventually.

'My people say they're genuine. Girl jockey in sex romps with TV bookie. It won't look good, will it?'

'I was drugged.'

'Fortunately all is not lost. I have a friend who's marginally involved in this business. The details are unimportant, but it really would help this friend of mine if you spoke to the police.'

Kelly had opened her eyes, and stared straight ahead of her. 'Go on,' she whispered.

'I think I can persuade my people to destroy the negatives if you just explained to the law how Ibn Fayoud approached you and persuaded you to bring his horses back from Tokyo with their special little packages.' Margaret held up her hand as Kelly tried to interrupt. 'You didn't know that drugs or smuggling were involved, of course. But it was Ibn Fayoud who was behind it all. Ibn Fayoud and no one else.'

'You're not a journalist, are you?' A harshness had entered Kelly's voice. 'You work for them.'

'Who I am is not your problem.' Margaret lightly touched Kelly's hand which still covered the photographs. 'But these are.'

Kelly withdrew her hand sharply, and Margaret picked up the photographs. She looked, almost tenderly, at the top print, which had been smudged by Kelly's damp palm.

'Why can't you just leave me alone?' Kelly said.

'But I will. When you've spoken to the police. I'll call you later to check that everything's all right.'

Like a zombie, Kelly Connor opened the car door and stepped out. She felt sick.

The car started and Margaret gave a chummy wave before driving away at speed, leaving Kelly standing at the side of road, wondering whether her life could get any worse.

Jack Butler had never done this before. All his life, he had ducked and dived, but he had never turned his back on the other side, however tough things were, never turned tail. He looked across at Roseanne who was singing tunelessly to a tape on the car cassette. It was a big adventure to her. Jack was a wild, romantic hero who had swept her off her feet like some knight in shining armour. He clutched the driving wheel and stared at the motorway ahead of him. Why had he involved this little girl? What was he, afraid to face them alone? In need of blonde company, even at this desperate stage? He smiled palely as she turned and touched his thigh.

Some knight in fucking armour. Up to his neck in it, sweating with fear, out of control and driving, fuck knows where, just driving. Running.

Chapter
12

Over the next few days she was haunted by the pictures. Her mind continuously flashed up the images of Jack Butler's naked body leaning over her. She felt physically sick every time it happened.

The rest of the time she thought of her father. The time when he had been there, advising and encouraging her, seemed now to belong to a distant, innocent age when life was harsh but simple. Since his death, she had ridden winners – no one who saw her on Shine On at York or in subsequent races could doubt that she had the ability and strength to make it to the top – but now that golden future was under a dark cloud of uncertainty. Violence, blackmail and corruption seemed to be following her every footstep.

The worst of it was that Kelly knew she had brought it on herself. If she had listened to the advice of Annie and others, the nightmare of the past few days would never have happened, or at least it would have happened to someone else rather than to her and those who worked with her. Kelly thought of Bill and Cy, bystanders struck down by events that crashed forward heedlessly, like a freight train on which the brakes had failed.

Once the press had picked up the story of Shine On's eventful return from Tokyo, the careers of the two seemed doomed. Both men protested their innocence at a magistrates' court and were committed for trial in a month's time at the Old Bailey. In the meantime, they were released on bail and, it was announced by the Jockey Club, were 'entirely free to pursue their careers until charges against them have been proved'.

Fortunately for Bill the majority of his owners were unwavering in their belief in him. Apart from the change of ownership to Ibn Fayoud's horses, which wouldn't affect him until the following season, there were no dramatic changes in the yard. Annie became more involved in the horses' training than ever before, partly because Bill was too preoccupied to do the job properly and partly through a discreet, unpublicized agreement between them that, should he be found guilty at the Old Bailey, she would immediately apply for a trainer's licence and continue to run the yard. Fiercely loyal to their employer, the lads found no difficulty in taking their instructions from the guv'nor's wife; in fact, some of them claimed that the horses were going better under the changed regime.

It was tougher for Cy. A freelance jockey, however senior, depends on good will; there's no room for sentiment or loyalty in his life. Some trainers neglected to book him because, they said, he had too much on his mind to ride at his best. Others claimed that their owners were unhappy to be employing a man suspected of smuggling drugs. But most of them didn't bother with excuses. McCray was out. Next season maybe, if he was given a clean bill of health by the beak at the Old Bailey, it could be a different matter. Until then, it was like he had the plague.

Kelly took to calling him most evenings. At first, he would answer the telephone eagerly, managing to conceal his disappointment that the call was not from one of his trainers offering him a ride. In those early days, he was like a man caught up in a nightmare, convinced that one morning he would wake up and find that his life had returned to normal. But gradually, the hope in his voice faded. Frequently, Kelly noticed a slurring incoherence which suggested that Cy was taking something to help him through the bad times – Valium perhaps, or grass, or even good old-fashioned alcohol. Whatever the drug was, it was changing him. He became surly, cynical, defeatist.

Just ride the horses. That was what Frank Connor would have said. They may be cussed and unpredictable but, compared to life outside racing, they were simplicity itself. His advice would have meant nothing to Cy, who had become obsessed with the cruel hand fate had dealt him and whose rides were now restricted to the occasional no-hoper, but it kept Kelly going through the dark days.

She also thought about Nick. She hadn't seen him since the day he'd collected her from the airport. He'd phoned a couple of times asking her out to dinner but she'd put him off. She still felt slightly uneasy about him, though she knew that it was thanks to him that she had not been implicated in the Tokyo scandal. As a result, she continued to receive offers of spare rides.

There was a hard, driven quality to the way she rode these days; the conviction that, sooner rather than later, her world, like Cy's and Bill's, would come crashing about her ears lent a recklessness to her race riding. Nothing mattered any more, only winning, only proving that she could do it before it was all taken away from her.

She won several races and, as the flat season drew to a close, she finally became a fully-fledged jockey, losing her claim. But she realized that she too, was running on a drug.

The drug was anger. In the weighing room, in the paddock, at the start, even during a race, images would flash before her eyes. The body of her father, the smiling face of Jack Butler, the bloody, broken remains of Damien Gould, the hunched figure of Ibn Fayoud in the back room of the Club Joey, the cool fingers of the woman in the Golf touching the back of her hand, and the photograph. Always that photograph.

The woman had not waited long before calling.

'Did you tell them about Ibn Fayoud?'

'Yes.'

'Just as I told you? He was the only person involved, no one else?'

'That's right.'

'You wouldn't be lying to me. I can check, you know. If you're jerking us off, those pics go straight to the press.'

'I'm not. How do I know you've destroyed the negatives?'

'You're going to have to trust me, aren't you? Just like I've trusted you.'

'Right.'

'We're watching you. Remember that.'

'I will.'

Of course, Kelly had said nothing to the police, or even to Nick about Ibn Fayoud. It would take time for the woman, or her people, to discover that the blame had not been placed fully on his fragile shoulders. The stories in the press had revealed that the police had been given a mere thirty minutes with him before he was bundled on to the jet bound for Qatar. Little would emerge of the investigations for days, maybe weeks.

But they would discover in the end and Kelly's career would reach its inevitable shameful conclusion; there appeared to be nothing she could do about that. It was for the sake of her father's memory that she had become involved in all this and to play along with criminals, simply because she was being blackmailed about something she'd never done, would be a betrayal of everything he had believed in.

Ride the horses, he would have said. Forget the world and ride the horses. And that is what she did.

Some time later she saw Nick at Windsor but he too seemed changed, distracted. At first, Kelly put it down to his own Jockey Club investigations into the case but, when Sheikh al Hassan made his announcement, she realized that drug-running was the least of his problems.

At the end of the season, the Sheikh would be withdrawing from English racing and setting up his international headquarters in France. Just like that. The vast network of breeders, trainers, jockeys, lads who were affected by the decision of the industry's biggest owner were treated to no more than a courteous expression of regret.

No wonder she had caught a distant, haunted look in Nick's face. Although he never spoke to her of his finances, she knew, as everyone in racing knew, that his bloodstock business was inextricably involved with the dealings of Sheikh al Hassan. If the cream of his mares and stallions were to be transferred to Chantilly and the rest sold off, he could be facing financial ruin. And the Jockey Club was not likely to retain the services of a bankrupt as a steward, particularly on the security side.

Typically, it was Annie who kept a sense of proportion.

'We never expected to get Ibn Fayoud's horses in the first place,' she said to Bill and Kelly at breakfast on the morning the news broke. 'From the racing point of view, it was a bonus.'

'If it wasn't for Ibn Fayoud, we wouldn't have gone to Tokyo,' Bill muttered drily. 'Some bonus.'

'And Shine On would have been sold outside the yard.'

'What will happen to him?' Kelly asked. 'Have you heard what the Sheikh plans to do with him at the end of the season?'

'Brompton-Smiley has said that, since he's been invited to run in the Washington Laurel International, he should go. The Sheikh will decide after that.'

Kelly nodded. It was open knowledge in the Templeman yard that Shine On, who had recovered well from the Tokyo Cup, was likely to run in America. What was less clear was who would ride him. Cy was in no fit state to compete in one of the world's great races.

Now Annie looked at her husband across the table. He nodded, then went back to reading his newspaper.

'Kelly, we think you should ride him in America,' she said.

'What about Cy?' Kelly was surprised at her coolness at the news.

'It's not that the Sheikh's influenced by the court case.' Annie smiled. 'He's sensible enough to see that Bill and Cy are innocent victims. No, it's simply that he's your ride and you should never have been taken off him in the first place. You know as well as we do that if you'd ridden him in Tokyo he'd have won.'

Kelly remembered her reaction when the tables had been turned, when Cy was put up instead of her for the Tokyo race. He knew it; she knew it. That was racing.

'Great,' she said quietly. 'When is it? A fortnight's time?'

Annie nodded. 'Just over.'

'You'd better win it,' Bill murmured.

'I will.' If the horse runs, Kelly thought. If I'm still riding. If the photographs don't reach the press before then.

There were times when she managed to forget, sometimes for as long as a couple of hours, and that afternoon, riding Warwick, was one of them.

Kelly had only one ride and, on any other occasion, she would have treated a two-hundred-mile trip to ride a mediocre horse in a small, low-value handicap as a routine chore but, since Gatwick, nothing was routine any more. The horse she was down to ride was Boardwalk, the one-paced gelding on whom she had failed to win a seller last time out at Ascot.

Kelly remembered that evening vividly. It had been her first ride since Pendero at Ascot, since her father's death. Mrs Prentice, the owner, had been thrilled with second place, but everybody else, including Bill and Annie, knew that she should have won. Today she would.

There were only four horses running, the race having cut up badly with the hard ground, but on all known form Boardwalk might as well have stayed at home for all the chance he had.

Driving to the races with Billie and Annie, Kelly had mentioned that Boardwalk lost his races by pulling his jockey's arms out over the first five or six furlongs. Since none of the other runners were proven stayers and were likely to be more bothered by the rock-like ground than their horse, why not let him go on? There was just a chance that he could give them the slip. At worst, they would give Mrs Prentice a good run for her money. After some discussion, they agreed.

It worked, even better than Kelly had planned. As the field raced down the straight, the favourite Mighty Quinn was in a group of three horses, each of whose jockeys were biding their time, waiting for one of the other two to make its run. The fact that they were all looking at the bony hindquarters of Boardwalk as he rattled along happily in front of them seemed supremely irrelevant. He'd be stopping soon, right enough, then the race would start in earnest.

Boardwalk and Kelly Connor had other ideas. By the time they were halfway round the lefthand bend heading for home, the rest of the field woke up to the realization that the one horse they had discounted as a threat was galloping, ears pricked, as strongly as ever. Almost comically, the three jockeys galvanized their mounts into action and set off in pursuit.

Kelly knew that, when Boardwalk came off the bit, the others would be running on but she trusted in his gameness and her strength to get him to the line before they caught him. He faltered with two hundred yards to go and the most seasoned gambler would still have laid odds on any one of his three pursuers overhauling him.

As she heard the thunder of approaching hooves behind her, Kelly roared at Boardwalk, who was now rolling wearily like a ship in a gale. Using her hands and heels, she kept him together and all but lifted him over the line as Mighty Quinn surged up to him and past. Had the winning post been moved twenty yards back, there would have been hundreds of happy punters at Warwick. As it was, the result was greeted with a sullen silence, broken only by wild cheers from Mrs Prentice. Boardwalk had held on to win by a neck.

These days Kelly avoided the post-race celebrations but on this occasion it was a pleasure to take a glass of champagne with Mrs Prentice who, even after the last race was finished, was still reliving her horse's victory and planning an impressive campaign for him next season. There would be a time when Annie or Bill would have to break it to her the way Boardwalk ran, his races hardly gave ground for optimism that he would make the transformation to a jumper, but now was not it. Smiling, they allowed their owner her moment of triumph and unbounded optimism. Reality could wait.

It was as Mrs Prentice recounted the race yet again that Kelly noticed Harry Short standing at the bar alone. Although he looked as red-faced and belligerent as ever, he seemed to be staring in her direction, occasionally jerking his large head in an unsubtle gesture of invitation.

'I think Harry Short wants a word with you,' Annie said softly.

'I was trying to ignore him.' Kelly stood up. Harry was not a person it was easy to ignore for long. 'This won't take a minute,' she said.

'Brilliant ride, Kelly.' Harry shook her hand with a smile that somehow deteriorated into a leer.

'Thank you, Mr Short,' Kelly said coolly. It was odd how the fat trainer unnerved her, even in a public place.

'Drink?' He turned towards the barman.

'No thanks, I'm with an owner.'

Harry frowned and looked around him conspiratorially like a joke villain. 'Wanted to give you a tip, darling,' he said. 'About your spot of bother.'

'Bother?' Kelly tried a smile but it lacked conviction. 'I've just ridden a 12–1 winner.'

'You know what I mean.' Harry was looking at her beadily, his little eyes sparkling unpleasantly above his fat red cheeks. It occurred to Kelly that he might be drunk. 'I've heard,' he continued, 'That your friend Jack Butler is in deep shit. Someone's after him, someone very big.'

'I don't see what – '

'If you want to know who was behind the Tokyo job, you better find Jack. He knows. But they're looking for him too. The word is they're not very pleased with him.'

'And who are they?'

'Can't help you there, darling.' Harry drained his glass. 'All I know is that a lot of money has been laundered through his shops. Naughty money. Drug money. And now Jack's lost his nerve. They say that it was Jack who tipped off the police about Tokyo.'

'Jack Butler? Why?'

'He wants out. And they're not happy about that.'

Kelly glanced back to the Templeman party. Bill was listening to Mrs Prentice, occasionally nodding with a polite smile. Annie was looking quizzically in her direction.

'I happen to know that it wasn't Jack who told the police about the Tokyo drugs run,' she said eventually. 'I think your sources may be stringing you along.'

'My sources are reliable. Take it or leave it.' Harry made as if to leave.

'Why tell me?'

The trainer hesitated, as if surprised by the question. 'Felt bad about the Pendero business,' he muttered eventually. 'Wanted to square it. Because, once they get Butler, they'll be after you. They don't like people who know as much you do.'

Annie was approaching the bar. 'Hi, Harry,' she said cheerfull y. 'How you doing?'

'Good,' he said. 'Just sussing out whether this young jockey of yours was interested in riding for me now and then.' He winked at Kelly. 'Give us a bell once you've thought about it, eh darling?'

'Of course.'

The two women watched Harry push his way through the bar and out of the door. 'Thought you might need rescuing,' Annie smiled.

'Thanks,' said Kelly thoughtfully. 'What would you say if I told you that Harry had just done me a favour?'

Annie shrugged. 'I'd say you needed a double brandy to recover from the shock. Harry's favours tend to be to himself.'

Kelly started back to the table where Mrs Prentice was still talking about Boardwalk's victory.

'Maybe it's just a day for miracles,' she said.

That night Kelly put through a call to Ireland and asked Dermot Kinane about hot money being laundered through bookmakers.

'Sure, you're a little terrier, you are. Don't tell me you're still on the snoop.'

'I owe it to Dad.'

'Laundering, is it?' There was a pause and, in her mind's eye, Kelly could see the Irishman sucking at his pipe before he continued. 'Well, it happens a bit.'

'What sort of people do it?'

'People with more money than they can account for. Thieves, drug pushers, anyone doing cash jobs that they don't want to declare to the Inland Revenue. Bookmakers, off-course as well as on the spot. It's a simple exercise with the right number of people working it for you.'

'So, do bank robbers use it?'

There was a sigh, as if Dermot were reluctant to reveal more. 'That's right. Irish bank robbers.'

For all his apparent vagueness, Dermot Kinane used words carefully but sometimes they needed to be decoded. The reference to Irish bank robbers was no pub joke. Before she could question him further, Kinane said, 'Kelly, we shouldn't be talking like this. Remember where I'm calling from. The lines aren't secure.'

'This is important, Dermot.'

'Hold on.' For a few seconds there was the sound of rustling paper. 'Call Mr Colm Hogan on this number. He lives near Royston. He can tell you something – in fact, he'll tell you a lot if you a buy him a couple of drinks.'

Kelly took down the number and hung up. Irish bank robbers. We shouldn't be talking about this. It was unlike the old man to sound so rattled, so edgy. Lines weren't secure.

Then she understood.

Colm Hogan answered the phone with the quiet suspicion of a man used to receiving only bad news. Kelly mentioned Dermot Kinane's name and suggested they meet. He showed little enthusiasm. Meet for a drink. Hogan laughed humourlessly and agreed.

They met that evening in a pub outside Cambridge. Hogan had been keen to meet at his local but, knowing that there was a stable yard in Royston and that some of the lads drinking at the pub might recognize her, Kelly had insisted he meet her where neither of them would be disturbed.

'Kelly Connor?' The man who approached her in the King's Head, Melbourn, was not at all what she had expected. Tall, pale and wearing a dark suit that had seen better days, he might have been an accountant, or a tax inspector fallen on hard times. Only the bloodshot, watery eyes behind the thick-lensed glasses and the high colour in his cheeks gave him away. 'Colm Hogan,' he said.

Kelly smiled and shook his cold, bony hand. Almost before she offered, he asked for a large vodka and tonic.

'Dermot sent his best,' she said as they found a table, outside in a beer garden. Hogan smiled wearily as if Dermot could send his worst for all it mattered to him. He drained his glass in one.

'What's it about then?'

'Just a spot of general information Dermot said you might be able to give me.'

'Is that what he said?' Hogan's voice was thin, correct with a fake gentility to it.

Kelly produced a fifty pound note and put it on the table between them. 'Another drink, Colm?'

He looked at the money and for a moment Kelly thought that the direct approach had been a mistake. But then he reached out and put the note in the top pocket of his jacket.

'That would be very nice,' he said with an insincere smile. 'Another large vodka for me and go easy on the tonic.'

She stood up and walked to the bar. She hoped Dermot had been right about this man.

On his third drink Hogan began to open up. He had known Kinane and Kelly's father at a time when they were riding and he was working for the Irish Jockey Club. He had trained as a laboratory technician and had been hired to test horses for dope after they had run.

'Interesting.' Kelly had decided that the best way to get information from this man was to take it slowly. On the other hand, she couldn't afford to wait so long that, by the time he reached the part of his story which concerned her, he was disappearing under the table.

Hogan shook his head. 'Worst decision I ever made. Should have been a scientist. Messing around with horse piss. Fucking horses.' The expletive sounded odd coming from him.

'What went wrong?' Kelly nodded in the direction of Hogan's glass. 'That?'

'No. I'd have the odd gargle, but nothing much. Not then.' He looked at her, challenging her to disbelieve him. 'Not until the boys got to me.'

'The boys.'

There was a long silence as Hogan looked around the garden. ' "Colm," they said. "You wouldn't be in the way of doing us a wee favour, would you? Nothing much. Just now and then making sure that the sample for this or that race is, like, exchanged for another. We give you the clean sample on the day of the race. You lose the real one, all right? You're on your own when you make the test. What could be simpler?" And I thought about it. These weren't just gamblers we're talking about. They were the boys.' A wheedling, pleading note had entered Hogan's voice, as if, right now, he was back in Ireland, trying to convince himself that he had no alternative. 'They had this sweet, sweet system of exchanging stolen money for nice, legitimate notes from across the counter. Plus a bit of interest. But,' Hogan sighed tragically, 'now and then it went wrong. Even when the boys had set up the race so carefully, when they had called up the trainers of the other horses and told them straight that, if they valued their kneecaps, their horse wouldn't win tomorrow – even then, there were mistakes. Fucking horses.' He pushed his glass towards Kelly.

When she returned from the bar, the Irishman needed no encouragement to continue with his story.

'It was easy,' he said, adding with a drunken smile, 'A piece of piss, you could say. Went on for two years. A truly sweet operation. Then,' Hogan's face clouded over angrily, 'Then it got untidy. Somebody else started calling me. They knew everything. I thought I was finished. But all he wanted was to join in the game. Did the same thing. The gambles that man landed.'

'Did you have any idea who he was?'

Hogan ignored the interruption. 'But it was getting silly now, silly. I couldn't understand how the stewards didn't see what was going on. I'd be getting calls from the boys, calls from this man – no wonder it got to me. I was telling the boys I was off the case. Said I'd work for them on the mainland if needs be. They didn't care. One day they'll call me. I'll get – ' Hogan frowned with concentration ' – activated. I'm a sleeper, you know,' he added proudly.

'What about the other man? What did he say?'

'Never heard from him again. Must have heard a whisper that I was off. Came here then. Started a new life.' Hogan stood up, swaying slightly. 'Must go,' he said.

'Who was he, Hogan?'

'I told you, didn't I? Just some fucking Englishman.'

Kelly watched through the window as Hogan weaved his way towards the bus stop. It would take a lot to activate him, to rouse this sleeper, but then the boys in the IRA were not without their powers of persuasion. She finished her drink and sighed. Colm Hogan, yet another loser.

Margaret Stanhope sat at Jack Butler's desk in Jack Butler's office and thumbed through his little red book. Conquests, contacts, conmen – it was all here. He must have been in one hell of a hurry to leave without it.

He wasn't holed up with a distant cousin, or a friend of the family, Margaret was sure of that. And with that little girl from accounts in tow, he was hardly likely to be hiding behind the skirts of one of his many ex-girl friends. Which left villains. The old con's network. It was a tough man's world, the criminal community but Margaret Stanhope was at her best in a tough man's world.

She was going to have to make some calls. It was dodgy, of course, the chance of messy misunderstandings occurring when you were dealing with thugs and hit-men was high but Jack's behaviour left Margaret with no choice. It was no good his doing a runner just when she needed him most. She had to get her hands on him one way or another.

At first, as she parked the car, Kelly didn't see the girl. When she did, a blonde, waif-like figure standing in the shadows, her instinct was not to get involved. The girl looked like some sort of runaway, a schoolgirl perhaps, and Kelly had troubles enough without that.

But then the girl walked slowly towards her as she was locking the car. Kelly saw now that she was older than she had thought, but her hair was lank and dirty, and there was a bruise on the side of her face. She was fumbling in her bag for something, talking to herself.

'Can I help you?' Kelly said.

'Letter,' said the girl, at last producing a crumpled envelope out of the bag. She put the envelope on the bonnet of the car and started walking away, quickly, unsteadily on her high heels.

Kelly picked up the letter which bore her name and the word 'Private' on the front.

'Wait!' she called out. But the girl had turned the corner. Kelly ran after her, but as she rounded the street, the girl was getting into a car. The driver – he looked like a man – drove off before Kelly could even take the number.

She swore and walked slowly back to the car, opening the envelope as she went. Inside was a note from Jack Butler.

Chapter 13

Dear Kelly,

I'm sure that by now somebody will have shown you pictures from the night of the Flaxton ball. It is the worst thing I've ever done in my life and I'm ashamed of myself. If you haven't seen them, I'll explain when I see you. I had no alternative, believe me. You're the reason why I've gone straight and why I'm being hunted.

I need to see you urgently. Please drive up and see me at the Coast House, Holkham, Norfolk (top bell) as soon as you possibly can. I want to tell you something important before I leave. You're the only person I can turn to who will understand. Please trust me. Tell absolutely no one about this note.

Yours,

Jack (Butler)

Kelly sat at the kitchen table and stared at the note. Neatly written in a careful, looping hand on cheap, lined paper, it might have come from a child. Jack (Butler). No longer the kingpin, but a fugitive, turning to her for help. It seemed absurd.

She felt weary, used. It was in this kitchen, at this very table, that she had read the letter from her father, his last message to her. What would he have done now? Believe a man who was corrupt, a bent bookmaker at the centre of an international dope-dealing ring? Trust him just this once? The shadow of a bitter smile crossed Kelly's face. Where had trusting people landed her, or indeed Frank Connor? Trust was a one-way street leading to compromise, danger.

And yet, she couldn't help thinking that Jack Butler was not the type to send fake SOS notes. He was on the run, Harry Short had already told her. Maybe, if she could reach him, he would provide the last piece of the jigsaw, allowing her to return to racing having laid her father to rest at last. She would drive to Holkham the following day, a Sunday, but she wouldn't just go without telling anyone.

She tried to get in touch with Annie, but she and Bill had gone to London for the weekend. Cy wouldn't be any use. She dialled Nick's number and cursed silently as she heard his answering machine. He was away at a bloodstock sale and wouldn't be back until Monday evening. After a moment's pause she said, 'I've heard from Jack Butler. He's in a place called the Coast House at Holkham. I'm going to see him tomorrow. I think it's got something to do with Tokyo.'

After she had hung up, Kelly found herself reflecting on the strange life of Jack Butler. See him on the television or on the racecourse, even at a social function like the Flaxton dance, and you'd say that nothing could shake his confidence, his control over every aspect of his life. Yet now he seemed to be on the run.

Some fucking Englishman. She remembered Colm Hogan's words. Presumably Jack knew the IRA was laundering stolen money through his bookmaking system and played them at their own game. But how, why, did he become involved in the drugs trade? Kelly opened the fridge and poured herself an orange juice. She could see the temptation. Once there were large amounts of cash being lost over his counters, there was a certain logic in expanding his operation. But why did he need to? Was it Ibn Fayoud's influence? It seemed unlikely. Or maybe his father, Reg Butler. Nick had told her that he was an old monster; made Jack look like a babe in arms, he had said.

It was madness. She was a sane, rational person, and yet here she was looking for excuses for someone who had drugged and virtually raped her.

She turned off the lights in the kitchen and went to her bedroom, thinking about Nick Morley and how little she really knew about him – his past, or the way he made his living in bloodstock, what he really wanted, how he felt about her. Nick was one of those Englishmen who hoard the personal like a dangerous secret weapon that could fall into the hands of some unseen enemy. What would he do if she needed help?

She thought about his guardedness, the way he withdrew into himself. It was not so surprising – in one way or another he had been involved in undercover work throughout his professional life. Racing, the army and, before that, if he was to be believed, childhood in a family deeply imbued with the English passion for privacy. As she undressed, she caught a glimpse of herself in the mirror. Thank God she was born Irish. Her father, Dermot, even Colm Hogan were possessed of an openness an Englishman of Nick's background would find alien. She wondered if Nick ever got drunk, ever spilt out his heart to an old friend, ever lost control, just for a moment. Somehow it seemed unlikely.

She put on her dressing gown, switching on the radio beside her bed. Although she had become used to living alone since her father's death, she didn't like the late-night silence of the empty flat. Maybe, when this was over, she would share a flat with someone – she needed company.

As she cleaned her teeth, the full absurdity of this idea occurred to her. Any day now, she could awake to find her name and her photograph splashed across the pages of some tabloid rag. The jockey who slept with a bookmaker. Kelly winced comically at her reflection in the mirror. It would be an inglorious end to her career. Perhaps, once she had heard Jack's side of the story, she would have the courage to tell Nick, even Bill and Annie, of the scandal that was about to break.

She wished Nick were here. They could talk, help each other. Although he was cagey about his army days, he would surely be able to shed some light on Hogan's story about the gambling activities of 'The boys'. Part of her longed to be able to pass over the responsibility of her knowledge to someone else but she knew that, until she talked to Jack, it would have to remain hers alone.

She turned off the radio and the bedside light, then slipped into her single bed. Staring into the darkness, she found herself thinking of Nick again. Perhaps it was companionship that she was missing, the sharing of a burden. Maybe, after tomorrow, it would be possible.

In the public bar of the Half Moon pub, Dagenham, a man sat nursing a pint of bitter. The look on his broad, ill-shaven face did not encourage small talk. At first glance, you might think he was a fat man caught up in some sort of daydream but look again and you'd see that the fat was muscle; you might even guess that nothing as innocent as a daydream would pass through the arid wasteland behind that low, furrowed brow.

Scag wasn't dreaming. He was remembering the job he had just done. What he'd be paid for in this very bar later tonight. Though, personally, he'd have been happy to do it for free. Because as jobs go, it was tasty – very, very tasty.

He shifted on his chair and belched happily. He was seeing something in his mind's eye – something that was better than the hottest, nastiest video. Because it had really happened to him that very afternoon.

The thing was, you didn't very often get the good stuff from Maggie. It was usually messy, cash-collection jobs. Flash gits who thought they could try it on with Jack Butler. Maybe Scag was going soft but brutalizing the older generation wasn't as much fun as it used to be. Once you'd seen one old geezer spitting his teeth out in a pool of blood on the floor, you'd seen them all.

But this was it. The good stuff. This made all the other crap he'd done for Maggie worthwhile. When he'd seen her, his girl, his blind date, walking down the street in that little dress, her face all puckered and worried, his heart just went boom-bloody-boom-bloody-boom. Was she a doll or what?

He followed her home, waited for a bit, then called from a phone box. Got a message from Jack, he said. Meet you at the pub. And she was out of the door, tip-tapping down the road, without so much as a second thought for her own safety. These young girls, no wonder they were getting into trouble all the time.

He wasn't rough. In fact, on the Scag scale of bad behaviour, what he did with Roseanne barely registered. He did slap her once, just after he had put her in the car but, after that, she was good as gold. Told him where Jack was when he'd told her to go home. Showed him the letter that he had sent to the Connor girl. And because she had been very good, he even drove her up to Newmarket to deliver the letter.

On the way, he'd tried to talk to her, but Roseanne just sat in the passenger seat and looked out of the window like it was the end of the world or something. Which was funny, because the way Scag had heard it was that they liked all that, girls. Bit of this, bit of that, bit of conversation, chatting up. But this Roseanne, she just would not be chatted up, moody cow.

Tell the truth, after they'd been to Newmarket, Scag had been well tempted to take her back to his gaff, maybe get a few mates round. But there was something about her little face, all smudged and defiant, that got to him. Basically she didn't look like a fun way of spending the evening. In fact, she might even have given him a spot of grief with the filth.

So he'd given her a friendly squeeze and pushed her out of the car round the corner from her house. She even sort of smiled at him and said thanks, like she knew that he was doing something rather beautiful, by his standards. It was one of the nicest dates Scag had ever had. And he was getting paid for it.

He pushed his way to the bar and ordered another drink. He had time to get another down him before Maggie's bagman arrived. It had been a very good day.

An autumn mist hung low over Newmarket as Kelly set off early that Sunday morning for the Norfolk coast. She had been there a couple of times with her father and associated the wide, wind-swept beaches, the acres of undulating dunes, with a peculiarly English form of holiday. The sea would be grey and distant, there would be the occasional families struggling with a picnic behind brightly-coloured canvas windbreaks. Even with the sun in the sky, it would never be quite warm enough. Beautiful but bracing, this stretch of coastland was ideal for the English at play. Of course, there would be fewer people than ever now that the summer holidays had ended.

The journey took longer than she had anticipated and, by the time she saw the North Sea, the sun was high in the sky and Kelly was hungry. Jack could wait. She went to a pub, ordered crab sandwiches and thought of her father. He had loved it here, saying it reminded him of County Kerry. Not for the first time, she wished Nick was with her. He would appreciate the wild beauty of the place, the quiet of a coastal town left at last to locals.

The barman told her that Coast House was a mile from the village down a long drive leading to the beach.

'Popular with folk that like to be left alone,' he said, his grin revealing an uneven set of yellowing teeth. 'Honeymooners and the like. Park at the end of the drive and walk another half-mile and you'll see it.'

Sensing the man's curiosity as to why a young woman on her own would be looking for such an isolated guesthouse, Kelly thanked him and returned to her car.

The barman had been right. The Coast House was an ideal hideaway. The only passers-by would be the few hardy souls who were visiting the distant beach. There were two other cars parked at the end of the drive, and neither of them looked like Jack Butler's. She walked down the narrow sand track and, after a few minutes, came to a bleak Victorian building set back among the pine trees. An ancient sign announced 'The Coast House, Bed and Breakfast, VACANCIES'. It had almost been obscured by windswept sand. There was no sign of life.

She walked to the front door and rang the top bell once, then, after a minute or so, again, more persistently this time. Eventually a middle-aged woman in an apron appeared from the back of the house. Kelly told her that she was looking for Mr Butler.

The woman looked puzzled. 'No Butler here,' she said. 'No one staying at all except Mr Reginald.'

Kelly asked if he was staying on the top floor.

'Maybe.' The woman approached Kelly, her hands sunk deep in the pockets of her corduroy trousers. 'I thought you wanted Mr Butler. Mr Reginald said he wasn't at home to visitors.'

'I'm not just a visitor. I'm a friend. He's expecting me.'

The woman shrugged. She knew about friends. A lot of friends stayed at the guesthouse during the season, ordering up breakfast in bed, messing up the rooms, whispering in the television room. It was good money, double rooms going for a lot more than singles, but she didn't like it, all this friendship that seemed to be going around these days.

'He's out,' she said eventually. 'Went for one of his walks this morning. Not back yet.' She pointed in the direction of the sea. 'You'll find him down there.'

Kelly thanked her.

'Seems he's got lots of friends all of a sudden,' the woman called after her. 'Doesn't see a soul all week and then it's two people in a day.'

Kelly turned. 'Two?'

'Met up with some feller down by the beach.' She looked sheepish. 'Saw them through the window a couple of hours ago.'

Although it was barely three o'clock, some of the weekend visitors were making their way back up the path from the sea, having stayed long enough with the wind and the waves to justify a cream tea beside a fire. Some of them looked curiously at Kelly, a woman walking alone towards a beach that was virtually deserted.

After half a mile the path divided up. The right-hand fork led to an expanse of beach where one or two families could be seen attempting to play beach football or to read newspapers in the wind. Kelly hesitated and took the left-hand path through steppe sand-dunes towards another part of the beach.

At first when she heard it, she mistook the scream for the cry of a gull above the wind, but then she saw two people running with unusual urgency towards a distant dune. She left the path, finding higher ground from which she could see a family group gathered round something on the ground. Although they must have been more than two hundred yards from her, Kelly sensed an agitation among them. This was no holiday adventure.

She started running.

As she approached, a boy in his early teens ran past her, panting, his eyes wet with tears that had not been caused by the wind. She could now see that three other members of the family were standing by the body of a man who lay, face downwards, at the foot of a sand-dune. The mother was leading her daughter away. The father glanced at Kelly as she ran up.

'My son just found him,' the man said helplessly. 'I sent him to fetch the police.'

'Come away from him, Peter.' The well-bred tones of the man's wife cracked with panic. 'There's nothing you can do.'

There wasn't. The way the body was lying suggested that the man had been kneeling in the sand and had pitched forward when he had been shot. The sand around the head was darkened by congealed blood. A bullet hole the size of a small coin could be seen at the back of the neck.

Kelly crouched beside the body. Half-concealed by the sand, Jack Butler's face looked at peace, as if the manner of his death contained nothing that had surprised or even frightened him.

'He's dead.' The man was now beside his wife and had awkwardly put his arm round his ashen-faced daughter. 'I don't think you should touch him.'

Kelly reached out to touch Butler's pale cheek. It was cold.

'Shot,' he muttered. The man had a gift for stating the obvious.

Round the bullet hole, the skin was dark, burnt. Kelly stood up slowly.

'Close range,' she said. 'If you hadn't found him, he would have been swept out to sea with the tide.'

'Nothing we can do.'

'No,' said Kelly. 'Nothing anyone can do.' She took one last look at Jack Butler, lying tidily in the sand with a tidy hole through his neck. He had died more neatly than he had ever lived. 'I'll make sure the police have got the message.' She set off through the pine trees. With luck she'd be able to reach her car before the police arrived.

'Right,' she heard the father saying with a final, despairing attempt at authority. 'We'll just stay here then.'

Sitting in her car, eyes closed as if to shut out thoughts of what she had seen, Kelly realized that it was pointless to run. She had been seen near Jack's body. It would take little – a photograph of her in the papers, a chance remark from Nick – to establish that she had been in Holkham on the day that Jack died. Running would only suggest guilt.

The body had been cold. If it was established that the murder had taken place during the late morning, Kelly's fears that she might be implicated in some way could be dispelled. She had been in the pub in Holkham. The barman with the bad teeth would remember her. She rubbed her eyes wearily. It had been lucky for her – and perhaps unlucky for Jack – that she hadn't driven straight to the Coast House.

She reached in her pocket for the note Jack had sent to her. *I want to tell you something important before I leave.*

Something important. Once, she had been certain that Jack held the answer to the most important question in her life, who had killed her father, but now it seemed that he too was a bit part player in the drama. He had used Ibn Fayoud as useful cover for his drug-running operation. He could even have been involved in the death of her father, of Gould, of Broom-Parker, but there was someone else giving him orders, someone higher up the chain of command.

Why was he running? Why did he have to die? Kelly remembered something Harry Short had told her; it was Jack who had blown the whistle on the Tokyo operation. She had dismissed the idea, knowing that Nick had warned the police, but maybe there had been two tip-offs. Perhaps, for some reason – lack of nerves, whatever – Jack was trying to extricate himself from an operation that had grown too big, too dangerous. It would explain why he had tried to stop her going to Tokyo, if it was him. Kelly was now certain it was.

So the person, or the organization, behind the drugs operation had decided that he was a liability. They had somehow tracked him down and murdered him. Except it wasn't just a murder – Kelly remembered the dark skin round the bullet hole in Jack's head – it was more like an execution. Her stomach knotted at the thought that she knew too much as well. Was this how drug barons punished offenders? It somehow seemed too military. Or paramilitary. The boys.

Three police cars approached at speed up the coastal drive. They pulled to a halt yards from where she sat and six policemen, two in plain clothes, emerged, slamming the doors of their cars. They seemed relaxed, as if they knew that death was no emergency, a corpse could wait.

Kelly got out and walked quickly to where they stood. 'You'll find him straight up the path, three-quarters of a mile beyond the house.'

'Was it you who found the body, miss?' one of the men in plain clothes asked.

'No,' said Kelly. 'But I know who it is.'

She rang Annie that night, as soon as she had returned to Newmarket and poured herself a brandy to steady her nerves. The police constable who had taken her statement had been irritatingly slow and sympathetic, as if obeying some procedural handbook concerning female witnesses of an ongoing murder situation.

She had told him everything directly relevant to the case. How she knew Jack Butler, his connection with Ibn Fayoud and the Tokyo run, the note she had received from him. Occasionally, as she dictated her statement, the constable would break off to greet colleagues – a deputation from forensic, an inspector from Norwich – before returning with a tolerant smile to Kelly and her story. Used to being given the dull, peripheral work, he seemed unable or unwilling to accept the significance of what she was telling him. Only when she haltingly told him about the photographs and how the woman calling herself Jill Turnbull had tried to blackmail her did the man raise his eyebrows in surprise. Sex, drugs, blackmail – this one had everything.

If, somewhere deep in his brain, the police constable had grasped that the woman from whom he was taking a statement had a motive for wanting to see Jack Butler dead, he showed no sign of it. His brief was to take a statement, not to rush about reaching conclusions.

No doubt the powers that be would want to talk to her further but, once she had completed and signed her statement, he let her go with a friendly, encouraging wink. By this time Kelly was seething. The constable was the wettest bastard she'd ever come across and she hoped to God the rest of the Norfolk Police weren't like him. If you phoned him in an emergency, you'd be dead before he realized anyone was calling.

Back in Newmarket, it was Annie, to her relief, who answered the telephone. As coolly as she was able, Kelly recounted the events in Norfolk, including details of the photographs.

Annie's reaction was to let forth a torrent of abuse about Jack. 'The creep got what he deserved,' she concluded. 'If I'd been here,' she went on, 'I would have come with you.'

'I left a message with Nick but he was out too.'

'Yes, he would be. There's a drinks party being held by Simon Brompton-Smiley at the Al Hassan stud tonight. He's meant to be explaining the implications of the Sheikh pulling out of English racing. Sounds like an exercise in window-dressing to me.' She laughed lightly. 'Bill volunteered to go.'

'Maybe I'll catch him there.'

'Except they won't let you in. This is an Arab function, remember. There will be tight security.'

Kelly thought for a moment. 'I suppose I'll just have to tell them I'm you.'

There was a pause from the other end of the telephone. 'You can tell them that if you like.'

'But you'd prefer me not to go.'

'Kelly, you're in enough trouble as it is at the moment. Why don't you just leave it all alone.'

'That's what I want to do,' Kelly said quietly. 'I think it's going to come out one way or another sooner rather than later. I want to hand my information over to someone with the power to do something about it.'

'Like Nick Morley.'

'Right. He knows the background, he's got the authority – '

'And you're in love with him.'

'No.' Kelly replied. 'I thought I may have been once, but not any more. No. We get on fine, but that's all.'

Annie sighed. 'We'll never win that bloody race in America.'

For a moment, after she had hung up, Kelly considered whether Annie was right. The Washington International could make her career. Although, on form, Shine On looked outclassed by an international field that included Badinage, the winner of that year's Arc de Triomphe, and Angel Dust, an American four-year-old that had been unbeaten in top-class company since he won the Laurel in the previous season, Kelly fancied his chances of running into a place. He had worked well since his return from Tokyo and, while other horses were losing their form after a long season, he showed no signs of going over the top. If he travelled well, if he got a good draw, if his jockey had her mind on the job, he could surprise them all. If.

She stood up and looked at her watch. It was almost seven thirty. She could get to the Al Hassan stud within the hour, speak to Nick and still get home early. In the morning, she was to ride Shine On for his last piece of work before he flew to America. This way she could wipe the slate clean, let Nick worry about the implications of Jack Butler's murder. It was time for her to be a jockey again.

It was eight fifteen when Kelly parked her mud-spattered Saab between a Porsche and a Mercedes outside the Fairfield Stud. She glanced at herself in the rearview mirror, and saw the face of a woman about to crash a party of Britain's racing elite, track down Britain's brightest Jockey Club administrator and tell him that Britain's best-known bookmaker had just been executed, possibly by Britain's most notorious terrorist group. And she hadn't even bothered to have a bath. Murder was a great motivator.

'Mrs Templeman,' she told the butler who opened the front door. 'I believe my husband's already here.'

The man directed her to a large room from where the hum of polite conversation could be heard. As she made her way across the panelled hall, she noticed him discreetly checking her name on a guest list on a table behind the front door.

For a moment, as she stood in the doorway of Fairfield Hall's reception room, Kelly thought her nerve might fail her. A glance around the room revealed several well-fed faces rarely seen outside the inner sanctums of the Jockey Club establishment; not only the racing managers of the rich and landed, the rich and landed themselves were here in force. In a corner, she could see her old friend

Colonel Beamish giving Ian Gardem the benefit of his opinions, while on the far side Bill, looking as bored as ever, was in a group which included General Winstanley and the steward Lord Chester. Kelly took a bucks fizz offered by a waitress and turned away – she had to reach Nick before Bill spotted her and asked embarrassing questions.

'Kelly Connor.' The booming voice of Charles Caldecott made her wince. She might as well have got the doorman formally to announce her.

She managed a smile. 'Hello, Charles.'

Caldecott came to stand before her, beaming aimiably. 'It's the mystery guest. Always turning up when least expected. What on earth are you doing here?'

'Feminine wiles.' Kelly sipped her drink. 'That, and the fact that I'm riding the Sheikh's horse in America on Saturday.'

Caldecott made a weak, whoops-silly-me face. 'Damn shame about the Sheikh pulling out like that,' he said, changing the subject quickly. 'A few people in this room will be sad to see him go, I'll tell you that.'

'Yes.' Kelly could see Nick across the room, deep in conversation with a man she recognized as Simon Brompton-Smiley. 'He paid quite a few salaries, one way or another.'

'Salaries? It's the unofficial trade that will be hit hardest, if you know what I mean.'

Nick had looked up and, Kelly sensed in an instant, had seen her. If she could just keep Caldecott talking, Nick would probably make his way unobtrusively to her. Once she had spoken to him, she would be out of here and on her way home before Brompton-Smiley became aware that he had an uninvited guest.

'Mmm?' She smiled warmly at Caldecott. 'I'm not sure I do know what you mean. What unofficial trade?'

'Come on, Kelly.' Charles Caldecott dropped his voice and spoke through his teeth like a bad comedian. 'When your employer has got so much money that your annual salary is what he'd pay one of his regular tarts in London or Paris, you have to look for the perks, the odd under-the-counter arrangement.'

In spite of herself, Kelly was intrigued by what Caldecott was saying. He seemed slightly drunk and unguarded, like a man talking about his wife now that he knew the marriage was over. The Sheikh was going, so a few spilt secrets would hurt no one.

'You mean tax fiddles?'

Caldecott frowned, as if his listener was being extraordinarily slow. 'No need for that.' He dropped his voice to a murmur. 'You're in Kentucky for the sales, all right? You're representing our Arab friend who's interested in a yearling by Northern Dancer. It's going to go for two million dollars. What's to stop you tipping the seller the wink that the Sheikh's prepared to go to two and a half million and splitting the extra after the sale. Suits him, suits you and the Sheikh's not going to worry about the odd couple of hundred thousand, is he?'

'That really happens?' Kelly noticed that Nick was no longer talking to Brompton-Smiley and was casually making his way across the room in their direction.

'Every time a horse is bought or sold, the agents rip these Arabs off a treat.'

Caldecott smiled as Nick approached. 'Talk of the devil.'

Kelly darted a surprised look in Caldecott's direction. 'Hi, Nick,' she smiled.
It was almost as if he had expected her. 'Delighted you could make it,' he said,
watching her warily as if warning her not to speak out of turn.

For a moment the three of them stood silently. 'Charles,' Kelly said finally. 'I
just need a quiet word with Nick for a moment. You wouldn't excuse us, would
you?'

'Of course.' Caldecott grinned knowingly. 'I'll leave you two to it.'

Nick looked at Kelly. 'What the hell are you playing at?'

Kelly had to hand it to him, knew how to keep up appearances. A stranger looking at them from a few yards away would have judged his manner to be that of
just another guest. Politely interested in the conversation, even slightly bored.

'I'm not playing at anything, Nick, if you just listened.'

He smiled and nodded. 'I can't listen here. Ring me tomorrow.'

'It can't wait.'

'Jesus.' He sipped at his drink casually. 'First I get a message on my machine
saying you're going after that bloody bookmaker, then you appear without warning or invitation at an extremely important drinks party. Have you gone quite mad?'

'Jack's dead. He's been shot.'

Nick raised his eyebrows and gave a convincing little laugh. She might have
been telling him a joke for all the emotion he showed. 'Did you tell the police?'

'They know. Listen, Nick, I know now's not the time but I must ask you this.
The gun to the back of the neck – it's an IRA execution technique, isn't it?'

A waitress appeared at Nick's elbow carrying a tray with food. 'Something to
eat, Kelly?' he said. She shook her head. Presumably Nick's intelligence training
helped him to behave like this but she found it unnerving. 'It's hardly the most
unusual way of killing someone, if that's what you mean. Could be anyone.'

'I think the people who killed him were the ones behind the drug run and probably the death of my father.' Kelly added more urgently, 'For Christ's sake, stop
smiling like that. Bill and Cy McCray are going to get to slung into prison unless
something happens.'

Nick turned slightly to acknowledge the presence of a plump middle-aged
woman who had caught his eye. 'Triona,' he said warmly. 'Have you met Kelly
Connor? The jockey?'

The woman gave a little squeal of pleasure. 'But I'm one of your greatest fans.
You ride for Bill, don't you?'

'Yes,' said Kelly. Nick was backing away.

'Keep me posted about that,' he told her. 'Don't do anything until I ring tomorrow.'

The woman was talking about Boardwalk's win last time out when Kelly interrupted. 'Sorry,' she said. 'Would you excuse me? I'm not feeling well. Got to go.'

She pushed her way towards the door, walked quickly across the hall, nodding
to the butler who said, 'Goodnight, Mrs Templeman.'

In fact, it was true. She was feeling ill. The contrast between the wild seascape
of Norfolk and the comfortable interior of Fairfield Stud, between the desolate
sighing of the wind and the sharp chatter of well-bred conversation, between the

lifeless corpse of Jack Butler and the coldly smiling face of Nick Morley had suddenly made her feel faint. And now she couldn't remember exactly where she'd left her car.

Breathing deeply, she leant against Nick's Aston Martin parked in the front row and squeezed her eyes shut. It had been a mistake to drink a strong brandy cocktail before she came here. In fact, it had probably been a mistake to come at all. She had merely antagonized the one man who could help her.

'Stupid, stupid,' she said, straightening slowly. It was getting dark now. She wiped her hands and made her way slowly towards her own car which she had spotted to her left.

Then she stopped. Something was wrong. She went back to the Aston Martin and ran a hand along the side of the bonnet. On the tips of her fingers were a few grains of sand.

'You're chasing the wrong fox, darlin'.' Dermot Kinane's voice was that of a man who had just returned from an evening's hard drinking at the pub and was unprepared for late-night calls about murdered bookmakers and suspect stewards. 'Nick Morley is not your man, I'm sure of it.'

'But the sand, Dermot.' Kelly remembered the wind and the way the sign outside the Coast House had been partially obscured by blown sand.

'All-weather gallops. Paddocks. There's no shortage of sand around Newmarket.'

Kelly wasn't convinced.

'I spoke to some people,' Dermot went on quietly. 'The Englishman who muscled in on Colm Hogan's set-up can't have been Jack Butler. He lived in the north – somewhere in Fermanagh, they say.'

'So there's no connection between – ' Kelly felt uneasy with the chummy euphemism used by Hogan ' – the boys and Jack Butler's little operation with Ibn Fayoud.'

'I didn't say that.'

'But – '

'Your man moved to the mainland but the word is that he still has Irish connections which are not strictly to do with racing.'

'You mean that the drugs operation had terrorist money behind it?'

'It's not just drugs. It's arms. I don't know how but they used to get hardware on to the mainland, using the trade in racehorses.'

'My God. So it was an execution. That was why Jack lost his nerve. He was playing out of his depth.'

'Kelly, listen.' Dermot sounded alert now, as if their conversation had cleared his mind. 'Nothing can stop these people. You're not dealing with some two-bit hoodlum with a grudge. These are Irishmen with a cause, working with Arabs. There's American business interests involved. For Christ's sake, you've found out enough about your dad's death to leave it there. Go to Washington and ride your race. Or you'll end up like Jack Butler.'

There was something in Dermot's tone which suggested that he knew more than he was letting on. Like many of his countrymen, he was torn between a belief in a united Ireland and a hatred of the viciousness and violence used to achieve it. Kelly knew that his contacts were a reliable source of information, that he wouldn't tell her so much over an open phone if he didn't know that the danger to her was real.

'You know who it is, don't you?' she said eventually. 'The Englishman.'

'I can hazard a guess. There was a man who lived in Fermanagh, a permit-holder who used to ride down in the south now and then. Suddenly, from being something of a loser, he starts doing very nicely. He goes back to England, gets on in the racing world. And now he's right at the centre of the Arab network. My hunch is that he's a puppet for the boys and they're working him, with or without his employer's blessing.'

'His employer?'

'Sheikh al Hassan.' Kinane paused. 'The man's name is Simon Brompton-Smiley.'

It was never beautiful, but it had never been this ugly. Snarling. Bitter. Nasty. And all with their clothes on. It was a shame it had to end this way.

Margaret Stanhope stood by the window of Room 501 in the Sheraton Park Hotel and stared down at the street below. She hadn't cried since she was a little girl until last night. Then she had cried a lifetime of tears for her one true love who had died, for the months and years of planning that had come to nothing, for the pain and disappointment of a wasted life.

It was her life she was thinking about. Trust that bastard Jack to get himself topped just when he was about to realize how much he needed her, just when it was all going to work out between them.

The flesh of Jack's flesh, Reg Butler, sat on the bed, thinking about his son. He looked old now – the idea of his even having a mistress seemed like a joke in poor taste. If it were not for the glitter of anger that shone in his eyes he might have been a pensioner reminiscing about the good old days.

Reg was bad at sorrow. When he was a young man, he used to be well known for striking out when he was down. It didn't matter who precisely he hit, it was just his way of expressing unhappiness. He liked to share grief, to pass it on to the next man.

Or woman. He had never hated anyone as much as he hated Margaret Stanhope right at this moment. Twenty-four hours ago, she had told him she had tracked Jack down. She had sent someone good, someone reliable to bring him home. Now the messenger had disappeared. Maybe some bastard had nobbled him, turned the messenger into a murderer. Maybe he'd got there too late, found the place stiff with filth, scarpered. It all boiled down to the same thing. His only son was gone. This bitch had screwed up.

'I need a name,' she said, like a sleep-talker.

'Fuck off.' Reg's voice was a cracked whisper. 'You're getting nothing.'

At first, when he had got the call from her, he hadn't believed she had the nerve to suggest a meeting. At a time like this. But then she'd asked whether he wanted to put her on to his wife right now or should she ring back later. She had dates of their meetings, notes about what they did, tapes even. Reg had just lost a son;

the idea of losing a wife made him feel sick to the stomach. Reg Butler, ending his life alone – it was unthinkable. The woman on the bed beside him had no heart.

'Don't think I wouldn't do it either, you stupid old bastard.' Margaret still had her back to him, but he could sense the cold obsessiveness in her voice. 'I didn't put up with you all those times for nothing. Give me the name and you'll never see me again. Otherwise – ' she sighed '– the missus is in for a nasty surprise.'

'The tapes, is it?' Butler reached for some prints. 'Like the photographs you took of my son with that little jockey – which you can't even sell now on account of dead bookmaker on the job being too tacky an item for even the scumbag press?' He tore the photographs into pieces and threw them on the floor. 'Some blackmailer you turned out to be.'

'Try me.' Margaret picked up the pieces and put them into her bag. There were some memories that should never be trodden underfoot.

Reg Butler sat for a moment on the bed, then stood up. 'Paper,' he said quietly.

Margaret watched him scrawling a name and a telephone number on a sheet of hotel writing paper. She wished he hadn't reminded her of Kelly Connor. If it weren't for that little bitch, Jack would have stood firm and would still be alive today. She had got to him that night even though she had been drugged out of her brain, she had infected him with something Margaret hated to the depths of her soul. Integrity. A sort of innocence. Love. And that had started the slide that ended with his death. Jack had been killed by love.

'He never fails,' said Reg, avoiding Margaret's eyes as he gave her the piece of paper.

She walked towards the door. 'Don't you want the tapes?'

The old man looked up. 'No.' He shook his head slowly, keeping his eyes fixed on her. 'The day you use them will be the day you stop living.'

Margaret paused. 'There weren't any anyway.' She opened the door. 'I hope he's good.'

She closed the door on Reg Butler, on part of her life.

Killed by love. Now it was Kelly Connor's turn.

Chapter
14

In the hot morning sun, Kelly was given a leg-up by Dennis, who managed a smile as Shine On arched his back in a skittish, good-natured apology for a buck.

'He's well enough,' he said, as horse, jockey and lad walked on to Washington racecourse. 'He may be one of the outsiders for tomorrow's race but, tell you what, I fancy him for a place.'

Kelly looked down at Dennis and smiled. It was odd but, since they had worked together in Tokyo, he had shown a new respect for her, as if he recognized that she wasn't just a jumped-up stable lass with nice legs and a pretty face but a fully-fledged jockey. 'A place?' she said patting Shine On's neck. 'What are you talking about, Den? We're going to win.'

Their optimism was not shared by the American press, who treated Shine On and his jockey as a novelty turn rather than as serious contenders for the Laurel International. The gossip papers were full of items referring to 'Britain's Knock-'em-Dead Racing Sensation' and 'The Jock With a Hollywood Smile'. The *National Enquirer* ran a scurrilous piece revealing that Kooky Kelly had been dating shamed drugs-bust American jockey Cy McCray, who had been helping prepare her for the big race. There was an invitation to appear on the *Johnny Carson Show* which Annie, who found herself acting as Kelly's minder, turned down. The last thing they needed was for Kelly to be transformed into a media star before she had even reached the start of the big race.

The experts in the more serious racing papers wrote with sober disapproval of the publicity, hinting that it had been encouraged by the race organizers and Shine On's connections. The Laurel International, they wrote, was too important a race to become a circus. The fact was that Shine On was among the outsiders, he had a bad draw and, for all her much-discussed good looks, his jockey was woefully lacking in experience. Those who took their racing seriously would be advised to ignore the fuss, which did little for the sport.

Kelly found it easy to dismiss the sillier stories – anyone who had survived the British press knew how to deal with gutter journalists – but she found the expert commentators' cool dismissal of her chances annoying. Annie helped to put their views into perspective.

'D'you know what these people said about Lester when he first rode here?' she said over breakfast at the Washington Park Hotel. 'The guy rides like a bum. He made them change their mind and so can you.'

She was due to work with Spritzer who had travelled over with Shine On from

Ian Gardem's yard. As she made her way over to where Ian and Annie were waiting, Kelly noticed a knot of onlookers in the stands.

Journalists. A few would be there to sniff out stories about her but most of them
wanted to see Spritzer who had won the St Leger last year. He had only been beat-
en once this season – last time out, in the Arc de Triomphe when, according to
many who saw him, he was unlucky to lose by a short head to the French colt
Badinage after being impeded by tiring horses in the straight.

There was no denying that Spritzer was impressive to look at, Kelly thought as
Bill Ryan, his jockey, greeted her in front of the stands. A big bay horse with an
intelligent, almost arrogant look to him, he had come into his own as a four-year-
old. Of course, he had had a hard race last time out, but on the other hand Shine
On had travelled halfway across the world and back. Never mind the home team,
or the French Derby winner Kernac or a highly fancied horse from Germany called
Millionaire's Row, Spritzer was going to take some beating.

Annie walked over to Shine On and checked his girths.

'All right?' she said.

Kelly nodded, thinking briefly how well Annie had adapted to her new role as
trainer. 'Yes, he seems in great form.'

'Just a pipe-opener, remember,' Annie said quietly. 'If Bill Ryan wants to go on
over the last furlong, let him. It's tomorrow that matters.'

Ryan was a quietly competent professional who had ridden against Kelly enough
not to be taken in by her looks or the fact that she was a woman. He spoke little
as they cantered down to the five-furlong marker but Kelly sensed, from the frequent glances in her direction, that he was assessing her horse. She smiled to herself – at least one expert was taking her chances seriously.

When they pulled up they let the two horses catch their breath and then turned
in together and came up the straight, stride for stride. Shine On was a good mover
but there was no denying that, beside Spritzer, he looked ordinary and Kelly felt
he was taking two strides to Spritzer's one. At the furlong pole, Bill Ryan looked
across at Kelly, said something she couldn't pick up and let his reins out a notch.
As Spritzer lengthened his stride, Shine On responded but Kelly kept a tight hold
of his head. By the time they passed the post, Ryan was three lengths clear.

Kelly smiled to herself as she let Shine On slow down to a walk. Doubtless the
journalists in the stand had the copy they were looking for; 'Class Brit horse
Spritzer sparkles in his gallop with disappointing Shine On.' None of them had
felt what she felt. Her horse had been pulling her arms out at the finish and had
worked as well as she had ever known him to.

'I think he'll go well tomorrow,' she said to Annie when she returned. Some
twenty yards away, Ian Gardem was talking to his jockey, running a hand down
Spritzer's front legs and patting him in a confident, satisfied way. It was doubtful
if he or his jockey were dismissing Shine On's chances as easily as the journalists
were, but their horse's wellbeing fully justified their confidence.

Annie walked with Kelly and Shine On back towards the stables. 'You've got
quite a fan club here, you know,' she said. 'Apparently the owner is coming along
tomorrow.'

'The Sheikh?' Kelly was surprised.

'He had to come to America for some business to do with Ibn Fayoud. Between you and me, I think he's less keen on moving his horses out of England than everyone thinks. I've had several calls from Brompton-Smiley asking about Shine On.'

The name brought Kelly up sharp. Preparation for the big race had proved to be the perfect distraction from the aftermath of Jack Butler's death. Shortly before she had left, two detectives had visited her and taken a further statement but, beyond that, she had managed to banish almost everything from her mind. This week was for racing; she would attend to the real world on her return.

'And your friend Nick Morley's here too. He's buying some mares and wants to look at American racecourse security.'

Her friend. Kelly winced as she remembered the last time they had seen one another. 'I know,' she told Annie. 'He's already been in touch. I said I'd meet him sometime today.' Maybe away from the pressures of home he would be different.

Back at the hotel, Kelly asked the desk clerk for her key. Apart from seeing Nick, she'd planned to do nothing except watch television, relax and read up the form of the following day's runners. The man behind the desk gave her the key to Room 1341 and invited her to have a good day. Kelly smiled and said she would.

In Room 1342, Margaret Stanhope sat reading yesterday's edition of the *National Enquirer*. She knew the story off by heart now – Kooky Kelly, indeed. She looked with loathing at the photograph of the Connor girl arriving at the airport earlier in the week. The jock with the Hollywood smile. Margaret narrowed her eyes. Tomorrow there would be an end to smiles.

There was a click from across the room. Donnell was at the desk, checking his gun yet again. Personally, Margaret could have done without the tedium of sharing a hotel room with a professional hitman with the conversational skills of the Statue of Liberty but it was simpler to get the room they wanted as a married couple. This was where they had spent their honeymoon night five years before. It was a romantic enough story to swing it, when backed up by a hundred dollar bill for the bookings clerk.

At least he didn't want sex; there was that. As soon as Donnell had been alone with her in the room, he had said, 'I sleep on the floor.' She had been polite, said they could both use the bed if he wanted but he had been like ice. 'I always sleep on the floor,' he said.

A gay hitman? Or was this some trick learnt in Vietnam where, Margaret imagined, Donnell had acquired his taste, his talent for killing? Don't talk, don't sleep on mattresses, don't touch women unless you happen to be murdering them at the time; the man was a crazy purist. Not that it made any difference, as long as he did what he was paid for. She watched the trim, balding figure of the assassin as he cleaned and assembled his short pug-like pistol, then fitted the silencer once more.

'All present and correct?' she said.

The man looked round at her, narrowing his eyes as if she were a stranger who had just come up and insulted the memory of his dear dead mother. For a moment, Margaret thought that he was going to kill her, just for the hell of it, even though she had only given him ten of the twenty thousand dollars he was to be paid.

He chewed thoughtfully on his gum, digging deep for precisely the right words.

'Shut the fuck up,' he said finally.

Margaret shrugged. She stood up and wandered out on to the balcony. A telephone was ringing from next door and, through an open window, she could just hear the voice answering it, laughing, carefree. Margaret smiled. Kooky Kelly. Soon to be the late Kooky Kelly.

As she listened to Nick's voice on the telephone, Kelly found herself wondering how she seriously could have suspected him of being involved in the death of Jack Butler. He sounded concerned, genuinely interested in the news about Shine On. He never said as much, but it was clear that he had timed his trip to Washington so that he could see her ride in the big race.

'Where are you staying?' she asked.

'Some people called Bruce,' he said vaguely. 'They've got a small palace in the north-west of Washington, where the diplomats and politicians hang out. I'm meant to be buying some mares from them.'

'When you're not dating jockeys.'

Nick laughed. 'Why don't you get a cab and come up here some time this afternoon? I've got to lunch here but afterwards I could show you the National Cathedral. It's spectacular.'

Kelly hesitated. She was hardly in the mood for sightseeing but the alternative of spending the afternoon in her hotel room or going over tomorrow's race yet again was even less appealing. 'Why the hell not?' she said.

They agreed to meet outside the main entrance.

Nick had been right. The National Cathedral was spectacular, a vast neo-Gothic celebration of American self-confidence. He greeted her by the main entrance, kissing her on both cheeks, holding her to him with an intensity which momentarily took Kelly by surprise.

'Shall we go in? Pray for your chances tomorrow?' There was something ironical and self-mocking in his smile, as if he were anxious not to reveal quite how pleased he was to see her.

'I'm a good Catholic girl,' she said. 'There's a time and a place for prayer.'

'Like down at the start.'

She laughed and they walked slowly into the great building. A boys' choir was practising in the crypt, and Nick and Kelly stood in the central aisle listening for a moment.

'Carols in October,' said Kelly. 'That must be a bad omen.'

'No.' Nick's voice was almost a whisper. 'They're boys from a local boarding school. It's famous for its singing. They'll be rehearsing every day from now on.'

Kelly looked at him. There was a strange glitter to his eye, as if he had been reminded of something distant and unpleasant. 'You're well informed,' she said.

He shrugged. 'I visit Washington quite a lot.'

He guided her to a pew where they sat, a congregation of two, listening to the carols. A young soloist had stepped forward. As he sang with all the confidence of youth, his voice echoed about the empty cathedral.

'Brahms,' said Kelly. 'It reminds me of my father. He loved carols.'

Nick was not listening to her but to the soaring voice of the chorister. 'The pure, unsullied voice of privilege,' he murmured, almost to himself.

'He's a good singer,' said Kelly, misunderstanding.

'And he'll be a good schoolboy, and good Ivy League graduate, and a good lawyer or businessman or politician until, in a few years' time, he'll be back here in the acceptable part of Washington. He'll take up the baton in national life, just as it was always intended he should. It's what Mom and Pop are paying for now.'

Kelly could hear that steeliness in his voice again. 'And some won't,' she said. 'Some will go their own way.'

'I was in the choir at Harrow.' In the darkness of the cathedral, Kelly could see that Nick was smiling now, an oddly cold smile.

'And you went your own way.'

'Yes.' It was as if he had suddenly awoken from a dream. 'That's what I did.'

The music had stopped now and the boys were collecting up their books, whispering and laughing in the crypt.

'I was going to be a lawyer,' Nick continued. 'That's what was planned for me. I had the brains, the education, the background. For some reason, maybe a fear of turning into a cold, loveless success like my father, I chose a career they would hate. They've never quite forgiven me.'

'They must be proud of you now.'

Nick looked at her as if she had understood nothing of what he had told her.

'Some go their own way,' he said and stood up.

Kelly felt a million miles from him. The music, the sound of the boys' voices had taken Nick into a cold, bleak land where she couldn't reach him and where she had no desire to go. He had business on his mind, and she had a race to win. She smiled to herself. Just ride the horses.

Blinking in the autumn sunlight, they emerged from the cathedral and turned left down the wide street.

'Now where are you taking me?' she asked.

He raised an eyebrow, once more his natural, charming self. 'Back to my place?' he suggested. 'For a cup of tea.'

'I think I ought to get back.'

'Don't be silly. You'll only be bored and my hosts have a magnificent house.

Like most of their neighbours, the Bruces, with whom Nick was staying, lived in style; theirs was not so much a house as a residence. In the large sunlit room where Nick and Kelly were served tea by a Filipino maid, there was a grand piano in one corner and photographs on the wall, most of which showed a plump, distinguished-looking man with various political and showbusiness celebrities.

Over tea, Nick explained that Virgil Bruce III was at his office downtown and his family lived most of the time in South Carolina. 'He's an old friend,' he said. 'We do a lot of bloodstock business and I have an open invitation to stay here.'

For a while, they discussed the Laurel International which Nick, like Kelly, thought was a more open race than many of the American commentators assumed. Last year's winner Angel Dust was a worthy favourite, having remained unbeaten all year and with the advantage of not having had to travel far, but the European challenge could not be ignored. They'd already won a handful of American races that season. Nick seemed distracted when Kelly spoke of Shine On's chances. Then, quite suddenly, he changed the subject.

'Have you heard anything more about the Jack Butler business?' he asked. Kelly looked at him, surprised.

She shook her head. 'The police took a further statement.' She thought of Jack lying in the sand. 'Did you know that he was involved with the IRA?'

'Jack Butler?' Nick sipped his tea. 'It wouldn't surprise me. There have always been links between terrorists and the criminal community, and even if he didn't quite fit into that category, his father certainly did.'

'It's more than that. An Englishman was involved in a betting ring in Ireland during the seventies. I've been told that he's remained active for them, that it was this man who was working Jack Butler and the drugs run.'

'An Englishman?' From Nick's tone of voice, they might still have been talking about Shine On and tomorrow's race, but he was now deathly pale. 'The boys use a surprising number of Englishmen.'

'This one lived in the north and was involved with horses. Now he lives in England.'

Nick looked at her, coldly, almost as if he were daring her to go further.

Kelly smiled. 'For a moment, I thought it must have been you, but now I've got the name.'

'Don't say it,' he interrupted her. 'I know.' He poured them both another cup of tea, saying quietly as he did so, 'I suppose I had better tell you everything.'

For five minutes, maybe ten, he addressed her coldly, succinctly, as if he were in a military debriefing session, only his eyes, which were alive with excitement, betraying the enormity of what he was saying.

Although he had left the SAS several years ago, he was still retained in a part-time capacity by a counter-insurgency unit at the Ministry of Defence. They had been aware for some time that the IRA were big-time players in the drugs business, the substantial rewards of which helped pay for their terrorist activities. Jack Butler had become involved out of sheer greed and ambition. First he allowed his shops to be used to launder drugs money, then he, or possibly his father Reg, had been persuaded to step up the stakes by pulling Ibn Fayoud into the conspiracy.

The Butlers had made sure that the young Arab, who was already in serious financial difficulties, become hopelessly indebted to them; the Pendero race at Ascot was just one of several gambles which had intentionally backfired on the Arab. Once they had him well and truly hooked, they used his cover to smuggle heroin through the diplomatic bag system, and also through racehorses travelling the world.

For some reason, Jack Butler lost his nerve. By the time Kelly alerted Nick to the Tokyo run, they were already aware of what was happening. He had been unable to tell her, although it had been his influence which had helped free her at the airport.

Kelly interrupted to ask about Cy McCray and Bill Templeman.

'They'll stand trial.' Nick shrugged regretfully. 'We can't blow our cover to help them.'

'You mean the smuggling operation is still continuing?'

Nick nodded. 'They killed Jack Butler, but he was small-time. The show will go on without him.'

'But I don't understand how Brompton-Smiley's involved.'

'You were right. There was an Englishman involved with the IRA during the seventies. We knew it was going on when I was on the front line, but we couldn't place who it was. It was after he began working for Sheikh al Hassan that our intelligence boys got on to him. He was the one who suggested Ibn Fayoud as cover. He's not as stupid as he looks; the reason why the Sheikh's moving to France is that he knows we're watching him. Even with Interpol co-operation, he'll have a clearer run over there.'

'If he goes,' said Kelly.

Nick looked at her sharply. 'How do you mean?'

'The Sheikh watched Shine On work this morning. He told Annie that, if he won tomorrow, he'll reconsider his decision to move to France.'

'That will spoil a few plans,' Nick said incredulously.

'It seems that Sheikh al Hassan is a bit of a romantic. He said that watching a small stable pitching for one of the big races was more exciting than anything he had experienced with his bigger yards.'

'So,' Nick smiled palely, 'It could all go into reverse if the wrong horse wins tomorrow.'

Kelly looked at her watch. It was time to get back to the hotel. 'Not that I'll be worrying about that as I pass the post tomorrow.'

'Of course not,' he said quietly. 'I'll order you a cab.'

Nick's explanation appeared to have solved the mystery of her father's death and everything else that had happened. But while he was out of the room phoning for a cab, she couldn't help feeling nagging, inexplicable doubt.

She stood up, cursing herself for being unable to stop the questions in her mind, even when the answers appeared to have been supplied. There was something wrong. It was somehow all too neat. She looked at the photographs on the wall. Virgil Bruce III with Richard Nixon, with Jack Nicklaus, with Henry Kissinger, with Frank Sinatra, with Ronald Reagan, with – Kelly paused by a shot of Bruce with a man whose face was familiar to her, yet which seemed out of context here. Grey-haired, a man of power with laughing, watchful eyes. Who the hell was he?

Nick returned to say the cab was on its way. He stood before her in the middle of the great room and reached out to touch her cheek. His hand was cold.

'I wanted to talk about us,' he said.

Kelly moved half a pace backwards, thinking of an excuse. 'Nick, I've got too much to think about right now. I've got a race to win. Will I see you there?'

'OK.'

The doorbell rang.

It was only when she was in the cab, driving down the wide avenues of Washington on her way back to the hotel that she realized he had never wished her luck.

She was right about him. When she got back to England she'd find herself a man with a heart. Someone who really cared about her. Not Nick Morley.

* * *

'Busy day, lady?'

Kelly assumed that the black cab driver had seen her picture in one of the news-papers. Yet there was something oddly appraising about the way he looked at her in the rearview mirror which went beyond traditional American openness.

'Not too bad,' she said.

'You guys work even longer hours than a cab driver. Afternoon with old man Bruce then back to the hotel bars. Shit, you sure earn your corn.'

It was a moment before Kelly understood what he was talking about. She laughed; it was the second time she had been mistaken for a hooker. She was about to cor-rect him in her most starchily British tones when it occurred to her that the driv-er might know something about the man with whom Nick was staying.

Misunderstanding her laughter, he went on, 'Jeez, the number of times I come to this district with young girls. I'm surprised the guys round here have time to run the country the way they behave.'

'Right,' said Kelly.

'And that Bruce guy, he's the worst, you know? Parties, girls.' The driver shook his head enviously. 'I don't know where he gets the energy from, that's the truth.'

'Maybe it's the southern air.'

'South?' The man sounded surprised. 'Old Virgil's been no further south than the Potomac. I read that he was born in the Bronx, changed his name when he moved from being an organizer with the Teamsters to setting up his own transport business. Irish family, he was. O'Brien or some such.'

Kelly heard Nick's voice in her head. An old friend. Old money. Certainly the house had old-world style. And yet there were no racing pictures on the wall, which seemed odd; just celebrity shots. It was then that she remembered where she had last seen the face of the grey-haired man in the photograph with Virgil Bruce III. It had been in a portrait in the house of Dermot Kinane.

Who did you believe? A security officer for the English Jockey Club who had saved you from arrest, or a Washington cab driver who read the gossip columns and thought you were on the game? Kelly looked out of the window. As if some evil genie had waved a wand, the wide sweep and lawns of the northern suburb had given way to dingy, inner-city squalor. Nothing was what it seemed.

Virgil Bruce III, old money, or O'Brien, an Irishman made good? She looked back at the driver's mirror and caught him darting another speculative look in her direction. Unlike Nick, he had nothing to gain from lying to her.

That picture. What would Virgil Bruce III be doing shaking the hand of the most famous President of Ireland in the Republic's history, a man celebrated not just as a politician but, in his youth, as a fierce fighter for the nationalist cause. Eamon de Valera.

Kelly smiled coolly at the cab driver and looked away. She wished that the Irish connection was a coincidence, but she knew that it wasn't.

'Dermot, the American business interests you mentioned. It involved Bruce, didn't it?'

It was difficult to tell whether Dermot's hesitation was caused by sleepiness – it would have been one in the morning in Ireland – or his characteristic wariness.

'What are you talking about, Kelly?' he said eventually. 'For the Lord's sake, can you not concentrate on the big race you're riding tomorrow?' The words sounded familiar.'

'Tell me, Dermot. This is important.'

There was another pause. 'The name I heard was not Bruce, that's for sure.'

'He calls himself Bruce but he was born O'Brien. He's in transport. Very rich.'

Kinane sighed, as if he were tired of the subterfuge, of trying to protect someone too wilful to see that the less she knew the better.

'All I can tell you,' he said, 'Is that there is an O'Brien who's known as one of the biggest sponsors of Noraid. He gives money to the IRA, maybe more than money but, heaven alive, it's a common enough name.'

'Where does he live?'

At first, Kelly thought Dermot had gone back to sleep. She repeated the question, raising her voice angrily.

'He comes from Washington.'

After she had bid Dermot goodnight, Kelly switched on the television without the sound and watched the flickering images of a game show as she pieced together what she knew.

Nick was staying with a man known to be involved with the IRA and possibly with drug-running. She thought of Brompton-Smiley's party in Newmarket, Nick's lack of surprise at the news of Jack Butler's death, the sand on his car. She closed her eyes and for a moment saw once again the image of Jack's body in the north Norfolk sand. He had trusted her with his hide-out address, she had trusted Nick, leaving the address on his answering machine. Suddenly everything was making sense.

Trust no one. The words from her father's letter returned to her. So plausible, so attractive, so human despite his position of authority. But on the night of her return from Tokyo, there had been that strange moment in his flat when she had felt not so much an accomplice as a victim. There had been something dangerous, triumphant about him that night. Unthinkingly, she had remarked that there were always more where the Butlers and Ibn Fayouds came from and he had become distant and distracted, had compared catching dopers and villains with defeating the IRA. It was the same thing for him, he had said.

Kelly remembered his manner that very morning in the National Cathedral, staring at the boys' choir as if lost in his own, inhospitable world. His parents had wanted him to be a lawyer and he had become a soldier. He had been bright at school, but he had elected to use low cunning and courage for a career. Doubtless his family expected him at least to join a socially acceptable cavalry regiment; instead he went into the SAS. Perhaps, when others looked to him to pursue a successful career as a soldier, he had once again moved in the opposite direction. What more perfect rebellion than to go over to the other site, to become rich in the service of the ultimate outsiders, a force beyond any civilized society. Some go their own way.

The telephone rang. It was Annie, checking that she was all right.

'I'm fine,' Kelly laughed and reassured her that the night spots of Washington could wait.

After she had said goodnight to Annie, she reflected that she had caught Nick Morley off-balance during their meeting that day. He had seemed put out, unnerved by the idea that Sheikh al Hassan could reverse his decision to pull out of English racing. Yet it was Brompton-Smiley who, he claimed, needed to move his base of operations to evade the natural curiosity of the Drugs Squad. A change of heart by the Sheikh would put those plans in jeopardy.

In other words, it was in Nick's interests for Shine On to be beaten in the Laurel International. It was possible that his involvement was nothing more than a figment of her talent for paranoia, but Kelly didn't think so. Unwittingly, by revealing Sheikh al Hassan's uncertainty about the move to France, she had set a trap.

The call came at eleven, shortly after Kelly had turned out her light.

'It's Nick.' His tone was brisk, wakeful. 'Can I come and see you?'

'No, I'm almost asleep.'

'Listen, this is important. I told you too much today,' he said. 'I've been in touch with London. We're in deeper than we thought. They need Brompton-Smiley to go to France and to make certain that he does, they want you to lose tomorrow's race. Kelly, you've got to realize that this is very important. Human lives, government matters are at stake.' He hesitated. 'It's absolutely essential. I've never asked anyone to do this before and I hate doing it, especially to you, but these are my orders and there's nothing I can do. You do understand, don't you?' There was more emotion in his voice than Kelly had ever heard before.

'Yes,' she said. 'I understand.'

Chapter 15

'It's gonna be a helluva horse race.'

The voice of Sam Dimona, an ex-jockey who was now America's best-known racing commentator, echoed over the public address system in the ballroom of the Washington Park Hotel. His words were clearly some kind of catchphrase because the journalists and photographers gathered for the Laurel International Breakfast whooped and cheered as if they were at the Troubadour in Vegas and Frank Sinatra had just ambled on to the stage.

Kelly caught the eye of Bill Ryan who nodded briskly and looked away. If he was taken aback by the publicity hoopla surrounding the race, he was determined not to show it. Beside her at the long table reserved for the trainers and jockeys of runners in the big race, Annie had the fixed smile of someone who wished she was somewhere, anywhere, else. She had warned Kelly that the hype surrounding the International was unlike anything seen in Europe, but nothing had prepared her for this.

They had reached the climax of proceedings, during which members of the press corps, who were restrained in an undignified rabble behind a silver rope, were invited to ask questions of the leading participants.

Kelly was relieved to see that most of the interest surrounded Eddie Marielita, the young Puerto Rican who had made his name as the jockey of Angel Dust and whose answers to the shouted questions belonged to the Lester Piggott school of economic communication. How was Angel? Fine. Was he going to win today? No problem. Who did Eddie see as his biggest rivals today? Anyone who started in the race was a rival. Was it true that his grandparents had flown up from San Juan to see him ride? Yes, it was. The track was riding softer than average today – would that worry Angel? No problem.

At one point, as the American journalists doggedly attempted to extract a quotable sentence from Marielita, Kelly thought she saw Nick at the back of the room but, looking more carefully, she realized that it was someone else. In spite of her determination to concentrate on the race, she had been unable to shake thoughts of yesterday from her mind. Maybe Nick was still working for the government. She remembered the feeling in his voice. Perhaps her own concerns, winning a race, even finding out who had killed her father, were insignificant beside the fight against terrorism. When all was said and done, today was just a question of one horse running faster than a few others.

The journalists were trying their luck on Paul Hiberdy, the pale, good-looking

French champion jockey who was riding Badinage. Every question was translated by the horse's trainer and followed by a lengthy discussion in French between the connections before a brief answer was supplied by the trainer. Annie muttered that, at this rate, no one was going to get to the racecourse.

In the end, Kelly reflected, she had to follow her instinct. No one – not Annie, nor Dermot, nor, least of all Nick – could help her decide. As the journalists moved on to the American jockey who was riding the fancied five-year-old gelding Space Cadet, she thought of the person to whom she had always turned for advice, whose quiet wisdom had helped her so much in the past and, in the end, had helped him so little. What would her father have said?

Her reverie was broken by the sound of an American voice calling out her name. 'Kelly Connor, how do you rate your chances today?'

She smiled and said she rated them highly.

Another journalist asked whether she had any thoughts about being on a horse ridden last time out by American jockey Cy McCray. Before she could answer, Annie spoke up to point out that Shine On had been ridden in all his races this season by Kelly except for the last one. Kelly added that Cy McCray was a fine jockey and a friend and that, after she had won, her first call to England would be to him.

When another reporter asked whether it was true that she had been offered $100,000 to appear in *Playboy*, she'd had enough.

'Grow up,' she said to laughter from the other journalists.

As the questioning moved on to Bill Ryan, Kelly rubbed her eyes wearily. For some reason, the press here had taken against her and now she had given them ammunition to use against her. Arrogant, snooty, abrasive. The bimbo bites back. It had been a mistake, but then she had hardly slept during the night.

Along the table, Eddie Marielita was staring at her. Almost imperceptibly, he gave a practised, see-you-after-the-show wink. His vulpine smile was not that of rival and was more eloquent than any words he had uttered minutes before. No problems.

Margaret Stanhope was not used to taking orders unless they were from someone she loved and the only person she had ever loved wasn't giving orders to anyone these days. All the same, when Donnell told her to get her bags out of the hotel by seventeen hundred hours and to meet him in the bar of the Holiday Inn that night at nineteen thirty because by then the job would be over and he'd be on his way, she asked no questions. The man was a jerk but he had his area of expertise, and Margaret had learnt to trust experts.

That morning, as the day's racing celebrities were given their highly public breakfast downstairs, she had wandered about the hotel room in her underclothes humming to herself. It wasn't that she wanted to do anything with Donnell – for her, social sex was only an occasional indulgence – more that she found his cold detachment something of a challenge. She still had a good body and liked to think she could influence the behaviour of most normal men by the promise of a share in her assets.

But Donnell was blind to her flat stomach, to her almost perfect breasts, to her long tanned thighs. She had sighed softly as she slipped on her nylon stockings, bitten her lower lip temptingly as she fastened her suspenders. But the bastard was as interested as if she were a slab of wet fish. She hated him – not as much as she would have hated him if he *had* tried to jump her, but she hated him all the same.

'So you'll do it when she comes back to the hotel?' Margaret looked at Donnell, who sat at the desk, staring out of the window. This was not a man, but a computer, a robot programmed to kill. Although he didn't seem to have stepped out of the light suit he wore, had slept in it as far as she could tell, he still looked as blandly immaculate as he had two days previously when she had first met him.

He gave the question serious thought and nodded.

'After five o'clock?' Margaret hesitated as Donnell narrowed his eyes. It annoyed her how those cold eyes made her flesh crawl – nobody, least of all a man, had frightened her like this for a long time. 'Or seventeen hundred hours, whatever you call it.'

'As soon as you get out of here.'

'So, by the time we meet in the Holiday Inn, she could have been found? The news might be out.'

Donnell stared at her. The publicity side of the job wasn't his problem.

'Fuck knows,' he said quietly.

If they had been in England, Kelly's big race build-up would have been simple – that is, the same as any other day, except for maybe arriving early to miss the extra traffic, then killing time chatting to the other jockeys outside the weighing room and studying the form. There was nothing strange or mysterious about it. Tennis players may hum their own special mantra, footballers may pray and cross themselves as they run on to the pitch, but jockeys just get on with it.

But they weren't in England. Here in Washington, on the day of the International, a jockey was news. Everything he said or she did was a potential quote or photo opportunity. Kelly was glad that she decided to walk the mile and a quarter course with Annie early that morning before the press were awake. The idea of going through the race before an audience of journalists more interested in her legs and face than in her ability as a jockey did not appeal.

It was a good galloping course and the going, which was on the soft side of good after some unseasonal rain, would suit Shine On. Since the race was run over a shorter distance than the horse had won over recently, Annie and Kelly decided it would be best to lie closer to the leaders than she normally did. They had been drawn one out from the inside track and the only way of ensuring a clear run would be to keep clear of the pack.

Force of habit had brought Kelly down to the racetrack again later that morning, and now she wished she had stayed in her room at the hotel. As she arrived, she found herself surrounded by photographers. She pushed past them, ignoring their shouted questions, and walked to the area adjoining the course where the horses were stabled. There at least she would be free of the publicity circus.

She showed her pass at the entrance to a barn-like building where all the foreign horses were kept. Unlike Tokyo, Kelly reflected as she walked the length of the barn towards Shine On's box, the security here seemed impeccable. Only the immediate connections of each horse were allowed into the barn, which had cameras covering every loosebox.

Kelly quickened her steps. She remembered Nick's reason for attending the meeting; the Washington security force were going to show him round. No one had a better entrée to the stables than he had and, if she was right about him, no one was more determined that Shine On shouldn't win.

Seeing Annie and Dennis at the stable, she breathed more easily. After a restless night, her imagination was running away with her.

'Shaken off your journo friends?' Annie asked.

Kelly smiled. 'Just about. I don't seem to have made too big a hit with the gentlemen of the press.'

'I'm not surprised after yesterday. But don't worry. It's just that you're not playing their game. In Washington, turning down the chance to appear on *Johnny Carson* is one of the Seven Deadly Sins. Everything is showbiz here – politics, sport, life.'

'Crime,' Kelly added to herself, thinking of Virgil Bruce and his collection of celebrity photographs.

'You'll just have to prove your point by winning the race. An American trainer was saying there's a question mark over Badinage's ability to stay the trip on this ground. He reckoned that Stir Crazy's here to make it a true run race for Angel Dust, so he's certain to get tested.'

'Could be.' Kelly had also heard that, although the American colt Stir Crazy had some good form, his owner was being paid to run him as pacemaker for his more fancied compatriot.

The two of them discussed the race for a few minutes before Annie glanced at her watch. 'Gotta run,' she said. 'Simon Brompton-Smiley wants to see me before the races.' She slapped Kelly lightly on the arm. 'See you in the weighing room. Don't go talking to any strange journalists.'

'Are there any other kind?' Kelly turned to Dennis. 'Will you be staying with Shine On all the time this morning?'

Dennis looked at her in surprise. 'You bet,' he said. 'No one gets to see this horse without seeing me first.'

'Fine.'

With time to kill, Kelly left the stables and took the lift to the top of the stands where, apart from a few early racegoers, it was deserted. She was looking across the green swathe of the racecourse, planning her race and fixing the course in her mind when she spotted Nick walking from the racetrack towards the stands, deep in conversation with two men. She wondered briefly what they were discussing. Security? Heroin? How to stop villains? How to stop horses? They were too far away for her to see Nick's face but she could imagine his expression – concerned, frowning, a man at work.

She remembered his late-night call and the urgency in his voice. Half the night she had tried to think of reasons why she should believe him, trust in the higher good which, according to his story, required her to throw today's race. We know best, he had been saying, trust us. It's more than a matter of racing, it's national security, life and death.

In the early hours of the morning, she had once more read her father's last letter to her – these days she always kept it with her. The men who had killed him had made it clear enough to him; 'Friends in high places' was the way they put it. But it was her father's own words which finally convinced her. 'In this war, there is no neutral territory. You're either with the enemy or you're not.'

Kelly recalled a story that her father had once told her about Dermot when he'd been younger and very much involved with the Cause. It was at a time when the fighting between the two religions was at its bloodiest. Dermot was taking a lunch break with eight workmates in a hut on a building site. Suddenly a man burst open the door and stood there with a mask covering his face and a machine gun held nervously in his hands. Everyone in the hut jumped to their feet in terror, anticipating the certain burst of fire.

'Everyone who's Protestant lie on the floor,' screamed the gunman.

Dermot had said they'd had no idea which religion the gunman supported. There could be no knowing and no pretending.

Dermot and two others remained standing. One wet himself with fear waiting for the ultimate verdict.

As Dermot put up his hand to make the sign of the cross, the man opened fire. Then he turned and ran out of the hut, leaving six men lying on the floor, their bodies torn apart by bullets. There were no half measures with these people.

The three men were approaching the stands. For a moment, Nick looked up and Kelly imagined briefly that he could see her, watching him. The enemy. It was difficult to see this man, who had once been her lover, as the enemy she was now convinced he was. She wondered how a mother could ever come to terms with a son who committed murder. She thought of her father, Damien Gould, of Jack Butler. Whatever devils drove Nick Morley – greed, ambition, or some deep-seated malaise of the personality that dated from his childhood – she'd been right; there was no place for humanity in his plans, no place for love.

Kelly turned to go back to the weighing room, taking a lift to the ground floor.

The doors opened and, as if her worst nightmares had become reality, the three men stood in front of her. The two men with Nick were broadly built and had brutally correct military haircuts. Villains, security chiefs – they all looked the same.

'Kelly.' Nick made no effort to stand aside. 'Ready to do your best for Queen and country?' Above the smile, the eyes were cold, professional.

Her mind was set. 'Of course,' she said, forcing herself to sound convincing. One of the men stood aside to let her through.

Although there were no other women riding in the Laurel International, Kelly was relieved to find that the women's dressing room was busier than it would be had they been in England. As she changed and prepared for the big race, several of the leading American women jockeys wished her luck. Maybe if the American press hadn't treated her like a joke contestant they might have put patriotism before sisterly solidarity but now they were right behind her.

It was a relief to ride out on to the racecourse for the pre-race parade. Now it was all over; the questions, the photographs, the speculation, the hype. Now it was a matter of horse and jockey. Away from the publicity circus, Kelly smiled and patted Shine On. She felt good, and so did he.

There were ten runners and, with the possible exception of Stir Crazy, they were all in with a chance. Angel Dust headed the parade and, from the reaction of the crowd, it was obvious that the tough, angular grey who had convincingly won the race last year was a big favourite. Behind him was Skillet, the American three-year-old who had broken the course record at Kentucky earlier in the season. The word in racing circles was that he was over the top, that he was half the horse he had been a month ago. As if to prove it, he was dripping with sweat. More impressive in the paddock had been Larkrise, a chestnut filly who had won her last two races, admittedly against moderate company, by six and ten lengths. Then there was Stir Crazy, pacemaker to Angel Dust.

The foreign challenge was the most formidable for years. Even if the chances of Shine On, last in the parade, were discounted, as they were by the majority of on-course experts, the claims of Badinage and Spritzer, first and second in the Arc de Triomphe, Kernac, the Chantilly-trained three-year-old who had won the French Derby, and even the German horse Millionaire's Row were undeniable. Looking at the horses ahead of her as they filed past the stands Kelly remembered the words of the pinhead back at the hotel. Yes, it was going to be a helluva horse race.

Down at the start, there was less chat between the jockeys than Kelly was used to. Of the Americans, only Eddie Marielita seemed to be enjoying himself, patting Angel Dust, grinning occasionally at Kelly in a way he clearly thought was seductive. Bill Ryan's face was set in an impassive scowl and Paul Hiberdy, the Frenchman riding Badinage, looked pale and tense.

With the odd numbers going in before the even numbers, from left to right, Shine On was put in the starting-gate first. There then followed a delay while the handlers tried to get Kernac loaded. The delay helped no one, but Shine On, having been incarcerated longer than any other runner, was most likely to break slowly. Kelly touched his ears reassuringly as the American handlers cursed Kernac. Thank God he was a seasoned professional for whom a delay in the stalls was merely part of the business of racing. Beside her, Ryan was keeping Spritzer on his toes – another one looking for a good break.

'Good luck, Bill,' she said.

The Englishman looked over. 'You too.'

Then Kernac was in.

The crack of the starting gun, crash of metal, the yells of the jockeys, the grunt of racehorses lurching out of the stalls and into their stride, the distant roar from the grandstand – they all came together as the starter pulled the lever that sent the runners of the Laurel International on their way.

Kelly had heard that race-riding in America was much more of a bodily contact sport than it was in England. From the thud of bodies and curses behind her, the reports had been correct. Shine On, willing as ever, had been first of the field into his stride, allowing Kelly the luxury of a place on the rails without close company to her right and in front of her.

For one awkward moment, she thought she was going to have to make the running but, after two hundred yards, Stir Crazy surged ahead with Millionaire's Row and Spritzer sitting in his slipstream. At some deep, instinctive level, Kelly noted that the race was being run at too fast a pace for the ground they were racing on, and as more of the runners went past her on the outside she abandoned her plans and let Shine On settle in towards the rear. There were only a couple of horses behind her and for an instant her mind flashed to two people in the stands. Annie would think that she'd gone totally mad, and Nick – well, who knew what Nick was thinking.

As they passed the halfway marker, Kelly breathed a sigh of relief as the early pace began to tell on some of the runners. The pacemaker had started to lose his position, but the jockey on Millionaire's Row had begun to move. Bill Ryan looked as confident as ever. The French horse Badinage was dogging his footsteps on the inside. There was no sign of Angel Dust. Then Kelly felt and heard another horse clipping Shine On's heels. She took a quick peek over her shoulder. The American horse was right behind her.

Shine On was good round bends but he preferred a right-handed track. It was as he moved half the width of a racehorse away from the rails, taking the last bend, that Eddie Marielita saw his chance. As they turned into the straight, Kelly became aware of the local horse making its run on her inside. It was time to remind Eddie that all's fair in love, war and racing. Letting Shine On quicken slightly, she closed the door on Angel Dust to a torrent of abuse from the American.

Three furlongs from home. British-trained horses were in first and second places, but it was beginning to look as if Ryan's determination to avoid the trouble that had cost him the Arc had asked too big a question of Spritzer. Kelly saw him change legs and moved to his outside. She could take him any time but the last thing she wanted to do was to hit the front too early.

Paul Hiberdy on Badinage solved her problem by switching his challenge to the outside. Kelly had started riding. Stride for stride with Spritzer, she was half a length down on the French horse. As they entered the final furlong, the crowd's roar was deafening – and then Kelly, Ryan and Hiberdy became aware of what was causing it. A grey spectre in the form of Angel Dust, Eddie Marielita hunched up his neck, hit the front as if the rest of the field was walking.

On her inside, Kelly heard one of Bill Ryan's few utterances – a multi-decibel obscenity aimed at Spritzer who was losing ground with every stride. Shine On had the edge on Badinage whose jockey was waving his whip like von Karajan going for the big finish in Beethoven's Ninth.

Shine On began to wander to his left and Kelly pulled her stick through to keep him straight. There was no need to hit him. He was running the race of his life. With less than a furlong to run Angel Dust seemed to have his race won, but Kelly could feel Shine On struggling to get back at him and she pushed harder than she ever had before to help him pull out a bit extra. He was like a tiger. Suddenly it was no longer a question of by how much the American hero would take his second Laurel, but whether he could hold on to win at all.

Limbs aching and lungs on fire, Kelly saw the post approaching as, stride by agonizing stride, Shine On pegged back Angel Dust's lead. Yards to go. There was a short head in it, if that. It was on the nod. As they passed the post, it seemed to Kelly that she had lifted the exhausted Shine On across the line. For seconds, as the two gallant horses pulled up, the roar from the crowd carried on. Kelly slumped forward as Shine On slowed to a canter, then a trot. Somewhere in the distance a photograph was announced, but she knew the result.

So did Eddie Marielita. As he turned back to the stands with her, the Puerto Rican pulled down his goggles and extended a hand. 'Eh, Playboy,' he said. 'I think you just won. You're a tough cookie.'

Slowly, as if from a dream, Kelly awoke to her immediate surrounding. Dennis was running towards her and, above the noise of the crowd, she heard him say – probably to Shine On – 'You did it!'

The generous American crowd, realizing that they had witnessed one of the greatest finishes to a Laurel International for years, applauded her and also Angel Dust as they made their way through the throng to the winners' enclosure. The American horse was still a favourite, but now they had another hero to cheer – the first woman to win the International.

There was a renewed round of applause as, some twenty yards ahead of her, Marielita took Angel Dust into the place reserved for the second horse. The cheer as she entered the enclosure was deafening. Kelly smiled at the flashing cameras, at the journalists already scribbling notes on their pads. So much for Kooky Connor – tomorrow the headlines would not be of the girl who said 'No' to Carson, but of a new super-jockette. No one could change horses midstream more adeptly than a pressman.

She dismounted as Annie, momentarily forgetting that Sheikh al Hassan was standing behind her, hugged her with delight. 'You were brilliant!' The Sheikh laughed and shook Kelly's hand. Above the clamour, he told her that no winner had given him more pleasure. Brompton-Smiley stood by his shoulder, nodding like a toy dog. She went to weigh in.

'Congratulations.' A familiar English voice cut through the furore as she stood down from the scales. She turned to see Nick standing before her, pale, unsmiling. For an instant, she held his icy look before returning to the dressing room. No regrets. Whatever Nick and his friends had planned for her, there were no regrets.

She hardly had time to change amidst the congratulations of the American women jockeys before she was called out from the dressing room.

'Hey, your very own press conference,' said one of the women, laughing.

Kelly smiled. 'Just what I always wanted.'

The man at the door looked familiar, but it was only when he was taking her to the lift that she realized where she had seen him before. That morning. On the racecourse, with Nick.

The doors of the lift closed behind her.

'Where's the press conference?' she said, as calmly as she was able.

The man looked at her coldly. 'Ain't no conference for you,' he said as the lift descended. 'You goin' on a trip.'

Kelly reached for the alarm button, but the man grabbed her hand and pushed it away contemptuously. He opened his jacket, like a man showing off the designer label on his suit. There was no label, only a dark leather shoulder holster containing a neat, black pistol.

'This is crazy,' said Kelly quietly. 'You'll never get away with it.'

'Wanna bet?' the man said as the lift came to a stop. 'Looks to me like we're getting away with it.'

Now Kelly saw where they were heading. Below the stands, there was a car park used by the racecourse employees. It emerged by the main entrance on to the drive outside the course. The man in the suit pushed her out of the lift and, at that moment, a dark, anonymous Chevrolet swept round the corner and pulled to a halt in front of her. The back door opened. Placing a hand on the top of her head like a cop bundling a criminal into his car, the man pushed her in and leapt in the front passenger seat. The Chevvy set off for the exit.

'Stupid.' Nick Morley, now in dark glasses, was in the back seat. He shook his head uncomprehendingly. 'So stupid.'

As they approached the way out of the underground car park and the Chevvy slowed down, Kelly lunged for the door. As she did so the man in the suit turned, brandishing a gun.

'Forget it,' he said calmly. Nick stared straight ahead.

They emerged from the car park; the main road was no more than fifty yards ahead but to reach it the car would have to pass the principal gate out of the course through which racegoers were leaving early to beat the traffic. Kelly sat forward in her seat, turning her face to the window.

Too late, Nick realized what she was doing. 'Sit back!' he hissed.

A middle-aged woman attempting to cross the road recognized her and shouted, 'Yo, Kelly, you did it!' and tapped on the window. Now Kelly could see a group of shabbily-dressed men, some of them with cameras, standing by the entrance. They looked in her direction – and started running for their cars.

'Shit.' The driver was trapped behind a stretch limo that was dawdling its way past the entrance. Kelly looked back and saw two, three, maybe four cars pulling out behind them.

Journalists. Kelly realized that her image as a publicity-shy star, the Great Garbo of the racetrack, had offered her a lifeline. Some pressmen, sensing that she might try to leave the racecourse without subjecting herself to their questions, had staked out the main entrance and were now in pursuit.

One car Morley's wheelman might have lost in the Washington traffic, maybe even two, but there was no way that he could shake off the pack that was now following them.

'Act normal,' Nick told the driver. 'Go to the Washington Park, We'll lose the journalists and leave by a back entrance.'

Kelly looked across at him. 'Why?'

The man in the passenger seat whirled round angrily. 'Don't say a fucking word,' he snapped.

'No,' said Nick, like a man under deep hypnosis. 'Don't say a word.'

Until that moment Kelly had been more angry than truly afraid. Now she was terrified.

At the Washington Park, there were more journalists waiting in the lobby. Kelly was about to scream when Nick forced his hand over her mouth and bundled her to a door at the rear, while the two goons made it look as if they were all just playing a game. As Kelly was taken upstairs the back way, Nick reappeared to explain to the journalists that she was tired but would hold a press conference in thirty minutes' time at five fifteen. Before they could ask any questions, he had collected her key and was in the lift heading to her room on the fifth floor. With cool professionalism, members of the hotel staff prevented the press from advancing beyond the lobby.

'Here's what we're going to do.' Nick double-locked the door to her room after the two thugs had left, took off his dark glasses and sat easily in a chair. Kelly had no doubt that he was armed. 'We wait here for ten minutes. I take you down the way we came in and out the back to where the car and my friends will be waiting. You go with them. I'll catch up with you later.'

Kelly looked at him. The light curtains were drawn but the early evening sun shone in, giving his deathly pale complexion an odd luminosity.

'You're mad, Nick,' she said. 'You've been seen with me. If anything happens to me now, you're up to your neck in it.'

Nick shook his head. 'I brought you back here. You told me you wanted to be left alone for a few minutes. I came down to tell the press that you might be delayed. I went back up and you were gone.' He shrugged. 'Anyway, my credibility is perfect. I'm in charge of security at the Jockey Club, I'm a former army officer.' He smiled wanly. 'I'm an Englishman.'

'Just tell me why.' Kelly was close to tears but she sensed that the longer she could keep him talking, the greater the chance that Annie would arrive. She would know that something was wrong the moment she realized that Kelly had left the course without seeing her and without her gear.

'I told you.' There was no trace of regret in Nick's voice. 'If the Sheikh gets out of English racing, I have an escape route. If you hadn't won, I was all set up. If – '

'Maybe he'll go anyway.'

Nick shook his head. 'He's staying and anyway, you know too much.' He sounded weary rather than bitter. 'It would have been so easy. I'd make a killing from inside deals on the sale of his horses and set up in France.' He looked at Kelly almost tenderly. 'We could have been happy, you know.'

'We?'

'I thought you might come with me. We would have been good together.' He smiled. 'Kelly Morley, champion international jockey – it sounds good.'

Kelly realized now that he was insane. She laughed humourlessly. 'I may be ambitious but I'd rather die than marry a dealer in dope, a murderer.'

'I'm not really a murderer. Your father was never meant to die. It was a mistake. I told Jack Butler's boys only to frighten him but one of them hit him a bit hard. Of course, he was an old jockey and his skull must have been thin.' He ignored the look of cold hatred that Kelly directed at him. 'And it wasn't going to be drugs from now on. There's more money in weapons. Ibn Fayoud gave me some contacts in Libya. The boys had the money for it. Shipping highclass mares around the globe was going to be the ideal cover.'

'And now you're going to kill me.'

'I loved you.' He moved close to Kelly as she sat on the bed and for a moment she thought he was going to kiss her. 'I would have done anything for you.'

Then something behind her seemed to attract his attention. He looked up, then back at her, as if torn by a moment of indecision. 'Don't move,' he said quietly.

At first, Kelly thought that it was a journalist who had somehow penetrated the hotel's security cordon, but then she realized that Nick was looking over her shoulder towards the balcony, out of the window.

It seemed to happen in a fraction of a second. Nick dived for the window, through the curtains, turning as he went so that his back shattered the glass. Against the evening sun, she saw the silhouette of Nick and a balding man in a light suit struggling. One of them was pushed back against the edge of the balcony and, at the moment when he began to topple backwards into the void, there was a muffled shot. Suddenly there was only one man left on the balcony. Slowly Nick turned towards her.

He stepped carefully through the shattered window and, as he smiled at her, she saw the small circle of red on his white shirt slightly to the left of his regimental tie.

'I loved you,' he said softly, before crumpling to the ground.

It was two hours before the police had finished with her, and now she sat in Annie's hotel room, pale and shocked.

'We must ring Bill, Cy,' she said quietly. 'They'll be free soon.'

'Later,' said Annie.

And Kelly sat, as Annie placed an arm round her shoulder and spoke soothingly about a future of horses and races and winners and no death. Free – now Kelly was free too.

'I can't understand,' she said yet again.

'Don't try. It's all over.'

Kelly thought of all the threats, the murders which had happened because of one man's restless unhappiness with what the world had to offer him. Maybe it had all been worth it. A trade in drugs, in weapons, in human misery had been terminated. Maybe she had been wrong, all those weeks ago, when she had said to Nick Morley – the late Nick Morley – that there was no end to evil, that wrongdoing would be there as long as there was greed in the world. Maybe it had all been worth it. Maybe.

At ten past eight, Margaret Stanhope, sitting alone in the bar at the Holiday Inn, sensed that it had all gone wrong.

She looked at her watch. She had given Donnell an extra forty minutes which, for a man of his precision, was more than enough.

She stretched her legs, carefully watching a group of three men who were deep in conversation at a corner table. Villains. Washington or the Wirral – she could tell a villain anywhere. Her hand smoothed down her skirt; she crossed her legs. The older fat one was calling the shots, the bald one was neither here nor there, but the younger guy, the one with the long dark hair – he was where tomorrow's power would reside.

Margaret stood up, draining her tequila. It was good to be a survivor. So the little Connor girl would live to ride her racehorses while she, sauntering now across the barroom of the Holiday Inn, would go back to riding her luck. Horses or luck. When it came to true future success – a Tudor mansion in the suburbs, a holiday home in Florida, servants, money like it didn't matter – Margaret knew where hers would be. The man with the dark hair looked up at her. She gave him her smile. Her best, winning smile.

'Hi,' she said.

STUD POKER

Acknowledgement

The author is grateful to Terence Blacker for his help in the preparation of this manuscript.

Inspiration and information for the poker scenes in *Stud Poker* came from Anthony Holden's superb *Big Deal*, (Bantam Books, 1991).

Chapter
1

Like most jockeys' valets, Jim Wilson could read racecourse rumour like a professional gambler could read a racecard. He knew what was true and what was bullshit. He knew the young jockeys who would still be in the weighing-room in ten years' time and those who would fade into obscurity after a season or two – or, as in most cases, a ride or two. He knew who was drinking, who was fighting a losing battle with the scales, who was in the pocket of the bookmakers. And, of course, he knew whose nerve had gone. There was something in the eyes of a jockey in those moments after he had weighed out for a novice chase and was waiting to be called to the paddock.

So when Jim Wilson, on a cold wet November morning, trudged through the car park at Plumpton racecourse carrying a suitcase full of breeches and saw Alex Drew sitting alone in his Audi Convertible with what appeared to be a fur coat on his lap, staring palely into space, he added the information to his vast storehouse of unofficial racing knowledge.

'Morning, Lex,' he called out, but Alex had seemed not to hear.

Jim glanced at his watch. Eleven-thirty. He was surprised to see Alex at the racecourse so early. His first ride was not until the fourth race and, until recently, he'd been one of the cool ones, turning up as late as possible in his flash car, exuding all the confidence of the young and talented.

Until recently. Wilson looked back at the Audi, parked in the far corner of the jockeys' car park. This season, something had happened to Alex. Two years ago, he had been no more than just another claiming jockey, an amateur with ambition. Last year, he had turned professional and a combination of luck – Ron Charlesworth's stable jockey had broken his leg in the first month of the season – and talent had marked him out as a possible future champion jockey. He had ridden over fifty winners, including a breathtaking success in the Champion Two Mile Chase at the National Hunt Festival on a horse of reckless brilliance called Spurgloss. Few, if any, of the top jockeys would have won on him.

But now something was wrong in the life of Alex Drew. Muttering to himself, the valet walked on to the racecourse, dismissing thoughts of Alex from his mind. Jockeys came, jockeys went. Promise turned to failure. It was life.

'He's gone.' Alex pulled back the mink coat and touched the blonde head that was resting on his lap.

'I was just beginning to enjoy it down there,' said Zena Wentworth, sitting up and checking her hair in the rear view mirror.

'Sorry.' Alex smiled palely. 'Jim's a bit of an old gossip. It's best to be careful.'

'Don't tell me jockeys aren't meant to be seen with girls before a race.' Zena put a well-manicured hand on Alex's thigh.

'Don't be daft.' Alex allowed a hint of irritation to enter his voice. Girls. That was a laugh. Zena Wentworth had stopped being a girl some time ago. In fact, even when she was a girl, to judge by some of the stories she had told him, she was doing wild, womanly things. 'It's just that talking to an owner's wife in the corner of the car park – people might misunderstand.'

'Spare rides?'

'Something like that.' A car drove by and parked some way in front of them. Two jockeys emerged, took their bags from the boot and walked briskly towards the racecourse entrance. 'Perhaps you had better tell me the message you've been asked to give me.'

'That won't take long,' she said. 'Just make sure that Dig For Glory doesn't win the handicap hurdle.'

'They've told me that already.'

'Something about keeping him on the inner, would that be it?'

Alex nodded. 'No problem. Paul always stays glued to the rails and I'll be on his outside making sure he can't squeeze his way through.'

'Make certain he comes unstuck.'

'Easy,' Alex said sarcastically. Of all the people in the world, Paul Raven was the one he wanted least to cut up on the rails – he was Alex's best friend. 'Piece of cake.'

Zena ran a hand up his thigh. 'It's only one race,' she said softly. 'No need to look so miserable.'

'I've been wasting,' Alex said. 'I have to do ten two in the last.'

'Ten to what?' said Zena, a coquettish smile playing on her lips as her hand came to rest. She raised a well-plucked eyebrow. 'You seem to be a bit overweight there, Alex,' she said, slipping down in the seat and pulling her mink coat over her head.

'Not . . . now.' But what he had intended as a protest came out as a sigh. Life had been saying 'Not now' to Zena for several years but, even at the age of forty-three, with the evidence of too many good times written clearly on her face, she had refused to listen. She wanted it now, she had never been good at waiting. While other women faced middle age with careers or children, Zena extended her competence exclusively in the area that she understood. Pleasure, taken and given. That – Alex looked down as the fur coat undulated like an animal stirring after a long sleep – yes, that she understood all too well.

A mere twelve months ago, he would have laughed at the idea of a secret assignation with an owner's wife in a car park at Plumpton. The idea of submitting to the eager caresses of Zena Wentworth would have been absurd, but not as crazy as the notion that he would stop Paul winning a race. Closing his eyes and gasping, Alex tried to forget his lost innocence, to think of this afternoon's last race, which he would win. The fur came to rest.

'That should help your weight problem,' said Zena, sitting up, daintily dabbing at the corners of her mouth with a long finger.

'I'd better go.'

'Fine.'

She checked her face in the mirror, saying, 'Do I look like a woman who's just had sex in the car park?'

Alex glanced at her. Zena Wentworth always looked like a woman who had just had sex in the car park. 'You look the perfect owner's wife,' he said.

'Thank you, jockey.' Zena opened the door and got out. 'I'll see you in the paddock.'

'Old Lex is here a bit early today, isn't he?'

Jim Wilson, limping slightly from the back injury that, twenty years ago, had ended an unpromising career as a jockey, laid out breeches, boots and colours in the weighing-room.

'Lex?' Paul Raven smiled. He was glad that he had Jim for a valet. Not only was he reliable, but he was a purveyor of the latest, twenty-two carat gossip – rarely malicious, but often useful. His only irritating habit, that of using the one nickname you didn't like, Paul found almost endearing.

'Yeah, Sexy Lexy. Sitting in his motor in the car park like he's in a fucking trance. Bit early, isn't he?'

Paul shrugged, recognizing the gentle probe of a professional gossip. 'Maybe he's got a spare ride in the first.' He sipped at the half-cup of sweet tea which, however light he had to ride that day, he would drink about an hour before his first race. He was worried about Alex – normally they travelled to the races together but today he had made some excuse and driven from Lambourn alone – but he was not about to discuss it all with Jim.

He looked up at the weighing-room clock. It was time to change. Unlike Alex, who took a cavalier attitude to routine, Paul liked order in his life, particularly on race days. He would arrive well on time, walk onto the course to check the going, have his cup of tea and stay in the weighing-room until it was time to weigh out for his first ride. It wasn't that he felt superior to the drifters and hangers-on who liked to pass the time with jockeys, simply that he preferred to concentrate on the job ahead.

He was riding Tidy Item in the second race, a novice hurdle. The horse had a chance if it remembered that it wasn't running on the flat any more and that there were eight hurdles to negotiate. He'd ride Dig For Glory in the handicap hurdle, a dream ride but a little lacking in speed. The guv'nor, Ron Charlesworth, was confident, in that gloomy, monosyllabic way of his, although Alex's mount, Big Mac, was also in with a chance. Then, in the last, all being well, he was due to ride a novice chaser trained by a permit holder who, after it had fallen twice under its regular jockey, had decided to use Paul. The joker in the pack. Still, there was a touch of class about the horse and there was nothing else of note in the race. If he could get it round safely it ought to win. Maybe he'd ride a treble.

That perhaps was Paul's secret. Every time he received a leg-up on to a horse in the paddock, whatever its form, whatever the competition, he believed it would win. This steely confidence, which older, more battered jockeys would call crazy optimism, helped earn him a growing reputation among trainers, and thirty-three winners last season. While others would accept less promising rides – the dodgy jumper in the last, for example – thinking only of the fee and survival, Paul saw each as another potential winner.

A tall man entered the weighing-room, his expensive tweed suit, the bag he was carrying and his general air of unease marking him out as an amateur. You could always tell the guys who were doing it for fun. Big and soft-skinned, it was as if they belonged to different species from the wiry, weather-beaten, professionals. Their gear was new; they fussed about with their silks and made frequent trips to the lavatory.

At first, Paul had assumed Alex Drew would be like that – a privileged, public school wally with a foppish hairstyle that came straight out of *Brideshead Revisited*. Paul remembered the first time he had seen him. It had been an early season meeting at Fontwell and Alex, who was riding in an amateur race, had behaved as if he had been walking in and out of weighing rooms for years, joking with the valets, chatting with the older jockeys with an easy, disrespectful charm. Paul had taken an instant dislike to him, had even permitted himself a smile when Alex's horse turned over at the last when challenging for the lead. Alex walked away, cursing, but back in the weighing room, bruised and mud-spattered, he was soon back on song, as if he couldn't wait for his next ride.

There was something else that had been different about Alex Drew; the way he rode. He was better than any amateur Paul had ever seen. On form, his horse – Paul couldn't remember the name – had no chance, and the cocky little bastard had taken him along easily at the back of the field, keeping the more fancied horses in his sights, unflustered by the ridiculous early pace, making his move with all the coolness of an experienced professional. At the last fence, he had been upsides but struggling, so he'd taken a gamble, asking his horse to stand off outside the wings and win rather than fiddle the fence and take second place. It hadn't paid off and Alex had taken a bone-crunching fall. But Paul was impressed. Judgement and nerve – it was rare to find those in a young amateur.

'Morning, Mr Wenty,' Jim Wilson called out to the tall man who had sat down and seemed uncertain what to do next. He smiled thinly at the valet. 'Clay, please, Jim,' he said.

'Right, Cleggy,' said Jim, bringing Paul his breeches and winking. 'How many rides have we got today?'

'Just the one. Skinflint in the fourth.'

Now Paul knew who he was. Mr Clay Wentworth, claiming seven pounds, successful property developer, unsuccessful amateur jockey, son of Sir Denis Wentworth who had last season bought Skinflint as a present for his son – a touching family gesture that had landed one of the best chasers in the country with one of the worst jockeys. It was a waste but, in racing as in life, money talked.

Paul drained his cup of tea. It was time to get changed. As he checked his weight on the weighing-room scales, he became aware that Clay Wentworth was watching him.

'Nice horse, that Dig For Glory.' To Paul, the son of a brickie in Wigan, Wentworth's voice jarred. Nasal and authoritative, it belonged in the paddock or the members' bar, not here among the professionals.

'He's not bad,' he said, returning to where his clothes were. To his annoyance,

Clay Wentworth followed him. The last thing he needed before a race was small talk, particularly with a man he didn't know.

'Fancy your chances?'

It was the apparently innocent question which all jockeys are asked. He shrugged. 'We've got as much chance as anyone,' he said.

'Thought of buying him once.' Wentworth opened a silver cigarette case which he waved, with a seigneurial gesture, in Paul's direction. Paul shook his head. 'We weren't sure he stayed the trip.'

'Oh yeah?'

'Needs holding up, they say.'

'Do they?' Paul smiled coldly. 'Thanks for the advice.'

As a general rule, cocaine and Plumpton Racecourse do not go together. Champagne at the bar: of course. Benzedrine in the weighing-room: perhaps. But a line of pure white powder inhaled through a rolled-up fifty pound note in the ladies' lavatory: no, not at Plumpton.

It was unusual, but then the presence of a moneyed pleasure-seeker like Zena Wentworth at a damp and modest National Hunt racecourse was in itself unusual. Zena needed something to help get her through an afternoon spent out of doors in the company of rat-faced men, large women with too much make-up, and horses. She was, by nature and inclination, a high-flyer and sometimes she needed help to fly as high as she liked to be.

Brisk and bright-eyed, Zena re-entered the bar, where a group of her friends were drinking champagne.

'Better, darling?' Lol Calloway, a former pop star who, even now that he was bald and pot-bellied, was occasionally recognized on the street by an ageing fan, gave her a knowing leer. 'Powder your nose all right, did you?'

His wife, Suzie, giggled.

'I just felt a little bit woozy,' Zena explained to a woman in a sheepskin coat who was sitting uneasily with them. The woman smiled politely. Owners were the worst part of training, Ginnie Matthews had decided some time ago, but since Clay Wentworth had brought something of a fan club with him, it had seemed ungracious to refuse the offer of a glass of champagne before the first race.

'D'you get nervous when Clay is riding?' she asked Zena.

'Not on Skinflint. He's as safe as houses, isn't he?'

'Almost.' Ginnie smiled, thinking that Clay Wentworth was capable of wrestling any horse to the ground, however safe.

'Zena's just a bit highly strung, aren't you?' A woman in her thirties with dark, cascading hair smiled at Zena. 'She has a lot on her mind, don't you, darling?' Alice Markwick smiled discreetly. She liked Zena, her sense of fun, the sparkle she brought even to a grey afternoon at a God-forsaken racetrack; the way, when she was in a really good mood, she let Alice sleep with her. Yes, she was fun.

'Look,' Zena trilled, pointing out of the window as the runners for the first race filed out of the paddock. 'Horses!'

'Did you have to get wired?' Clay Wentworth muttered as, a dark blue coat over his silks, he sat down with the group. 'Couldn't you stay straight for one after-noon?'

'I was nervous. There's so much riding on this.'

'Did you see Drew?'

'Yup.' Zena smiled at her husband, her eyes sparkling. 'He knows exactly what he has to do.'

'A winner for me, a loser for Paul Raven.' Wentworth lit a cigarette and inhaled deeply. 'Just what the doctor ordered.'

Racing journalists had taken to describing Paul Raven as 'cool', 'dispassionate', and 'machine-like' and it was true that, beside the sport's more extrovert charac-ters, he might have seemed taciturn, possibly even dull. If you dressed him up in a suit and put him on the 8.20 from Surbiton to Waterloo, he would pass for a young, good-looking articled clerk on his way to work in the City.

Paul didn't care. To him, riding horses was a job, a way to escape the harsh poverty of his family background. As the other lads at Ron Charlesworth's yard could testify, he had a quiet, wry sense of humour and, unlike other jockeys on the brink of success, he was prepared to help the newer lads in the yard, giving them advice, intervening on their behalf when they were on the receiving end of Ron Charlesworth's icy disapproval.

He knew what it was like to be an outsider, to be starting on the lowest rung of the ladder in one of the harshest sports in the world. Like any large stable yard, Ron Charlesworth's had its hierarchy, its harsh traditions. Charlesworth himself, a tall, trim man with the cold, blue eyes of an executioner, was pitilessly ambi-tious – his horses and the men he paid to ride them were no more than part of a career plan.

His head lad, Jimmy Summers, a wiry Scotsman with a legendary temper, under-stood his boss as well as anyone. In racing, there was no gain without pain and Jimmy was an expert at ensuring that the lads under his care – particularly the teenagers stupid enough to think that shovelling horse-shit and riding out in sub-zero temperatures was the road to stardom – understood all about pain.

Watched by a handful of racegoers including the Wentworth party in the Members' Bar, Paul rode Tidy Item onto the racecourse.

'He's in great form; you could win this, you know, Paul.' Bill, one of the older lads, chattered away as he led the horse out. 'Just need to give him a view of the hurdles, hold him up, he's got the speed and . . .'

Paul turned out, as Bill told him yet again what he already knew. Tidy Item, a lightly-framed bay four-year-old, already had a great future behind him. In his first season as a two-year-old, he had won a decent race at Goodwood. The following year, his Timeform rating had plummeted and, by the end of the season, he had won only a moderate handicap over a mile and a half at Nottingham. As if aware that appearing in a novice hurdle at Plumpton, a gelding, was hardly what was expected of a horse of his breeding, Tidy Item had a listless look about him, his coat was stary and dull. For the first time today, he was wearing blinkers.

'Cheers, Bill.' As the lad released him Paul turned and cantered down to the start.

Tidy Item had a long, rangy stride which made him an easy ride on the flat. It was the hurdles which bothered him. The first couple of times Paul had schooled him at home, he hadn't had a clue what to do, hurling himself at them in panic. These days, he took the marginally safer course of galloping straight through them, often losing lengths in a race, shattering the hurdles as he went. Getting in close and fiddling a hurdle was something Tidy Item knew nothing of.

But he could win. 'Try jumping them this time, fella,' Paul muttered as he showed the horse the first flight, patting him on the neck. His seven years riding racehorses had convinced him that the best way of getting winners was the quiet way: settle them, relax, let the other jockeys scream and swear. Riding Tidy Item over hurdles might be like surviving eight earthquakes but, when he wasn't kicking bits of timber into the air, he was a good ride. Yes, he would win. Paul was confident.

The race followed the pattern Paul had anticipated. A couple of horses set a smart pace which had several runners, bred less aristocratically than Tidy Item, off the bit from the start.

Paul allowed Tidy Item to dawdle near the back of the field tight on the inside rail, a position which gave him little view of the hurdles but since even if the horse had the entire racetrack to himself he would crash through every flight, taking him the shortest way made sense.

Despite destroying six flights of hurdles, Tidy Item entered the straight at the back of the leading group still on the bridle. Paul let the leaders run off the bend and then let him run through smartly on the inner. He was going so easily it was almost embarrassing. As if sensing that the unpleasant experience of smashing timber at speed was soon to be over, Tidy Item lengthened his stride approaching the last hurdle and, by his standards, jumped the last well, diving through it a foot above the turf, and actually made ground doing it. Paul didn't even have to ride him out, as he won pulling the proverbial cart.

'Cocky bastard,' Dave Cartwright, who had ridden the second horse, called out as they trotted back having pulled up. No one, even at Plumpton, likes another jockey to get up their inside. 'You could have won that by ten lengths.'

'Somebody's got to ride them.' Paul trotted on. He didn't care what other jockeys, or journalists, or lads or even Ron Charlesworth said to him.

He had won it; and that was what mattered.

The bastard was cool. Clay Wentworth sipped the one bucks fizz he allowed himself on days when he was riding and watched a TV screen on which, in silent slow motion, Tidy Item was once again being gathered up after his mistake at the last hurdle.

'So *cheeky*.' Zena's voice, like a distant mocking soundtrack, penetrated Clay's thoughts. 'Why don't you try and win like that, darling?'

He smiled wanly without taking his eyes from the screen. For a moment, he had managed to forget that, in a little over an hour, he would be riding Skinflint. 'Maybe I will,' he said.

Where did it come from, the coolness, the poise, that converted the will to win into the ability to win? Nobody wanted to win races more than Clay Wentworth did but his determination was panicky and ineffective. Whereas jockeys like Paul

Raven looked in a finish as if they were part of the horse, its powerhouse, he flapped about like a duck landing on ice with a broken wing. Occasionally his horse won a race but it was always in spite of his efforts, not because of them.

'Clay's psyching himself up,' Lol Calloway was saying to Zena and to Alice Markwick. 'It's like a big gig at Madison Square Garden. I'd get the band together and say "Guys, we're gonna fuckin' blow them away tonight, right?" They'd go, like punch the air, and say "Yeah, right, Lol!" Then, after I'd done a line and fucked a groupie, we'd go on like well psyched.'

At a nearby table, a local doctor and his wife, who liked an afternoon at the races, muttered poisonously to one another before draining their drinks and moving away.

He hated it, that was the truth. Clay Wentworth, never one for deep self-analysis, knew this at least. He hated the weighing-room where suddenly he was no longer the boss but some sort of junior. He hated the walk out to the paddock, the cold, the wet, the pervasive smell of horse shit and cigar smoke. He hated the moment he was given a leg-up, when he was left all by himself with the horse to canter down to the start. He hated circling round at the start, hearing the starters' roll-call – 'Mr Wentworth,' 'Sir.' He hated, Christ he hated, the moment when the field jumped off and there was no escape and the first fence, getting bigger and bigger, loomed up before him, the kick, the lurch, the shouts and curses all around him. After the first, it got better, particularly if he were riding Skinflint, but he never liked it, not until he was back among the racegoers, preferably in the winners' enclosure. There was nothing like the feel of the ground beneath his feet when he dismounted.

Clay took another sip of his drink. No, he sighed quietly to himself, he was not a natural.

That was what made Alex Drew the perfect patsy. The moment he had joined the Circle, playing poker like he rode horses – with style and bravado – Clay had known what had to be done. They needed someone who rode as a professional, competent enough to stop another horse, straight enough to keep himself out of the stewards' room, weak enough to bend under pressure.

Alex discovered that poker is not like racing, but he discovered too late. Nerve and skill are not enough. You have to know how to bluff, how to cheat, your every move must be informed by rat-like cunning and deception. That cheerful openness, which served him so well on the racecourse, had betrayed him at the table.

Zena had worried. What if someone got hurt? What if Alex's career was destroyed? Clay had frowned as if considering the moral options. There was no reason for things to go wrong. The risks were as low as the stakes were high.

He smiled. It was a lie, of course – as big a bluff as he had ever played at the table. If someone's career hit the rocks, he was certain it would be Alex's. If someone's body paid the price of Clay's ambition, there was no better body than Alex's.

'Everything all right, Clay?' As usual, it was Alice who understood better than anyone what was going through his head. Her dark, smoky voice carried concern but Clay was aware that there was nothing personal there. Alice's concern was always financial.

'He's thinking about his race, ain't you, Clay?' said Lol Calloway. 'Trying to decide whether to sneak up on the rails like the last winner or to take it easy and win by ten lengths.'

'Of course,' said Alice. 'It's a big day, isn't it?'

Clay Wentworth nodded. 'Yes, it's a big day.'

Paul Raven had never known Alex like this. In the early days, he had distrusted Alex's high spirits, his ability to make a joke even when things were going badly. Alex was an amateur when they had first met and it was as if the years of money and privilege had come bubbling to the surface in an excess of optimism and good humour.

Three years later, he knew better. Joking had been Alex's way of dealing with stress. Once he was in the saddle and the flag went down, he was a different person. It seemed odd now that it was Paul who was doing the talking before the fourth race, as Alex sat, pale and distracted, like a man facing a death sentence.

'That Tidy Item's going to bury me one day,' Paul said. 'When they send him chasing, the ride is yours.'

Alex didn't reply. He wanted it to be over, or at least to explain to Paul before it was too late and explanations were superfluous.

It was unusual for them both to be riding for Ron Charlesworth in the same race. Ron was good at placing his horses and, unless he was giving one of them an easy ride, or a fancied runner needed a pacemaker, he avoided sending out two runners to compete for one prize. This two-and-a-half-mile handicap hurdle had been intended for Freeze Frame, Alex's ride. It was only when the weights had been announced, allotting Dig For Glory an absurdly generous ten stone three, that Dig For Glory had been included. He needed the race to be fully fit but his owner Lady Faircroft had been anxious to see him run. Reluctantly, Ron had agreed.

The two jockeys sat together, having weighed out, the brickie's son and the former amateur, one dark and wiry, the other with the cherubic, long-haired look of an overgrown schoolboy. They were an unlikely couple.

'What's the problem then, Alex?' Paul asked. 'Anybody would think you were nervous or something.'

'You must be joking.' Alex tried a smile, but it was an unconvincing effort. 'I'm fine.'

With anyone else, Paul might have suspected normal jockey problems – money, weight, an unhealthily close association with bookmakers – but he knew Alex, for all his wild talk, was too sensible for that.

'Just tell me if I can help, that's all.'

Alex looked at him oddly. 'Thanks, Paul,' he said.

The bell sounded for jockeys out.

'Paddock, jockeys.' A bowler-hatted official stood at the door and the riders for the fourth race at Plumpton filed out to make their way to the paddock.

'Good luck, boys,' said Jim Wilson.

'Cheers, Jim,' said Paul.

Alex said nothing.

Chapter 2

Peter Zametsky had thought he was getting used to the English way of doing things. He had sat in pubs where Londoners gathered to complain about life. He had travelled by underground where they stared ahead of them, not acknowledging the existence of other human beings despite being pressed up against them in a position of forced intimacy. He had been to a football match where they stood up and swore at one another. He had visited a church on Christmas morning where they had seemed ill at ease except when booming out tuneless versions of the carols.

But nothing had prepared him for a betting shop.

There was a reverence here which had not been evident in the church. Through the pall of cigarette smoke, under the bright strip lighting, men – and just a few women – were staring, staring upwards as if praying for a miracle. Some held slips of paper in their hands; others were seated in front of newspapers. Around the room were television screens which were showing some sort of dog race. The murmur of a commentary could be heard, but Peter understood little of what was being said, although certain numbers seemed to be repeated like a mantra.

'Go, on, number three.' A tall West Indian, standing in front of Peter, was muttering. 'Go on, my son.'

'Excuse me, sir.' Peter was unsure of the procedure on these occasions, but his three years in England had taught him that no one helped you unless you asked first. 'To place a bet?'

The man seemed to be suffering from some kind of attack. 'Yes,' he said, occasionally looking away from the television screen as if the mystery unfolding there was too much for him to take. 'Yes, my son. *Here* he comes.'

As Peter waited patiently for an answer, the man gave a sort of moan and then, with intense loathing, balled the piece of paper he had been holding and threw it onto the floor in a gesture of terminal despair. 'Bastard,' he said.

'Where to place a bet, please?'

As if coming out of a trance, the man turned his bloodshot, tear-stained eyes in Peter's direction and burped. Peter, a small bespectacled man in his thirties, with thinning hair and a dreary suit, moved through the crowd of punters.

'To bet?' he asked an elderly woman who was staring into space. She nodded over her shoulder. 'Over there,' she said.

Peter made his way to a counter at the back of the shop.

'In the two-thirty at Plumpton,' he said nervously to a plump girl behind the counter. 'I'm wanting . . .'

'Slip,' said the girl. As Peter frowned helplessly, she pushed a piece of paper across the counter. 'Fill it in,' she said loudly. 'Comprende?'

Peter found an empty corner in the betting-shop and sat down on a stool. There was a small, slightly chewed biro on the ledge in front of him which he looked at, as if it were a specimen in the lab, before picking it up. 'How is it, Peter,' his wife used to say, 'that in some things you are so brilliant, in others so completely foolish with your frown and so innocent eyes?' Klima was right: at work, Peter was almost masterful, as he sat at his bench, crouched over a microscope or tapping easily at his computer. It was real life that caused him problems.

He looked up at a screen. Four to one. He was not by nature a gambler but he had confidence in his work. Carefully, he wrote on the betting slip. 'FREEZE FRAME – £100 (win), Plumpton, 2.30', adding as an afterthought, 'Ridden by A. Drew'.

Once you're in the saddle, it's just another job of work. From his earliest days as an amateur, Alex had learnt to exclude the personal from his race-riding. Cheerful and outgoing before the race, the chat and the jokes were put on hold as soon as he was in the paddock. As for the other jockeys, they were no longer friends or enemies but simply part of the job. It was the two-ride-a-week merchants that were the trouble. Most of them were all over the place in a race, just like weekend drivers. It was beyond some of them to ride in a straight line, which when you're doing fifty miles an hour towards a fence doesn't make life easy, especially when the horse you're riding doesn't jump very well. As for the bends, well, if you were foolish enough to be on the girth of one of them there, then you deserved whatever happened.

Those were relevant considerations; character – friendship, in particular – needed to be forgotten until after the race.

And yet. Cantering down to the start, Alex watched the orange and black colours of Mrs T. Farquhar, worn by Paul on Dig For Glory some five lengths in front of him. And other images of Paul flashed before his eyes – the quiet lad at Charlesworth's yard taken for granted by everyone, the workaholic, the jockey glancing across at him as they raced knee to knee on the Lambourn downs, helping him to polish up his riding, the friend who was always the first to say well done when he rode a winner and most important, the one who always came to make sure he was all right after a fall. On paper, there was little to separate Freeze Frame and Dig For Glory although, given the choice, Alex would have chosen Paul's horse, a big five-year-old whose inconsistent form last season due to weakness had ensured that he was well down in the weights. Dig For Glory had developed over the summer months and, even though the ground had been firmer than he liked, he had run promisingly in a two-mile handicap hurdle at Leicester. The soft ground and the extra half-mile at Plumpton would suit him. Under normal circumstances, Alex would have fancied Paul's chances.

They pulled up at the start and Paul glanced across at Freeze Frame, who was sweating up slightly. 'He looks well,' he said quietly.

Alex smiled, patting Freeze Frame. The horse was small and a brilliant jumper but he lacked finishing speed. Ron Charlesworth's instructions had been to lie up

with the leaders and make the best of his way home from three flights out but –
Alex felt a wave of nausea as he remembered the task before him – today he had
other priorities.

'Where are you going?' he asked.

Paul looked at him, surprised. If there was anyone in the world who knew that
he always rode his races from the inside, hugging the rails, it was Alex.

'Guess,' he said.

'There are some bad jumpers in the field.' Alex tried to sound casual. 'I'd keep
him out of trouble on the outside.'

Paul grinned. 'Nice try, Alex,' he said. It was at that moment, as the jockeys circled around the starter, that Paul realized that, for some reason, this race was not
like all the others. He couldn't put his finger on it, but something wasn't right.
Everything seemed the same as normal – the other jockeys chatting, the sound in
the distance of the racecourse loudspeaker, but something was different.

'Smith.' The starter's voice was briskly military.

'Sir.'

'Drew.'

'Sir.'

It was Alex, that's what was different. He had sensed it on the gallops, in the
yard – that look of a man haunted by something stronger than ambition or friendship, but it had never happened on a racecourse before.

'Raven.'

Keep him out of trouble. What had Alex meant, what was he trying to say?

'*Raven.*'

'Sir.'

'Wake up, we haven't got all day.'

The starter, still grumbling, mounted the steps and brought them under orders.
Paul took up a position directly behind Happy Fella, who usually made the running. As the tape rose and one or two of the jockeys slapped their horses down the
shoulder, helping them into their stride, Paul banished all thoughts of Alex from
his mind and concentrated on the race before him.

The race was a good one, considering the state of the ground, and, by the time
the field streamed past the stands with two circuits to go there were one or two
struggling to lay up. Dig For Glory was going easily in sixth place, some eight
lengths behind the leaders. Paul looked at the horses ahead of him and noticed
with some surprise that Freeze Frame was not among them. As they turned away
from the stands, Alex loomed up beside him, on a tight rein.

Paul looked over. 'They're not hanging about. I hope I'm going this well next
time around.'

'So do I.'

By the time they'd completed another circuit, the pace had slowed considerably,
Paul had Dig For Glory precisely where he wanted him, in fifth place on the rails
with the leaders, including Freeze Frame, well within striking distance and that
was where he stayed as they raced down the hill on the far side for the last time.
A good jump at the third last took Dig For Glory even closer. All four jockeys in
front of him were now pushing hard for home, and Paul began to niggle at Dig

For Glory. The ground and the pace were taking their toll and Paul wasn't certain Dig For Glory's stamina would see him home. As they rounded the bend and turned towards the finish, Alex and Freeze Frame looked beaten and Paul called to his stable companion to lay over and leave him the inner. Alex immediately pulled Freeze Frame to his right as Paul urged Dig For Glory through the gap. They were within two strides of taking off for the second last when Alex suddenly shut the door. Dig For Glory, whose heart was bigger than himself, was suddenly faced with a large, solid wood wing and instead of slamming on the brakes made a vain attempt to jump it. There was a sickening sound of splintering wood as horse and jockey went crashing through to the ground, where both now lay motionless.

'Dig For Glory, a faller at the second last.' The commentary from Plumpton to betting-shops throughout the land laconically recorded the facts without dwelling on the human drama behind them. 'Over the last it's Happy Fella and Sweet Charity with Freeze Frame getting into it. It's going to be close, they're all tired, but it looks like Freeze Frame's going to do it there at the line. Freeze Frame the winner. Happy Fella second. Sweet Charity third.'

Peter Zametsky stared at the slip of paper in his hand. It had worked. The one gamble in his life had paid off. He would buy Klima new shoes, perhaps a fridge, clothes for the baby. Yes, it had worked. Peter felt sick.

In a trance, he walked to the counter and passed the betting-slip to the teller.

'Not weighed in yet,' she said.

Peter frowned. 'Weighed in?'

The woman sighed. 'You wait five minutes. Then we give money and you go and don't come back, okay.' She turned to the young man sitting beside her at the counter. 'E's won £500 and doesn't even know what weighed in is.'

'Please,' Peter ignored the man standing behind him who was muttering impatiently. 'What happened to the jockey?'

'*Jockey*?' The woman leaned forward as if talking to a child. 'I expect he's very happy now. Celebrating, you know.'

'No, not him. Can we see the television again?' Peter pointed to a nearby screen on which, once again, greyhounds were racing. 'The other jockey. The one who fell. Is he all right?'

'What's he talking about?' the woman asked her colleague. 'Only races here, mate. Just winners and losers and odds, d'you understand?' She looked over his shoulder to the man behind him. 'Next.'

Only the ignorant or those greedy to collect their winnings hurried away from the grandstand after the two-thirty at Plumpton. The binoculars of most regular race-goers were trained on the second last flight where Dig For Glory and his jockey Paul Raven still lay motionless.

Alex was not the praying type. At a Christmas carol service, he might pray for a hat-trick on Boxing Day; the next day, perhaps he might pray that his modest turkey dinner wouldn't show up as overweight when he sat on the scales, but these were light-hearted, insurance prayers intended for any Superior Being who happened to be tuned in to him.

But he prayed now. 'Let him be all right,' he whispered as he trotted Freeze Frame past the stands, standing in his stirrups in an attempt to see what was happening down the course. 'Just let him be okay.'

An older jockey, Dermot O'Brien, who had finished way down the field, cantered up to him.

'Nice one, Alex,' he said, pulling down his goggles.

'Cheers, Dermot.' Alex smiled thinly. O'Brien was one of the old school, a tough Irishman who had broken every bone in his body and had little time for small talk or sentiment.

'Sure, I couldn't have done him better myself,' he added with a trace of admiration in his voice.

There was a subdued welcome at the winners' enclosure where, to Alex's surprise, he was met by Liz Charlesworth, the plump and apologetic wife of his trainer.

'Where's the guv'nor?' Alex asked, dismounting.

'On the course.' Even by her standards, Liz seemed distracted and unhappy. 'It doesn't look good.'

Bad news reaches the weighing-room fast. By the time Alex had weighed in and returned with his saddle, the word was out. An uneasy silence greeted him as he walked in.

Jim Wilson took his saddle, unusually avoiding his eyes.

'How's Paul?' asked Alex nervously.

The valet looked up at him accusingly. 'If he hasn't broken anything it'll be a miracle.'

'It was an accident,' Alex said quietly. 'He went for a gap that wasn't there.'

Dave Smart, whose horse Sweet Charity had finished third, stood in front of Alex. 'The gap was there. I was a couple of lengths behind him. You did him.'

Alex shook his head in weary denial.

'Some fucking friend,' Smart muttered, wiping the mud from his face with a towel.

Five long minutes later, one of the jockeys told Alex that his trainer needed to see him outside the weighing-room.

Ron Charlesworth was not an emotional man – love, regret, sadness and humour played an insignificant part in his life – but on the rare occasions when he was angry, it was plain for all to see. Although his voice remained as dry and precise as that of a solicitor reading out the details of a particularly unfavourable will, two vivid blotches of colour appeared high on his cheekbones, remaining there until the rage had subsided.

So, although he smiled at Alex as, with an arm around his shoulder, he led him to a corner away from the scales and the ever-alert ears of racing's gossip-mongers, Alex knew that he was in deep trouble.

'I should give you the fucking sack,' Charlesworth said quietly. 'You don't deserve a job in racing.'

'I've just ridden you a winner.'

'You've just killed one of my best horses.'

Alex looked at Charlesworth, expecting news of Paul from him.

'What were you playing at? Did you two have some sort of lovers' tiff? What the fuck's going on?'

Running a hand through his thick hair, Alex closed his eyes. 'How's Paul?' he asked.

'You're damned lucky they've got lenient stewards here. They're having an enquiry and it isn't going to look good and I ought to let you take what you deserve for this.' The trainer made no attempt to conceal the disapproval in his voice. He paused for a moment. 'Trouble is I'll lose the race if I tell them what I think, so I'll just say that the horse has a tendency to duck to his left and we'll stick to that.'

'It was an accident,' pleaded Alex, trying to convince himself more than Ron.

Charlesworth looked at him coldly. The normal pallor was slowly returning to his cheeks. 'I hope so – for your sake.'

'How's Paul?'

'Hospital.' Charlesworth shrugged as if another injured jockey was the least of his problems. 'You'd better get ready for the fourth. You're lucky I'm not jocking you off.'

Lucky. Alex felt the unluckiest man alive. As he returned to the weighing-room, the jockeys for the amateur race were being called out to the paddock.

The tall figure of Clay Wentworth loomed up before him. 'Well-ridden, Alex.' Although the voice was neutral, there was mockery in his expression.

Alex looked away, apparently muttering to himself. Only Clay Wentworth was close enough to hear the words, 'Debt repaid.'

Alex was just pulling on a new set of colours when he was called to the enquiry. As he watched the head-on of what he'd done to his best friend he felt sick. A jury could have found him guilty of attempted murder. The stewards took no action.

It was cold. It was wet. Something rather disgusting seemed to have become attached to the sole of her Gucci shoe. The noise in the Members' Bar was like feeding time at the zoo. The company at her table was neither intelligent nor attractive enough to be remotely interesting. She hated horses.

All in all, Alice Markwick had decided, National Hunt racing was not for her. She glanced at her watch. One more race – Clay's big moment – and she would be off. There was work to do back home. Then, later tonight, she would slip down to Heaven, her favourite club, to pick up someone soft and understanding. God knows, she deserved it.

Beside her, Zena was conducting a coke-fuelled monologue that had already covered a variety of topics including the excitement of the last race, except for what happened to that poor jockey who fell off, how she loved to go racing when Clay was riding, why she needed to buy some more clothes, a woozy reference to a night she had once spent with Alice, a discussion of how cocaine and champagne worked together, a scurrilous commentary on a group of men standing at the bar, her husband's obsession with work, a brief attack on that cold, sinister bastard her father-in-law, and some rather sordid story involving a jockey in the car park before the races.

Alice smiled at Zena, her thoughts miles away. The great advantage of substance abuse was that it required no effort from the other person. A woman on coke was her own best company, entirely self-sufficient. In her thirty-five years, Alice had learned that to make love to someone so wired that she was on another planet was a ghastly, monotonous, exhausting experience but, when it came to conversation, the stuff had its uses. Red-eyed, her chin working overtime, Zena would dribble on like a running tap until it wore off and she returned to the civilized world.

'There he goes,' Zena trilled, pointing to the racecourse where her husband was cantering down to the start on Skinflint. 'He's in the lead, Alice!'

'I don't think they've started yet.' Alice sighed. She was no expert but even she realized that, with one horse walking and another trotting, these were mere preliminaries.

'Haven't they?' Zena laughed girlishly, then covered her mouth. 'Where's Lol gone?'

Alice sighed. Even the short-term memory was going now. 'They've gone to watch the race from the course,' she said. 'Remember?'

'Aha, yup, right. *God . . .*' Zena looked wildly around the bar. 'They're so serious in here, why aren't they excited? *I'm* excited, and sort of nervous at the same time –'

It was a long way from Prague, Alice thought to herself, as Zena resumed her monologue. Yet even this, a grey afternoon at Plumpton, represented a new start. Alice was not nostalgic – she rarely looked back to the days when, as simple Alzbeta Flaishman, she had arrived from Czechoslovakia to make her life in London. After all, there were a few good memories, apart from the day when, by some act of an ever-merciful God, her husband had suffered a heart attack and died, leaving her a legacy that only now, over fifteen years later, was coming to fruition.

Alice thought of the humiliations that she had suffered to reach this point, of the freedom and riches that lay ahead of her. What a strange place this was for your life to change. She must have drifted off into a distant world of moneyed fantasy for it seemed only seconds later that she became aware of Zena gripping her hand and bouncing up and down in her seat. And there, down on the racecourse, she saw men on horses galloping past the finishing post. Ahead of them, by some ten lengths, also bouncing up and down, was Clay Wentworth. Even to Alice's untutored eye, Clay looked absurd, more like a drunk trying to direct traffic than a jockey riding a finish.

'He won!' Zena's eyes sparkled. 'He *won* the race, Alice.'

'Isn't that just great?' Alice smiled. 'Today, everyone's a winner.'

More than once, as Alex sat in the reception area of Lewes Hospital, he was asked if he needed Casualty. He had the look of a patient – deadly white and apparently in shock.

'No,' he shook his head. 'I'm waiting for a friend.'

It was early evening and he had been at the hospital for over an hour. On his way out to ride an undistinguished young horse in the novice 'chase, the second last race of the day, a reporter had walked beside him and asked him for his version of the incident involving Dig For Glory and Paul Raven.

Alex had walked on, declining to comment.

'They say he' pretty smashed up,' the journalist had said, adding quickly, 'there's been a press release. No limbs broken but badly shaken.'

Alex looked at the reporter. He might have been making it up but that phrase 'badly shaken' had the ring of truth to it. If some of the racecourse officials had been 'badly shaken' in the way that jockeys had been, in that phrase they used so easily, they would be on the way to the mortuary.

'D'you know anything more?' Alex asked.

'One of the press boys claims that he was still unconscious when they took him off to hospital.'

Alex closed his eyes for a moment. Then, remembering he had a race to ride, he walked towards the paddock, wondering whether Ron or Liz Charlesworth knew anything more. Knowing the guv'nor, he would be driving home by now. Alex touched the peak of his cap as Eddie Marwood, a small West Country trainer whose horses he sometimes rode, gave him his instructions.

Within moments of finishing well down the field in the novice 'chase, he was back in the weighing-room, giving Jim Wilson his mud-spattered gear before changing and hurrying out to the car park.

'He's not going to be able to see you tonight.' A young nurse stood before Alex.

'I'll wait,' he said.

'He's really not very well.' The girl was slim, with her short blonde hair tied back severely. She seemed too young to endure the daily sadness of a hospital. At any other time and in any other place, Alex would have been thinking of ways to get her telephone number.

'Is he conscious?'

'Yes,' she said quietly. 'He's conscious, but we're keeping him in intensive care for the time being.'

Alex rubbed his eyes wearily. To his surprise, the nurse sat down beside him.

'What about you?' she asked. 'You don't look so good yourself.'

'I'm all right.'

'You're a friend of his?'

Alex nodded, reflecting with a wry smile on the kind of friend he had been that afternoon.

'Go home,' the nurse said. 'Perhaps you could call his family to reassure them. Ring in tomorrow morning. He might be able to see you then.'

'No,' said Alex. 'I'll wait here.'

Dr Michael Evans had had a bad day. He estimated that he had worked a daily twelve hours for the past six days and he was on a late shift again tonight. He had had enough sick people to last him a lifetime.

And now even the healthy were giving him grief. When Nurse O'Keefe had asked him to speak to some idiot jockey in reception, he could hardly believe it. If Dr Evans had his way, little men with bandy legs who cluttered up the hospital every time there was racing at Plumpton would be sent to a special clinic for racing fools.

'There's absolutely no point in your staying here,' Dr Evans said loudly as he walked into reception.

Alex looked up at the man with tired eyes and a white, unbuttoned coat.

'I'd just like to see him,' he said.

'Impossible. Even if you were his long-lost brother, we couldn't let you in.'

'But he's conscious now, is he?'

Dr Evans sighed. 'Yes of course he's conscious. He just had a bang on the head.'

'So, if he hasn't broken anything and he hasn't serious head injuries, he might be out of here soon?'

'He won't be out of anywhere soon,' said the doctor impatiently. 'At least, not under his own steam. It looks like he's broken his back.'

Chapter
3

Life had been hard on Ginnie Matthews. Born some forty-seven years ago into a racing family, she had never known her mother who, when Ginnie was three years old, had run off with a travelling salesman to live in Scotland. From the age of five, it seemed to her now, she had looked after her father whose unpromising career as a trainer near Malton in Yorkshire had been seriously impeded by an ever-increasing dependence on whisky. Ginnie remembered him as a kind, weak man, awash with whisky and self-pity.

By the age of sixteen, she had learned the art of lying to owners, a talent that would stand her in good stead later in life. Daddy was a bit tied up at present. Daddy was out at the stables. Daddy was seeing another owner. Her best efforts were finally in vain. When she went racing, people smiled at her politely but their eyes said it all: Daddy was a loser, a piss-artist heading hell-for-leather for the gutter. Daddy was finished.

Owners deserted him. Horses were taken away. Lads sought other employment. Eventually, Ginnie left, too. At the age of seventeen, she came south and worked in a yard near Lambourn.

She was slim in those days and had a certain chirpy competence that men – particularly weak, mother-fixated men – found attractive. Four years after she had left home, she married Harry Matthews, who was assistant to the legendary Arthur Williamson, by general consent the most successful trainer of his day.

It was early morning, two days after Skinflint had won at Plumpton. Ginnie stood by her Range Rover, watching the string making its way through the early morning mist towards her and thinking about the only man she had ever slept with.

On the face of it, Harry Matthews had been quite a catch. A charming, good-humoured man, whose ten years in the army had left him with an easy manner with employees and a faintly ludicrous moustache which suited his healthy, high-coloured face. Harry was a card, a character; he was good company, always popular on the dinner-party circuit. Despite their age difference – he was forty when they married – she fell for his charms, ignoring the rumours that he had something of a weakness for fun and fast ladies.

'Charm,' Ginnie muttered as she stepped forward, standing in the centre of a circle formed by her horses like a ringmaster at a circus. 'Down with charm.'

She ran an expert eye over the horses, noting which were carrying too much weight, which needed building up. Ginnie prided herself on turning out horses that not only won races but that looked well too.

'How is he?' she called to the lad riding Skinflint.

Pete, a quiet lad who had worked for Ginnie five years now, smoothed Skinflint's coat behind the saddle. 'I don't think he knew he was in a race.'

Ginnie smiled. 'I'm not sure he was,' she said.

It was Wednesday, the day when most of the string were given half-speed work over a mile. Today Rock Steady, a four-year-old hurdler recently acquired by Clay Wentworth, was being schooled over hurdles. Mr Wentworth was not an amateur jockey who was prepared to tack his horse up and ride him out with the rest of the lads. He liked all that to be done for him so that he could drive to the gallops, work his horse, then return to London. Today, as usual, he was late.

As the horses cantered away from her to the end of the gallops, Ginnie found herself wondering why, at this of all times, she had been ambushed by reminiscences of the past. Under normal circumstances, she rarely looked back – the past, as far as she was concerned, was not just another country, but an alien, distant land hardly worth considering.

It was the thought of a visit from Clay Wentworth that had done it. He was the sort of owner her former husband had cultivated for social as well as financial reasons. Beefy, empty-faced officers, flabby City men, the occasional farmer made good – they had flocked to Harry Matthews when he established his own yard in Lambourn. He had loved it, spending night after night with these idiot amateur jockeys, flirting, getting drunk, frequently returning the following day, leaving Ginnie to look after first and second lots. He called it a sales drive and, for a while, she had believed him.

But Harry's amateur friends let him down. The officers were late paying their bills. Every time the economy dipped, the City men sold their horses – almost always out of the yard.

In the distance, Ginnie saw Clay Wentworth's Mercedes making its way up the lane by the gallops. Harry would have liked Clay. Doubtless he would have joined the famous Wentworth poker circle, if he were still in charge of the yard, if his charm hadn't let him down in the end.

After ten years of marriage, Ginnie had concluded that, perhaps through some odd psychological need, she had managed to find a husband who, in his way, was as big a loser as her father had been. The other women she could just about understand – her infertility was the excuse he used for his philandering; the booze she could live with. It was the lying and incompetent dishonesty that she hated.

Harry lost owners. Like many other trainers, he tried to escape financial ruin by setting up gambling coups. Even that, he screwed up. Horses that were meant to lose, won; good things turned out to be bad things. The Jockey Club took an increasingly close interest in his affairs and, after a particularly transparent act of fraud, took away his licence for two years.

At that moment, Ginnie had decided she was through with charm. She filed for divorce, borrowed enough money to buy him out of the yard, and began to rebuild.

Now, seventeen years later, she was one of the most successful trainers in the country, and her only use for men was as employees. She had learned the hard way.

'Ginnie, the top of the morning to you.' Clay Wentworth emerged languidly from his car. To Ginnie's surprise, he was wearing a pin-striped suit.

'Are you schooling like that?' she asked.

'Bit stiff after Plumpton.' Clay arched his back, wincing slightly. 'Thought I'd let one of the lads have a go.'

Ginnie nodded. She had often wondered why Clay put himself through this. His nerve was bad and he lacked any natural ability or understanding of horses. There was something apologetic about his tall, slightly stooped figure, particularly when his father was present. She glanced in the direction of the Mercedes and there, sure enough, was Sir Denis, sitting stonily immobile in the passenger seat.

'Morning, Sir Denis,' she called out.

The old man nodded curtly.

'My father was wondering why you were working Skinflint.' Clay smiled weakly. 'I mean, hasn't he done enough this week?'

Ginnie looked away towards the string as it came up the gallops. She couldn't stand owners who thought they knew better than she did. 'He thrives on work,' she said eventually. 'A half-speed will relax him.'

'That's what I told Dad,' said Clay.

'I've entered him in a couple of decent handicap 'chases in the New Year,' she said. 'If he's well in at the weights, we might consider giving him a crack at the big guns.'

'Excellent,' said Clay, adding as an afterthought, 'We don't want too light a weight, of course.'

She said nothing.

'I'm a bit strapped to do anything under twelve stone, to tell the truth.'

As she watched the horses trot back towards them, having pulled up at the end of the gallops, Ginnie swore silently. An owner, for whom money and the pleasure of having a top-class horse in his name, would have understood what she was saying. There comes a time when the owner should step down and make way for a professional jockey. Skinflint had the ability to beat the best in the country over three miles but, under the dead, uneven weight of Clay Wentworth, he was nothing special.

Unfortunately Clay and his ill-tempered old father were not interested in prizes or the pleasure of ownership; they wanted to see a Wentworth riding into the winners' enclosure, whatever the cost in money and wasted opportunity.

Clay patted Skinflint, who was hardly blowing after his exertions. 'Good boy,' he said. 'We're going to win lots more races together, aren't we?'

'Pete, can you get on Rock Steady and pop him over a couple of hurdles with old Home Boy?'

While the lads exchanged mounts, Clay muttered, 'You do understand why I want to ride him, don't you?'

'He could be a Gold Cup horse.'

Clay smiled. 'Maybe next year. This year it's the Kim Muir. A big amateur race at Cheltenham – it's not bad, is it?'

'No.' Ginnie smiled wearily. 'It's not bad.'

Some horses are lucky with owners – the great Arkle was owned by the Duchess of Westminster throughout his racing career. Others are less fortunate. As a four-year-old hurdler, Skinflint had been sold out of a yard in Newmarket to a Colonel Gilbert, an old enthusiast who kept a few horses with Ginnie.

By the time the Colonel died two years later, Skinflint was a top novice 'chaser with the temperament, toughness and turn of foot to become a Cheltenham Gold Cup prospect. When Mrs Gilbert, who had always resented her husband's interest in racing, put all his horses on the market, Ginnie had worked hard to find a new owner who would keep him in training with her. Clay Wentworth, who had just sent her a young hurdler called Rock Steady, had seemed ideal.

But Ginnie had underestimated Clay's – or rather, his father's – ambition.

'Will Sir Denis want to come over to the schooling ground?' she asked.

'He'll watch from here,' said Clay. 'He just likes to feel involved.'

Together, they walked to the schooling ground, an area of about twenty-five acres with lines of hurdles and fences of varying heights. They watched Rock Steady canter down to the far end of the gallop with Home Boy. Both horses were shown the first flight of hurdles.

'Do we know who are going to be our two main rivals in the Kim Muir?' Clay asked.

'Not officially, but I could take a pretty good guess.'

'You couldn't be terribly kind and jot them down for me, could you?'

'Jot them down?' Ginnie looked at Clay with some surprise. 'Can't I just tell you?'

'No, put them down – with owners and trainers. On a piece of paper. Know your enemy and all that. Besides, with my memory I'd forget them.'

She shrugged, as the two horses turned towards the first hurdle and set off at smart gallop.

'Here they come,' she said.

The more they talked of miracles around Paul's bed at Lewes Hospital, the more depressed he became about the future. It had been a miracle, Dr Evans had told him, that the impact of a racehorse falling at racing speed on top of him had not been fatal. It was a miracle that he had recovered consciousness so quickly. It was a miracle the way his body was responding to treatment so that now, five days after his fall, he was out of intensive care and back in a ward.

Then, subtly, the emphasis began to change. It would be a miracle if he were out of hospital within six months, and – the one that went through his mind a thousand times a day – it would be a miracle if he ever walked again. Three days after he had been brought into hospital, Paul had asked Dr Evans when he would recover the movement in his legs. 'Tell me what's going to happen,' he asked. 'Without the miracles.'

And the doctor, normally so direct, had been evasive, explaining with the help of X-rays he extracted from the folder he was carrying that the problem was a series of crushed vertebrae at the base of the spine. 'If the damage had been two inches lower,' he said, 'the risk of fundamental damage would have been less. As it is, we have to wait for your body to recover from the shock of the fall and for the swelling to subside, before we can conduct an exploratory operation. Only then will we know what the future holds for you.'

'Fundamental damage.' Through a haze of morphine Paul sensed the reason for Dr Evans' uneasiness. 'Does that mean I'm out for the season – or for ever?'

Dr Evans gestured to Nurse O'Keefe, who was standing at the foot of the bed. The nurse drew the curtains around the bed.

'Listen, let's take one step at a time.'

'What about walking?'

'I honestly don't know, only time will tell.' The doctor paused.

Paul had closed his eyes as the doctor had explained, as dispassionately as a science master, the medical advances in the field of spine damage.

'We find that attitude's important.' Dr Evans tried a smile but there was something chilling about his bedside manner, as if somehow Paul had brought this on himself.

Attitude. Paul understood that. After Dr Evans had left to continue on his rounds, he stared ahead of him at the plastic curtains which the nurse had left closed, thinking of the path which had led him to this hospital bed.

His family had laughed when he had told them his ambition. They had been having tea as usual, after his father had returned from work at the building site and the mood had been jovial, it being the end of the week and times in the building trade being good. His two older brothers, both in their teens, had been unenthusiastic about the idea of work but had grumpily given the impression that, like their father, they would work in construction. Mary, Paul's sister, wanted to be a nurse.

'I'm going to be a jockey,' Paul had said. He was five at the time.

But, to the Raven family's amazement, Paul's obsession with horses had grown stronger as he grew up. He watched racing on the television, discussing form with his father from the age of seven. There was a riding-school on the outskirts of Wigan and, ignoring the taunts of his schoolfriends, he worked there during the school holidays. He was even allowed to compete in the local shows and, although the ponies he rode were less well-fed and schooled than those ridden by the sons and daughters of local farmers, he won his fair share of show-jumping classes.

It took attitude to overcome the opposition of his father, who wanted him to serve an apprenticeship on the site like his brothers, and his teachers, who claimed he was too bright to leave school at the age of sixteen, and to come south, looking for a job in racing.

He had rung three trainers for work and luckily it was the fourth, Ron Charlesworth, who had agreed to take him on. Surly and mean, Charlesworth believed in bringing on his own lads, and that had been the making of Paul Raven.

Maybe he should have stayed in Wigan, he thought. His father and his two brothers were on the dole now; his sister was married with two children; but at least none of them faced a future in a wheelchair.

'How are you feeling?'

Nurse O'Keefe stood at the foot of his bed. Paul was grateful that she wasn't wearing the hospital smile, an expression of phoney sympathy that he found increasingly irritating.

'Numb,' he said. 'I can't take it in. I keep thinking that the drugs have got to me and I'll snap out of it.'

The nurse walked around to the side of the bed. As she was tucking in his sheet,

she said quietly, 'If you need someone to talk to, just say the word.' She smiled at
Paul in a way that verged on the unprofessional. Then, as if the sister had just
walked into the ward, she said more loudly, 'That's what we're here for.'

'Thank you, nurse.'

'Angie.'

'Thank you, Angie.' Paul watched the slim, pale figure as she made her way
down the ward to see another patient. 'Angie,' he said, and for the first time for
five days, he smiled.

That night, Angie O'Keefe had agreed to go out for a meal with some of the other
girls but, when they knocked on her door in the nurses' hostel, she told them she
was tired, she had a headache. Eventually, she agreed to meet them later at the
restaurant. Now she sat on her neatly-made bed, thinking of the quiet, dark jockey who, Dr Evans said, could be paralysed for life.

Angie's small room was a credit to the convent in Berkshire where she had been
educated: neat, well-dusted and decorated only with photographs of her parents
and two younger sisters. Unlike many of her contemporaries, she had never reacted against the discipline of her education by running wild in her late teens. Now
twenty-one, she had avoided drinking to excess, swore only occasionally and she
was a virgin. Not that sexual purity was something to boast about – Angie felt
almost jealous when she heard tales of heart-thumping promiscuity from the other
girls – she simply preferred to wait for the right man.

She saw the dark, even features of Paul Raven in her mind's eye and shook her
head firmly. On every count, he was Mr Wrong. First of all, he was a patient and
it was a golden rule among the nurses not to make a difficult job worse by falling
in love, or even flirting, with one of the customers.

Then he was a jockey. Angie smiled as she remembered the scandal of one of
the old girls who was said to be dating a bookmaker. Fast men who made a questionable living out of fast horses: nothing could be more dangerous for the purity
of a girl's soul.

His connections hardly inspired confidence. Two days after Paul had been admitted, his mother, a short angry woman who seemed ill at ease away from the north,
had appeared in the ward. Mrs Raven had not exactly told Paul to pull himself
together and stop moping about like a big girl's blouse, but she was hardly sympathetic, implying to her son – and, indeed, to the rest of the ward – that, if he were
daft enough to ride horses for a living, what else did he expect but to end up in
hospital? Like the majority of people, she had no perception of the word
paralysed.

The same day a Mrs Charlesworth, the wife of Paul's trainer, had shuffled in.
Ron was away racing, she said. Ron needed him back as soon as possible. Ron
had been in a filthy mood ever since the race at Plumpton. Without enquiring into
Paul's state of health, she had eaten the grapes she had brought, then scurried out
of the ward, leaving it smelling faintly of the stables.

Slowly, Angie unbuttoned her nurse's uniform. She walked across the small
room to a basin in the corner above which there was a mirror. Angie had never
been vain – she had never understood why men looked at her the way they did –

but now she stood before the mirror, taking in the pale skin, the athletic figure, the shadows of tiredness under her eyes, the practical, no-nonsense haircut. She ran her hands over her hips as if smoothing down an invisible skirt.

Above all, there was the third reason why Paul Raven should be erased from her thoughts as soon as possible. Angie was a good nurse, but she was no Florence Nightingale. When she gave herself to a man – and she hoped it would be soon – she was old-fashioned enough to hope that he would sweep her off her feet, take control. There was little chance of Paul being able to do that. Caring and convalescence belonged at work, not at home.

Yesterday the other jockey, Alex – the one several of the nurses were talking about in the staff room – had visited Paul once again. There was something wild and distracted about the man; his conversation was too loud and cheerful to be entirely natural. While they were talking, Angie had called by to check that Paul's drip was still working and, as she walked away, she had sensed that they were discussing her. Paul said something quietly, and she had heard the clipped tones of Alex Drew, saying, 'You know what they say, Paul. There are only two certainties in life – death and nurses.'

She had been unable to resist glancing back. To her relief, Paul wasn't laughing.

That evening, after Alex had left, the customary calm had descended on the ward as the patients watched early-evening soaps on the television. For the nurses, this was about the only time during the day when they could relax, confident that, for a few minutes, the sun-drenched domestic dramas of Australian suburban life would distract the patients' minds from their own troubles.

Angie noticed that Paul never bothered with these programmes. Tonight he seemed quiet, more distant than usual, as if the visit from his friend had unsettled him. Most of the lights in the ward had been switched off, the curtains drawn, so that, briefly, it was lit only by the light from the television.

'So you're not an addict.' Angie smiled, sitting on the chair which Alex had left beside the bed.

'Can't follow the plot.'

She laughed softly. 'How are you feeling?'

'Alex is taking this badly. He keeps going over the race, talking about it. He knows I can't remember anything about the fall but it's as if he wants me to blame him. I've seen the video of the race and there's no doubt he stopped m deliberately. What happened was a chance in a million, but it's eating him up. He looks terrible.'

Angie remembered his remark about nurses, the confident tone of the young middle-class male. 'He seemed all right to me,' she said.

'You don't know him.'

Paul was staring sightlessly in the direction of the television. In the gloom, he reminded Angie of some wounded hero of an old black-and-white film, his dark troubled features against the white of the pillow, his eyes catching the light and seeming to sparkle feverishly. A dying member of the French Resistance, perhaps, even a consumptive poet. Raven – he was well named.

'Tell me something, Angie,' he said. 'Not as a nurse but as a friend. Assuming the worst – that I'll never walk again – ' He paused then plunged on. 'Does that mean that I'm finished as a man too?'

'No. It doesn't.'

He had turned to look at her, surprised by the confidence of her reply.

'You understand what I'm asking?'

'You're all right,' she said. 'If you had no feeling in your legs, there would be a problem. As it is, your – ' Angie hesitated. 'The rest of it will be unimpaired.'

'You're sure about that?'

'I'm sure.' In the semi-darkness, she lay a hand softly on his. 'I asked the doctor myself.'

Back in her room, as the warm water filled the basin before her, Angie remembered the conversation with Paul. She rubbed her hands on the soap, then carefully washed her face. Once she had prided herself on being in control of her life. Too many of her friends had fallen in love with the wrong men at the wrong time and in the wrong way. Not her, she had always vowed. Now she wasn't so sure.

She rinsed her face. Perhaps, after all, she would join her friends at the restaurant. She felt like company.

'Fifty to come in.'

Clay Wentworth pushed a small pile of plastic chips into the middle of the table and allowed his large, fleshy features to assume the expression of relaxed inscrutability he felt was appropriate for these occasions. He stared at the suit – king and five – he held in his hands, as four of the other players – Lol Calloway, Alice Markwick, Digby Welcome and Harry Biddulph – came in.

Clay felt lucky. They were playing his favourite form of poker, Texas Hold 'Em, and already he was seven hundred quid up on the night, thanks to a combination of good hands and cool play. The dealer for the game, Perry Smythe, rolled two more kings and another five and laid them in the middle of the table. Yes, it was his night. When Clay bet £250, the maximum allowed on Thursday Poker Night, Alice, Digby and Biddulph folded. With his usual confident smile, Lol raised it to five hundred.

Lol couldn't handle poker politics. Never had and never would. Clay glanced across and for a moment he was fixed by Calloway's hooded eyes. There was something impressively sinister about him, his bald pate and long, lank hair giving him the look of a bank robber rather than a former rock star, but he was no card-player.

It was time for a spot of Wentworth bluff. Clay glanced down at his hand, frowning as if his best plan was going horribly wrong. He chewed his bottom lip for a moment like a man whose every instinct told him to cut his losses and fold.

Lol Calloway had never been able to read a bluff. Clay looked to him for a 'tell', some small tic that would betray the strength of weakness of Lol's hand, and found it. When the God of poker was smiling on him, Lol would purse his lips, draw the cards together, then re-open them. This, Clay had learned over the two years in which he had been doing poker nights with Lol, was a sure sign that he held a good hand. Despite appearing in cameo roles in the occasional TV detective series, the man was no actor. He drew his cards together, shook his head, and looked at them again.

A certain etiquette had evolved on Thursday Poker Nights. A player who had folded, or who was sitting out the game, was not meant to comment on proceedings, however light-heartedly. Now Alice, Digby Welcome and Harry Biddulph sat at the table, silent and straight-faced, as Clay called Lol's five hundred and re-raised him another six hundred.

Two cards remained to be shown. Clay judged that Lol must hold the last king and possibly an ace. To match Clay's full house, he needed an ace from one of the next two communal cards. Smythe the dealer dealt the top card, laying it aside face down – an entirely unnecessary touch of melodrama since no one, on Thursday Poker Nights, had been known to cheat – then rolled the top card. It was a four. Lol closed his eyes briefly then nodded. Smythe dealt again. A jack.

'Fuck.' Lol threw down his cards, revealing a king and a nine, and with a passable show of nonchalance wandered over to an open fire on the far side of the room near which there was a drinks trolley. He poured himself a large whisky. 'A whole day's fucking PR receipts. You are one lucky bastard.'

Clay smiled as he raked in his chips, estimating over a grand of clear profit on the game. Sure, he was lucky – not so much with the cards he was dealt but with his poker partners. Over the past two years, a small but significant percentage of Lol's massive earnings had found its way into his pocket and those of the other Thursday regulars. It was as if Lol were punishing himself for making so much money so effortlessly. Three good years as a guitar hero in the early seventies, some clever management of his diminishing assets and the new obsession of advertisers for revising old tunes had yielded a salary that hit the half million mark – on a bad year.

'It's called skill,' Clay said amiably, leaving the game and placing his chips on a side table. That was the great thing about the Thursday game. From Lol Calloway, for whom losing fifteen thousand pounds in ten minutes was mildly irritating but soon forgotten, to Digby Welcome, for whom an equivalent crash-out would be three hundred or a week's drinking money, the regulars knew how far to take it. Maybe that was why they were regulars – the guys who lost it, who went 'on tilt' as they say in gambling circles, desperately throwing good money after bad, tended not to last long.

'We need new blood in the school,' Lol muttered, as if reading Clay's thoughts. 'Another fuckin' Alex Drew. Otherwise it's always going to be me that's turned over.' Clay sat in the armchair opposite Lol and crossed his long legs.

'Couldn't you tell I was looking at a full house? You were crazy to follow me up.'

Lol stared gloomily into the fire. 'You looked so fuckin' depressed,' he said. 'I was thinking, it's got to be bullshit. No way has Clay got a king in the hole and a five. No one can get that lucky. Oh well – ' he slurped noisily at his drink. 'Can't win 'em all.'

'No, you can't.'

'Heard from Alex, have you?'

'Had a couple of calls.' Clay noticed that, even though Digby, Harry Biddulph,

Alice and a couple of the newer members of the group had begun another game, the focus of attention in the room had shifted from the poker table to the conversation. 'He's not a happy boy. In fact, he's rather upset about what happened.'

'Too right,' said Lol. 'A broken back's a fuckin' bummer in any language.'

'As I understand it,' said Digby Welcome, without taking his eyes off the two cards in his hand, 'the boy Raven has crushed vertebrae. Not what I'd call a broken back.'

A silence descended on the room. It was odd, Clay thought, that Digby, the one Thursday night regular who claimed to understand racing, to have it in the blood, was the person least concerned by what had happened. Even Alice, in her glacial way, had noted that there had been what she called 'an unscheduled casualty'.

He didn't like Welcome, but then few people did. For a moment Clay watched the stout figure, whose comical little legs hardly reached the floor, as he played his normal tight, careful game of poker. If it was true that in every fat man a thin man was trying to get out, the inner Digby was a sour, ungenerous bastard strangely at odds with the roly-poly exterior and the flushed round cheeks.

'I fold.' As was his custom, Digby decided that discretion was the better part of valour and left the game at an early stage. The man was a dull poker player, meanly backing good hands while taking few chances. Every Thursday, he gained between £100 and £200 – but then again he probably wasn't there for the money.

No one knew the truth about Digby Welcome. He claimed to be an old Etonian but this, like so much of his personal history, might have been a fraud. By guile and cultivating the right contacts, he had, it was said, established himself as a National Hunt trainer and had a fairly successful yard in Sussex during the 1960s. More surprising still, he had married the reasonably attractive daughter of one of his owners.

It went wrong, but not in the usual way of racing failures – Digby's was not a gambling yard. His innate meanness found him out. The horses were underfed, the lads underpaid. As the winners dried up, owners deserted him and so, amid rumours of unseemly marital demands in the Welcome bedroom, did his wife. Digby gave up his habit of paying bills late, opting instead for not paying them at all. The withdrawal of his trainer's licence was followed, within a month, by bankruptcy.

These days, Digby Welcome represented a small and somewhat shady manufacturer of horse tonics, travelling in his Volvo Estate from stable to stable. He still went racing, but had more enemies than friends and was frequently to be seen drinking alone at the members' bar.

Having left the game, he placed himself in front of the fire, his short, tubby figure shielding Clay and Lol from the warmth.

'That's racing,' he said, almost sitting in the fire in an attempt to warm his over-generous behind. 'I always used to warn my jockeys about coming up on the inner. Raven's been around long enough to know the dangers.'

'Do me a fuckin' favour, Digby.' This was too much, even for Lol Calloway. 'We all know there was more to it than that.'

Clay darted a warning glance in the direction of the table where the two new members of the Thursday Night school were still playing with rapt concentration. 'Not all of us know that,' he said quietly.

'Well, I feel bad about it,' Lol muttered.

Briefly Clay looked troubled. 'There's nothing we can do now,' he said.

They were on their last game for the night when the call came through. It was almost four o'clock, and Clay was back at the table, taking some money – off Perry Smythe and one of the stockbrokers who had recently joined the school. Alice was just about breaking even and Digby had made his almost statutory two hundred pounds. Only Lol was by the fire, moodily nursing a large glass of whisky.

He looked at his watch without any particular surprise as the telephone continued to ring.

'Must be the fuckin' Coast,' he murmured as he made his way unsteadily across the room. In Lol's world, the only time it was inconsiderate to call was during daytime working hours when he was normally asleep.

''Ullo.' He swayed backwards and forwards like a sailor in a storm. 'Who the fuck is this?' he asked. The answer appeared to take some time. 'Oh, it's you. Why didn't you fuckin' say so? He's in the middle of a game right now.' Lol winced and held the telephone away from his ear. 'All right, all right, keep yer 'air on.' He turned towards the table where the game was taking its course. 'It's for you, Clay. Alex. Says it's important.'

Clay frowned, laid down his cards and walked over to the telephone.

'Alex,' he said silkily. 'Where are you? We were expecting you.'

The call took ten minutes and when he put down the receiver, Clay's good humour had faded. He returned to the table, looking pale and weary.

'Alex Drew wants to talk,' he said.

Digby looked up from his cards. 'He should have come round this evening. A touch of poker therapy would have done him the power of good.'

'To the authorities, I mean.' Clay sat down slowly, still deep in thought. 'I think I dissuaded him.'

'There's not much to talk about.' Alice looked only mildly concerned. 'Nothing can be proved.'

For a moment, there was silence in the room, and from outside the first early twitterings of birdsong could be heard.

'Fuckin' dawn chorus,' muttered Lol.

Clay threw his cards into the middle of the table. 'I'm out,' he said.

From his chair by the fireside, Lol gave a little, drunken laugh. 'Alex was well gone. That little bastard was feeling no pain.'

Clay stared into the dying embers of the fire. 'If only that were true,' he said.

Alex Drew sat on the side of his bed, pressing the mobile telephone to his forehead as if it were a poultice. He didn't cry – he was past all that – but he muttered to himself, again and again. 'No going back. No going back now.'

In his twenty-three years, Alex had experienced his share of good times. He had been to all-night parties. He had lived hard and wildly, drinking and making love. He was no stranger to the more fashionable of recreational drugs – cocaine, amphetamines, even, on a couple of occasions, heroin had assailed his senses. It was life – at least, it was life if you were young, good-looking and from a family where money was never going to be a problem.

And yet he had retained the smooth-faced innocent look of a grown-up choirboy. One day maybe his body would protest, fast-lane wrinkles would appear on his face. Then again, maybe not.

Carefully, Alex switched off the telephone and laid it on the bed. Anguish and guilt had marked his face in a way that too many parties never had. There were rings under his eyes, the once-smooth cheeks were unshaven, the hair, which he wore longer than most other jockeys, was lank and dull.

Like a man preparing for an execution, he stood up, took off his jeans and slipped into his riding-out clothes – jodhpurs, boots, a dark polo-neck sweater. He took a trim jacket from the wardrobe, picked up his car keys from the dressing-table and left.

It was light now. Within an hour the lads would be arriving at Charlesworth's yard to prepare for first lot. Alex unlocked his Audi and, driving with a care that was unusual for him, set off towards Lambourn.

A horse-box was already in the yard, and Alex cursed softly. Having told the guv'nor that he was ill, he hadn't ridden out for three days. Presumably one or two of the horses were running at a distant race-meeting today and needed to set off early.

'Och aye, he's back at last.' Jimmy Summers, the head lad, was putting a couple of hay-nets in the horse-box. 'Better, are you?'

Alex kept walking. 'Much better,' he said.

'You look fuckin' terrible,' said Jimmy cheerfully.

Behind the stables were some farm buildings. He needed to get there and back to the car without arousing Jimmy's suspicions.

'Who's running today then?' he asked.

'Och, it's the big time,' Jimmy smiled. 'We're taking Smile Please and Pretty Marie up to Fakenham. Fuckin' waste of petrol if you ask me.'

The head lad disappeared into the horse box and Alex continued on his way across the yard.

'No going back now,' he said, as memories, unwelcome memories, flashed through his mind.

Someone, somewhere had said to him, as if revealing one of life's eternal verities, that those who play must pay. It had stuck in Alex's mind as being as stupid a cliché as he had ever heard.

The girl – yes, it was a friend of his older sister who, during her brief and otherwise forgettable affair with Alex had allowed herself to get pregnant – had really believed it. She had actually held out her hand and, for a moment, he had failed to understand the precise nature of the payment she was looking for. She was more specific. The cost of the abortion was down to him. He had given her £300 in cash, which was the cost of the operation plus £50 for her trouble – an uncharacteristically spiteful touch, but then he had only been eighteen at the time.

If that was how those who played paid – with a trip to the bank – Alex was unconcerned. Life had given him a blank cheque. The world was his plaything.

By the time he had first met Paul Raven, Alex had decided that there was only one activity about which he would be wholly serious. When he rode horses, the nonsense, the laughter ended. He had ridden his first winner under rules, an amateur hurdle at Devon and Exeter, when he was eighteen. The following year, he was champion amateur and, to the dismay of his father, a wealthy and shrewd Scottish landowner, he had decided on a career in racing.

The idea of becoming a professional jockey – of riding for money – had come later. Until he was twenty, Alex had assumed that he would work among the ranks of racing's tweed-suited elite – an assistant trainer perhaps or something in blood-stock. His father, a generous man who believed that youth should have its fling, paid for Alex's year at Ron Charlesworth's yard, confident that, by the time he reached his twenty-first birthday, his son would be ready to embark on a serious career.

It had been Paul who changed all that. At Alex's request, he was treated like a normal stable lad at the Charlesworth yard, living in the chilly hostel and spending long, harsh hours mucking out stables and cleaning tack. It was a far tougher baptism than Alex had expected, for his accent, his clothes and, above all, his sports car set him apart from the other lads and made him an obvious target for persecution. Only Paul, the quiet northerner who had already ridden several winners for Charlesworth and other trainers, recognised that behind the soft-skinned facade of a privileged amateur, beyond the playboy image, there was a steely determination.

They should have been enemies. Their backgrounds, their characters, the growing competition for spare rides from the stable seemed sure to set them on a collision course. But, as they rode work together, discussed the horses in the yard, the qualities of the top jockeys they both admired, a mutual respect developed between them.

'Leave him be,' Paul would say with quiet authority. 'Just 'cause he doesn't talk like you, it doesn't mean he can't do the job.'

Gradually the jibes subsided, Alex established his position at the yard and the professional regard between him and Paul developed into friendship.

'How come that leery bastard runs for you when he won't do a tap for me?' Paul had asked half-jokingly after they had worked a couple of three-year-olds over a mile and a half.

'I talk to him nicely.'

'Typical.' Paul had smiled. 'Even the horses are snobs round here.'

Thanks to Paul, Alex had the confidence to join the ranks of professional jockeys and, thanks to him, he had the strength to withstand the storm of disapproval that broke over his head when he told his parents. In a way, he owed Paul everything.

Larks were singing in the pale morning sunlight over the downs as the Audi made its way up the lane beside the gallops. It stopped at a point where there was a hedge beside the track, on the far side of which was Ron Charlesworth's schooling ground.

Moving more deliberately than was his habit, Alex got out and lowered the roof of the convertible. He reached on to the back seat, picking up the rope that he had picked up in Charlesworth's farm building. He glanced up the gallops to ensure that no early morning joggers or dogwalkers were watching and briefly he heard the thunder of hooves as the string made its way up the slight slope towards where he stood. Then, shaking his head as if to rid himself of memories, he took the rope and adeptly formed a loop at one end, smiling to think how the knowledge of knots he had acquired when sailing as a boy was being put to belated use. Laying the coiled rope on the back seat of the car, he took its other end and attached it to the trunk of a stout oak that formed part of the hedgerow. He tugged at it twice then walked slowly back to the car and sat in the driver's seat.

For a moment, it was as if he had drifted off into a trance. Then he reached behind him, took the end of the rope and, as carefully as a woman trying on a hat in a shop, he placed the noose around his neck, tightening it so that the knot rested against the back of his neck.

He glanced at the coils lying on the back seat, then fastened his safety belt. Twenty yards, and in a car with powerful acceleration. It would do.

Alex switched on the engine, gunned the car, priming it as if it were a sprinter in the stalls. He slipped it into first gear, saying quietly, 'Those who play must pay.' This, at least, was true payment.

Taking the handbrake off, he closed his eyes and pressed the accelerator to the floor, drowning out the singing of larks for ever.

Chapter
4

'The VART man?'

There were times when the deep and husky voice of Alice Markwick became aristocratic in its disdain, when a stranger might be forgiven for assuming that she was the daughter of a White Russian countess rather than of a factory worker in Prague.

'The VAT man, yes.' Norman Little, her secretary, stood in the door to her office. A neat, unambitious man in his late twenties, Norman was used to Mrs Markwick's ever-changing moods and had learned to ignore them. 'He claims he has an appointment.'

Alice looked at the leather diary on her desk. 'He is wrong. Tell him to come back next week. Say it's a bad moment.'

Norman touched his temple with thumb and forefinger, like a man sensing the first twinge of a migraine. 'I think that would be unwise, Mrs Markwick. They can make life very awkward, these VAT people.'

'V.A.T. spelt G.O.D. This country's bureaucracy gets more Eastern European every day. Ask Simon to show him the books. He wants the finance director, not me.'

'He insisted that he should see you.'

'Hell and damnation. Get me the books and the last company accounts. And show him into my office – after a quarter of an hour or so.' Alice grimaced as her secretary shook his head disapprovingly. 'All right, five minutes.'

'Yes, Mrs Markwick.'

'And give him a cup of tea – or whatever VART men drink.'

Norman smiled. 'Already done,' he said, retiring from the office like a well-trained butler.

'Bloody VAT.' Alone in her office, Alice closed the desk diary and lit a cigarette. She had nothing to hide from any government money snoop and, if there was one thing you learned from being brought up in Czechoslovakia, it was how to deal with bureaucrats. All the same – Alice stood up and walked to the window – it was bad timing. She felt uneasy, as if some small part of her carefully laid plans had gone wrong, but she didn't know how.

Perhaps it was the jockey. Just over three weeks ago, Alex Drew had committed suicide. There had been an absurd amount of fuss – Alice had never understood the seriousness with which violent death was taken in this country – and the press had pored over his last days in a way which briefly had unnerved her.

'Another casualty,' the fool Wentworth had said when he had rung her with the news. Barely keeping hysteria at bay, he had described how a torso had been found in Alex's car by the lads riding out for Charlesworth. His head had later been discovered in a hedgerow, near a noose.

'How frightfully macabre.' She had tried unsuccessfully for a lightness of tone. 'There were no notes or anything, I hope.'

'I don't think so.'

And there hadn't been. Alex may have been as flashy in death as he had been in life but at least he had been discreet. His death changed nothing, in Alice's view. He had served his purpose.

'You know how your saying goes,' she had said to Clay. 'The one about making omelettes, breaking eggs.'

'Yes.' Clay seemed to be pulling himself together now. 'You're right, of course.'

'Remember. It's some omelette we've got cooking.'

Alice looked down at the laboratory, across a yard from her office. It was a modest set-up, a complex of ill-designed modern buildings, entirely in keeping with the other small businesses run, mostly by Asians, in this particular part of Willesden. Only the discreet but highly sophisticated security system suggested that Markwick Instruments plc was anything out of the ordinary.

The door opened behind her.

'Mr Birtwhistle,' said Norman. 'From the local VAT office.'

'Ah, good.' Alice turned, smiling, even shaking her dark curls with a hint of coquettishness. This, after all, was an occasion for charm. 'So sorry to have kept you waiting, Mr Birtwhistle.'

After two decades in England, Alice could still be surprised. The young man standing before her eyes was not at all her idea of a Mr Birtwhistle from the VAT office. With thick dark hair slicked straight back, a raffish moustache, and smooth, even features, he looked a successful City man, a broker or commodity man with a mobile phone, a Porsche and a string of girlfriends. Even his dark, pin-striped suit seemed rather too well-tailored for a VAT inspector in Willesden.

'The apologies are mine,' he said, a suggestion of a south London twang in his soft voice. 'I was thirty minutes late myself. I had a bit of bother with the address.'

'It's a warren round here.' Alice sat behind her desk, gesturing in the direction of the guest chair nearby. 'People can get lost for days.'

Birtwhistle sat down, laying his shiny black briefcase on his knees. 'I'm still a bit of a stranger to the area,' he said.

'When did you arrange the appointment, exactly?'

'Must have been last Monday.' The VAT man had opened his briefcase and had taken out a form. 'The lady I spoke to assured me this morning was clear for you. Now I needn't detain you long. My department is involved in a background briefing exercise involving businesses in the area whose turnover exceeds half a million pounds and which . . .'

Alice nodded politely as the young man recited his well-rehearsed lines. He was sounding more as she had expected now. Perhaps his manner and style of dressing were merely a sign of the times – these days, even VAT inspectors were upwardly mobile.

He had been talking for about a minute when Norman entered the office, bearing a number of files which, with an apologetic smile, he hid on the desk with a muttered 'The books, Mrs Markwick.'

Birtwhistle paused until Norman had left. 'Sorry,' he said mildly. 'I should have explained. I don't need the figures today – just a few details from you.'

'Details?'

'As I've explained – it's for our local firm profile operation.'

'Ah, yes.' Alice glanced at her watch. 'Well, my late husband set up the firm in 1964. He was a physicist, specialising in optics, in particular early research into lasers. By the time he died we were selling optical instruments to a number of medical establishments and engineering firms throughout the United Kingdom.'

Birtwhistle looked up from the form on which he was making notes. 'He died when, precisely?'

'1972. Heart attack.'

'And you were . . .'

'We had married in 1969. I had been his secretary.'

'It must have been a great shock.'

'Yes.' Alice quickly closed down that line of questioning which had nothing to do with anybody but her. 'He was only forty-three. But – ' she smiled bravely ' – he left the firm in good shape, with some excellent researchers.'

'Local people, I imagine?'

'They came from all over. Some from England, some from my native country. If they knew about lasers, I didn't care where they were born.'

'And you continued to run the firm.'

'I have a good team. Our turnover topped five million last year.'

'D'you take on defence work?' Birtwhistle asked casually. 'Lasers can be used as a weapon, as I understand.'

Alice smiled. 'Not our type of lasers. We work to make people better, not to kill them.'

'I see.' Birtwhistle took some time to note it down. 'Perhaps you could show me round – when we've finished.' His smile was boyish, almost mischievous.

'Of course,' Alice said. 'I have a meeting in fifteen minutes. Until then – ' she returned his smile with a hint of professional flirtatiousness ' – I'm all yours.'

'One more step.'

Angie O'Keefe stood behind Paul, a hand on each of his hips, ready to catch him should he fall backwards from the walking frame on which he was leaning.

'Jesus.' Paul gritted his teeth as, with effort which seemed to wrack his whole body, he willed his right foot forward. 'Whoever said nursing was one of the caring professions?'

Angie laughed. 'Cruel to be kind,' she said. 'Go on, Paul. One more – for me.'

It wasn't really a step. It was a desperate, unsteady, old man's shuffle which covered barely six inches of the shiny floor in the Physiotherapy Room – but for Paul it felt more important than his first winner. As time had passed and the swelling reduced, relieving the pressure on his spinal cord, so the feeling in his legs had gradually returned. There was no paralysis, but the injury to the bone was quite extensive.

'Enough,' he gasped, as Angie placed his wheelchair behind him. He swayed as she took away the walking frame and stood in front of him. He placed his arms around her neck, saying with a weary smile, 'We can't go on meeting like this.'

She lowered him gently onto the wheelchair.

'I'm exhausted just looking at you,' she said.

Paul smiled. Love and rage were a potent combination, motivating him to push himself faster than ever the doctors wanted.

Thanks to a contribution from the Injured Jockeys' Fund, he had been transferred to the Croydon Rehabilitation Centre where he devoted his every waking hour to walking once again.

Angie had taken to visiting him on her days off work, talking through his despair, helping him to look to the future, always encouraging him.

'Thanks, nurse,' he said. 'I don't know what I'd do without you.'

Angie stood in front of the wheelchair smiling, her arms crossed. 'All part of the service,' she said.

Paul looked away. 'Don't feel you have to visit me,' he said. 'You should be going out – this must be just like work for you.'

'I'm not a health visitor,' she said leaning forward and touching his cheek briefly with her hand. Then, as if she had suddenly made some rather important decision, she kissed him – at first tentatively, then with a firm, deep insistence.

When she stood up, there was colour in her normally pale cheeks.

Paul smiled. 'What do I get after walking six steps then?' he asked.

'I've never kissed a man like that before,' Angie said distantly. 'I mean – it's not like me to make the first move.'

Paul looked into her clear blue eyes, so close to him as she stood, one hand on each arm of the chair. Her face, framed by the short blonde hair, seemed younger, more vulnerable than when he had first seen her in the hospital. 'If you hadn't, we might have had a long wait on our hands,' he said.

Slowly, she pushed the wheelchair down the corridor and back to his small room. Only when she had closed the door behind them did Paul finally speak.

'I need your help,' he said hesitantly. 'I've no right to ask you and I'll understand if you refuse.'

'Don't be . . . '

Paul held up a hand. 'I'm not talking about . . . all this.' He paused. 'I've got to know what happened to Alex.'

Angie turned away to a desk on which there lay some newspaper cuttings. A headline – 'JOCKEY IN SHOCK SUICIDE MYSTERY' – caught her eye. Paul had reacted with incredulity to news of Alex's death but, in time, grief had turned to anger. Although he had been unable to speak of his friend until now, she had noticed the look of quiet determination, almost of anger, that crossed his face when the memories returned.

'What can we do?' She laid a hand on Paul's shoulder. 'Alex is dead. You saw how he was after your fall. He was obsessed with guilt about what had happened.'

'I'm not saying he didn't kill himself. Just that – he was involved in something before the race at Plumpton. I think – I know – that if my fall was just an accident, he would never have killed himself. He was too strong for that. He was a survivor.'

'How long had you been friends?'

'Three years. When he first came to work for Charlesworth, I couldn't stand him – he was so jaunty, so confident. The lads took against him – the way he talked, his good looks, his car. And of course he was an amateur.'

'That matters?'

'It matters. A few years ago, trainers used to put amateurs up on their horses to save the cost of a jockey's fee. These days, they have to pay the Jockey Club so that amateurs and professionals are competing on level terms but the idea that somehow they're taking bread out of the mouths of lads who have worked their way up the hard way lives on.'

'I can understand that. If it weren't for his father's money, Alex would never have made it as an amateur. Compared to someone like you, he had it easy.'

'Didn't matter to me. It wasn't his fault that his parents were rich. But it was never his background that made him different from the lads – it was the fact that he rode better than them. I knew he'd turn professional that first time I rode work with him. It was the only thing he really wanted to do – ride horses and win races.'

'You encouraged him.'

'Of course. We were a bit guarded, at first, but soon we got on well.

'Although we were different, in many ways we were in the same situation – more than lads, once we started getting rides, yet not fully-fledged jockeys. That brought us together. And we trusted one another – in racing, that counts for something.'

Angie sat down at the desk and picked up one of the cuttings. For the week following his death, there had been lurid speculation about why a young jockey, on the brink of a successful career, should commit suicide. There were rumours of gambling debts, problems with a girlfriend, a rift with his father and mother. A couple of reporters had even tried to talk to Paul but he had refused to comment.

'A few days after Plumpton,' Paul said, 'a reporter from the *Guardian* wrote to me in hospital. It was before it had been announced how badly I was hurt. He had seen a video of the race. He knew nothing about horses, he said, but he was surprised that there was no investigation.'

'Why?'

'He seemed to think Alex put me through the wing deliberately. He wanted my view.'

'What did you say to him?'

'I said he stopped me getting up his inner, which he is entitled to do, and that there was no way he could have known Dig For Glory would take on the wing. Anyway the article he was writing didn't interest me at the time – he was an anti. Believed racing should be banned. He seemed to be more interested in poor old Dig For Glory than he was in me.'

For a moment, there was silence in the room. Outside, a number of patients in wheelchairs were making slow progress down the drive. It was like a procession of war veterans.

'I read the piece,' Angie said eventually. 'It mentioned your race. I thought – '
she hesitated ' – I thought he had a point. Over two hundred horses were killed
last year – it seems a lot for a sport.'

Paul glanced at her, surprised. 'Don't tell me you're an anti too.'

'I have an open mind.' Briefly, she had the look of a sixth former asked to defend
her position in front of the class. 'Perhaps now's not the best time to discuss this.'

'I kept the article.' Paul wheeled himself to the desk and leafed through the cuttings until he found it. 'I was wondering if this man – ' he glanced at the byline
'– Gavin Holmes – knew anything. If he's right – and Alex wanted to stop me in
that race for some other reason – it would explain a lot. Why he was so distracted that day. Why he was so concerned about how I was going to ride the race.'

'Why he killed himself.'

'Could be.'

Angie took the cutting and, folding it carefully, put it in the back pocket of her
jeans. 'As your nurse,' she said, 'my advice would be to look to the future, not the
past.'

'But you're not my nurse any more.'

'No.' She smiled and kissed Paul lightly on the lips. 'I'm not your nurse any
more.'

One day, Clay Wentworth thought, he would live in Ireland. He liked the pace of
life, the sense that nothing – not jobs, not politics nor your home life – was quite
as important as horse-racing. One day, when his father died – if his father died, he
was tempted to say – he would sell up, buy some land in County Limerick, and
breed horses for the rest of his life.

Leaning on the rails at Leopardstown racecourse, Clay felt at ease with the world.
He was more of a countryman than his father had ever been. On the rare occasions
Sir Denis Wentworth gazed at a green field, his only thoughts would be of the
number of houses it could accommodate and what percentage profit the development would earn.

'Silly old fool,' Clay muttered, as the runners for the Dunraven Handicap Chase
cantered past him on their way to the start. Clay was never happier than when a
stretch of deep blue seawater stood between him and his father.

He respected Sir Denis, of course. He was immensely grateful for what he would
give him one day. The son of a Luton warehouseman, his father had trained as an
accountant, then during the 1950s he had become interested in buying and selling
property. Thirteen years later, thanks to energy, enterprise and a winning way with
corruptible local councillors, he had become a millionaire, one of a new generation of tough industrialists. A knighthood followed and soon, all talk of corruption and ruthlessness forgotten, Sir Denis Wentworth was a pillar of the
establishment. Leaning languidly on the rails at Leopardstown, his only son could
hardly resent that – nor the considerable fortune to which he was heir.

Clay made his way from the rails to the grandstand. This was the race he had
come to see and he had no intention of being jostled by over-excited Irishmen during its closing stages.

Ballina Lady was the last to go down and, taking his position, Clay followed her progress with binoculars. The publicity surrounding the mare had not been exaggerated – she was impressive-looking, a good seventeen hands and powerful with it. Although she was only six and this was her first season over fences after a successful career as a hurdler, there was an intelligence, an authority to her which suggested real class. There was a stir of interest from the crowd as she cantered down, ridden by the top Irish amateur, Tim Heaney.

It was occasions like these that made Clay aware that he was happier in a warm tweed suit, standing in the grandstand, than out on the course, the reins in his hands and half a ton of horseflesh beneath him.

Clay had been unable to resist a small bet of a hundred pounds on the second favourite. Although he knew little of its form, the prohibitive price on Ballina Lady – three to one on at the bookmaker Clay had used – had pushed out the odds of the other eight runners. On paper, the mare would have little trouble recording her fifth successive win of the season – her jumping was impeccable, the going was as she liked it and, even with a penalty from her last win, she was well handicapped.

There was a buzz of anticipation as the racecourse commentator announced that the field for the Dunraven Handicap 'chase was under orders. As the starter let them go, Clay felt the same clammy-handed expectancy that he had experienced before the race at Plumpton – only now he could enjoy it in the knowledge that today he wasn't riding in a later race.

It was clear why Ballina Lady demanded such a following from racegoers. Ears pricked, she made the running, taking lengths off the other runners at every fence. As the field passed the stand, led by some five lengths by the favourite, one or two racegoers were unable to resist applauding her as she went.

She jumped from fence to fence and seemed to take one stride for everyone else's two. At the end of the back straight for the last time, with three quarters of a mile to run, the race had become a procession, with Tim Heaney hunting the mare along easily, now some fifteen lengths to the good of her nearest contender who was fading.

As Ballina Lady rounded the final bend, with two fences to go, Clay raised the binoculars to his eyes.

Later, they said the roar of the crowd had distracted her. Others claimed that, in the split second before she took the fence, the mare had suffered a massive heart attack. She had met the fence right, Heaney riding her as strongly and confidently as ever. But then she seemed to falter, to lose her way at the last crucial moment. Instead of taking off for the fence, she crashed through it, cartwheeling before landing awkwardly on her neck on the far side. Heaney, thrown clear by the fall, lay still as the rest of the field galloped past him, then sat up on the damp ground.

Ten yards from him, the best horse he had ever ridden was not so lucky. It took one look to see that the mare would never race again. Ballina Lady had broken her neck.

Clay Wentworth lowered his binoculars. The horse he had backed had jumped the last fence well clear but Clay had forgotten about the race. He reached into the inside pocket of his jacket and took out a handwritten list. Carefully, with his gold-plated biro, he crossed out one of the names on it.

* * *

'Fucking horses.' Gavin Holmes sat slumped in front of his screen on the vast open-plan floor at the *Guardian*'s Farringdon Road office. He was tired, he needed a drink and the editor had wanted yet another update on his racing story. Yesterday, at some poxy racecourse in Ireland, another nag – apparently a good one too – had gone belly-up. There were rumours that a member of the RSPCA Executive was about to launch a campaign to ban steeplechasing. One of his stringers was trying to find out how many horses were killed in training every year.

Gavin looked at his watch. It was six o'clock and his piece was complete and on-screen. In the unlikely event of his date for the night coming up with something tasty, he could always phone it in.

Gavin, who was thirty-five but had the muscle tone and liver of a man ten years older, stood up, hitched his jeans over the beginnings of a paunch and slipped on the leather jacket that had been draped over the back of the chair. His reputation as a ladies' man surprised some of the younger journalists – he had the jowly, pallid look of a man allergic to any kind of healthy living, he dressed like a slob and he was distinctly light on romantic charm, 'Are we going to do it or what?' being one of his more subtle approaches.

He made his way to a corner office in which his news editor sat, checking copy, a cigarette dangling from his mouth.

'Checking out a lead, Harry,' he said, standing at the door. 'I'll ring in any changes to the racing piece.'

'Hope she's worth it,' said the news editor without looking up.

Gavin took the lift to the ground floor. Once upon a time, he'd enjoyed his reputation for wildness but now he was discovering that today's tearaway is tomorrow's randy old drunk. Once he had been discussed as a future foreign correspondent; of all his contemporaries, Gavin Holmes was thought most likely to land his own column – witty, informed, knowing. Instead he was still on home news and his only claim to fame was that he had bedded a healthy percentage of his young female colleagues. 'Better than nothing,' he muttered, stumbling out of the lift.

Standing outside the *Guardian* building, the journalist patted his pockets. He had his cigarettes, he had his tape machine and, the eternal optimist, he had in his wallet a packet of condoms. Gavin smiled as he hailed a taxi. Maybe it was true what they said about girls and horses. Maybe tonight, he would get lucky.

'I don't ride horses myself. I – my boyfriend does.'

Angie felt uneasy as she sat across from the overweight, chain-smoking journalist at a corner table in a city bar. All around her, there was noise and laughter, punctuated by the occasional pop of a champagne cork. Somehow she had found herself backed against the wall, her knees unavoidably touching those of Gavin Holmes. If she tried to move them, she had no doubt that he would misread her body language as some kind of response and move in closer.

'Tell me about him. Your lover.'

Gavin filled the two glasses in front of them with champagne, drained his glass, and refilled it. In the ten minutes since they had met, he had smoked two cigarettes, made light work of a bottle of Moet et Chandon and casually dropped the names of several politicians and actors with whom he appeared to be on first-name terms.

'He comes from the north,' Angie said. 'He's a jockey. He's brave.' Angie was unhappy at the way the discussion was going.

'Will he ride again?'

'Probably not. He can't really walk yet.'

'Poor bastard.' Gavin waved at the barman and, ignoring Angie's protests, ordered another bottle of champagne. 'Where do I come into this?' he asked.

'In your article, you mentioned a video – taken head-on at Plumpton.'

'Right. I used a contact on the racecourse staff. He gave it to me.'

A waiter brought the second bottle of champagne to the table, filled Gavin's glass and poured a polite drop into Angie's which was already full.

'I thought your friend would have wanted to see it. What does he think?' Gavin asked. 'It looked deliberate to me.'

'He thinks – ' Angie checked herself, her head was aching now from the smoke and champagne. 'He thinks there's more to it than just one jockey stopping another.'

Gavin looked at Angie with his best knowing smile. This girl was cute – very cute. Young of course, and a bit shy, but he liked that.

'So it's a favour he's asking,' he said.

'A small favour.'

Angie closed her eyes, as the journalist moved his knee up and down against hers. She decided, for Paul, to give it one more try, then to leave.

'There may be a story in this,' she said. 'A big story. Paul would give you first shot at it.'

Suppressing a belch, Gavin muttered, 'Stories – who needs fucking stories? I've got stories up to where my hair used to be. They're the last thing I need – particularly if they're anything to do with sodding horses.'

'Fine.' Angie picked her bag off the floor. 'It was just a thought.'

'On the other hand,' Gavin said quickly. 'You never know. Why don't we talk about this over dinner? Maybe we could – ' the hint of a leer entered his voice '– work something out.'

'I have a train to catch.'

The journalist muttered, 'How about a quickie then?' Misunderstanding, Angie smiled politely. 'No, I've drunk too much already. I really ought to go.'

'I'll get you a taxi later. The paper'll pay.'

Angie tried to stand up but found her way barred.

'I think I might be able to help you with that favour,' Gavin was saying. 'Maybe two favours.'

Angie pushed back the table and, trying to ignore the hand that touched her thigh as she passed, paused briefly. 'Two favours?'

The journalist smiled. 'He can't walk, you say, your lover. Disabled. It must be tough on you. No nooky.'

Ignoring Angie's angry look, Gavin added quietly, 'I'll get you back in the morning. You and me, eh?'

She turned and walked quickly out of the bar.

* * *

The photographer sat in his BMW, some thirty yards away from the entrance to Markwick Instruments plc. He was a heavy man but the watchful look in his eyes and the slightly tanned face suggested that, should he ever be required to, he could defend himself in a tight corner. He had risen early that morning and now, at ten thirty in the evening, he looked unshaven and tired.

Peter Zametsky emerged from the front door of the office building, looked quickly left, then right, and walked towards the car. As he approached, the photographer got out, handed him the keys. The two men spoke briefly and quickly in their own language. Then the photographer crossed the road, unlocked an old Jaguar and drove off at no particular speed.

Peter sat in the BMW and spoke into the car telephone. When he had finished he drove the car towards the office building. As he approached, the metal gates that led to the office yard opened, allowing the car through.

After they had closed, a man watching from the darkness of a nearby alley walked away quickly down the gloomy side street towards the lights of Willesden.

Chapter
5

Racing likes its heroes dead and dignified, or alive and winning. It has no place for the halt and the lame. If Paul had been killed by Dig For Glory's fall at Plumpton, his tragically brief career would have been commemorated by an annual race at the course – the Paul Raven Memorial Hurdle or something similar. If he had walked away unharmed, the calls from trainers would have continued to come in. As it was, he was no more than a distant memory. In the harsh, enclosed world of racing, there's no place for fellow travellers.

It was a month after his discharge from the Home in Croydon and, on the face of it, he had much for which to be thankful. With the help of two walking sticks and occasional pain-killers, he could walk, albeit slowly and uncertainly. The doctors, whose experience had taught them to be pessimistic about back injuries, had found themselves revising their prognoses as, step by painful step, Paul proved them wrong. Those who once confidently predicted that he would never be free of his wheelchair admitted that a few, shuffled paces a day would be a possibility. When Paul walked twenty, then thirty, then fifty yards, they admitted they may have over-estimated the damage to his vertebrae. On the day he discharged himself from the Home, they warned him of the consequences but, among themselves, they were pleased to see him go. He was a difficult patient. Bloody-minded. He had never done what he had been told.

Yes, he was thankful to be away from the men in white coats, thankful to be walking slowly, still with two walking-sticks but more confidently now, down Lambourn High Street. He was home and, although he could do nothing to help in the yard, he had been allowed to stay in the small flat rented by Ron Charlesworth for his more favoured staff. This, by Charlesworth's standards, was an act of almost unprecedented generosity.

It was too early to say what he would do with his life. Angie, who visited him on her days off, believed he should get out of racing altogether, but Paul knew he couldn't. Not yet at least.

He turned into a newsagent where an elderly man handed him a *Sporting Life* with a cheery 'What do you know, Paul?'

'Not much, Bill.' Paul smiled. Like several of his friends in Lambourn, Bill Preston overcame the embarrassment of his disability by refusing to admit it existed. Every day, he was as eager for tips from Paul as if he were on his way to the races, at the centre of things, as he had been in the old days.

He took the paper and glanced at the headlines, the tips and whispers about the day's runners. No, Angie was wrong – racing was in his blood. Until he knew what had happened to Alex, it would stay there.

Paul was greeted by a couple of stable lads from Charlesworth's yard but resisted the temptation to ask them of any news. Although the trainer was making use of freelances, it could only be a matter of time before he signed up a new stable jockey. For their part, the lads seemed uneasy, hurrying on after exchanging a few pleasantries with Paul, as if his bad luck could be catching.

A dirty yellow Rolls Royce cruised down the High Street. It passed Paul, then stopped some twenty yards ahead of him. The driver had made no attempt to park, leaving the car some two feet from the kerb. A woman, blonde and in her late thirties or early forties, emerged and half walked, half ran, a fur coat billowing behind her, tripping on high heels towards where Paul stood. To his surprise, she held out an elegant hand.

'Mr Raven?'

'That's right.'

The woman smiled, perfect capped teeth gleaming behind the lipstick.

'Zena Wentworth. We haven't met.'

Guardedly, Paul hooked the walking-stick over his arm and shook her hand. The woman's breezy confidence and cut-glass tones were not endearing. 'How can I help you?' he asked.

'It's about Alex Drew,' she said. 'I was a friend of his.' Behind her, several drivers, held up by the badly parked Rolls, were sounding their horns. 'Dickheads,' she said conversationally.

'How did you know Alex?' Paul asked.

Zena flashed another smile and glanced over her shoulder. 'The natives appear to be getting restless,' she said. 'Let me give you lunch.'

Paul thought for a moment, then nodded. 'All right,' he said. 'Let's go to a pub.'

Zena Wentworth wasn't used to pubs. Three had been rejected on the grounds of being too smoky, too common and too full of darts players before they found a hotel on the outskirts of Wantage which she found acceptable. A fast driver, she had kept up a monologue, rarely interrupted by Paul.

Half listening, while gripping the side of his seat, Paul had discovered that Zena was married to Clay Wentworth, that she had not the slightest interest in racing and that she appeared to be on first name terms with most of the well-bred wallies whose faces Paul had seen in gossip columns and glossy magazines.

It was only when they were sitting in the dining-room of the Bell Tavern, Wantage that Zena mentioned Alex Drew. Already, she had made it clear that the quiet, unpretentious atmosphere was not what she was used to, bewildering the young waitress by asking for a tequila before settling sulkily for a large vodka and tonic. When the waitress brought them the menu in a plastic folder, she had opened it, placed a hand over the typed contents and said, 'Let me guess. Steak and chips. Gammon and chips. Plaice and chips.' And she was right, of course.

After the waitress had taken their order, she lit a cigarette. 'God, I hate the countryside,' she said cheerfully. 'This is the sort of place Alex used to take me to.'

Paul watched her as the cigarette smoke caught the winter sun shining into the half empty dining-room. There was something odd about Zena Wentworth, a tension which suggested that her sophistication and worldliness were a disguise, a cover.

'How did you know Alex?' he asked again, quietly.

'Met him at a party in London,' she said vaguely. 'Usual thing. Boy meets girl. We – ' she gave him a knowing smile ' – clicked.'

'Are you telling me – ' Realising that his incredulity might be taken for rudeness, Paul hesitated. 'But he had a girlfriend.'

'Everybody has a girlfriend. And everybody cheats.'

The waitress brought the drinks. Zena raised her glass before drinking deeply. Paul sipped at his tomato juice, thinking about Alex. That his friend had been unfaithful to Joanna was hardly a surprise. But Zena Wentworth? She could have been his mother.

'What's this got to do with me?' he asked.

Zena seemed more relaxed now that she had a glass in her hand. 'I heard – a little birdy told me – that you wanted to know more about Alex's death.'

Paul nodded. For all her apparent lack of interest in racing, Zena Wentworth seemed well-informed. Over the past month, he had been ringing around his contacts, people who knew or had worked with Alex. The story had always been the same. Until the beginning of this season, Alex had been fine. Since then, as Paul had noticed himself, he had become less reliable, turning up late for work, struggling to make weights that last season would have been easy. Like Paul, no one seemed to know what his problem was. But there was something outside racing that had been distracting him. Paul had spoken to Joanna but she had seemed embarrassed by the call, as if Paul's interest was no more than a morbid obsession with the past.

'I want to know why he killed himself,' he said. 'I haven't been able to do much – I only started driving last week – but I'm convinced he was involved in something.'

'There's a little man I know who's become rather interested in Alex's story. A somewhat unsavoury journalist called Gavin Holmes. I believe you know him.'

'I know the name,' Paul said carefully. 'I wouldn't have thought he was on your circuit.'

Zena gave a contemptuous little laugh. 'He isn't, thank God. A couple of years ago he developed an interest in the scandalous use of drugs in society. Some little prig gave him my name. We developed what you might call a working relationship.' She paused, as if expecting a question. 'Like most journalists, the man's infinitely corruptible. I hadn't heard from him for a while until he called the other day. It appears that he's taking an interest in Alex. He told me that a little friend of yours had seen him.'

'Yes. He wasn't helpful.'

'Tell me why you're so interested.'

'I need to be convinced that it was an accident.'

'Did you know Alex gambled?' Zena asked suddenly.

'He didn't gamble. I'd know if he was in the pocket of the bookmakers. Stewards may not be able to tell the triers from the non-triers, but one jockey can't fool another, and believe me, he always did his best.'

'Not bookmakers. Cards. He fancied himself at stud poker, poor boy.'

'I know. He used to play with the other jockeys in the weighing room. He was quite good. How did you know he played cards?'

Picking unenthusiastically at her microwaved plaice and chips, Zena told him about the Thursday poker nights – how Alex, at first an occasional player, had over the months before his death become a regular. When Paul shook his head incredulously, she said, 'He wanted to be a grown-up, poor boy. He wanted to be one of the big guys.'

'Did he win?'

Zena shrugged. 'You should understand that, in my marriage, communication is limited to the practical. Clay would no more tell me about his poker nights than I would tell him about my . . . private business. I understood from Alex that he was in some difficulty. He didn't like talking about it.'

'What sort of people go to these poker nights?'

'They're either rich and bored, or on the make. The only regulars that I know of are Lol Calloway, the clapped-out rock star, and a man called Digby Welcome. I can try to get more names, if you want.' She smiled, lighting up another cigarette although Paul was still eating. 'Maybe we could work together on this.'

'The names would be useful, although I still don't see the connection between Alex's gambling and what happened at Plumpton.'

'Nor me.' Zena picked up the leather bag that she had laid beside her chair. 'I must be going. I'll see if I can find out any more for you.'

'How?'

Zena Wentworth gave a histrionic little shudder. 'I don't even want to *think* about it,' she said.

Later, driving back to London, Zena thought about Paul Raven. She had, of course, told him only part of what she knew, but the information would revive his faltering attempts to discover what had happened to Alex Drew.

She was coming down, the couple of pills she had taken that morning to get her through the day had been nullified by the vodka. Zena accelerated, pushing the Rolls up to a hundred and ten as she fumbled in her bag. Expertly, she removed another pill from a small bottle and tossed it back into her mouth.

She smiled at the thought of Paul Raven's expression when she had left. For a man who rode horses, he was no fool. He realised what she meant. He was so young, so innocent. For him, the most simple of sexual transactions had a deep significance. Zena tried to remember what that purity had been like, but failed. It was all so long ago.

She thought of Alex, of how she and Clay, in different ways, had corrupted him and felt a fleeting pang of guilt. Yes, what she was doing was right. Paul Raven was a bonus. On the racecourse at Plumpton, he had seemed just another scrawny jockey but weeks of inaction had filled out his face. Pain and anger had made it interesting.

'Just once,' she said. 'Once is all I want.'

*   *   *

In America, Alice Markwick had always thought, they organized things better. If her first stop from Prague had been New York rather than London, she wouldn't have found herself dealing with bungling, weak amateurs, with the astonishing complexities of Britain's subtle class system, with the obstacles placed in her way by interfering government bureaucrats.

Behind Alice's large desk, a cold winter dusk was settling sullenly on the streets of Willesden. The workers from the factory below were making their way home, doubtless cursing her name and dreaming of a time when their futures would not be bound up with that of Markwick Instruments plc.

She didn't give a damn. Dispensing human happiness had never figured among her priorities. Once, three or four years ago, she had employed a Personnel Officer but he had disagreed with her on a matter of basic policy – as to whether to treat personnel like human beings or expendable units – and she had fired him within the month. Her firm was no place for tenderhearts.

She pulled a small white telephone on her desk, her personal line, and stabbed out a number. It was time to put a call through to the man who made even her short-lived Personnel Officer seem like a tower of strength.

'Clay,' she said. 'Alice. I hear we're in business again.'

At the other end of the telephone, Clay laughed nervously. 'Went like a dream,' he said.

'No problems at all?'

'There are one or two comments in the racing press but everyone puts it down to bad luck.'

'It's a funny old game,' said Alice flatly.

'D'you have the *Sporting Life*?'

'I'm not a regular reader, I'm afraid, Clay.'

'Let me read you their report.' There was the sound of rustling paper and Alice imagined Clay in his large office, the huge photograph behind him showing Mr C Wentworth as he jumped the water at Kempton on Skinflint. She sighed. A captain of industry. God help England.

'Here we are,' he said finally. ' "JINX HITS CHELTENHAM HOPE . . . . The extraordinary run of bad luck that has befallen the season's contenders for the top amateur prizes continued yesterday at Huntingdon when the highly fancied Brut Force failed to finish after a bizarre accident in the Valentine Hunter Chase. The experienced nine-year-old, who started at eleven to four on, appeared to be making light work of the field of six when, after jumping superbly throughout, he entered the final turn with a ten-length lead only to fail to negotiate the bend, crashing through the stand side rails in a horrific fall. His young amateur rider Jamie Saunders, who was miraculously uninjured, was mystified by the normally reliable Brut Force's lapse. 'Until then, he hadn't put a foot wrong,' Saunders told me. 'But, as we came out of the bend, he seemed to panic and I couldn't steer him.'

' "Trainer Charlie Dixon had been mystified as to what went wrong and added that the horse appeared to have injured his back and had lacerations to his hindquarters.

' "Brut Force won't run again this season," he said, "but we hope to patch him up for next year."

' "Brut Force is the latest of a series of horses fancied for one of the major amateur races at the National Hunt Festival which have been forced to withdraw, after the tragic deaths over the last month of the Irish mare Ballina Lady and the crack northern 'chaser Whataparty." '

'Accidents will happen,' said Alice. 'Perhaps we should leave it there. We don't want to stretch coincidence too far.'

'One more,' Clay said briskly. 'Thursday, Wincanton. As we agreed.'

Alice sighed. 'At least there's no danger of a post mortem this time,' she said.

'Right,' said Clay. 'Are you coming to play poker this week?'

'I hope so.'

After she had hung up, Alice sat at her desk, deep in thought. True, Clay was a bungling amateur, but he was a useful bungling amateur, and expendable. After all – she glanced at the photograph of a frail-looking man that was given pride of place in the office – bungling amateurs had served her well.

Not that the late Dr Eric Markwick was an amateur in every way. As a scientist, he had been years ahead of his time. It was real life that caused him problems.

As Alice's ambitions had begun to seem realizable at last, she found herself thinking more and more of Eric. Doubtless he would have thought her plans dangerous, immoral even. His risks and gambles rarely extended beyond the theoretical and scientific; his weakness was not for money or power, but simply for Alzbeta Flaishman, an innocent little Czechoslovak girl trying to find her way in a wicked western metropolis.

Alice smiled. She must have been innocent once, when she was Alzbeta, but she really couldn't remember when. Prague during the 'fifties and 'sixties was no place for childish illusion. Her father worked in a munitions factory, spending what little he earned on vodka, occasionally venting his rage against a grey, unjust world on Alzbeta, her older brother Tomas and, above all, on her mother. Partly to earn extra money and partly to escape from the bellows and the flailing of her husband, Alzbeta's mother Irina had taken a job, cleaning government offices in the evening and late into the night.

She was beautiful. No misery could extinguish the sparkle of those dark eyes, the long dark curls, the frail but womanly body.

Their life changed. Mr Flaishman was given promotion and an honorary post in the local party. The family was able to move to a larger flat in a better part of town. Maybe, when she was seven or eight, Alzbeta might have believed that this was the way life was – you worked, you were rewarded – but there was something in her mother's eyes that told her differently, that spoke of corruption and compromise.

There was one moment that changed it all. One night – Alzbeta was just ten – word came from the local bar that old Flaishman had hurt himself, having become involved in a brawl. A neighbour had seen the fight and ran to tell Alzbeta and her brother that their father had been taken unconscious to the local hospital. Tomas had gone to the hospital while Alzbeta went through the dark streets of Prague to the Central Party offices where her mother was working.

It was ten-thirty when she arrived in the vast building. Frantically she had asked a couple of crones sweeping a downstairs corridor where she could find Mrs Flaishman. Her question had caused much hilarity, but eventually they had directed her to the top floor.

The building was five floors high, there was no lift and by the time she reached the top, she was breathless and tearful. She tried office after office, nervously opening each door in the brightly-lit warren of corridors. It seemed a lifetime but it must have been five minutes at the most when she pushed open the large door to a corner office.

The man was large and wearing the grey uniform of a senior officer in the army. His face was red and transfixed by an ugly smile, or perhaps a grimace. His fat hand, like that of a priest conferring a blessing on a communicant, lay on her mother's head as, kneeling – crouched under the pendulous bulk of the man's paunch – she worked on him, nodding like a doll with a broken neck. As Alzbeta stood there, the man tightened his grip on her mother's head, not allowing her to turn towards the door. 'Welcome, little one,' he said thickly. 'Have you come to join the party?'

She stood there for twenty seconds, perhaps thirty. Then, without a word, she had turned, rushing blindly down the corridor, almost falling down the stairs and into the icy cold night where she had run, tears streaming down her face, back to the flat.

Because everyday existence in Prague was full of such humiliations and sleazy compromises, nothing much changed among the Flaishmans after that night. Alzbeta's father recovered but, whenever the mood was upon him, would blame Irina for not visiting him in hospital that night. But then little Alzbeta had failed to find her. While old man Flaishman grumbled and Tomas mocked Alzbeta for her ineffectiveness, the two women of the family had caught one another's eye and each had looked away quickly, unwilling to acknowledge the guilty secret they shared.

When she grew up, she came to think of her mother as a heroine, abasing herself night after night, an unofficial whore, so that her family could survive. But then, with the clear, unforgiving eyes of childhood, she felt nothing but a deep sense of betrayal – of her father, of the family, above all, of her. A coldness entered the home as little Alzbeta extinguished the warmth and laughter she had once brought to it.

Seeing her mother kneeling before the soldier changed Alzbeta's life for ever. She knew, even at ten years old, that she had to get away from the family, possibly even from the country. Never political, she spent her teens begging her parents to be sent to the west to study, professing a deep interest in the ways of capitalism. An exit visa, of course, was impossible; the Flaishman family had little enough money without the expense of sending a daughter abroad.

And here was the ultimate compromise. Alzbeta knew the way things worked in Czechoslovakia. She understood that her mother could win her escape only one way, yet she asked for it. While treating her mother with cold disapproval, she accepted the rewards of whatever Irina did at the government offices into the early hours of the morning. On her eighteenth birthday, Alzbeta was given an exit visa and one hundred pounds in English money. When she cried, her father and Tomas assumed it was out of gratitude. Only Irina knew the truth.

Something else changed that night when old Flaishman got drunk and was taken to hospital. As the girl became a woman, as beautiful as her mother, with the same dark curls and slender waist, Alzbeta knew with a deep certainty that, whatever else she did, she would never make love to a man. She would lose her virginity, of course, she would use her beauty, but in submitting to men, she would be the exploiter, not the exploited. She might smile, flirt, feign desire but it would be done with a clear-eyed coolness that had nothing to do with love. The idea of being penetrated was loathsome to her; it was a foul invasion, for which she would demand, and receive, the highest price.

The heating in the offices of Markwick Instruments had been turned off, and Alice shuddered. 'Poor Eric,' she said quietly, as she tidied the papers on her desk. Poor Eric had only discovered that too late.

Turning off the lights in her office, she made her way downstairs, across the yard to the laboratory. Zametsky would be there, of course. Despite the young wife and baby whom he worshipped, Peter usually worked late, so absorbed in his work that he would hardly have noticed that the sun had set, that his colleagues had gone home. Sometimes he worked until nine or ten at night, the light in his corner cubicle shining like the beacon of pure research into the grubby gloom of Willesden.

Pure research. Alice Markwick smiled as she entered the laboratory.

'What about that poor wife of yours, Peter?' she called out as she made her way down one side of the lab, switching off work-lamps.

There was a distracted grunt from the direction of Peter Zametsky's desk. Sometimes, when she had interrupted him as he worked on a problem, stabbing at the keyboard of his computer, making swift, feverish notes on a lined pad on the desk, he had seemed in a different world, had turned to her with a look of fierce concentration, the light in his eyes fading slowly as he turned back into the dull world of reality. He should have been at a university where such intensity was regarded as normal but there again no university could give Peter Zametsky what she could offer.

Alice was about to leave the genius in his laboratory, working for the good of human knowledge and Markwick Instruments – though not necessarily in that order – when she noticed through the frosted glass of his corner office, that he appeared to be sitting on his chair. Then she saw a foot, trembling slightly, obtruding from the office.

He was lying on his back, his legs awry and his hands palm downwards on the floor, clawing at it. His shirt appeared to have burnt around the chest and neck but Peter's head was hidden behind the desk. As Alice stepped, his body shook epileptically. Then she saw his face – or, at least, what remained of his face under the bubbling, suppurating purple surface that had once been his flesh. The eyes were gone, the nose was no more than a white bone extending from a featureless mass. His hair, like the carpet beneath his head, had been burnt away, but the mouth – a lipless, gaping cavern – was open in a silent scream of pain.

Alice stepped back. She took a deep breath, swaying slightly. Then she walked quickly to a nearby telephone, stabbing three digits quickly. Her voice, when it came, had only the hint of a tremor.

'Ambulance,' she said.

Digby Welcome was asleep in his deep and comfortable single bed when the call came through. He had had a busy day – a full five hours work on the daytime job, followed by a late evening trawl among his Kensington contacts, and he was tired. As his head touched the pillow, he was off, enjoying the profound, untroubled sleep of a man with no conscience.

'Is it a bad moment?' The voice at the other end of the telephone was Clay Wentworth's. He sounded more than usually rattled.

Digby looked at the leather-cased alarm clock by his bed. 'Two thirty in the morning is always a bad moment, dear boy.' He sat up in his bed and switched on the light. In his well-cut flannel pyjamas covering his globe-like stomach, he looked almost cuddly. 'But I'm not fucking anyone, if that's what you mean.'

'We have a problem. Alice's senior boffin appears to have been attacked. She's spitting – thinks there's been some sort of security leak.'

'Bloody fool. Why does she think that has anything to do with us?'

'It appears she's had her suspicions for some time. She rang me a few days ago about some taxman snooping around. She had managed to convince herself that he was part of the opposition. Just turned up out of the blue, claiming to have made an appointment through a female secretary.'

'I thought she only employed male secretaries.'

'Precisely. Then this chap Zametsky had told her that he thought the offices were being watched – cars parked across the road and so on. Next thing she knows the guy's had some sort of acid splashed over him.'

'Oh shit.' It was an utterance of vague annoyance, like that of a man finding he hasn't a clean shirt in the morning.

'She's managed to keep the police out of it. Luckily the acid came from the Markwick stores so she managed to persuade the doctors that it was an accident. Anyway, I promised her I'd ring round. You haven't been talking have you, Digby?'

'Don't be absurd. I may not be good for much but my discretion's phenomenal. Have you tried Lol?'

'He said the same thing.'

'Zena? No one could be less discreet than your wife when she's on the stuff.'

Clay Wentworth gave a humourless laugh. 'She knows nothing about this.'

'Well then.' Digby yawned, running a hand over his large stomach. 'No problem. Probably Alice getting the jitters. You know how she is. What about her chap – the one with the acid? Has he said anything?'

'He's in intensive care. Alice seems to think that he won't make it.'

'Poor bastard,' said Digby cheerily, promising to see Clay at Wincanton.

'Yes, poor bastard,' he muttered after Clay had hung up, but he was thinking of himself now. He was awake, his fat frame full of an unmistakeable restlessness for which there was only one known cure. He reached into a drawer in the bedside table, taking out a small black book. He found a number and dialled.

Chapter
6

It was a long, painful walk from the car park at Wincanton to the weighing-room. Even now that he had graduated from two walking-sticks to one, Paul could shuffle only slowly, and with many rests. Then there was the pain: in spite of Angie's protests, he had weaned himself off painkillers, determined, in an obscure, unmedical way, to fight his handicap on his own terms.

There was another kind of pain. It was Paul's first return to a racecourse after his fall at Plumpton and he had to endure the sympathy and covert, sideways looks of those who had known him when he was fit and on the way up. A few pretended not to notice him and hurried by, but most of them – particularly the trainers and jockeys – paused to talk to him, their voices unusually loud and hearty, their eyes betraying embarrassment, fear and, worst of all, pity.

Angie helped. She walked beside him slowly, with the easy amble of one who's happy to take her time. She asked him questions about racing – innocent daft questions that, had they been asked by anyone else, Paul would have found irritating. It was the first time she had been racing and her clothes – a light girlish shirt, a beret on her head, a bright green scarf wrapped around her neck – gave her away. Paul glanced at her and smiled. She looked sexy, fashionable, and desirable. On the whole, people who came racing at Wincanton in February were none of these things.

'You look good,' he said quietly, as they made their way onto the course.

'I'm not sure I approve of all this. I might stage an anti-racing demo in the paddock.'

Paul laughed. 'That would be the end of a beautiful friendship,' he said.

'Bloody hell, I thought you were crook, Raven.' The unmistakeable, booming tones of Ginnie Matthews interrupted their conversation.

Paul stopped, leaning briefly on his walking-stick, as the trainer sized him up, as if he were one of her charges after a spot of work. 'Not finished yet, Mrs Matthews.'

Ginnie glanced at Angie. 'So I see,' she said, introducing herself to Angie with a smile. 'Better go and see my fella at the stables. How about a drink later? Catch up on the news.'

'That would be good.' Paul smiled. For all her bluff heartiness, Ginnie Matthews was one of the few trainers who wouldn't make him feel uneasy. 'Just the one runner today?'

'Skinflint. We should win the amateur race.'

'Tanglewood's useful.' Ginnie dropped her voice to what she assumed was an undertone but still made nearby heads turn. 'Which is more than could be said for our jockey.'

'Who's the jockey?' Angie asked, after Ginnie had left.

'A man called Clay Wentworth,' said Paul. 'It was his wife who came to see me.'

'Small world.'

'Yes. Everybody knows everybody else's secrets.'

'Which should make it easier to find out what happened to Alex.'

'Let's hope so.'

Paul took Angie to the bar where he bought her a drink and found her a quiet table. 'I'm going to the weighing-room,' he said. 'I need to talk to someone. I'll be back in a few minutes.' Then, seeing the look of uneasiness that crossed Angie's face, he added, 'Don't worry. It's one of life's golden rules – no one gets picked up at Wincanton.'

Angie looked around the bar, where men and women were earnestly discussing the day's racing. Apart from the occasional, distracted glance in her direction she might have been invisible. 'Don't be long,' she said.

It was strange re-entering the weighing-room, leaning on a stick, a bystander to the day's action. Already, Paul felt an outsider. Although the official at the door, who was only supposed to admit jockeys riding that day, had nodded him through, there was a hint of sympathy to his smile; there was no mistaking the warmth of the greetings given to him by his fellow jockeys and by the valets but here, for the first time, in the smell of cigarette smoke, linament and saddle soap, he became aware of the void that would be left in his life now that he was unable to ride any more. Suddenly he was an outsider, a hanger-on, a has-been.

'You look better than ever, Pauly.' Jim Wilson sat down beside him during the brief lull that followed the jockeys for the first race trooping out of the weighing-room. 'If it weren't for that stick, I'd be laying out your gear as if nothing had happened.'

Paul smiled. 'And I'd be getting into it. I can't get used to this spectator lark.'

'When will you be back? End of the season?'

'They don't know.' Paul looked away. He wasn't in the mood to discuss his future. 'Tell me what the lads have been saying about Alex.'

'Lex.' The valet wiped his hands with the cloth he was carrying. It was an odd, uncharacteristic action and he suddenly seemed older and more fragile than his years. Alex, Paul remembered, had been one of Jim's favourite jockeys. 'Now there's a thing for you.'

'Someone must have an idea what made him do it.'

'He was in a bad way. We all knew that. Even before – ' Jim hesitated ' – even before Plumpton, he had been acting strange. But you know how he was, he'd keep on joking, never letting on what was really happening.'

'Bookies?'

'No. I asked around. He didn't bet – at least no more than any of the lads did. I have a feeling it was something to do with his life outside racing.'

'I saw the head-on of our race at Plumpton,' Paul said quietly. 'There's no doubt that he was up to something.'

'You mean he put you through the wing.'

'Let's just say he could have given me more room.'

'I can't understand it. He was your mate.'

'Nor can I. But if he did put me through the wing and then thought that I'd never walk again, it could explain why . . .' Ambushed by obscene imaginings of his best friend, Paul stared ahead in silence.

'I saw him alone in the car park that day. Then one of the lads said he was talking to Digby Welcome near the Members' Bar.'

'Welcome?' Paul was incredulous. 'That bastard offered me two grand to stop a horse at Lingfield once. What would Alex want with him?'

For a moment, the two men sat in silence, thinking of Alex Drew. Then Jim stood up. 'Is it a good idea, this?' he asked. 'Maybe you should be thinking about your own future, rather than digging around in the past.'

'I'll have plenty of time for that.'

'Better get on, Pauly.'

'Let us know if you hear anything, right?'

Jim nodded. 'I'll do some asking round,' he said.

Angie had always considered herself an easygoing, gregarious sort of person who could adapt to most social environments. A couple of years ago, her father had taken her to Henley where she had smiled her way through a tiresome afternoon of straw hats and champagne without too much difficulty. One of her first boyfriends had been obsessed by grand prix racing – hours at Silverstone spent jostled by men in sheepskin coats with their willowy girlfriends against a background of screaming engines had posed no problem. A passing-out parade at Sandhurst, a *thé dansant* at the Savoy, a fashion show in aid of Africa's starving millions, an acid house party in a disused hangar off the M25 – Angie had endured them all with the same sweet tolerance.

But National Hunt racing on a Thursday, particularly now that Paul had left her on her own while he visited old friends, was proving to be a trial. Wherever, she went, she felt eyes following her, as if no one young and well-dressed had ever been seen here before.

In the bar, she had been ignored until two men in officer issue overcoats had, after a languid enquiry in her direction which she had failed to understand, sat down at her table to conduct a hearty conversation about breeding and bloodstock. Occasionally one of the men had glanced at her with undisguised suspicion so that eventually, feeling like a spy, she had left the table and stood at the bar to wait for Paul.

There was only one group of racegoers, Angie decided, that belonged to a world that she recognized or understood. Some ten yards away from her was a table already laden with champagne bottles. Two women – one dark and with her back to her, the other a jaded blonde who was doing most of the talking – sat across the table from a long-haired man, whose face seemed vaguely familiar to Angie, and a red-faced, pot-bellied character whose glittering little eyes darted around the bar-room as if looking for someone he recognized.

It occurred to Angie that, despite the ease with which they were working their way through the champagne, these people, like her, were outsiders.

'Hullo, darling. Come 'ere often, do you?'

Angie turned, her social defences at the ready, to see Paul, smiling.

'Thank God you're back,' she said, laughing uneasily.

'What happened to your table?'

'I was joined by two middle-aged men who started talking about sex.'

'Sex? At Wincanton?'

'Between horses.'

Paul laughed. 'That's all right then.' He told her about the conversation with Jim Wilson. 'I need to see one or two people. Then we'll have that drink with Ginnie Matthews and be off.'

Angie looked away. 'I don't like being the little woman, Paul,' she said quietly but firmly. 'It's not my style.'

'Give me until after the second race. Why not get away from these idiots and go onto the racecourse. Stand by a fence. You can find out whether racing's as cruel as you think.'

Reluctantly, she agreed. Sometimes these days she wondered about Paul Raven. The icy, almost obsessive determination that had helped him out of the wheelchair onto his feet was praiseworthy enough, but he could be cold. Nothing would stand in the way of his need to find out what happened to Alex. The desire for revenge was there, at the centre of Paul's life; perhaps, Angie thought now, not for the first time, it excluded the potential for love.

'Talk of the devil.' Paul was looking across the room to the party of two men and two women that Angie had noticed.

'Which devil is that?' she asked quietly.

'A man called Digby Welcome. Sitting with Zena Wentworth, the blonde woman on his left.'

'Wasn't she the one who came to see you?'

'Aye.' Paul smiled as Zena looked in his direction but she pointedly ignored him. 'But it seems she's forgotten me already.'

So, with a reluctance that she hoped was obvious even to Paul, Angie agreed to watch a race by herself and made her way to join a small crowd of spectators and photographers standing in the centre of the course by the last fence. She looked at her racecard. Twelve horses were running, including Skinflint, the horse Paul had discussed with the hearty woman trainer. Its owner-rider was Mr Clay Wentworth.

Angie shivered slightly in her light overcoat. At least she had an interest in one of the runners.

It's not easy to follow a man when you can hardly walk, and Digby Welcome, despite his bulk, moved with the sprightly gait of the school fat boy heading for the tuck shop. Briefly Paul had considered asking Angie to tail him but he knew that was impossible. Besides he had something to tell Welcome in person.

After he had seen Angie making her way onto the course, he returned to the bar, just in time to see Digby pushing back his chair. 'Time for a little punt,' he said, patting Zena Wentworth on the shoulder, and scuttling off.

Slowly, Paul followed in the direction that he had gone, watching the broad back as it was engulfed by the crowd of racegoers who were making their way to the Silver Ring to put on their bets before the second race. Although he couldn't stay with him, Paul noted the name of the bookmaker, Bert Lomax, at whose stand Digby placed a bet. Then he turned and made his way back to the bar.

Paul played his own small gamble. Digby had consumed a fair amount of champagne. Even that fat gut would need relief sometime. Pushing his way through a door marked 'Gents', Paul selected a cubicle and waited.

There was no mistaking the approach of Digby Welcome. He wheezed like a tired steam engine approaching a station. Paul heard the sound of a zip being undone and a heavy sigh, before silently drawing back the bolt.

It was perfect. There was no one else there but Digby, his little legs apart, humming to himself, enjoying the moment of relief.

Paul turned his walking stick upside down, swung it back in an easy golf swing, and brought the heavy curved handle up sharply between Digby's legs.

It wasn't a scream of pain, or a gasp – it was the surprised yelp of a brutalized puppy. Digby collapsed, his face sliding down the urinal before he lay on the ground clutching at himself, his normally flushed face drained of colour.

Recovering his balance Paul took the handle of his walking-stick, placed its point on the side of Digby's neck and leaned forward, pinning him to the ground.

'Not me,' Digby managed to say, his eyes squeezed shut with pain and fear.

'Get in the toilet,' Paul said with quiet urgency.

'Wha – ? Wha – ?'

'Get your fat arse off the ground and into the cubicle.'

'Can't . . . move.'

Paul jabbed the end of his stick and Digby gave another little yelp as he dragged himself towards the cubicle.

There was wetness down the front of his trousers. 'For fuck's sake, put yourself away,' Paul muttered following him. 'Sit on the seat.'

Digby opened his eyes now and shook his head as he scrambled miserably onto the seat of the lavatory. 'There's been some mistake,' he whispered.

Outside, there was the sound of voices approaching. Paul closed the door of the cubicle, holding up a warning finger to Digby. They heard voices outside, two men discussing the amateur race. By the time they had left, a mottled unhealthy colour had returned to Digby's cheeks and he was breathing more easily.

'Would you care to explain why you've assaulted me, Mr Raven?' he said with a feeble attempt to retain his dignity.

'No.' Paul held his stick to Digby's neck, pushing him back against a pipe behind him. 'Tell me what you know about Alex Drew.'

'Racing. I used to see him racing.'

Paul jabbed the walking-stick. 'Friends, were you?'

The normal look of evasive cunning had returned to Digby's eyes. He was no hero but, now that the throbbing pain in his groin was receding, he could see that a man with a walking-stick – a man who had difficulty walking – was hardly in a strong position.

'We met occasionally,' he said. 'And unless you let me out of here, I'll report you to the stewards.'

Paul laughed. 'Get me warned off, will you? Excessive use of the walking-stick?' He lowered his voice. 'I know things about you that would destroy you. I just need information.'

'Alex wasn't the saint you seem to think he was.'

'Go on.'

'He couldn't keep his hands off women. He was addicted to it.'

Paul shrugged. 'People don't kill themselves for getting too much sex. Was he stopping horses for you?'

'Not his own. He was too ambitious for that.' Digby took the point of the walking-stick and, with an ironic wince, pushed it slightly aside.

Slowly lowering the stick, Paul asked, 'So he gambled, right?'

Digby Welcome nodded, as he attempted fussily to adjust his clothing.

'I don't understand why having the occasional punt on a horse should have destroyed him.'

Checking in his top pocket, Digby took out a betting-slip as if to reassure himself it was still there, then returned it to the pocket. 'Punt?' he managed a pained smile. 'It wasn't horses. It was poker – stud poker.'

Paul reached into Digby's top pocket a nd examined the betting-slip. 'Got a good thing for the next race, have we?'

The fat man swallowed hard. 'Steal that,' he said quietly, 'and you won't have heard the last of it.'

'Mmm.' Paul examined the slip. 'Sounds like a very good thing – but I'll resist the temptation. Jockeys aren't allowed to bet.' He pulled back the bolt behind him and backed out of the cubicle. Holding the betting-slip before him, he tore it up, throwing the pieces into the next-door toilet and flushing it away.

Hearing the rushing water, Digby darted into the cubicle in a doomed attempt to retrieve the slip. His hands wet he turned red-faced to where Paul was standing. 'You don't know what you've started, Raven,' he said.

Paul smiled coldly. 'I'd tidy yourself up before you go back to the Members' Bar,' he said. 'You've got piss in your hair.'

The crowd was thinning as Paul made his way down to the Silver Ring. Glancing down the course, he could see the runners and riders, circling around the starter in the last moments before the 'off'.

Although unlike many jockeys, Paul had always considered betting too risky a way of supplementing his income to justify breaking the rules of racing, he had a nodding acquaintance with the bookmakers whose pitches were frequently on courses where he was riding.

Bert Lomax was one of the old school. A small hunched man with the lined, expressive face of a lugubrious music-hall comedian, he rarely smiled and, when he did, it was while the rest of the world was cursing. An odds-on favourite that broke its leg, a housewife's choice going arse over tit at the first fence in the Grand National – these were moments when there would be the faintest trace of facial movement around the fat cigar Bert invariably smoked. 'Lovely job,' he would say before his features settled back, into impassivity, like mud disturbed by a passing gumboot.

'Wounded hero, is it?' Bert Lomax glanced at Paul as he approached. 'When you going to start riding again, Paul? We need a few more beaten favourites.'

'Thanks, Bert,' Paul smiled. 'I knew I could count on you for a few encouraging words.'

Bert puffed at his cigar without removing it from his lips. 'Bloody shame it was,' he said. 'Bloody diabolical.'

Paul looked at the bookmaker's board. In the field of eight for The Gentleman Jim Handicap 'chase for Amateur Riders, two horses – Skinflint and Tanglewood – were joint favourites at six to four. Punters had seemed to give the other runners little chance, the next most fancied horse being Drago's Pet at six to one.

'Busy?' Paul asked.

'Not bad for a bumper,' Bert said. 'Lot of late money for Tanglewood.'

'Nice horse,' Paul said. 'I rode it once in a novice hurdle. I always thought it would make a chaser.'

There was a scurry of activity as the racecourse commentator announced that the field was under orders. As Bert had said, most of the money seemed to be going on Tanglewood. 'They're off.' Bert wiped the chalked prices off his board and stepped down from the small ladder on which he had been standing.

'Did Digby Welcome have a bet with you?'

'Yeah, the fat bastard.' All the bookmakers knew Digby and most disliked him. 'Had to lay it off too. He had three grand on that Skinflint and a couple of ton on Drago's Pet. He must be flush. Tight bastard usually. Fancy Tanglewood, do you?'

'Don't know about that.' Paul smiled at the bookmaker. 'They've all got a chance until the tapes go up.'

He made his way slowly back to the grandstand. If he had been a betting man, he would have ventured a few bob on Tanglewood, the big bay he saw bobbing along the outside of the field as they jumped the fence in front of the stand. Although he was held on form by Skinflint, he had two great advantages over him: a pull of eight pounds in the handicap, and the fact that he wasn't being ridden by Clay Wentworth.

With mild interest, Paul watched the runners as they wheeled right-handed into the country. Wentworth was easy to spot – he was the one standing up in the stirrups like a policeman directing children across the road. Even two hundred yards away the man exuded incompetence.

There were even more people at Wincanton than usual, local racegoers having been tempted by the bright, wintry weather and the prospect of seeing several fancied candidates for the big prizes at Cheltenham running for the last time before the National Hunt festival. Paul trained his binoculars on the second last fence where Angie stood in a small group of spectators, a splash of colour against the grey and brown.

Maybe she would learn to like racing, discover that there was more to it than small men lacerating horses with their whips, more than broken bones and heartbreak. Paul smiled. She had been nervous about coming. She'd embarrass him, she had said – use the wrong terms, say the wrong things, she would be an outsider. As if that mattered.

The field was strung out on the far side of the course. As happened so often with amateurs, the early pace had been too fast, and already the horses or jockeys who needed the race were losing touch. With a mile to go, one of the outsiders, thirty lengths behind the field, tumbled wearily over a fence, unseating its jockey as if protesting against the whole absurd business. Tanglewood had moved closer to the leaders but was still a couple of lengths behind Skinflint who, in spite of Wentworth's worst efforts, was gaining ground with every fence.

At least, Paul thought, the face that Angie saw at close quarters from the racecourse was unlikely to reveal the sport's harsher face. There was a gentility about the way amateurs rode: most of them lacked the killer instinct that caused crashing falls over the final fences, and excessive use of the whip was beyond their area of capability. Amateurs of the type Alex Drew had been were rare. Of those riding in this race, only Bill Scott, the young farmer's son who was on Tanglewood, had any hope of turning professional.

Of course, Jim Wilson was right. The obsession with Alex's death, with the past, could lead him nowhere. A sensible man would weigh his assets – youth, a passable brain, a loyal girlfriend – against his liabilities – the small matter of a broken body – and look to the future. Acting the avenging angel, he risked losing more than he had already lost.

Four horses were left in it with a chance. Snow Leopard, a big grey who had made all the running and whose lead had been narrowed to a couple of lengths, Drago's Pet who was being tracked by Tanglewood and Skinflint. Distracted by thoughts of Alex, Paul trained his binoculars on the leading group as they took the turn into the straight.

It was one of the favourites' race, that was for sure. Although Skinflint was going the easier, Clay Wentworth seemed intent on making the cardinal error of riding against one horse in particular. Glancing across at Bill Scott on Tanglewood, he pushed Skinflint half a length up so that he was challenging Drago's Pet. The grey was now falling back as if he had decided that two and three quarter miles was quite far enough to gallop at racing speed.

As they entered the straight, Paul found himself watching Clay Wentworth. Every few strides, he glanced back, taking Skinflint wider and wider of the bend, as if inviting Bill Scott to challenge him on the inner. Sensibly, Scott had followed Skinflint so that, as they approached the third last fence, the two favourites were on the stand side, leaving Drago's Pet to approach the fence on the inner. The crowd in the grandstand stirred in surprise and some amusement. There was no reason for jockeys to take the long way home – the going was good on both sides of the course – and for the leaders to be dividing, leaving ten yards of course between them, was inexplicable.

'Prats,' Paul muttered to himself as he watched Clay bump uneasily over the second last fence. There was no doubt in his mind that, barring accidents, Bill Scott had his race won – Tanglewood had a fair turn of foot while Skinflint's jockey would be nothing but a handicap in a tight finish. He was watching the two favourites so closely that at first when he heard the gasp from the stands, he thought something had happened to one of the backmarkers. Then he trained his binoculars down the fence. Drago's Pet lay motionless on the landing side; his jockey had rolled under the rails but at least he was conscious.

Paul lowered the binoculars. The spectators by the fence had backed away but he could see the slash of green that was Angie.

He had started shuffling towards the fence by the time Tanglewood and Skinflint passed the post. It had been a closer race than Paul had anticipated, Skinflint having put in a stupendous leap at the last, but on the run-in the wild efforts of Clay Wentworth, which defied all laws of rhythm and gravity, had pulled the horse back and Tanglewood, ridden coolly with hands and heels by Bill Scott, had stolen the race. Even pulling up, Clay conspired to look inept, looking over his shoulder as if to see how and where he had managed to lose the race he should have won.

Angie stood before him, having run across the course towards the grandstand. She looked pale and was breathing heavily. Paul wanted to say something, to explain that falls as heavy as that of Drago's Pet were unusual in racing but words seemed inadequate.

'Can we go?' she said quietly.

Peter was lost in a nightmare of pain and darkness.

He knew little beyond the fact that he was in hospital, that his skin was on fire and that he was afraid. The morphine they gave him induced wild, technicolour dreams but slowly the memory of how he came to be here became clearer, like a ship of death, looming through the fog.

Twice they had changed the bandages on his face and his hands, and the black before his eyes had changed to a dark and muddy yellow but, beyond that, he had no sense of time. At least, they had left gaps in the bandages so that he could hear the sound of the hospital – the muttered consultations of the doctors, the chatter of the nurses, the soothing tones who had visited him three times, the cries of fear of the baby which gave the only clue to how he looked.

No policemen. That surprised him.

Once he had tried to communicate with Klima to tell her what happened but his words come out as a rattle, behind an eerie monotone. He had moved his chin but felt only pain where his lips should have been.

'Another visitor, Peter,' the sing-song voice of one of the nurses interrupted his thoughts. 'You're popular today.'

He turned his head slowly in the direction of the voice. Klima had just left. The Markwick woman was unlikely to call. The police – it had to be the police at last.

'It's your brother,' said the nurse. 'Come to see how you're getting on.'

'Poor old Peter. You look like an Egyptian mummy.'

'Not too long,' warned the nurse. 'He's still very weak.'

Peter raised an arm feebly, as the nurse with a cheery 'I'll leave you lads together, then,' left the room. He heard the squeak of her rubber soles as they receded down the corridor.

'So how are we, Bruv?'

Breathing heavily, Peter let his head fall back against the pillow. He was beyond fear, yet his heart thumped painfully in his chest. Helpless, he listened to the voice of a stranger.

'As it happens, we didn't want this,' the man said. 'When I asked a friend of mine to lend me a spot of acid, I thought he'd give me the stuff they put in car batteries.'

The man paused, as if expecting Peter to interrupt.

'I had no idea that it would take your whole fucking face off.'

Peter struggled to remember where he had heard that voice before. It was villainous, plausible and would have suited a new-style City broker as easily as it would a bank robber.

'Still, look on the bright side, eh? At least this way we know where we stand. You've got what we want and you're going to tell us how to get it. We want to deal with you, not Alice. She can be so unreasonable.'

There was the slightest pull on the drip leading into his arm. The man, he was sure now, was trying to cut the supply of morphine which kept the waves of pain at bay.

'So you get well soon, eh? I'll be back as soon as you're talking.'

'Don't touch the drip, please.' The nurse's voice, as she returned, was brisk.

'I thought it wasn't working,' the stranger said. 'I can't bear to think of my brother in pain.'

The nurse dropped her voice. 'I think you'd better go,' she said. 'He gets very tired.'

'Right.' The man stood up. 'I'll be off, Bruv.' Then from the direction of the door. 'I'll give Klima your love. I plan to visit her soon. Family's got to stick together, hasn't it?'

After the man had gone, the nurse turned to the bed. Peter seem disturbed, upset. He kept making that odd, keening sound though his lipless mouth, almost as if he were trying to tell her something.

She checked his drip once more and straightened his sheets. Poor man. He would be unrecognizable when the bandages came off, but he would never be able to see that horror his featureless face would cause in others. Sad because, if he had been anything like his brother, he must have been a good-looking man before the accident.

Still, at least he had a family to look after him.

It had not been a successful day. Paul had hoped that Angie would be won over by the atmosphere and excitement of a Saturday's racing. Instead, her worst prejudices had been confirmed by a horse turning over at speed only yards from where she had been standing.

They drove back to Lambourn in silence. Angie was still distracted by what she had seen and Paul's back ached from the hours spent standing up. Doubtless the tussle with Digby Welcome had hardly helped.

He parked the car beside her Mini on the street outside his flat. Remembering that she was working on the early shift at the hospital, he asked, 'D'you want to go home?'

'Not yet.'

'I can offer you supper. Frozen chicken pie à la Raven.'

She smiled and he saw that she was sad, not angry. 'My favourite,' she said.

There was a tension between them that evening. They talked little, like a married couple who had fought and were carefully choosing topics of conversation in which there was no risk of renewed hostilities.

After they had eaten in the kitchen, they sat on each side of the open fire, Paul nursing a whisky while Angie, who had seen too many road crash victims to risk a drink when she was driving later, sipped a cup of coffee.

'I spoke to Digby Welcome today,' Paul said eventually. 'A friend of mine had told me that Alex had some connection with him.'

'What's he? A jockey?'

Paul smiled. 'Hardly. He's the sort of character you find on the fringe of racing. Part fixer, part crook. A hanger-on.'

'Doesn't seem Alex's type.'

'Alex was a good jockey, but he was no angel. He wanted to be in the fast set – parties, girls, his face in the gossip columns. Whenever he had a spare moment, he would be into his car and up to London. He wanted me to come but I couldn't live like that.'

'And that's how he knew this Welcome man.'

'Everybody knows Digby Welcome. If you're sensible, you keep your distance. There's a corruption about him that's catching.'

Angie found herself thinking of Gavin Holmes, the journalist. 'I know that type,' she said.

'I asked him whether Alex was in trouble with the bookmakers. He said something strange – something about stud poker. That Wentworth woman mentioned poker too. When I asked if he had stopped horses, he said, "Not his own." '

'Which would confirm your suspicions about your race. You think he had been told to stop you.'

Paul stared into the fire. 'I don't understand it. When a jockey's been got at, there's gambling involved. Yet at Plumpton, there was nothing unusual in the betting pattern; I checked with the Betting Officer – no late support for Freeze Frame, Alex's horse. More importantly, Dig For Glory's price never drifted. It seemed that everybody thought I'd win.'

For a moment, Angie watched as he poked at the fire, the glow lighting up his dark eyes. She wanted to go to him, to hold him and tell him that nothing could come of this obsession with his friend's death, but something held her back. 'You're really hooked now, aren't you?' she said.

Without a word, Paul stood up and, with some difficulty made his way to the telephone. He dialled a number.

'Mrs Matthews,' he said. 'Paul Raven. Sorry I couldn't make that drink. My . . . back was playing up a bit . . . Yes, some other time. Sorry about Skinflint. Thought you were a bit unlucky there.' He laughed quietly. 'He's no Lester Piggot in a finish that's for sure.' Angie heard the raised tones of Ginnie Matthews as she enlarged, with a string of obscenities, on the performance of Clay Wentworth as a jockey. 'Somebody told me he was a bit of a poker player,' Paul added casually. 'They asked me if I wanted to join some sort of gambling party.' He listened for a minute or so before saying, 'Aye, perhaps you're right, Mrs Matthews. Bit out of my league.'

After he had hung up, Paul turned to Angie. 'Wentworth has a poker evening once a week. High stakes. You need to be invited.'

'What's that got to do with Alex?'

'A couple of times I've seen Welcome with Clay Wentworth. It would explain how Alex knew Zena. If I could get into the poker circle, maybe I could find out what was going on.'

'School. It's a poker school.'

Paul smiled. 'Don't tell me you're an expert.'

'I know a bit.' Angie gave a self-mocking woman-of-the-world smile. As she looked up at him, Paul noticed that the top button of her blue dress, so wrong for Wincanton and so right for now, had come undone revealing a pale throat, the shadow of a breast. 'It was about all I learned at school.'

'Will you teach me?'

'While you were making that telephone call in the middle of our conversation – ' smiling, she held up a hand to stop his interruption ' – I reached two decisions. The first was that I'm leaving the hospital. If you're serious about finding out what happened to Alex, you're going to need help. I'll do agency work – it's better paid and I can work the hours I want.'

Paul looked at her in amazement. 'Angie, that's crazy. You don't have to do that for me.'

'It's not for you, it's for me.'

'And the second decision?'

'Ah, that.' Angie looked away and Paul thought he could see a heightened colour in her cheeks. 'For the second decision I'll need a drink.'

'But you're driving. What about – ?'

'That's the second decision.' Angie turned to him solemnly, her lips slightly parted. 'Tonight I'm not driving anywhere.'

It wasn't how she had imagined it. In her fantasies, she had imagined a power-ful man, his heavy weight on her. She had expected fear and pain with the pleasure.

Instead, when she came to Paul's bed, her athletic body caught by the lamplight from the street outside, his body dark and taut against the white sheets, she was the seducer, the conqueror.

'You realise you're going to have to do this,' Paul said quietly.

'That's what nurses are for,' she said, and she knew as she caressed his body with her hands and her lips that this, all along, was how she had wanted it. Her fears of doing the wrong thing, the last vestige of shyness, disappeared as she made love to him, gasping more with pleasure than pain, when she lowered herself onto him, sighing with relief, and gentle aching desire, her days of waiting for the right man, for Mr Right, over at last. The girls had never told her that at the end, she would cry with happiness.

Afterwards they lay together for several minutes. 'Where did you learn all that?' Paul asked at last.

'I learned that at school too.'
And, in the semi-darkness, they both laughed.

Chapter
7

There were some virtues left within the soul of Gavin Holmes; not honesty, or industry, or fidelity – which he had outgrown within his first year on Fleet Street – but he still had one quality in which he took a certain amount of pride. He never bore a grudge against a woman who had refused to sleep with him.

In this, he was unusual. Most of his male colleagues would express their frustration and guilt by spreading unpleasant rumours about the woman who failed to be attracted by them. Not Gavin – he almost admired someone who had the spirit to reject him. From that moment on, she moved out of the sexual arena to become something else – a friend, a rival, a person. Oddly enough, he had more difficulty with the ones he *had* slept with, who either wanted to do it again when he would rather forget the whole thing, or if he did happen to fancy a spot of auld lang syne, pretended nothing had ever happened. That was another point in his favour – he never forgot the face of someone he had taken to bed, however drunk he had been at the time, however messy and unfortunate the subsequent experience.

'In fact, I'm full of fucking virtues,' Gavin muttered to himself, sitting in the wine bar where his blundering attempt to seduce the O'Keefe girl had gone so wrong. Yet here he was, waiting for her again – only this time she was bringing her boyfriend.

A story, she had said. Gavin drank deeply at the glass of wine in front of him. They always had a story.

'Not more gee-gees, please,' he had said, when little Angie O'Keefe had rung him at the office.

'We think we have something which could interest you. About the death of a jockey. It's confused but we think Clay Wentworth's involved.'

He had asked a few more questions, the answers to which had faintly quickened his interest. Money seemed to be involved. Maybe even sex. The equestrian element had seemed to be mercifully small.

Angie had asked him about a man called Digby Welcome and, after an hour of punching up a selection of old stories from the information service database, he had become more confident. Yes, it was distinctly possible there was a story here.

'Gavin, this is Paul.'

The journalist looked up from his drink, and there was Angie, her hand resting gently on the arm of a dark, good-looking man carrying a walking-stick.

'Hi, Paul.' Gavin extended a hand, nodding curtly in the direction of his legs.

'How's it coming on?'

'Not bad,' Angie laughed as she drew up a chair for Paul.

'According to the doctors, he should still be in a wheelchair.'

She was hardly recognizable as the pale, edgy girl whom Gavin remembered. There was an openness about her, a warmth in the eyes that seemed entirely new.

'What's his secret cure?' he asked, a hint of irony in his voice. Nothing made Gavin more nervous than young love. It made him feel his years. Angie blushed, looking at Paul as if the question were absurd.

After a waitress had brought two more glasses, and Gavin had poured, he said 'Okay then, what's the story?'

Paul looked across the table with an unnervingly direct gaze.

'First,' he said, 'tell us what you know about Digby Welcome.'

It took a lot to rattle him. Over the years, after more tumbles and setbacks than most men were forced to endure in a lifetime, Digby had learned to roll with the punches.

Some five miles west of the bar where his chequered career was being discussed, he sat in a restaurant at his usual table, eating his usual meal and wondered how best to discourage Paul Raven. Contacts, of course – Digby had plenty of those. Violence, almost certainly. He shifted his bulk uncomfortably, wincing with pain as he did so. Yes, the jockey had certainly done enough to be damaged a little bit more than he was already.

A dark girl in the tight white tee-shirt that the waitresses were required to wear when working at the restaurant hurried by, pointedly not looking in Digby's direction. Languidly, he held up the empty wine bottle on his table, letting it swing between two fingers. On her return, the waitress hesitated nervously and took the bottle. Digby held onto the neck and looked up, his greedy little eyes taking their time to work their way up her body.

'Everything all right at home, is it, Diana?'

The girl took the bottle and said in a heavy East European accent 'Is good, Mr Welcome, thank you. Another bottle wine?'

Digby nodded slowly. These girls, he sighed. The trouble they caused him.

'It's as if he's had several incarnations.' Gavin was interested enough in the case of Digby Welcome to slow down his drinking for a while. 'I kept reading these Digby Welcome stories from the archives to find a different character popping up each time.'

'I would never have thought that he was that interesting,' Paul said.

'First of all, he was at Eton – his name keeps cropping up whenever some nobby businessman or cabinet minister is asked about his schooldays. Apparently he was something of a card – a practical joker, smart but lazy. They say he was good-looking then.'

'Bloody hell,' Paul muttered.

'He was expelled for some prank. Joined the army. Appeared to be something of a high-flyer until he left under a cloud when he was in his mid twenties.'

'More pranks?'

'No, the army can handle that. Something more serious – money or sex, I suspect.'

'Then he got into racing.'

'Yes. Again it all looked very promising. He got a yard on the Sussex Downs when he was quite young, trained a few winners, seemed to be going places. The next thing the cuttings reveal is that he was banned from all racecourses for two years. Something about not paying bills.'

'Right.' Paul nodded. 'That's the part I know about. He was a tight bastard – not unusual in racing, but he didn't pay wages, his cheques bounced. He underfed the horses. In the end, even his friends at the Jockey Club couldn't ignore it.'

'So there he was – fat, nearly forty and famous for all the wrong things. He had a marriage that had gone wrong – his wife divorced him for mental cruelty. He ended up in a part-time job selling horse tonic.'

'It doesn't make sense,' Paul said. 'Clay Wentworth only hangs out with people who are useful to him. And another thing. If Welcome was so chronically mean, what was he doing putting three grand on a horse in an amateur race?'

Gavin shrugged. 'Maybe he was doing it for someone else. Clay, for example.'

'There's no rule against amateurs betting. Clay would have an account with a bookmaker.'

'Unless Digby has yet another incarnation.' Gavin filled his glass. 'Another source of income.'

'Something mucky, I imagine,' Paul said.

Gavin smiled. 'Could be very mucky. I asked one of my colleagues about Digby. He had heard some nasty rumours. Apparently our friend's popular on the coke and champagne circuit. They say he's an ace supplier.'

'Dope?' Angie laughed at the idea of the tubby buffoon in tweeds as dealer in narcotics to the fast set.

'Not drugs.' Gavin sipped at his wine, enjoying the drama of the moment. 'Girls. Wives.'

Zena Wentworth wandered from room to room like a restless and unhappy ghost in the large house in Harley Gardens. She felt empty and alone, trapped by a gloom so deep that not even a trip to the medicine cupboard where she kept all kinds of mood-changing pills seemed worth the effort. A couple of those brightly-coloured items might pick her up, propel her out of the door to a place where there were lights and music only to slam her back down to earth in the desolate early hours of the morning. These days, the pleasure of going up hardly seemed worth the pain of coming down.

Barefoot, in a dark red kimono, she ran a finger along the mantelpiece in the high-ceilinged sitting-room. Her eyes scanned the invitations, some for Mr Clay Wentworth, some for Mr and Mrs Clay Wentworth, none for Mrs Zena Wentworth. She hooked a finger around the bronze figure of a horse and jockey driving for the line.

'Whoops,' she said, pulled it slowly over the edge so that it fell with a clatter on the marble fireplace below. 'Favourite's down.'

Zena picked up the bronze, noting without much interest that the jockey's head had been bent to one side, giving him a comical look as if he were wondering what all the fuss and effort were about. She ran a long finger down his bronze back, around the back of his bronze thighs, thinking vaguely of Paul Raven.

'Horses,' she said, looking at the painting on the wall, the ornaments on tables. 'Nothing but bloody horses.'

The house was unusually quiet. Emilio and Maria, the Spanish couple who lived in the basement and looked after the Wentworths, had gone out to some obscure spot in the suburbs where Spaniards met on their nights off. When Clay and Zena had moved into this house, shortly after their marriage, the idea had been that it would be filled with children. Now, ten years later, the quest for a family was over, giving Clay and that creepy old father of his yet more reasons to despise her.

Slowly Zena crossed the hall, ruffling her faded blonde hair like someone who had just awoken from a long sleep. She entered a small room which smelt of stale cigars – her husband's study, his little retreat. She sat on the leather chair, leaning back and placing her bare feet on the desk so that the kimono fell back, revealing her long slender legs. Yes – Zena ran a hand over one smooth thigh, and then the other – at least she still had good legs. Not that anyone cared.

There were two photographs on Clay's desk. One showed her husband on Skinflint, taking a water-jump. Zena smiled – it had taken quite a search to find a shot that made Clay look like a real jockey and even this one showed him with his mouth open like a goldfish – but it was good enough to be blown up and featured above his desk at the office. Poor, foolish Clay.

The other photograph was an old portrait of Sir Denis, taken shortly after he had received his knighthood. Against the background of what seemed to be a setting sun, he stared out at her with his cold tycoon eyes.

Creepy. Zena pointed a toe like a ballerina and pushed the framed photograph off the desk.

He had always hated her. He had distrusted her looks, the way she exuded pleasure in the good things of life. Even in the early days, when she had acted the proper daughter-in-law, he had shown her little respect, hardly bothering to talk to her, introducing her to his important friends with an apologetic mumble. Then, as it became obvious that she was unable to fulfil her most important function – to provide an heir for the Wentworth millions – he had ceased even to acknowledge her existence, drawing his son into the business and away from her.

Clay, as was his habit, took the line of least resistance. Torn between father and wife, he returned to the cold bosom of the family. He spent evenings with Sir Denis, still the little boy desperate to please Daddy.

Languidly, Zena pulled open the top drawer of the desk and took out her husband's Filofax. She flicked through the pages, forlornly hoping to find signs that Clay was more than a cypher in his father's plans. There were notes about race meetings, business addresses but – unless Clay had shown an intelligence and cunning uncharacteristic of him – not the slightest hint of adulterous behaviour. Zena sighed. Her husband had always regarded sex as yet another chore life had burdened him with.

A small scrap of paper fell onto her lap. It had been folded many times and contained a list of names, written in an unfamiliar hand. The first three items on the list had been deleted with a line. The last, 'Tanglewood', had been circled heavily with blue biro.

It took a few seconds for Zena to remember where she had heard the name Tanglewood. Of course – that had been the horse that had beaten Clay in his last race.

She looked more closely at the list and noticed, written faintly in a corner, in pencil by her husband, the words 'Dig For Glory'. They too had a line through them.

Zena put the Filofax back in the drawer, which she closed. She stood up and, fanning her face with the slip of paper, made her way out of the study and up the stairs to her bedroom. In her handbag was a small notebook, which she flicked through until she found what she was looking for. She dialled a number on a telephone beside the bed, then drummed the long fingers of her right hand as she waited. 'Bloody machine,' she muttered.

'Paul, this is Zena Wentworth,' she said. 'I think I have something which might be of interest.' She paused. 'It's to do with Alex. Perhaps you could call me as soon as possible.' She gave her number and hung up.

Smiling, she folded the piece of paper and put it in her bag. Maybe she was being disloyal to her husband. Perhaps the list meant something.

At least she'd be able to see Paul again.

It was a tremendous game – the best game Digby Welcome had ever played. The fat man puffed out his cheeks as he cupped his hands around a brandy glass, gazing into it as if he could read his future there.

It was almost eleven thirty. The kitchens were closing, customers were being turned away at the door. Soon the waitresses – including Diana and Juljana, both of them his girls – would be dividing up the evening's tips and going home to lives of sweet, if not entirely simple, domesticity. At about the same time, Roberto the manager would amble over to his table, sit down and spend a few minutes chatting with him. Business might be discussed – girls who needed Digby's help.

Other games – at school, in the army, on the turf – had tended to end in tears, those in authority frequently failing to share his sense of humour. But in this game, he was in control. He called the shots.

It had been so easy, such an obvious development of Digby's personal interests – money, food and, of course, people. In the early 1970s, after his career as a trainer had been terminated, Digby had taken to dining out in restaurants in the Kensington and Chelsea area. His easy charm and teddy-bear looks had encouraged the girls to chat to him. One – he forgot her name now – had, late one night, opened her heart to him. Her student permit had expired, the immigration people were after her, yet she would rather die than return to the grey and cold of Warsaw. She needed a husband within a week – she could pay £2,000.

Digby helped her. He knew plenty of Englishmen happy to lose their bachelor status for the three years required in return for instant cash. The girl had a friend with the same problem, which Digby also solved.

His strength was that he never asked too many questions. Where the money came from, for example, or whether the husbands he provided – some of whom were frankly rather dubious characters – demanded more of their new wives than mere cash.

Since then, he had become a familiar figure around the restaurants of London. It turned out that Eastern Europe was full of families who had sent their girls to make their way in the West, and London, of course, was not short of husbands.

Digby's unofficial marriage bureau had flourished and – even allowing for kick-backs to managers like Roberto – he had flourished too. The only disadvantage to this part-time job was that some evenings he was obliged to eat two or even three dinners and that, for Digby Welcome, was no great hardship.

He looked across the restaurant to where Diana was talking to the manager. She was a nice little thing – dark, slim, with a look in her eyes that promised much in the way of diversion – but these days Digby resisted the temptation to combine business with pleasure. Once he used to demand a non-fiscal bonus with some of his more attractive girls, but it hadn't been a success: the demands he made of them had been rather too sophisticated – too much of a culture shock – to be accept-able. After one tearful scene too many, he had decided not to jeopardize the busi-ness. There were experienced business girls he could call – girls who took him for what he was, warped and all.

The door opened behind where Roberto and Diana were standing, and a slight girl with short blonde hair entered. Digby was trying to remember where he had seen her before when he noticed, standing behind her, the face of a man he knew all too well.

Roberto was telling the girl that the restaurant was closed, but Paul Raven had seen him, and the manager smiled and gave a nod as if to say that any friends of Mr Welcome were friends of his.

The couple approached, the girl waiting for Paul to make his way slowly past the tables.

'Digby,' said Paul. 'Here you are. We heard this was one of your watering-holes.'

Digby scowled as the girl pulled back a chair for Paul, then sat down herself.

'This is my friend Angie,' Paul said conversationally. 'Angie, this is Digby Welcome. We met one another briefly at Wincanton the other day.'

'What do you want?' Digby avoided Paul's eyes. 'I was just going.'

'We know all about you,' Paul said quietly. 'Your little business looks like it will be getting some belated publicity in the press.'

'Business?'

'Your work as Agony Uncle.'

'I don't know what you're talking about.' Digby swirled the brandy around in his glass before drinking it back in one gulp.

'Invite me to one of your poker evenings,' said Paul. 'And we might be able to keep your nasty little secret quiet.'

An ingratiating little smile played on Digby's lips, as if he couldn't believe his luck. 'They're not my poker evenings. They're Clay's.'

'Well, get me invited.'

Digby took a calling-card from his top pocket and scribbled an address on it. 'Next Thursday,' he said. 'I'll tell Clay you're my guest.'

Paul took the card and, glancing at it, gave it to Angie. Leaning heavily on his walking-stick, he stood up. He looked at the stick as if suddenly remembering something.

'How are they by the way? Still sore?'

Digby's face turned a darker shade of red. 'Very amusing,' he said.

After Paul and Angie had left, Roberto came over to the table. 'Nice girl,' he said easily. 'One of yours, was she?'

With a distracted stroke to his head, Digby muttered, 'No – just old friends, you know.'

'Can we talk business?'

But Digby was staring at the door of the restaurant like a man who knew his gravy train had just left the rails. 'No business tonight, Roberto,' he said.

'Puttana!'

The tall, thin man stabbed the table with a knife, leaving it quivering like an arrow until a passing waitress removed it with a muttered *'Idiota'*. The man watched her walk away. He was only young and his chiselled good looks had caused many a female customer of his small pizza parlour to return in hope and lust, but his cold green eyes gave him a harsh, forbidding maturity.

He was sitting with two other men, one in his sixties who was examining his carefully manicured nails with a look of intense concentration, the other in his late twenties with a dark moustache, good-looking but with a pale, apologetic smile on his face. 'Giorgio,' he said quietly, 'we've only just begun.'

The young man, Giorgio, darted a look around the room. The last customers in the small cellar, a popular haunt among the young and upwardly mobile of Wandsworth, had gone home, leaving the three Italians alone, except for one waitress who was cleaning the tables. 'Every time she tricks us,' he said.

'We know where it is,' said the man with a moustache soothingly. 'Our little Polish friend has not responded well to his acid bath.'

'What about his wife?'

'We know where she lives. I could – '

'No.' The older man spoke for the first time. 'There's no point in that.'

'We're losing time, papa,' Giorgio said quietly.

'Salvatore has done well, Giorgio.' The grey-haired man picked at one of his nails with a fork. 'You know the layout of the factory, right?'

The man with a moustache nodded. 'But I can't be a VAT man again. She was suspicious last time.'

'Hurting the Polak's wife would be counter-productive. Perhaps we should turn our attention to other members of the syndicate. The man Wentworth. Or Calloway. We know we can reach Welcome.'

'Time, papa!' There was anger in Giorgio's voice, and a hint of panic.

'We have three weeks.'

'There's another problem,' said Salvatore. 'I have heard that someone else is interested, is snooping about.' He reached into the inside pocket of the jacket of his dark suit and took out a photograph torn from a newspaper. He unfolded it, laying it in the centre of the table.

'Who's she acting for?' the older man asked.

Salvatore shrugged. 'He's some kind of jockey.'

'Jockey?' Giorgio said softly. 'What's a jockey got to do with this?'

'We had better discourage him,' his father said mildly.

Salvatore reached for the photograph. 'I'll ask if anyone has heard – '

'No!' Giorgio spoke sharply. 'There's no time for that.'

The waitress marched across the room and, with a reproachful look in the direction of the manager, began to clean the table. As if it were contaminated, she picked up the photograph, glancing as she did so at the dark features of Paul Raven.

'Mmm,' she muttered. '*Che bel tipo.*'

'Not for long,' said Giorgio. 'Not for long.'

Chapter
8

'It wasn't the first time she had returned to Czechoslovakia since the day she had left to find her future in the West but, every time that she alighted from the plane into the greyness of Prague airport, a touch of claustrophobia, of a deep, psychic anxiety, gripped her.

Whatever the changes – to her, to the motherland, to the world – the dark, crumbling buildings and the weary, watchful eyes of the Czech officials always meant the same to her. It was a trap. This time she would not escape. The sins of her past – those deeply capitalist sins of greed, lust and selfishness – would come back to haunt her.

With the other passengers, she was herded into an airport bus, which smelt faintly of cheap, stale cigarettes and disinfectant. The engine sounded unhealthy and the driver drove with contemptuous speed towards the main terminal as if, whatever the politicians might say, the old disapproval of the soft, decadent ways of the West still endured. Around her, the other passengers seemed uneasy – perhaps the bus with its crazed driver would head out of the airport, take them without a word to another, more sinister destination. A middle-aged businessman tried a joke about local driving standards, but no one smiled and his words died on his lips.

Sitting on one of the few benches on the bus, Alice noticed, were two teenage girls, one of whom – with dark, cropped hair and fine features – she might, under other circumstances and in another country, have tried with a smile. Not here: it was strange how even her most natural instincts went into retreat in her cold, forbidding homeland.

In the main building, there were queues. The English thought they understood patience – they boasted about their queues – but they were amateurs compared to her countrymen. Here you stood in a line for everything: sometimes you queued for a permit to join another queue and, by the time you reached the front of it, you'd forgotten what you had wanted in the first place. Alice shivered – she hated coming back – and gathered her fur coat more closely around her.

On this occasion, she was met by a government functionary, a middle-aged man with shifty eyes and a coat too thin for the climate. 'Miss Flaishman?' he said, as she walked towards the queue.

'Markwick,' she said.

The man nodded. 'Please follow me,' he said.

It was better. Every time she returned, she was treated with more respect. Twenty years ago, the man would have called her by her surname, holding her eyes with the stare of a man with power over her, perhaps even allowing himself a speculative glance at her legs. Now she was in charge; he avoided looking at her. Conversation would be minimal.

The man nodded to passport control officials as he took Alice past the queue through the hall of the terminal and into a large car that was waiting at the entrance. Sensitive to the essential signs of social and political importance in Czechoslovakia, she noticed that the car was not quite the most luxurious available. Those had been reserved for the party officials and were now used by the new brand of politician scrambling for power under the free, post-communist constitution.

New. Free. Settling back in the adequate comfort of the car, Alice smiled. They were just words. Nothing had really changed.

On the way to the Ministry of Defence, the car drove past the huge government building where, all those years ago, Alice's mother had once worked. There was something desolate about it now as if its power to terrify had gone for ever. Alice stared at it without feeling any of the old dread and disgust. That ghost, at least, was dead.

Josef Petrin, her contact, was waiting in his large, chilly office when she was shown in by the official. He smiled, extending his arms in a phoney gesture of welcome which, when he saw the icy disapproval in Alice's eyes, became a brisk handshake. They exchanged pleasantries about the journey, as he escorted her to a chair in front of an ancient gas fire, which had been installed in the ornate fireplace.

'Now, Mrs Markwick,' Petrin smiled ingratiatingly. 'You cannot keep us waiting any longer. Tell me when we take possession.'

'Quite soon.' Alice spoke slowly as she placed her briefcase on a table in front of her and fiddled with the security lock.

'How soon?'

The question contained an undertone of impatience, perhaps even threat. Petrin was the new breed of official but, while his suit came from Savile Row, his shiny black shoes from Rome, and his slick smile owed much to Madison Avenue, he was not that different from his predecessors, only younger – in his late thirties – and marginally more plausible. Briefly Alice wondered whether he demanded intimate overtime from office cleaners. No, the modern way was a hunting-lodge, complete with young mistress, in the forest nearby – such was progress.

Alice took a folder out of her briefcase and gave Petrin a videotape. 'The tape I promised,' she said, choosing to ignore his questions. 'You have the machine?'

Petrin nodded and, taking the tape, crossed the room to a table on which there was a television and a video machine. He stood in front of the machine as a sequence of films was shown. Occasionally he gasped and laughed, like a little boy watching a circus.

'Excellent,' he said, after the television screen had turned to grey. 'You use peculiar clinical models but that is your choice.'

'We had our reasons.'

'And afterwards? Any problems with the post-mortems?'

'Nothing.'

'Of course, we need a human test. As you promised.'

'Humans talk.'

'We have humans that don't – or won't, if we ask nicely.'

'No. Leave it to us. We'll manage something.'

'Fine.' Petrin smiled once more like a barrister addressing a hostile witness. 'When?'

'You'll have your evidence in a week. If you're still happy, we deliver at the end of March.'

'Not before?'

'There's still work to be done.'

'And we're exclusive? That's what we're paying for. My colleagues will be very unhappy to hear of models going elsewhere. We're depending on you for this.'

Alice closed her briefcase with a click. 'Trust me,' she said. 'Remember I'm a Czech.'

'That's what worries me,' said Petrin, and they both laughed guardedly as he showed her the door.

There were three hours before her plane left for London, but Alice had only one call to make. She told the driver to take her to the west side of the city, a square mile where the houses were painted and had heating that worked even in the winter when, as if by tradition, the power in the big housing blocks used to fail, sometimes for days at a time. This was where the foreign diplomats lived, and senior civil servants and politicians. There were few shops and no bars for the poor to gather and drink vodka and talk of future freedom. It was the acceptable face of the new Czechoslovakia.

At first, Alice's mother had objected when, as a condition of dealing with the government, her daughter had secured her a two-bedroom house in the suburbs. Since her husband had died some seven years previously, she had lived alone, depending on neighbours and the occasional visit from Tomas, her son, for company. The new house might be comfortable, she argued, but she would be lonely. But Tomas had a car these days and, aware that one day he might inherit the house, he had promised to bring his family to see her every weekend.

The car drew up outside the house and Alice told the driver to wait for one hour.

'Alzbeta.' The old woman opened the door and embraced her daughter, then held her at arms' length, stroking Alice's fur coat. 'My daughter.'

The two women sat in the kitchen drinking tea while Alice gave her mother a sanitized version of her work in London. Her mother, as usual, became tearful and asked her when she would be coming home for ever.

'One day,' Alice said, 'when I've made my fortune.'

'Money.' Her mother looked away, ashamed by the memories that swarmed in. 'It's always money in our family, isn't it?'

And, with the faintest shiver of repulsion, Alice agreed. Yes, it was always money.

At first, when Ginnie Matthews had written to Paul suggesting he ride out for her, he had assumed it was her idea of a joke. Although the doctors were pleased with his progress, he could still only walk slowly and his legs felt as unsteady and weak as those of a new-born foal.

Then, when Paul had rung her, Ginnie had explained that she had an old hunter in the yard called Monty who needed exercising. He was dead quiet and Paul would be able to sit on him and go where he wanted. He could even come up to the gallop and watch her horses working. To his surprise, the specialist raised no objections. Nor, less surprisingly, did Ron Charlesworth. Still he hesitated.

'Try it once,' Ginnie had said. 'What's the problem?'

At that moment, Paul knew what the problem was.

'I'll be there,' he said quietly. 'What time d'you need me?'

Under other circumstances, it would have been comical. Paul Raven, the ice-cool jockey, afraid of the idea of mounting a fat and ancient hunter. Yet as, early the following morning, Monty was pulled out and led by one of the lads to a mounting-block in the corner of the yard, Paul felt sick with fear. He climbed the steps of the block slowly, like a man going to his execution.

'Hold him up for the first couple of miles, then give one behind the saddle,' joked the lad. 'He's got a great turn of speed.'

As Paul hesitated on the block, the reins in his hand, Ginnie walked towards him. 'Step one of Raven's comeback,' she said loudly. 'Don't hang about, Paul – you're not at Charlesworth's now.'

Paul lowered himself across the saddle and slowly pulled his right leg over. Ginnie helped him adjust the stirrups. 'All right?' she asked.

Paul nodded, his face pale.

And it was. Although he felt weak, he followed the string out in the cold morning mist and, even when the horse in front of him had shied violently, causing his lad to curse at him, the old hunter had hardly turned a hair. As the string worked at half-speed over six furlongs, Ginnie had watched with interest, noting how they had all gone, and it crossed his mind that if he couldn't race again, then, despite all the problems, maybe he would try training. Cheltenham was now two weeks away and Ginnie had three fancied contenders for the big prizes – The Smiler for the Trafalgar House Hurdle, Harry's Champ for the National Hunt 'Chase and Skinflint for the Kim Muir.

Looking down the hill to the all-weather gallop, Paul noticed Skinflint, pulling hard, at the back of the string. 'He must have a decent chance,' he said.

'Yes.' Ginnie narrowed her eyes as if not entirely comfortable with the subject. 'The race has cut up badly.'

There seemed to be an easiness about the lads who worked for Ginnie Matthews. Behind the jokes about 'the missus' and her booming voice, there was none of the edgy competitiveness that Paul remembered from Charlesworth's yard. As the string made its way back, the sun showed through the mist and one or two of the lads had lit up cigarettes. The talk was of racing and horses and women. Paul smiled and patted Monty's neck. It was good to be back.

These days, although Alex's death was still at the front of his mind, so was his own future. His mother had taken to sending him letters advising him to find a desk job while there were still vacancies – she didn't actually spell out that soon Paul and his racing successes would be forgotten and he would be just another applicant, but she didn't need to. He had thrown away the pages from the local paper with jobs circled without even looking at them. Maybe one day he would become a tea-boy or an office clerk, but not yet.

Strangely enough, it had been Angie who had convinced him that only when he had settled his mind about what had happened to Alex would he be able to start a new life. She was working out her notice period at the hospital but, since the night Gavin Holmes had told them about Digby Welcome, she had become quieter, more subdued.

He thought of the message from Zena Wentworth on his answering-machine. It had been two days since he had heard from her but something – perhaps a wariness about her motives – had prevented him calling her back. Whatever Zena could tell him, Paul was convinced he could find out more by attending one of her husband's poker evenings.

On returning to the yard, his back was aching but he insisted on unsaddling Monty himself. The old hunter had done him more good than all the doctors put together, and for the first time Paul began to feel more like he had before the accident.

Zena Wentworth was bad at waiting at the best of times and now wasn't the best of times. The previous night Clay had stayed out late, having dined with his father and Lord Wallingford, another bent peer with property interests, at one of their dull gentlemen's clubs. On his return, Clay had been more monosyllabic than usual. She had even accused him of cheating on her. Clay's face had been such a picture of astonishment that she had had to laugh. Clay Wentworth an adulterer – there was certainly something comic in that.

Two days she had waited for Raven to respond to her bait but there had been nothing, not a nibble. After Clay had gone to bed, she had taken a pill and stayed up all night watching television. At six, she had had a bath, washed her hair, put her face on. By eight o'clock, she was in the Rolls heading down the M4.

She had been surprised to find that he was out, but her patience had paid off when, twenty minutes after she had parked outside his door, Paul had drawn up behind her in his car. Zena watched in her rearview mirror as he lifted one leg and then the other onto the pavement, before pulling himself out. She checked her face one more time, then opened the door.

'Riding again?' she asked breezily.

Paul looked surprised, and less than pleased, to see her.

She smiled and walked lazily towards him. 'You look good in your . . . togs.'

'Thanks.' Paul walked slowly to his door and Zena followed him.

'I drove down from London to see you,' she said.

'Why?'

'You didn't answer my call. I wanted to help you.'

Paul unlocked the door and hesitated as he opened it. 'Help me?'

'I admire you,' she said brightly. 'There aren't many wounded heroes where I come from. Can I come in?'

'All right.' Paul sighed. 'I have to be going soon, though.'

'Pity,' said Zena quietly.

As Paul put on the kettle, she sat at the kitchen table, crossed her legs and glanced into the sitting-room next door. 'Cosy.'

'It does. Why don't you tell me what you're here for.'

'Two reasons.' Zena opened her crocodile skin bag and took out a small folded piece of paper, which she laid on the table. 'What horse were you riding at Plumpton?'

'Dig For Glory.'

'I found this in my husband's desk. Why d'you think he's written the name of your horse on it?'

Paul turned and looked at the list of names. 'Did your husband write this?' he asked.

'No. That's a woman's writing. Apart from Dig For Glory, what are the other names?'

Paul looked more closely at the list and frowned. It was strange. 'Just horses,' he said quietly.

'Wasn't Tanglewood the horse that beat Clay at Wincanton?'

'That's right.'

'And it's the only one that's not been crossed out.'

'So it seems.'

Either Zena knew more than she was letting on or – and this seemed more likely – she was too stupid or uninterested in racing to see the connections between all the horses whose names had been deleted from the list. All had died in racing accidents over the past two months. As he gave Zena a cup of tea, he glanced at her, catching her eyes on his legs.

'They suit you, those jockey trousers,' she said.

'They're called jodhpurs – I never thought of them as a fashion accessory. What was the second thing?'

'Mmm?' she smiled, parting her painted lips.

'The second reason you came down here.'

In reply, Zena leaned forward and extended a hand across the table, placing it on Paul's hand.

'You know the answer to that,' she said.

He tried to withdraw his hand but found that her grip was surprisingly strong. 'I'm very good, Paul,' she said. 'Alex could have told you that.'

'Aye.' Paul wrenched his hand back. 'And look what happened to him.'

'I'm serious.'

'And so am I. Drink up your tea, Mrs Wentworth. I have things to do.'

'Mrs Wentworth.' Zena spoke coldly. She took a sip of tea then stood up, smoothing the front of her skirt down her thighs. She brushed his cheek with her long fingers. 'Mrs Wentworth wants you, Paul. And what Mrs Wentworth wants, she gets.'

Paul watched Zena as she strolled to the door, with a lazy swing of the hips, and let herself out without a backward glance. Outside, there was an angry purr and a squeal of tyres as the Rolls set off back to London.

What was her game? Paul was used to fending off the attention of libidinous older women but there was a dangerous, driven quality to Zena that worried him. He reached for the slip of paper, which lay on the kitchen table. After a moment, he picked it up and walked slowly through to the sitting-room. At his desk, there was a copy of Chaseform, a small plastic-bound book whose weekly supplements recorded every race in the calendar.

Apart from Dig For Glory, whose fate Paul knew all too well, there were four names on the list – Ballina Lady, Whataparty, Brut Force and, undeleted and with a heavy circle around it, Tanglewood. Paul flicked through the pages to find Ballina Lady's last race, the Philip Cornes Handicap 'Chase at Leopardstown. The summary beside her name was succinct. *'Always going well. Fell second last. Destroyed.'*

Whataparty had run on Boxing Day at Haydock Park and he too had failed to finish. His final entry read, *'Settled early, improved rapidly at half way. Led third last clear and going easily when fell last. Destroyed.'*

Paul recalled Brut Force's last race – his accident at Huntingdon had made the headlines in the sporting press. Once again Chaseform's summary was brief and laconic: *'Always with the leaders. Left in front at the third last. Ducked out at last bend. Destroyed.'*

There was no need to look up Tanglewood's form. Paul remembered the race well, Bill Scott tracking Clay Wentworth until they approached the last fence, then riding his horse out with hands and heels while, behind him, Clay did his imitation of a drunken bandmaster wielding the baton with impotent fury. Another image flashed across his mind – Angie, staring with undisguised horror as the other horse in contention, Drago's Pet, lay motionless a few yards beyond the second last fence. He too had been destroyed. Even in a sport where equine casualties are the norm, it seemed too much of a coincidence.

Paul reached for the telephone and dialled. He hadn't warmed to Gavin Holmes – there was something seedy and unhealthy about the man – but, for the moment, they had a shared interest. The woman who answered his extension laughed incredulously at the idea that Gavin should be at work at ten. She'd try to get him to call back when he made his customary late-morning pit-stop at the office before wandering off to lunch.

Hanging up, Paul looked once more at the piece of paper Zena had left him. The writing seemed somehow familiar. He shuffled among the papers on his desk before finding what he was looking for.

He put the letter he had received last week beside the shopping-list of ill-fated horses. There could be no mistaking the bold, round strokes, the way the cross on each 'T' floated oddly above the perpendicular, the confident 'F' on the name Brut Force.

Few village gossips were as effective, as ruthless professionally, as Joe Taylor. While others might happen upon an interesting titbit which was broadcast, suitably embellished, to anyone who cared to listen, Joe hoovered up the gossip at Lambourn and passed it on to one or more of his contacts. And, because horse chat can often be converted into money, Joe made a good living.

The word about Paul Raven riding again was hardly vintage material – no one was going to get rich on a broken-backed jockey – but it had a bit of colour to it, brought a smile in a grim and grey month, so, as soon as he heard about it, within a matter of hours of Paul alighting carefully from Monty's back, he rang one of his journalist contacts. It was a soft story but it would make a paragraph in the morning's gossip column and provide Joe Taylor with a handy £25, so all things considered, Paul Raven's return to the saddle was good news for everyone.

A profound restlessness assailed the heart of Digby Welcome. It was nine in the evening and, instead of working, he had spent most of the day worrying about developments in his life. On a normal night, he would be out there on his territory, bringing a harsh and chilly relief to Dianas and Juljanas all over West London, setting up marital deals that would keep them one step ahead of Immigration. There was work to be done – just because the authorities in Eastern Europe were happier to export the young and ambitious than they had once been, it didn't mean their counterparts in England would ease control on human imports – but tonight Digby hadn't the strength to engage in his own peculiar form of social work.

He sat in front of a fake coal fire warming his neat and chubby hands on the gas flame. Already he had tried different forms of distraction – a brandy and ginger ale, a quiz show on television, a few minutes on the crossword puzzle – but his mind kept returning to the mess of grimy deals and petty corruption that was his life.

If only his business and personal affairs were as ordered as the neat bachelor flat off the Old Brompton Road where he lived. Digby sat back in his armchair and closed his eyes to it all. With those glittering little points of greed extinguished, he appeared almost amiable, a red-faced, roly-poly character in an expensive tweed suit, the sort of man you might see asleep in a corner of one of London's better clubs – a card, a joker, a gentleman.

Digby drummed the short, well-manicured fingers of his right hand. Wearily he opened his eyes and reached for a telephone on the table beside him, placed it on his knees. He dialled Clay's private number – the number to which crazy Zena had no access – and waited.

'Clay,' he said eventually. 'Can you talk?'

There was a brisk and not entirely friendly reply from the other end of the telephone. Whatever else he was, Clay was no gossip. Besides, few people spent more time chatting to Digby Welcome than was strictly necessary.

'Ran into that chap Paul Raven the other day. Mmm. Met him at the sports.' On occasions like these, Digby's voice became plummy and distracted. 'No, didn't say a word about poor little Alex. He seemed to have heard about our Thursday nights. I said he could come along, try his luck.' He winced comically as Clay, with a certain impatience, presented his objections. 'I don't know, old boy. Felt sorry for him, I suppose. His back and all that kit. Perhaps a spot of gambling would take his mind off it.' An effete and deeply insincere chuckle shook Digby's frame. 'I don't know where he gets his money,' he said. 'Maybe the Injured Jockeys' Fund is more generous than we thought. That's his problem. Hmm. My guest, of course. I hear what you're saying, old boy, but I can't believe that one night can do any harm. Well done, good kit, see you on Thursday.' Digby hung up. 'Fucking bastard,' he drawled with quiet vehemence.

What he had never understood was how men like Clay – or indeed women like

Alice Markwick – managed to get through life without the disastrous, crippling setbacks that seemed to afflict him. While his career could be seen as a juddering switchback ride, theirs was a straight line, an inexorable upward graph. He was brighter than they were – brighter, at least, than Clay – yet there was something about him that invited distrust and, after distrust, disaster.

He reached into a drawer and took out a box of expensive cigars which he kept hidden in case one of his rare guests at the flat expected to be offered one. He lit up, puffing at the cigar restlessly as if, within moments of indulging himself, he wanted it to be gone.

He thought of school, army, his racing stables. The pattern was always the same. Up, then down. Boom, then crash. Order, then confusion. The business in which he had been engaged over the past decade or so had been good to him but now – Digby knew to the core of his substantial frame – it was all about to go wrong.

He was sensitive in that way, with the crook's instinct for the job that he shouldn't do, but always will.

Briefly, Digby considered ringing Alice Markwick. He didn't like the woman but if his other business interests were about to hit the rocks, it was important that his investment in Markwick Instruments paid the spectacular dividends that he expected. 'Alzbeta,' he said quietly. How she had changed over the years.

Laying the cigar in an ashtray, Digby pulled himself out of the armchair and walked slowly towards the bedroom.

Something bad was coming. He just knew it.

The organization had many divisions, each of them catering in a highly efficient way for different forms of human weakness. Drugs, ranging from the recreational and mind-expanding to the more serious and death-dealing, was an ever-buoyant area. Fraud, funny money games played with neat, hi-tech sophistication, was demanding more and more attention. And, of course, there was sex – there was always sex.

Maria Curatullo checked her make-up in the mirror of a Maida Vale flat, then looked, with a brisk professionalism, in the leather carrier bag on the floor beside her. Seven days she had been waiting in this grey city where the men watched you with dirty-little-boy stares and the women scurried home from work as if they had sand in their knickers.

Maria had worked most of the cities in Europe. She liked Paris, which was like a flighty and expensive mistress; she was always happy to return to Frankfurt, a sharp and ambitious teenage whore of a town, ready for anything at the right price. Rome, of course, was like her – a big, generous woman of the world who understood pleasure. But London? She was a sour old widow, shrivelled up with repressed and twisted desire. Only for very special cases did Maria come to London.

The dark Rover that waited for Maria Curatullo outside her flat might have belonged to a senior sales director of an international firm, just as the young man in suit and tie who sat in the driver's seat might have been a professional chauffeur. The organization liked to look after its executives.

There was no need to give the driver the address to which he was taking her. The words '*Al lavoro*' were good enough. The waiting was over, the time-killing expeditions to shops or cinemas were behind them. The young man, an apprentice in the organization, risked a glance at his passenger in the rearview mirror. Despite the night outside, the signorina was wearing dark glasses.

Behind the shades, Maria's face showed no interest in the streets of London as they sped by. Once, when the Rover stopped at a red traffic light, two men in a nearby car stared across, laughing uneasily at her menacing sexuality. Maria ignored them. With the self-knowledge of a true professional, she knew that her eyes were most effective when hidden. Without dark glasses, she was no more than a handsome woman with a knowing look, a wife even; with them, she was forbidden and dangerous.

From the early days, when she was recruited as a teenager to work for the organization, she had fallen into the habit of giving her punters nicknames. It made the work easier, these private labels. The job tonight was on 'Il Grassone', the fat one.

Maria pulled the leather hold-all closer to her at the thought of the task ahead. Once she had needed no more than her own body but, as the years went by and she became known for experience and skill rather than youth and beauty, she needed props, a bag of tricks. Some of the older women she saw stepping into limousines in Mayfair, or Les Halles or on the Via Veneto, were practically carrying suitcases. In that sense, Maria considered that she was lucky. Sex was no longer her exclusive area of expertise – she had diversified, made herself useful to the organization in another way.

The car pulled up and Maria told the driver that she would be an hour, maybe slightly more. Relaxing at last, he watched the signorina as she walked up the steps towards the block of flats. She still had good legs – the man smiled – despite the miles on the clock.

Maria pressed a button on the intercom at the entrance. 'Mr Welcome,' she said, 'Ees me.'

There was a pause of some seconds before the door clicked open.

By the time the lift had taken her to the third floor, Il Grassone had left the door to his flat a little ajar. With a slight sense of foreboding – you never lost the smallest frisson of fear the first time with a new man – Maria pushed the door and entered a small, dimly lit hall.

'I was expecting Nicola.'

Il Grassone was standing at the entrance to the sitting-room, his hair slicked down, wearing a maroon silk dressing-gown – an English client of the traditional variety.

Maria slipped off her coat and threw it over a chair. 'Nicola ees eell. You got Maria,' she said huskily. 'I go away?'

He stood there taking in the statuesque body in the black Armani dress. She was too big. Too old. Too much of a woman.

'Did you talk to Nicola? About me?'

'Yes, Deegby. I talk. I know.' She stepped closer to him. They never changed their minds – once they had made the call, slipped the leash from their sick and feverish desires, there was no going back.

'So you know how you are required to oblige me?'

Il Grassone had stepped back, as if afraid of being touched. She knew nothing of this Nicola, except that, just this once, she had been taken off the case; but experience told her what the man needed.

'Oblige me? What means this?' she asked.

'Bloody hell, they've sent me someone who doesn't even speak English.'

Maria glanced at her watch. 'You want conversazione, I fetch someone else,' she said.

'No.' Il Grassone's pleading, glittering little eyes told their own story. Anger was precisely what he wanted.

'Maria.' He seemed to cower slightly. 'I've been a very naughty boy.'

'To bedroom,' she said like a school matron. 'Get ready for Maria.'

Il Grassone ran a nervous tongue over his lips, then turned towards the bedroom.

'*Fai presto!*' she hissed, reached for her leather bag. *Dio*, these Englishmen were all alike.

Her right arm ached. She was getting bored. For twenty minutes she had been working on Il Grassone who lay face down on his bed, the acres of white flesh now striped with red marks from the whip. As he whimpered, it wobbled like some disgusting English summer pudding.

He had had his fun. He was relaxed. It was time for business.

'Turn over, you fat peeeg,' she said.

Nervously, painfully, he lay on his back, exposing his vast belly and pitiful manhood to Maria's scornful gaze. His eyes, wet with tears, widened as she took two pairs of velvet-lined handcuffs out of her bag. 'That was antipasto,' she said, clicking them onto his wrists. Roughly, she wrenched the cuffs upwards and attached them to the bedhead. 'Now is time for main course.'

Caught between fear and pleasure, Digby whispered, 'Sorry, Maria.'

Briskly, she reached into the bag, this time bringing out a small cassette recorder which she placed on the bedside table, then an electric lead, a plug on one end, two naked wires on the other. With genuine alarm, Digby tugged helplessly at the handcuffs.

'*Allora*'. Maria switched on the cassette and, as loud disco music filled the room, plugged the lead into a nearby socket. Humming softly to herself, she looked into the hold-all once more and took out a piece of paper which she unfolded. 'I have to ask you some questions, Deegby.' She ran the hand holding the live wires across his hairless chest and down over his stomach. 'Ees true what you say. You were a vairy naughty boy.'

She turned the disco music up louder.

At the pizza house in Wandsworth, three men sat at the corner table. Conversation was flowing less easily tonight, as if all three of them sensed that what, they had assumed, would be a simple task, had proved to be a problem.

When the telephone rang at two-fifteen, it was Giorgio who walked to the bar, picked it up and listened. 'No,' he said eventually. '*Si*.' He hung up wearily.

'*Niente*,' he said, returning to the table. '*Assolutamente niente*.'

The three men sat in silence for a moment, before Salvatore asked a question, a casual afterthought.

Giorgio shrugged. '*Naturalmente*,' he said.

Personally, Maria had nothing against Il Grassone. He had been an easy patient, succumbing to electricity with only slightly more noise than he had made under the whip. And it was hardly his fault that he had been unable to give her the information the organization needed on the whereabouts of the Markwick machine, whatever it was.

Personally, she would have left it there but Giorgio had insisted and, above all, she prided herself on her professionalism.

Maria shifted slightly on Il Grassone's face. Luckily he was tired and, when she had settled on him, placing one foot each side of his great white stomach, he had writhed only for a few moments. She glanced at her watch. In half an hour's time she would be at the airport hotel for four hours' sleep before she left to catch her flight home. It would be good to get away from this odd, depressing country.

Il Grassone trembled once more and was still. Maria sighed. Sometimes she felt she was growing too old for the game. Once sitting on a man's face had meant pleasure, not death.

Neither the sex nor the killing came as easy to her as it used to.

For a few more seconds, she sat there heavily, lost in thought, like a middle-aged washerwoman astride a log. Then with a quiet, 'Bye-bye, Deegby,' she lifted herself off the dead man and prepared to leave for the airport.

Chapter
9

It wasn't Watergate, but it was interesting.

Eyes closed, Gavin Holmes braced himself as another wave of nausea broke over him – but it took more than a Force Nine hangover to deflect him from a story once it started to buzz. 'Touch of 'flu, is it, Gav?' Shirley, one of the younger reporters, called out as she walked briskly past his desk.

'There's a lot of it about,' he muttered, carefully placing a third finger and thumb on his eyelids, as if to check the eyeballs were still in place. He opened his eyes to gaze blearily at Shirley's legs as she walked away. Maybe her turn would come.

He heaved himself back in front of the word-processor to look once more at his notes. On the screen, he read

DEAD NAGS

Five names on list given to Paul, all but one dead.

Except for Dig For Glory, all ridden by amateurs.

All fell towards end of race, three at a fence, one on the flat.

Postmortem: only two taken to Newmarket Veterinary College. Contact there – Heather O'Connell – claims neither horse, Whataparty or Brut Force, showed signs of substance in the bloodstream. Heart and lungs appeared to be entirely healthy.

Quote: 'It's a dangerous game and the majority of serious falls occur over the last half mile. Our conclusion was that these fatalities were the sort of thing that happen in National Hunt racing, no more, no less.'

Gavin sat back and massaged his eyes once more. It was just the sort of remark which, a week ago, he would have used but since then his area of interest had changed. 'The sort of things that happen in National Hunt racing.' That was yesterday's scandal. He punched some keys on the word-processor and more notes appeared on the screen.

Linked characters??

Clay Wentworth. Background – see Who's Who 1991. Chairman of Wentworth

Properties and amateur jockey. Riding on the day Dig For Glory killed (not in same race). Also in race won by Tanglewood, the only surviving horse on the hit list. Ambitious?

List found in his possession?

Raven claims that Alex Drew used to play poker with him.

Strange (strained) relationship with wife Zena.

It wasn't much to go on. Gavin was as prepared as anyone to doorstep the great, the good and the guilty in pursuit of a story but the connection with Alex Drew's death seemed tenuous, even – Gavin remembered seeing photographs of Wentworth on financial pages – unlikely. He tapped in one more word onto the computer report.

Weak?

Gavin's notes on Zena Wentworth and Digby Welcome took him no further on the case. Zena, a former model, was said to have had a drink problem which developed into a fidelity problem – there was nothing new or unusual there.

Digby, the late Digby, was more interesting. According to Gavin's police contacts, the murder of Digby Welcome was being treated as a sex and robbery case. The flat had been turned over, a few items and possibly some cash had apparently been removed. The received opinion at Chelsea Police Station was that a business girl had got greedy and had graduated from prostitution to murder. Not even the fact that Digby was handcuffed to the bed, that his poor, abused frame showed signs of a beating and electrocution to sensitive erogenous zones, had aroused particular interest. The world was full of punishment freaks. The velvet-lined handcuffs, it was said, were made in Italy.

Gavin sat back and closed his eyes. The thought of Digby Welcome writhing around in pleasure as some hard-eyed tart goosed him with electric wires did nothing for his hangover. But it wasn't Digby's death, which he put down to the journalistic version of Sod's law – your best lead always dies – that interested him, but the connection with Clay Wentworth. On the face of it, they were ill-matched characters with no more in common than an interest in racing and, from what Gavin had heard, Digby was not one to spend time on normal social relationships. For him, friendship was always a means to an end£

There was another oddity. Paul Raven had discovered that Digby had put £3,000 on Skinflint to win, yet he was said to be funny about cash – after all, it had been chronic meanness that had finished his career as a trainer. Gavin didn't know much about racing but you had to be blind not to see that putting three grand on a horse ridden by Clay Wentworth in an amateur race was high-risk gambling bordering on lunacy.

Unless Digby had known that Tanglewood couldn't win, that after that race, the horse would be dead or injured and its name would be removed from Clay's list. As it was, Tanglewood won, although Raven had mentioned that there had been another casualty in the race.

He dialled Paul's number, but the boy wonder was out or busy with cute little Angie, because Gavin found himself listening to his soft northern tones on an answering machine. He decided to leave a message.

'These nags that bought it,' he said, as if they were in the middle of a conversation. 'What did they have in common which Tanglewood didn't? I was wondering if there was anything odd about the Wincanton race. The boffins at Newmarket are fucking useless, by the way. Give that darling girlfriend of yours a kiss or something from me . . .'

He hung up. Gavin preferred the company of women to that of men but he couldn't help admiring a man whose body had been broken but who was already walking, who was obsessively searching out the person behind his friend Drew's death and who, despite several disabilities – a lack of significant movement in the legs, a career in ruins, a family that came from north of Watford – had still managed to pull Angie O'Keefe. Gavin respected the man; in a world where words were cheap, his quiet determination was unusual.

He punched up more of his notes onto the screen.

OTHERS POSSIBLY INVOLVED

Ginnie Matthews (trainer)

Lol Calloway (rockstar)

Alice Markwick (businesswoman)

With a grunt of effort and pain, Gavin stood up. He wandered across the large open-plan offices of the *Guardian* until he reached a group of desks where the staff covering the business pages worked. 'Sorry to wake you up, Peter,' he said to a man who sat, his feet on the desk before him, staring indifferently at the Teletext on the screen before him with the unmistakeable smugness of a journalist who has already filed his copy.

'I'm thinking,' said Pete Morrow, assistant business editor.

Gavin sat on the edge of the desk. 'What d'you know about Alice Markwick?' he said.

Kevin Smiley had once loved racing, but now he hated it. Fourteen years ago, he had left school with a dream in his heart of becoming a successful jockey. He had worked in a small yard near Leicestershire before trying his luck in Newmarket. He grew too heavy to get rides even in apprentice races, so he moved on yet again to a jumping stable outside Royston.

He was twenty-five before he began to realise that the dream was never going to come true. At first, he had thought it was his weight. Then he had convinced himself that the Head Lad disliked him. After that, he blamed himself – he was moody, sometimes giving the Guv'nor of the moment a piece of his mind.

Now that he was thirty, Kevin had discovered the truth that others had known for years. His problem was not on the scales, or in his character or attitude, but in the saddle. He wasn't exactly useless – sometimes he could look quite neat as he rode work

– but he would never wear silks. He hadn't the judgement, or the balance, or the brains to ride competitively. His past, his present and his future were as a lad, not a jockey.

At first, he took his dissatisfaction out on the horses, prodding them with a pitchfork as he mucked out, jabbing them in the mouth as he rode them in the string. He became unpopular with the other lads, making trouble for them, bullying the younger apprentices, particularly if they showed a talent that he would never have.

Kevin was bent before he had come to work for Ginnie Matthews, supplying information, helping out when a certain runner needed to be slipped a certain untraceable substance with its morning feed. The fact that the Matthews stable was straight and the Missus trusted her staff implicitly changed nothing.

Kevin was part of racing's secret and corrupt network. He was a sleeper waiting to act on behalf of vaguely criminal elements. In return, he would receive money and, more importantly, experience the simple pleasure of doing someone harm.

'Morning, Kevin.' Paul Raven made his way slowly across the yard on his way towards the Missus' house. 'Riding out second lot?'

'Nah.' Kevin looked away. 'You?'

Paul smiled. 'I'm giving Monty a half-speed over six furlongs,' he said.

'Right,' said Kevin, watching as Paul rang the bell at the Missus' front door.

Slo-Mo, he called him to the younger lads who were too afraid of him not to laugh. 'Here comes old Slo-Mo,' he'd say as Paul pulled himself out of the car before second lot.

He walked round to the tack room and reached for a bucket. Glancing around to check that no one was coming, he took some powder from his pocket and carefully poured it into the bucket which he half-filled with water.

He hadn't understood his instructions but he was confident that, somewhere along the line, he would be helping to cause a fair degree of pain and disappointment to some bastard who had it coming. Kevin smiled – it was good to feel wanted.

'How's Skinflint going?'

Breakfast with Ginnie Matthews was not a social affair – conversation tended to be minimal or non-existent – but there were two reasons why Paul had accepted the casual invitation, muttered the last time he had ridden out. The mixed grill cooked by the Irish maid was astonishing and Paul needed to resolve a question in his mind.

'Fine.' Ginnie hardly bothered to look up from her *Sporting Post*, tucking into the heaped plate before her as if she hadn't eaten for days. Manners had never played a great part in her life and, ever since she had lived alone, her breakfast behaviour had gone into a sharp decline. Through a mouth full of food, she added 'He'll win at Cheltenham if the jockey doesn't make a balls up.'

'The race has cut up badly.'

Ginnie nodded, as if to say that Paul had exhausted her supply of early morning conversation.

Paul persisted. 'Extraordinary how many of the fancied horses have gone wrong.' He looked away as the trainer did something mildly disgusting with a fried egg before shovelling it into her mouth. 'Died in fact.'

Ginnie glanced up and, below the thick make-up on her face, there appeared the hint of a blush. She finished her mouthful, reached for a napkin and wiped, not entirely successfully, the traces of egg from the sides of her mouth. 'Yes, I've noticed.'

Paul reached into the pocket of his jodhpurs and passed a slip of paper across the table.

'Who gave you this?' Ginnie asked eventually. She seemed more surprised than guilty.

'It doesn't matter. The writing's yours, isn't it?'

'Looks like it.' Ginnie pushed the paper back to Paul and busied herself spreading a thick layer of butter on some toast.

'The horses whose names are crossed out have all been destroyed,' said Paul.

'Bloody hell,' Ginnie boomed. 'I may be keen on getting winners but I don't go around killing horses.' There was an edgy, unconvincing humour in her voice. 'The list is mine,' she added, 'but I didn't cross the names out.'

'What was it for?'

'An owner needed it.'

'Clay Wentworth?'

Ginnie nodded as she chewed on her toast. 'Some time back, Clay wanted to know the main contenders for the Kim Muir. I jotted them down for him.'

'Why Dig For Glory?'

'God knows. If you look at your piece of paper there, you'll see that name's in different writing. Anyway I wrote the list after your fall.' She glanced at her watch. 'Time for second lot. Or are you too busy playing detective to exercise poor old Monty for me?'

Paul stood up. 'How did he do it?' he said, almost to himself.

'It seems a bit efficient for Clay,' said Ginnie. 'I've always thought he lived like he rode – weak and ineffective.'

Paul smiled. 'He must have help.'

Ginnie walked briskly out of the door. Either she was a better actor than he would ever have believed or she was entirely innocent.

There were few advantages in being a part-time jockey on the mend, Paul reflected as he made his way out of the house towards the yard, but at least he was spared the drilling discomfort of riding out in the gloom and cold of first lot at seven o'clock. Now, as the lads pulled out the second string, a wintry sun was taking the bite out of the morning. There was another small privilege – Monty was tacked up for him by one of the younger lads.

As Paul approached Monty's box, a figure scurried out, carrying a bucket and sponge, whistling cheerily as he made his way back to the tackroom. Paul opened the stable door and, looking at Monty, noticed a dark stain on his chestnut hindquarters under the tail. Nothing unusual there – the Missus took a robust, old fashioned view of turn-out and had an eagle eye for dried sweatmarks behind the girth or a trace of muck on the hindquarters. The only surprise was that it was Kevin Smiley, not normally a perfectionist, who was attending to Monty.

The string had made its way past the farm buildings and neighbouring houses that backed onto the yard when Monty first swished his tail and lifted his hindquarters.

At first, Paul laughed. 'Who's been feeding up this old bugger?' he called out. 'He's trying to drop me.'

Pat, the Head Lad, who was riding in front of Paul in the string, looked around. 'You all right?' he asked.

Paul nodded. The old horse was jigging about like a two-year-old and, for the first time since he had resumed riding, Paul was nervously aware of his insecurity in the saddle. He laid a calming hand on Monty's neck and was surprised to find that, despite the cold, he was beginning to sweat.

There was a matter of seconds between Paul's realization that there was something wrong and the moment when it was too late to do anything about it. As the string turned right up a side road towards the gallops, Monty started to dance sideways, his eyes fearful, his mouth flecked with foam.

'Get off him, Paul,' Jamie called out. 'He must have something under his saddle.'

Paul kicked his feet out of the irons. The horse grunted, kicked the air and, before Paul could dismount, Monty had set off, first at a trot, then, snorting with pain, at a gallop away from the string. Like a clown on a circus horse, Paul clung to the mane, unable to grip enough with his legs to control the horse.

Pat set off in pursuit but pain had given Monty a surprising turn of speed and, before Paul could reach him, he had rounded a bend and was making for the main road.

Paul knew there was no choice. As pain wrenched his back, the wind whistling past his ears, he saw, drawing ever closer, the cars and lorries speeding along the road before him. Closing his eyes and doing his best to ball himself up as he fell, he dived to the left, hitting the ground a matter of yards before the main road.

Seconds later, Pat pulled up, alighting from the saddle. He crouched down beside Paul, gently turning him over.

From the near distance, there was the sound of the blaring of car-horns followed by the unmistakeable sound of metal impact at speed.

Pat glanced towards the road, then back at Paul , registering the flickering of consciousness in his eyelids.

'Lie still,' he said. 'Don't move a muscle.'

Those who knew Alice Markwick well, a small and exclusive group, rarely guessed her true weakness. Although she had a deep and sincere affection for money, it wasn't financial greed. As for the trips to Heaven in search of someone young, firm and dressed in a leather skirt, that was controllable: her libido, while powerful and slightly odd, was not allowed to dominate her life.

The flaw in Alice's personal armoury was simple – she wanted to belong. All her life, she had been an outsider. Now, after two decades of work and discreet corruption, she felt it was time she became part of the inner circle where your place of birth was no more than an exotic extra, where the way you had made your money was irrelevant. Others slipped easily into Britain's legendary class system: why couldn't she?

She could have married again, of course, but that was an unacceptable option. For five years she had endured the demeaning reality of heterosexual sex. The day that she had stood by the coffin of Dr Eric Markwick, she had promised herself that never again would she allow her flesh to be invaded by a repulsive male presence. Sex with Eric had been like submitting to a herd of eager slugs, one of whom was carrying an absurd and disgusting prong. No, never again – not even as a means to acquire the respectability she so longed for.

Alice sat in a deep armchair in her spacious and tastefully decorated Islington flat, flicking restlessly through a glossy magazine. It was about ten thirty; normally she would have been at the office for two hours by now but today, she deserved a morning off. Today she would take one step nearer society, *le tout Londres*.

She found herself thinking of Clay's father, Sir Denis Wentworth, whom she had met a couple of times. Like her, he had been an outsider, although he lacked her sophistication and looks. And, despite the fact that he was no more than a hard and humourless businessman, he had entered the magic circle with apparent ease. Why? Because he was rich? Because he was English? Because he was a man? Certainly charm had had nothing to do with it.

The bell rang. Checking her appearance before a large mirror, Alice walked to the intercom. 'Who is it?' she asked.

'Gavin Holmes. *Mail on Sunday*.'

Alice pressed another button. 'Top floor,' she said.

It had only been a matter of time. With her looks and contacts and professional success, fashionable exposure in the right places had to come. When the man from the *Mail on Sunday* had rung her at the office and asked whether she would contribute to a series of profiles called 'Me and My Roots', she had jumped at the chance. A Sunday magazine, complete with colour photograph – it was too good to be true.

'Mrs Markwick?' the man at her door had the unhealthy pallor that she associated with journalists. He extended a hand. 'Gavin Holmes. So kind of you to spare the time for our little feature.'

'What about the photographer?' Alice asked.

Gavin shrugged apologetically. 'He'll call you later to arrange a time for the pictures,' he said, entering the flat and making his way into the sitting-room. 'We'd only have been in each other's way if he'd come this morning.'

The man talked. As Alice gave him coffee, hoping that he would note that it was the best Italian blend served in softly hand-painted porcelain manufactured in Longchamps, she listened to him explaining at length the rationale behind the piece. It wasn't muckraking, he said, more lifestyle, a positive, life-affirming, upbeat story full of human touches, surprising, intimate, that would reach –

'Why don't you just ask me the questions and we'll take it from there?' Alice smiled, settling back into her seat like a charming English hostess. Noticing the flicker of sexual interest in the journalist's eyes as she leaned forward, she took off her shoes and curled her legs under her, affording him a better view of them. She smiled. A ladies' man; this was going to be easy.

Gavin took out a notebook. 'Perhaps you could tell me about your childhood in Prague,' he asked.

'Ah, Prague.' Alice allowed a shadow of unease, suggesting painful memories, to cross her face. 'I was born into a poor working family. My father worked in a factory. My mother, a beautiful woman, was an office-cleaner. It was a hard life . . .'

She spoke eloquently, her husky, slightly accented voice presenting the vivid picture of her youth which she had perfected over the two decades in which she had been in England.

The journalist jotted notes onto his pad. 'So you came to London. What sort of work did you do?' he asked without looking up.

'Au pair. Washing-up. Translation.' Alice smiled. 'The usual things.'

For a few minutes, Gavin asked questions about London in the sixties. It was wild, wasn't it, something of a party? Alice was evasive. Not in her circles, it wasn't. As if talking to himself, Gavin spoke of the fascination the old permissivenes held for *Mail on Sunday* readers. The music, the drugs, the laughter.

'You're asking if I had lots of boyfriends? The answer is no,' Alice said more cooly.

'Did you know Digby Welcome?' The question came out of the blue, attended by an innocent smile.

Alice frowned. 'The name seems somewhat familiar,' she said eventually. 'Have I read something about him?'

'He was murdered recently. I read somewhere that he had introduced you to your future husband.'

Alice felt the colour draining from her cheeks. She leaned forward and took the journalist's cup. 'More coffee?' she asked. 'I'm rather pleased with this blend. Rozzo di Palermo. Bought it in Harrods Food Hall.'

Gavin smiled, but made no note on his pad.

'I thought this was a lifestyle piece,' she said lightly.

'Colour. A little mention of Welcome would give the piece what we call "contemporaneity". The feature editor likes that. So you knew him?'

'I worked in a restaurant. I think Welcome might have invited me to the party where I met Eric. It was a long time ago.'

'And you kept in touch?'

'Good Lord, no. The man gives me the creeps.'

Gavin frowned, allowing a moment of silence before speaking again. It was clear that Alice Markwick had nothing more to say on the subject of Welcome.

'So,' he said. 'Tell me about your husband.'

'Ah, Eric.' Alice relaxed, a distant look in her eyes. 'A sweet, brilliant man.'

It was another half hour before Gavin Holmes left the flat. Although Alice knew little of journalism – she rarely bothered to read beyond the financial pages of *The Times* – the interview had surprised her. She had been expecting something rather gentler, a light-hearted tour of the flat, some harmless chat about her past, her work methods, where she shopped. Instead Holmes had asked prying, insistent questions about the work carried out by Markwick Instruments. He had been alarmingly well-briefed.

Then there was Digby Welcome. How on earth had he known about that?

There were certain memories which Alice had tried over the years to erase from her mind – useless, negative memories of events which, even these many years later, made her feel sick to the stomach.

Staring out of the window, she heard once more the smug and sinister tones of Digby Welcome – 'your guardian angel, my dearest', he used to call himself in the early days. And, of course, he was right. If Digby hadn't been there to rescue her from the smoky Knightsbridge restaurant where she was working, she would never have reached where she was today. Marriage wasn't a problem; but Eric, by some freak of chance, had been perfect. He was brilliant, he was gullible, he fell in love easily and – the best kept until last – died at an early age, leaving his firm to Alice.

Once Digby had something on you, he never let go. At first, it had been easy – Alice shuddered as she thought of Digby's skin netted with the red lash marks from her whip – but, as if he had understood that hitting a man was a positive pleasure for her, he had given that up, taking instead some share options in the firm. The fact that, because of his mysterious demise, Digby Welcome would not be picking up his share of the big pay-off caused Alice no disappointment whatsoever.

Her instinct told her that there was something not quite right about Gavin Holmes. She picked up the telephone book and, having leafed through its pages, walked to the hall telephone and dialled.

'Features editor,' she said.

At the other end, the phone rang for some time before a woman picked it up. The features editor was in conference at present, she said.

'My name's Mrs Markwick, I'm sure you could help me.' Alice put on her most ingratiating voice. 'Your man Gavin Holmes has just been interviewing me for your "Me and My Roots" feature. He told me I'd be visited by a photographer. I really need to know when he's coming round.'

'Holmes?' The woman at the other end seemed confused. 'I think he's on the *Guardian*. He doesn't work for us. Anyway we wound up that feature last month. Who did – '

Alice hung up. It wasn't often that she was taken in by a man and she didn't like it. She dialled another number.

'I think I've found Petrin's guinea pig,' she said.

Clay Wentworth put down the receiver as if it were a piece of rare china, and tapped his rolled gold biro on the desk. He didn't like Alice Markwick and he certainly didn't like depending on her. There was no point of contact – not class, not sex, not humour. All that bound them together was the project on which they both, in different ways, depended. She was too cold, too hard – she seemed to relish the danger of their plan, the pain it caused to others. He thought of her luckless employee, Zametsky. Alice had known that there was some connection between what had happened to him and her own dubious plans, yet she had insisted it had been an accident. Zametsky had, for some reason, seemed too afraid to tell the truth. In the end, it had been Clay who had sent his wife £1,000 in cash. The money was nothing when your face was missing but it made him feel slightly better.

'Lunch.' His father stood at the door of the office, leaning on his walking-stick. As usual, his short frame and glittering blue eyes emanated wordless disapproval.

Father and son went through to the boardroom of Wentworth Properties plc, where a plump and nervous girl, the daughter of a shareholder, served them with a beef casserole taken from some Cordon Bleu cookbook for executive lunches. As usual, Sir Denis's portion was microscopic and, after the girl had gone, he looked at his meal with distaste before poking at a piece of meat and fastidiously putting it in his mouth. His old jaws worked slowly.

Sometimes, during these meals, Clay would look down the length of the long mahogany table and think, 'Die, you stupid old bastard, choke on it.' Then he would think again. Not yet. Not quite yet.

'Who was she?' Sir Denis spoke little these days so that, when he did, his words came out in a slow guttural rasp, like the voice of a Dickensian villain.

'Who, father?'

'On the phone. In the office.'

'Just business.'

For a moment, the boardroom was silent except for the sound of silver on china.

'Business.' Sir Denis pushed a bit of meat around his plate. He understood Clay well enough to know that no mere matter of profit or loss would preoccupy him for long. His son had never understood the importance of money. 'You're poking, I suppose,' he said.

'No, father. I'm not poking, as you call it.'

Chewing slowly, Sir Denis looked at his son with chilly contempt. 'I don't suppose you are.' An odd, birdlike sound, somewhere between a laugh and a death rattle, came from him. 'Never much of a poker, were you?'

A flush of anger appeared on Clay's cheeks. He could just about take his father when he was lecturing him about company matters; when he moved into the personal area, he was impossible. Ever since Lady Wentworth, a quiet, blameless woman, had died in the early 1970s, Sir Denis had lived in a flat in Knightsbridge alone apart from the butler who looked after him. The spartan simplicity of his life had allowed him to comment, almost always unfavourably, on Clay's domestic arrangements.

'Ditch the bitch,' Sir Denis said as if reading Clay's thoughts. 'New young wife. Children. That's what you want.' A drop of dark gravy hung on his lower lip. 'She's poking, you know.'

'Told you that, has she, father?' Clay pushed away his plate. 'You talk about poking with my wife?'

'Ditch her. You'd make an old man very happy.'

Maybe, when this was all over, he would. Living with a crazed, pill-happy, middle-aged woman was almost as depressing as working with his cold and sinister father.

He watched as Sir Denis toyed with his meal. It would be another fifteen minutes before Clay was free to return to his office.

'Maybe I will,' he said, thinking of freedom, a new start in life. It wouldn't be long now.

This story had led to some of the worst places – a cold stableyard, the backstreets of Willesden, and now the casualty ward of a run-down rural hospital. It wasn't what he'd become a journalist to do.

Gavin walked down the ward to a bed beside which sat Angie, a ray of beauty in a grim, off-white world.

'Gavin,' she said, smiling. 'Kind of you to visit.'

'My pleasure,' he lied. Reluctantly, he turned to the bed where Paul lay. 'You prat,' he said. 'What is it with you and horses?'

It had been twenty-four hours since Paul had been admitted. His face was decorated by vivid bruises and his right arm and shoulder were bandaged up. 'It wasn't an accident, Gavin,' he said quietly.

The journalist pulled up a chair and slumped into it. 'What do the docs say?' he asked.

'That he was a bloody fool to be riding in the first place,' said Angie.

Paul smiled weakly. 'It could be worse,' he said. 'Light concussion, fractured collar-bone. The back's shaken up a bit. I fell in the right way.'

'You seem to have lots of practice.' Gavin produced a packet of cigarettes and was just about to light up when he remembered where he was. Swearing softly, he put them away again. 'While you've been trying to kill yourself, I've been making myself useful.'

'A trainer called Ginnie Matthews made that list,' Paul interrupted. 'She gave it to Clay Wentworth.'

'You think she's involved?'

Paul shook his head, wincing slightly. 'She suspected something was going on but I'm sure she wasn't involved.'

'Yet it was at her yard that you had your accident,' said Angie. 'It seems a bit of a coincidence.'

'No, maybe Paul's right,' Gavin said. 'There seems to have been very little gambling involved in these races. I think the people behind it are outside racing.'

He told them of his visit to Alice Markwick, pointing out the connection between her and Digby Welcome.

'Markwick and Welcome used to go to Wentworth's poker evenings,' said Paul. 'But why were they involved in killing horses?'

'To help Clay win races?' Angie remembered the tall man she had seen in the bar at Wincanton. He had hardly seemed the ruthless type.

'And how?' Paul asked.

Gavin smiled triumphantly. 'As part of my profile, I asked Alice about the research being done by Markwick Instruments. It's into the use of lasers in surgery – particularly in eye surgery. She was evasive, claiming that she was a businesswoman who knew little about the technical side.'

'Eyes,' said Paul quietly. 'That's how they did it. They blinded the horse they were after as it approached the fence.'

'No, I checked with Newmarket,' said Gavin. 'According to the lab, there was nothing irregular about the horses' sight.'

'How do they do it then?' Angie asked. 'And what's their next target?'

'I've got to get to that poker school,' Paul muttered.

Gavin smiled. 'I wish I could help but both Alice and Clay would recognise me.'

'No,' Paul said. 'I'll go.'

'We need to get to Alice Markwick. Find out how they're blinding the horses – I'm sure that must be what they're doing.' Gavin sounded evasive, as if he had an idea which slightly embarrassed him.

'But how?' Angie asked.

'There is one way.' The journalist was looking at her in an odd and slightly alarming way. 'But it's ever so slightly tacky.'

'Surprise us,' said Paul.

There were times when Kevin Smiley cursed the day his father took him racing. He had been thirteen at the time and it had changed his life. The action, the atmosphere, the smell of courage and money – even though it was Haydock on a chilly Saturday, it had been enough to infect little Kevin. 'I know what I want to be,' he had said to his father, driving home that night. 'I'm going to be a jockey.'

And, sure enough, he wasn't.

As Kevin packed his few belongings into a suitcase, he thought of the cold mornings and casual humiliations that were the sum total of his racing career. 'You're fucking useless, Smiley,' one of the older jockeys had told him when he was still in his teens. 'You haven't got it.'

The bastard had been right. Whatever the 'it' was – that magic ingredient that turned boys into jockeys – he didn't have it. Kevin glanced at his watch and looked his last at the bedsit that had been home for the last couple of years. He was thirty. It wasn't too late to start again. He'd go to London, find a job. He'd tell his parents later.

Kevin felt an uncharacteristic pang of guilt. It was true that he had let a few people down. His mum and dad, who had always believed in him, Mrs Matthews, who had turned a deaf ear to those who had told her that Smiley was a wrong 'un and taken him on all the same.

He thought of the last time he had seen his employer. She had been talking to the vet the day after the business with Paul Raven. Later, as he cleaned tack, one of the lads told him the rumour going round the yard.

'Weren't no accident, were it?' he had said. 'Fuckin' vet only found acid on poor old Monty's hindquarters. No wonder 'e went fuckin' apeshit. Burnin' into 'is flesh, weren't it?'

'Acid?' Kevin had acted as casually as he was able.

'Slow acting. Reacted with horse's body sweat, is what I heard. The more he sweated, the more it fuckin' ate into him.'

'So someone did it on purpose?'

'You're fuckin' quick, ain't you?' the lad had said. 'The Missus'll find him, that's for sure. Can't have her darlin' Paul buried like that, can we?'

It was hardly a glorious note on which to end his career but, if he had learned nothing else in a life of ducking and diving, Kevin knew when to cut and run. He clicked the suitcase shut and, leaving the light on and closing the door, he made his way down the stairs.

His car, a Ford Granada, drew up within seconds of Kevin appearing at the front door of the hostel.

'Minicab?' Kevin asked, as the driver opened the passenger door.

'For Mr Smiley,' said the driver.

'That's the one.' Kevin put the suitcase on the back seat and climbed in. 'Swindon station please, mate.' He sat back and closed his eyes, relaxing at last. It was good to get away.

It took a minute or two for him to realize that the car was heading the wrong way.

'Sorry, mate,' Kevin said uneasily. 'I said Swindon.'

In reply, the driver accelerated, flicking an electric lock on his door.

'What's up mate? What are you up to?'

'Child lock,' said the driver, his handsome dark eyes watching Kevin in the rearview mirror. 'Child lock for a very bad boy,' he said.

For a moment, Kevin was confused. Then he sat back and asked quietly, 'What exactly d'you want from me?'

'Nothing,' said the driver. 'Assolutamente niente.'

Chapter
10

The photographer sat in his rabbit-filled bunker, thinking about the future. It was a small room, brightly lit by strip lighting, with a workbench in one corner and, occupying most of the floor space, the animals' play area.

He had enjoyed designing their little assault course. It had reminded him of when he was a small boy in Warsaw, of the toys he would make in the small back room of his mother's apartment, except here the toys were alive and, for a while at least, warm.

Of course, the rabbits were predictable in the stupid, panic-stricken way that they responded to scientific stimuli.

'Want to play, Fi-Fi?' The photographer spoke in the well-bred undertone of a man who had spent much of his life in university libraries and laboratories. He took a white and brown rabbit from a cage, placed it carefully into a corner of the play area enclosed by wire and turned to a control board on his desk. Humming softly, he pressed a couple of switches.

The prod flashed red, then green, then white as it approached Fi-Fi, causing her to cower against the wire. As it touched her white fur, the shock of an electric current jolted the rabbit's body. The prod withdrew before, flashing brightly once more, it advanced again. Fi-Fi was relatively intelligent and soon the first bright flash induced her to leap backwards against the wire in the knowledge that where there was light, pain would follow soon afterwards.

The photographer opened a small door, allowing her to escape into the rest of the cage. For a minute or so, he watched as she dashed backwards and forwards in her new-found freedom. He liked Fi-Fi – her rabbitty will to survive made her a good target. He reached for the camera on his desk.

It was too heavy, in his opinion. Zametsky had developed the prototype and had been indifferent to the photographer's complaint that, while it looked like a camera, a security guard or customs official merely needed to hold it to be suspicious. These people were trained to look for bombs and, although the camera was far more dangerous than mere explosives, its weight was a serious design flaw. Zametsky had smiled. Cosmetics, he had said, could come later.

Fi-Fi's efforts were tiring her. With a soft 'tut' of impatience, the photographer activated two more prods, one of which caught her, enlivening her performance. He weighed the camera in his hand, then took aim and shot.

The noise was good. The click and whirr was just like a real camera. Fi-Fi kept running, only this time she hurled herself against the wire. The photographer activated the flashing lights on the two electric prods. Frantic as she was, the rabbit made no effort to avoid them, running blindly into the first one and then the other. In a relatively short time, she lay in a corner, her sides heaving with exhaustion. The photographer moved the prod slowly towards her. It flashed red, green and white, but Fi-Fi no longer reacted.

Perfect. The photographer left the prod flashing before the rabbit's unseeing eyes and checked his watch. Four minutes. Fi-Fi would come round within the next sixty seconds.

At first, he hadn't believed that there was no trace, that the beam of Zametsky's gismo could penetrate the corneal cortex and freeze the iris without long-term damage. It was a miracle of technology, a laser that incapacitated yet was untraceable. The photographer felt proud to be a part of it, privileged.

There was a scrabbling from the cage as the life came back to Fi-Fi's eyes and she saw the flashing horror before her.

The photographer smiled at the rabbit's clownish double-take. Throwing the switches on the control board, he said, 'Good girl,' and opened the run and picked Fi-Fi up. Her eyes, if anything, seemed brighter than they had been before the experiment. Smoothing down her ears, he put the rabbit back in her cage.

It was good. He was ready for the next job. The photographer hoped it would be on something more interesting than a horse.

It had been a long time since Zena Wentworth had been needed. Now and then, she might get a call from one of her part-time lovers who, in that presumptuous way that men had these days, told her that he needed her now, right now – but that wasn't need, it was boredom, like you needed a gin and tonic, or a holiday in the sun.

Paul Raven wasn't like that. When he rung her and explained that he needed her help, she was almost down the stairs, in the Rolls and on her way before he had explained the precise nature of his need. When he did, she had hesitated, briefly unsure, assailed by a certain illogical loyalty to her husband.

Then she agreed. Bloody hell, she had needs too.

Paul had seemed surprised that she intended to visit him. She could phone him, he said.

She had insisted. She had something to give him.

Zena parked the Rolls down the street from the flat and walked briskly, her mink coat hanging off her shoulders, towards the flat. She rang the bell, tapping her foot impatiently as she waited.

After what seemed an age, the door opened and Paul stood in a dressing-gown, his right arm in a sling, and leaning heavily on a walking-stick.

'Sorry,' he said. 'I've got a bit slower since I last saw you.'

'Your poor face.' Zena made to reach out for him, then, remembering that Paul was uneasy with flirtation, stopped herself.

'Better than it was.' He turned slowly back into the flat. 'Only been out of hospital a couple of days.' He made his way through a small, comfortable sitting-room. 'I'll have to talk to you in the bedroom. Doctors have told me not to move about for a while.'

'Who looks after you?' Zena picked up a framed photograph on the table. It showed Paul upsides over a hurdle at Cheltenham. The other jockey she recognized as Alex Drew.

'Angie comes by after work.' Paul made his way into the bedroom and, with some difficulty, eased himself into bed. 'I feel bloody daft,' he said. 'Make yourself a coffee if you like.'

'I won't bother.' Zena took off her fur coat, threw it across a chair and sat on the end of the bed. 'The next meeting of the poker school is at this address.' She opened her bag and handed him a piece of paper. 'I suggest you ring Clay and explain that Digby invited you before his . . . accident.'

'You won't be there yourself?'

'I'm not welcome. My husband says I talk too much. Don't take it seriously like I should.' She smiled. 'Our marriage isn't close.' She looked at Paul, who had his dressing-gown wrapped around him to his throat, and smiled.

'What was the other thing then?' he asked, eager to break the moment.

'Apart from an invitation, there's one requirement for joining Clay's poker school. You have to have a minimum of a thousand pounds in stake money.'

'I'll borrow it,' Paul said.

Zena took an envelope from her bag. '*Voila*,' she said. 'Your entrance ticket. Two thousand pounds.'

Illogically, Paul felt a surge of anger within him. 'It's your husband's money.'

'Don't be so ridiculously old-fashioned. We're married. We share. He goes to work, I look after the domestic side – send Christmas cards, book restaurants, that sort of thing.'

'He earned it.'

Zena laughed harshly. 'My husband has earned nothing in his life. He's waiting for his darling daddy to topple off the perch. The money comes from the highly dubious enterprises of Sir Denis Wentworth.'

Paul felt uneasy at the woman's casual intimacy, the way she was half-lying now at the end of his bed, pinning down the blankets so that he was unable to move his legs. 'I couldn't gamble with your husband's money,' he said.

'Why are you going to Clay's poker school?' Zena asked, casually kicking off her shoes.

'Because I want to know what happened to Alex. I have a feeling your husband was involved.'

'What scruples you have. You think he might have been involved in finishing your racing career and causing your best friend's death and you can't bring yourself to use his money against him.'

'You're very bitter.' Paul tried to move his legs but, now that Zena was kneeling at the end of the bed, he felt powerless. His shoulder was aching and suddenly he wanted to be alone.

'Use Clay's money. Nothing would give me more pleasure.' There was a sparkle in Zena's eyes as she leaned forward, proffering the brown envelope with her left hand. As he took the envelope, she shifted quickly, trapping his free hand beneath her. Paul gasped. Zena reached under the blankets and, before he could do anything about it, slender, knowing fingers were working their way up his bare thigh under his dressing-gown. 'Or almost nothing would give me more pleasure,' she added.

'Don't.' Paul looked at her coldly, then shuddered as her hand darted upward and found him. Zena closed her eyes ecstatically. He said, more threateningly, 'Get your hand off me.'

'Don't be like that,' she said, with a catch in her voice. 'I like you very much, Paul. You won't have to move.'

Paul swallowed hard. Trying to move his hand merely caused a searing pain in the other shoulder. To his horror, he felt his body responding.

'Everything else in working order, I see,' she purred. 'I'd really like to get your bit between my teeth.'

As she leaned forward, Paul gritted his teeth and jerked his left hand free, brushing her off the bed. 'I'm not interested in being raped,' he muttered.

Zena stood by the bed, barefoot and contrite. 'Not even. . . ?' She gave an eloquently suggestive pout, her tongue across her upper lip.

'Bugger off out of it,' said Paul. 'And take your money.'

She put on her shoes and slipped into her mink coat. She walked over to a mirror and, checking and making some minor repairs to her make-up, she seemed cooler now, philosophical, as if such things happened to her every day.

'I'll leave the money,' she said lightly. 'You'll need it.' Without looking back, she swayed out of the bedroom.

Paul relaxed at last and closed his eyes with relief that she had gone. He glanced at the envelope still in his hand before becoming aware that Zena was back, standing at the door.

'Let me know if you change your mind,' she said. 'I have a feeling that we could be *very* good.'

The squire of Lenbrook Hall was out shooting on his estate. So far that afternoon he had zapped three rabbits, a couple of hares, five pheasants and a couple of smaller brown birds which he hadn't ever shot before. 'Not zapped, Lol,' the squire muttered to himself as he approached a cottage. 'Bagged.' He banged on the door with the butt of his shotgun like a sheriff making a house call, 'Ere, John,' he called out.

An old man wearing moleskin leggings and slippers opened the door. 'Mr Calloway,' he said. 'How did you get on?'

Lol thrust a black dustbin liner forward. 'That's what I bagged, John. Not a bad bit of bagging, eh?'

With a hint of a sigh, the old man opened the dustbin liner. 'Very good, Mr Calloway.'

''Ere, what's 'em little brown fellas, John? Grouse, are they?'

The gamekeeper held up a small bird. 'They would be mistle thrush, Mr Calloway.'

'Get away.'

'Tricky devils to shoot, sir.'

The squire looked disappointed. 'On the bird-table, weren't they,' he said sulkily. 'You can keep them. The old lady gets heavy about bodies in the kitchen.'

'Thank you, Mr Calloway.'

'Cheers, John.'

To tell the truth. Lol wasn't sure about that old bastard. There was something leery about him, like he was laughing up his sleeve all the time. He was good at his job, ensuring that the animals on the estate were plump, docile and slow, but he had an attitude problem: no respect. If the squire of Lenbrook Hall didn't deserve respect, who did?

Lol broke his twelve bore, took out the two cartridges and put them in the pocket of his Barbour, as he slouched across the lawn towards the house. Although the owner of what the papers called a 'luxury Elizabethan mansion', he still didn't feel entirely at home there. Still, what with the leisure complex at the back and the conversion of the library into an indoor swimming-pool with jacuzzi en suite, it was getting there. He opened the french windows into the sitting-room and, leaning the twelve bore against the television, kicked off his green Hunter boots and trudged towards the kitchen.

'Cooee, darlin', I'm home,' he called out in the hall. There was no reply. 'Out playing Lady Fuckin' Bountiful, down the village, I suppose,' he grumbled.

Back in the seventies, Suzie had been the hottest groupie around. She was class, could do things that that geezer Kama Sutra had never dreamed of, and nice with it. You didn't mind waking up beside Suzie which, in Lol's extensive experience, was rare in a groupie.

But, ever since they had moved to the hall, she had been different. The middle-class background she had once been so ashamed of had re-established itself. Village fetes, the fucking Women's Institute, sending the kids off to nobby private schools. She had even objected when he changed the name of the house from Chevenham Grange to Lenbrook Hall, after his bassist Len Brook who had tragically died inhaling his own vomit back in 1969. Worse than all that, Suzie had become sniffy about the better things in life, like mind-expanding drugs. Lol laughed quietly. Now the only thing that was expanding was her bum.

Lol paused in front of the large oak mirror, which Lady Muck had bought for an arm and a leg the previous year. He pushed the deer-stalker to the back of his head and, as if to compensate for his bald pate, fluffed out the big brown locks around his collar. Whistling a song from the sixties, Lol pushed the door to the basement where he had built a games room. A touch of snooker, that's what he felt like; maybe a spot of indoor croquet.

It was as Lol was pouring himself a whisky at the customized cocktail bar in the corner that he became aware that he was not alone. Beyond the glass case containing his guitar collection, across the stretch of purple astroturf with yellow croquet hoops, there was a rocking-chair he'd bought in San Diego. It was rocking.

Stealthily, Lol backed towards the billiard table, keeping his eye on the chair. The door clicked shut behind him. 'Mr Calloway?' The voice was mellow and relaxed, like the voice-over for a coffee advert. There was a slight accent there. Lol turned slowly. From behind the door, a man in his early thirties stepped forward – his dark, even features, carefully tended moustache and well-cut suit suggested respectability, but the man's build, his broad and muscular hands, were not those of an office worker.

'Who the fuck are you?' Lol asked.

In reply the man stepped forward, picked up the billiard cue that was lying near Lol's right hand and broke it across his knee. Casually he threw the two bits onto the astroturf. 'I don't like snooker,' he said.

'How did you get in? The gate's locked. There's security.'

'Why so shy?' The man in the dark suit sat on the edge of the billiard table. 'You need security?'

'Fans. Autograph hunters.'

The man laughed humourlessly. 'There didn't seem to be many when I climbed over. Maybe the gate's too high for their bath chairs and walking-frames.'

'You didn't tell me who you are.'

'Call me Signor Salvo. I'm here to get your support for a good cause.'

'My wife – '

'Shut the fuck up and listen.' The man paused, as if slightly taken aback by his own outburst. 'I haven't got all day,' he said more quietly. Placing both hands on the side of the table, he lifted himself up like a gymnast on the parallel bars, landing on his toes. He walked over to Lol's guitar collection.

'All you got to do is give me some information,' he said. 'Then I'll leave you alone.'

Lol glanced towards the door. He might make it – a dash upstairs to the old twelve bore in the sitting-room – but then again he might not. With Signor Psycho here, it was no time for heroics.

'I believe you belong to a business syndicate.' Salvatore's hands were in his pockets now. 'You have an interest in a certain product being developed by Markwick Instruments.'

Lol shrugged.

'Right. My employers want your product. We want it exclusively and we want it very, very soon – before it gets into the wrong hands. And you're going to help, right.'

Lol was no stranger to violence – he had been yards away when his bouncers had clubbed an over-enthusiastic Hell's Angel to death during the 1970 tour of the States – but he didn't like it at first-hand, one to one. Suddenly he felt old and afraid.

'I have a lot of business interests,' he said. 'Maybe I am involved with Markwick. Why don't I talk to my people . . .' He hesitated as Salvatore ambled over to the purple croquet lawn and picked up the heavy end of the broken snooker cue '. . . and get back to you.'

Salvatore tapped on the glass in front of the guitars. It was like the window of a music shop, with no less than ten gleaming instruments on their stands. 'Are you going to open this or am I going to smash it?' he asked. 'I'm interested in music.'

'They're of purely historic interest, but – '

A sharp crack, followed by a tinkle of falling glass interrupted him. Salvatore put the snooker cue down and kicked in the rest of the glass. He reached into the display and took out a large red guitar, with the vulgar, extravagant curve of an old American car. Lol took a step forward, like a mother anxious about her child, but paused, as Salvatore froze him with a look. 'I've always hated rock and roll,' he said conversationally, picking clumsily at the strings.

'Different strokes for different folks, eh?'

'Jazz, that's what I like.' Salvatore turned the guitar over and tapped its shiny back. 'You know who the last decent guitarist was?'

Lol frowned, desperately trying to think of jazz guitarists. 'Pat Metheny? The blind Canadian geezer?'

'Django Rheinhart, dickhead.' Salvatore was holding the 1955 Gretsch by the neck as if it were a baseball bat.

'Ah,' Lol smiled. 'The gypsy.'

'*Not a gypsy!*' The guitar was held aloft a brief second before it fell like an axe, shattering on the side of the billiard table.

'Cool it, Luigi!' Lol had seen a few smashed guitars in his time – in fact, he'd stomped on a few himself as part of his stage act, but this was different. 'Jesus, man,' he sobbed, 'Scotty Moore played that axe.'

'Not a gypsy.' Salvatore turned the wrecked instrument over with his toe. 'A romany.' He seemed calmer now. 'And my name's not Luigi.' He glanced at the display case, as if choosing which guitar to destroy next. 'You feel like talking now?'

'I'm an investor in Markwick, that's all,' Lol said quietly. 'I don't know what's going on. There's this thing called Opteeka B – sort of camera-type gismo that their boffins have been working on.'

'We know all. What's the timing?'

'They've got a prototype they've been testing. They're going to sell it to some Czech geezer. Alice Markwick's information was that the Ministry of Defence here and the Pentagon were a bit iffy about a weapon that blinded people.'

'When's it being handed over?'

'Soon.' Sorrowfully, Lol picked up the remains of the old Gretsch. There was a guy in Ealing who reconstructed guitars but, apart from the neck and the chrome machine-heads, this one was a goner. 'I'm just the money,' he said. 'They don't tell me nothing.'

Just the money. As Lol examined the mess of wire and wood, turning it over in his hands, memories of his ill-fated investments of the past crowded in on him. The independent record company. The rock magazine. The film company. All he had wanted was a safe home for his royalties, a bit of financial security, yet every time it went wrong. Opteeka B had seemed too good to be true, too easy. 'I'll help you if I can get my money back.'

'We might give you some compensation,' Salvatore said, 'when we take possession.'

Lol nodded wearily.

'You tell us where to find it, okay? I'll call you in a week's time. If you speak to the others – Markwick, Wentworth, Raven – it won't be your Gretsch that's destroyed. Remember what happened to your friend Digby.'

'Raven? Who's Raven?'

'The jockey – he isn't with you?'

Lol shook his head. 'Never heard of him.'

'One week.' Salvatore walked to the door. 'You're with us now, Lol.'

'Right.'

'By the way, what are those tests?'

'I dunno. Horses, mostly.'

'*Horses*?' Salvatore laughed. This was going to be like taking a toy from a baby. 'Be in touch, Mr Rock and Roll.'

'Sure, man.'

With a final look of contemptuous pity, Salvatore turned on his heel and left.

The place was going downhill and no mistake. Goods in the shops seemed shabbier and more expensive, the assistants less respectful. You held up your hand on a corner in Regent Street and taxis swept by as if a better class of passenger, with a bigger tip, awaited them around the corner. The locals had an edgy, defeated look to them as they went to work. In the evenings, the restaurants were virtually deserted, and the windows of the residential flats were illuminated by the glow of a million television screens. Outside there were beggars – disgusting, black-toothed creatures, toting some dog or baby, as they extended a grimy hand from their cardboard shelter in the entrances to shops. Policemen walked in twos, with surly expressions on their faces. The traffic moved with the speed of a glacier. Public transport was a joke in exceedingly poor taste.

'Two months ago.' Josef Petrin drummed his fingers on the counter of a gentleman's tailor in Savile Row. 'Surely to goodness you people can manage to put together a tweed suit in such a time.'

A grey-haired man with apologetic eyes, hunched by a lifetime of measuring inside legs, explained that there had been 'flu among their employees, and layoffs. If Mr Petrin could give them another fortnight –

'Heavens above, man. I could be anywhere in two weeks' time. I really can't build my schedule around the health of your staff.'

The tailor simpered some more. Maybe ten days was possible, quality was so important, it was vital not to hurry the final work on the suit.

With some difficulty, Petrin extracted a date from the man and left the shop exuding righteous indignation. There was no doubt about it – London was in terminal decline.

By some miracle, a black taxi deigned to stop for him. 'The Ritz,' he said.

The taxi-driver, a youth with the cropped hair of a football hooligan, nodded moodily. Whatever happened to the cockney, Petrin wondered as he settled back in the cab – the cheery red-faced character full of vulgar working-class charm, the bloke who addressed you as 'Guv'? Nothing was simple any more.

The tea-room at the Ritz was full of Arabs and ancient women but, after a five minute wait, Petrin was shown to a table. Without waiting for Green, who would inevitably be late, he ordered tea.

He was on his second scone before Bernard Green, an overweight producer of what they called 'Talks' at the BBC, flapped into view and, with much huffing and puffing, slumped into the chair opposite Petrin.

'Bloody meetings,' he explained.

Petrin decided not to give Green the benefit of a smile but poured him a cup of tea. The producer eyed the scones like Bunter, the famous English schoolboy whose adventures Petrin had read while at university. 'Help yourself,' he said drily.

'So.' Green took a scone onto which he heaped a mess of butter and raspberry jam. 'How goes life in Prague now that you're liberated from the embrace of the Bear?'

It was always like this – the paunchy Englishman pretending, perhaps to himself, that they were meeting on BBC business. Petrin smiled at last. He enjoyed the irony of playing host to this unhealthy-looking fool, so old for his forty-odd years, wearing the cheap ill-fitting suit. Mao had been wrong – power does not grow out of the barrel of a gun but out of carefully maintained political contacts. 'Less has changed than you might think, Bernard,' he said. 'You'll be glad to hear.'

A look of unease crossed the Englishman's face. On Petrin's last trip to London, Bernard had casually suggested that *perestroika* had swept away the need for secret alliances. Petrin had dismissed Bernard's pathetic attempt to resign his commission with an airy wave of the hand. Astonishing as it was, he was quite a big wheel in the BBC, his radical past now no more than a distant memory – distant, but not forgotten. 'There's always room for unofficial diplomacy,' he said, adding more firmly, 'We still need you.'

Bernard was building up his cholesterol level, shovelling back scones and cakes with the determination of a man who'd like to be struck down by a heart attack before tea was over. 'What do we want to know?' he asked.

'There's a woman called Alice Markwick who runs a company specializing in lasers. She has a rather ingenious device which we covet.'

'A device of aggressive intent?'

'If you mean a weapon, yes. We're due to take possession within the next few weeks. I have a suspicion that Mrs Markwick might be contacted by someone else.'

'Like who?'

'As I say, it's an ingenious piece of technology. There might be interest from the Americans, or the French, or even some branch of private enterprise.'

Bernard winced. 'Weapons,' he said heavily. 'Haven't we outgrown weapons yet?'

'Maybe at your Television Centre they value your inquisitive spirit, your charmingly ineffective liberalism,' Petrin said more sharply. 'We just want you to do what you're told. The weapon, as it happens, has considerable political credibility. It's not in the least bit messy.'

'What do you – ' Bernard hesitated. 'What do we need to know?'

'Who the opposition is. Can we trust the Markwick woman? Is this thing any bloody good? Perhaps you could discover these things without alerting ten camera crews and the national press.'

Bernard nodded.

'I'm here for a few days.' Petrin stood up. Lowering his voice slightly he said, 'Let's not have one of your legendary British cock-ups this time, eh?'

Bernard ran a broad finger across his plate and licked the crumbs off it.

Not telling Angie about his visit from Zena Wentworth was the easiest decision Paul had ever had to make. Since his fall, she had been trying to persuade him that to risk future injury trying to discover what had happened to Alex Drew was putting death before life, the past before the future. Gavin's sleazy scheme to entrap Alice Markwick had alarmed her further. The news that Zena Wentworth had attempted to rape Paul on his bed of pain might have been the final straw.

'Welcome to the evil empire of Crazy Mary.' Angie held open the door of her Fiesta as Paul, whose arm was still in a sling, heaved his legs round and out of the car. He looked up at a discreet sign reading 'The Empire Club'. There was a burly uniformed doorman standing by the entrance of the club, stamping his feet in the cold.

'Looks respectable enough to me,' Paul said.

Angie smiled and slipped a hand through his free arm. 'Wait 'til you meet Mary,' she said.

It had been her idea to come up to London the night before the poker game. It would get Paul away from the flat, she said, tune him into the ways of the metropolis. They were staying in the Putney flat of an old school friend, whose work as an air stewardess took her away much of the time. Then there was the briefing session with Crazy Mary.

'We're here to see Mary Chivers,' Angie told the doorman. 'The croupier.'

The doorman showed them down the stairs, into a large room full of roulette and backgammon tables. Apart from a few cleaners, the place was deserted. The smell of the previous night's cigars hung heavily in the air.

The short, dark girl who walked towards them in a navy blue suit and flat shoes might have been a stockbroker.

'Hi, Chiv,' Angie said. The two girls brushed cheeks in greeting. 'This is Paul.'

'Hullo, Mary.' Paul extended his left hand.

'It's a bit grim at the moment.' Mary glanced around the brightly-lit room. 'We're only closed for three hours out of twenty-four. The punters will be back this afternoon.'

They went to a small office where, over coffee, the two girls talked of friends from school. As far as Paul could gather, most of them had gone wrong: one worked for a discreet and exclusive escort agency, another had run away to Spain with an ageing bank robber, a couple had hurried into marriage and out the other side.

'What was this, a reform school you went to?' Paul interrupted at one point.

Mary shrugged. 'Convent girls,' she said, as if no other explanation was necessary. 'You wait – you'll discover Angie's hidden vices in the end.'

'I've discovered a few already.'

Angie blushed, but smiled with pleasure. 'It's Mary here who's the fast one. Don't be taken in by the respectable suit.'

'Croupiers have to be above suspicion,' Mary said. 'One hint of a relationship with a punter and you're out.'

'That's why they call her Crazy Mary.'

The croupier frowned, as if surprised by the nickname. 'You become a bit of a control freak working in a casino. Once every few months, I take time off with some of the other girls to work on transatlantic cruises.' She shrugged. 'I seemed to have acquired something of a reputation.'

'She'll try anything once,' said Angie.

Paul smiled nervously. He felt ill at ease with this casual talk of misbehaviour.

As if she sensed that now was not the moment for confessional reminiscence, Mary opened the top drawer of the desk and took out a new, unopened pack of cards, which she unwrapped. 'Right,' she said, shuffling the cards like a magician. 'Crazy Mary's crash course in stud poker.'

Chapter 11

There were times when Ginnie Matthew's love affair with racing went through a rocky patch, when she envied those friends of hers whose children were growing and whose husbands, becoming balder and duller by the minute, at least provided a stolid kind of security.

It was four o'clock on a chilly afternoon in late February. The racegoers at Lingfield Park were drifting home after a day's racing which had provided the Matthews yard with a disappointing third in the novice hurdle and a faller in the two mile 'chase. She walked briskly towards the stables where Skinflint and a decent five-year-old called Above Par were being saddled up for some post-race work. There had been two spare places in the horse-box and, once the Lingfield authorities had given her permission to gallop two of her horses on the track after the last race, she decided that Skinflint – and, more significantly, his jockey Clay Wentworth – would benefit from one last outing before Cheltenham.

'Looks well, don't he?' Pat, the Head Lad, stood beside her as Clay led Skinflint out of his stable.

Ginnie stepped forward and patted the horse, running a hand down his shoulder and his front legs. 'Could be worse,' she smiled, knowing Skinflint had never been in better condition. The Kim Muir had come just at the right time for him – but the same could be said of the Cheltenham Gold Cup, which was to be run the day after. The greed of owners, the vanity of amateur jockeys – Ginnie sighed, as she watched Clay Wentworth hold up a leg so that Pat could give him a leg-up into the saddle. He looked soft, slightly overweight and nervous; not for the first time, Ginnie found the comparison between Skinflint and his jockey painful to contemplate. At last she had a top class horse in the yard – and it was doomed to be ridden by Clay Wentworth.

From the next door box, Dave Smart led Above Par, checked his girths and hopped into the saddle. Dave wasn't the greatest jockey of all time but he was a good professional, honest and tough. He deserved the ride on Above Par in the Ritz Trophy at Cheltenham.

'See you in front of the stands,' she said.

Watching them as the two horses made their way onto the race-course, Ginnie found herself reflecting that although Skinflint was her favourite horse in the yard, she would have mixed feelings if he won at Cheltenham. There was something tainted about his success this season. It was as if his progress was inextricably linked with the misery of others – horses that were destroyed, the suicide of Alex

Drew, the ending of Paul's career.

'Wish I'd entered that horse in the Gold Cup,' she said to Pat, who was walking beside her.

'With Mr Wentworth on board?'

'No,' Ginnie sighed. 'He'd need a jockey.'

It was never the professionals who caused her problems. It was when outsiders became involved, dabbling in racing for their own peculiar reasons, that it became confusing, demoralizing. Bent jockeys, corrupted stable lads – there was inevitably the hand of someone outside racing working them, misguided, greedy amateurs.

'I heard from Kevin Smiley's parents yesterday,' she said. 'They seemed to think what happened to him was our fault.'

'It wasn't suicide, that's for sure.'

The trainer and her Head Lad walked on, each thinking of the inexplicable death of Kevin Smiley. It was clear, even to the police who had seemed reluctant to treat his drowning as murder, that it was Kevin who had put acid on Monty's hind legs that morning. Possibly he knew the gravity of what he was doing; more probably, he took the money without asking questions.

A local mini-cab company had confirmed that he was due to be taken to the station that evening, but when the car turned up, there had been no sign of him. Next morning his body was found floating in the River Kennet, some eight miles away. A post-mortem had revealed alcohol in the blood and bruising to the side of the head consistent with a heavy blow.

'Who was he working for, that's the question?' Pat said.

Ginnie looked down to the racecourse, where Clay and Dave Smart were walking in a circle, waiting for her. 'Whoever it was seemed to be after Paul,' she said. 'And if they could do that to him, bumping off poor little Kevin was hardly going to worry them.'

'But why Paul?'

'Why indeed?' Ginnie thought of the note she had written for Clay, of Paul's determination to find the person behind Alex's death. Yes, sometimes she wished she had never set foot in a racing yard.

She glanced back to the grandstand, where a group of race-goers was lingering, watching her two horses through binoculars as the crowds thinned. A few would-be journalists and professional gamblers, but the majority would be the clueless addicts of racing whose dreams of a great gambling coup would never be realized.

'No shortage of spies, I see,' she said.

It was true. Ginnie never gave her horses trials. The punter and journos doing overtime at Lingfield would discover no more than what the more knowledgeable of them already knew – that the Matthews yard never sent a runner out for one of the big prizes who wasn't jumping out of its skin with health and fitness.

Sitting by the rails, hunched on a shooting-stick like an ogling vulture, sat Sir Denis Wentworth.

'I see Daddy's here,' Pat muttered.

Ginnie laughed. 'All teeth and smiles, as usual,' she said. The relationship between Clay and his father was a mystery. Neither particularly liked the other but, wherever the son went, the father seemed to follow. Yet Clay never objected.

A generous interpretation would be that a cold, undemonstrative kind of family love was at work but there was no hint of affection in Sir Denis's pale watery eyes as he watched his son.

Ginnie stood beside the old man. 'Looks well, doesn't he?' she said.

Sir Denis moved his jaws as if he had been given something unpleasant to take. 'Very,' he said eventually.

'Hack on round to the two-and-a-half-mile start. Pull them up and let them get a breather and then carry on the rest of the way round.' She called out to Dave Smart and Clay. 'You can let them stride out the last couple of furlongs but don't go mad.'

As the two jockeys cantered their horses to the far side of the course Ginnie heard a guttural mumble emanating from Sir Denis. He might have been clearing his throat, or maybe making some comment to himself. The words sounded suspiciously like, 'Bloody fool, he is.'

She decided to ignore him. Ginnie had more important matters to worry about than Wentworth family relationships.

It was his first visit to a British racecourse and Gavin Holmes wasn't impressed. The afternoon had seemed to consist of a lot of standing around punctuated occasionally by equestrian events of highly questionable entertainment value. A large majority of the racegoers were the type of Englishman, goofy and over-confident, that he had until now thought were an endangered species. They honked, they drank, they talked about horses, they honked some more.

'Get on with it, you stupid *bastards*,' he muttered to himself, stamping his feet on the ground to keep the circulation going. Clay Wentworth and the other jockey seemed to be taking an age to do whatever they intended to do.

A ferret-faced little man, an ex-jockey, perhaps, looked up at him in slight surprise. Gavin smiled apologetically.

The only way he had managed to survive the afternoon was by putting away a bit at the bar. Bucks Fizz, during those brief early moments when he had felt he should behave himself; champagne to celebrate the completion of the first race; brandy and ginger ale, followed by brandy. It was one way to spend an afternoon at the races – in fact, it was the only way.

As the two horses had pulled up on the far side of the race-course, Gavin put the binoculars he had borrowed from a colleague at the office to his eyes. He had difficulty focussing them, or maybe it was his eyes that couldn't focus any more.

To work while terminally pissed was a basic journalistic requirement. Over the years, Gavin had taken this skill one step further so that now he could only work while pissed. During the afternoon he had chatted easily with barfly racegoers, concentrating on the career and character of Ginnie Matthews. Was she ambitious? Was she ruthless? Was she bent?

The general consensus, gleaned from an in-depth survey at the Lingfield Park bar, was that Mrs Matthews was marvellous, bloody *marvellous*. Troubles in the past, of course, with that shit of a husband of hers, but good old Ginnie hadn't let that hold her back. Bent? Good God, no – she was straight as a die.

'Here they go,' said the ferret beside him in the grandstand. Gavin managed to focus his binoculars accurately enough to follow the two horses as they galloped down the back straight. Maybe, to the cognoscenti, the way the animals were moving had deep significance, but to him they looked like any other horses doing the sort of thing that horses do.

Gavin let the binoculars drop, and looked down to the rails where, broad-backed in her sheepskin coat, Ginnie stood between one of her employees and an old man Gavin guessed was Sir Denis Wentworth.

After the fourth race, he had ventured out of the warmth of the bar down to the sort of clubhouse from where the jockeys appeared. One of Ginnie's horses had taken third place in the race which had just finished and he managed to talk to her briefly outside the winners' enclosure.

'Mrs Matthews,' he had said. 'Gavin Holmes, *Guardian*. D'you have a moment?'

'Holmes? Are you new on the racing page?'

'It's a general feature. We want to profile your owner, Clay Wentworth. A half-page on a businessman at play, that sort of thing.'

Ginnie Matthews had frowned. 'Businessman at play? Doesn't sound very *Guardian* to me.'

'It's a departure,' he said, noting that she was more perceptive than most of the people he had met racing. 'How is Mr Wentworth preparing for his big race at Cheltenham?'

'You'd better ask him that.'

'I have a meeting with him later. He suggested I watch him ride here, then we could talk afterwards. But you could tell me if, say, he goes to watch the horses he'll be racing against.'

'For example?' Ginnie seemed more interested now.

'Brut Force, was it?' It was lucky he had done his homework. 'Ballina Lady. Whataparty.'

The trainer looked away, then said more quietly, 'The businessman at play, eh?' There was nothing evasive about the way she had looked at him. 'Why don't you ring me this evening and we can talk about this at more length?'

It had not been the remark of a guilty woman.

'Look at that fucker go.' The ferret standing beside him in the grandstand muttered to himself. The two horses, Gavin saw, had just entered the home straight but, while Dave Smart was niggling at Above Par, Clay seemed to be having difficulty holding Skinflint. By the time they passed the stands, Skinflint was eight lengths to the good and still pulling.

'What a flying machine, eh.' Watching Skinflint go through his paces seemed to have cheered the man standing beside Gavin. 'He's got a wally on board, he's giving the other horse a stone and a half and he still trots up. Talk about a good thing for Cheltenham.'

'Right.' Gavin glanced at his watch. It was time to ask the wally a few pertinent questions.

As the taxi moved slowly through the streets south of the River Thames, caught up in the late afternoon traffic, Josef Petrin stared out gloomily onto the damp streets outside. Ant-like, the workers scurried into the underground stations, grabbing evening papers, ignoring one another in their feverish need to get home to television, a drink and some ghastly English meal. 'Don't hold your breath,' the taxi-driver had said. 'Bad time of day to be heading out of the centre of London. Early rush hour.'

Petrin smiled wanly. Did they really call this crawl a 'rush-hour'? Not for the first time, he found himself wondering whether his country's relentless move towards capitalism was such a good idea. There may have been queues and shortages in Prague, free speech might have been somewhat curtailed, but at least there was a kind of security in hopelessness. Here in London, no one was satisfied with his lot – jealousy, greed and resentment seemed to seep from the very brickwork.

The cab jerked forward as his driver neatly headed off a car trying to filter onto the main road in front of him. 'English – very bad drivers,' he said over his shoulder. 'Very dozy, right?'

'Right,' said Petrin.

'You wanna watch yourself down where you're going, mate,' the driver said.

'Yes?'

'Bandit country. Walk down the street in that overcoat, in those shoes, carrying that briefcase, and you'll be in dead schtuck, mate. Brixton, Stockwell – mugging's like the local industry down there. Everybody's at it.'

Petrin looked at his slim, expensive black briefcase. Perhaps it had been rather naive to venture out of central London with it.

'They have mugging where you come from, have they?'

'No,' said Petrin in a tone he hoped would discourage further conversation. 'Not yet.'

He wasn't nervous as he noted, as he neared his destination, the increase in litter on the streets – paper, tin cans, not to mention debris of the human kind – just mildly concerned. It was not that he was incapable of looking after himself – you didn't work your way up from the factory floor to the senior reaches of government in Prague, as he had, without learning about self-preservation, but he disliked fuss. Over here, the press was not as accommodating as it was back home.

'How long you going to be?' asked the cab-driver.

'Ten minutes maybe.'

'Tell you what. Pay me for the trip and I'll wait outside for you.'

'That would be most kind,' said Petrin.

The street in Brixton where the Zametskys lived was pleasingly grimy. The old communist in Petrin – part of him that he rarely mentioned these days – took satisfaction in reflecting that it was for this that the man Peter had fled his motherland – this was his precious freedom. The taxi drew up outside a forbidding two-storey house with dustbins tipped over by the front door and a window boarded up.

'Sure you've got the right address?' asked the driver.

'Yes.' Petrin stepped out. This was home sweet home for Mr and Mrs Zametsky.

As soon as he stepped into the cold, high-ceilinged room with its peeling wallpaper and yellowing posters, he knew it was going to be a depressing experience.

'Peter.' The plump Polish girl with the peasant eyes spoke softly. 'We have a visitor.'

He had never been a squeamish man when he was young, yet these days Petrin found he avoided visiting friends in hospital. Driving by an accident just outside Prague and seeing the body of a lorry-driver laid out beside the road had made him feel really quite nauseous. He put it down to middle age.

So he hesitated when he first saw the thing on the bed. It was particularly unfortunate that, while the parts concealed by a suspiciously off-colour blanket had presumably been unaffected by the accident, his hands and, more disgustingly, his face, were horrifically disfigured.

Hairless, wearing dark glasses, his flayed skin red and shiny on the cheekbones, Peter Zametsky was making an odd sound through the lipless void that was his mouth.

'Hullo, Mr Zametsky,' Petrin said, drawing up a chair some way from the bed. 'My name is Josef Petrin. We've not met.'

Klima, his wife, sat on the bed and laid a soothing hand on the scarred right hand. 'He wants me to stay,' she said. 'He's been very nervous of strangers since the accident.'

An angry sound came from the figure on the bed.

'Sorry, darling.' Klima smiled apologetically as she turned to Petrin. 'My husband believes it was no accident. You aren't the police, I suppose?'

In a way, thought Petrin. 'No,' he said.

'Somebody did this to my husband.' The woman's pale and placid features showed signs of animation. 'He was visited in hospital by a man, threatening to do worse. Even though the nurse gave them a description, the police have put it down to the effects of the acid.'

Peter made another incomprehensible noise.

'Yes,' said his wife. 'They think he's mad.'

Briefly, Petrin considered confiding his disappointment with the state of Britain, perhaps comparing it to the new vitality of Eastern Europe, but he restrained himself. It would seem like crowing; another time perhaps.

'I'm an acquaintance of Mrs Markwick,' he said. 'I'm here to offer some help.' Laying his briefcase on his lap, Petrin opened it and took a sealed white envelope which he gave to Klima. 'Please open it,' he said.

The woman blushed as she saw the £50 notes, as though she had already done something mildly immoral to earn it. 'It's money, Peter,' she said. 'This gentleman's giving us money.'

'A thousand pounds.' Petrin smiled. 'Not much, but a start perhaps. It's a sort of insurance payment.'

Peter stretched out a hand. His wife gave him the envelope. He said something, then hurled the money across the room.

'The money doesn't come from Mrs Markwick,' Petrin explained smoothly. 'It's not compensation or guilt money.' From a distant room, he heard a baby cry. 'I'd keep it if I were you.'

Klima walked across the room where the £50 notes had spilled out of their envelope onto the bare boards of the floor. 'What do we need to do?' she asked.

'Alice and I are old friends. For some time now, we have been discussing the acquisition of her secret project, the development – ' he nodded in the direction of the shape in the bed ' – thanks to Dr Zametsky, of Opteeka B.'

There was a question from Peter, which his wife interpreted. 'He's asking how you know about Opteeka B,' she said.

'I am Alice's client. As you probably know, she has been talking to the Czechoslovak government. Once Opteeka B has completed its tests, I take possession of the prototype and the design plans. My problem is that I very much fear that there are others who may sabotage my agreement.'

'The people who did this to Peter.' Klima was holding the money as if, at any moment, she would have to hand it back.

'Precisely. They're remarkably unpleasant people. Civilians, I suspect. Whereas we would mass-produce Opteeka B for entirely legitimate military use, these people are nothing less than criminals. I dread to think what they have in mind.' The sound of the child crying was beginning to irritate Petrin. 'D'you want to fetch the baby?' he asked. 'I'm in no hurry.'

Klima hurried out of the room, returning moments later with a child, red-faced from its wailing. Without a word, she unbuttoned the front of her dress. Petrin looked away queasily but not before he had caught sight of a billowing, blue-veined breast.

'So.' As Klima looked from her baby to Petrin, her face became edgy and mistrustful. 'What do we have to do for the money?'

'It's yours.' Petrin smiled, forcing himself to look at the baby. 'It was the least we could do. You could – ' he hesitated, as if a thought had suddenly occurred to him ' – maybe earn a little bit more.'

For a moment, the room was silent but for the sound of the baby as it sucked noisily. Petrin swallowed as his sensitive nostrils were assailed by the sweet, sickly smell of mother's milk.

'Yes,' he said. 'If you were able to tell me how Opteeka B is going to be tested, and where. That would help me forestall any last-minute hitch in the arrangement with Markwick Instruments.'

'What about Mrs Markwick?' Irina asked. 'Why don't you ask her?'

'It's complicated. She denies there's a problem of security.' Petrin opened the briefcase and took out another envelope which he weighed in his hand thoughtfully.

'He's got some more money, Peter.'

There was an odd moaning sound from the bed. Peter Zametsky took off his dark glasses and, with the red stubs of his fingers, wiped a tear from his light grey, sightless eyes. He repeated the sound more loudly.

'Paper.' Klima stood up, holding her baby to her. 'Yes, that's right. You'll need some paper.'

It was twenty minutes, not ten, before Josef Petrin closed the heavy door behind him and, with just one glance down the street, stepped into the taxi.

'Sorry,' he said. 'My business took a bit longer than expected.'

'All right, squire.' The taxi-driver put down his evening paper and started the engine. 'The meter was running so I wasn't worried.'

'Of course.'

'Where can I take you then?'

'The Ritz.' Petrin had seen enoug of Brixton to last him a lifetime. 'As quick as possible.'

On this story, Gavin had given himself so many false identities that he had almost forgotten who he was. Deception was part of the job, of course – it went with the territory – but he preferred distorting a few facts on the page to inventing aliases for himself. Written lies were somehow easier to live with.

Gavin poured champagne into the glasses of Clay and Sir Denis Wentworth, then filled his own, fighting back his need for a brandy. 'Cheerio,' he said raising his glass. 'Here's to Skinflint at Cheltenham.'

Lifestyle expert he had been with Alice Markwick; now he was a human interest journalist, contributing to the business pages. Gavin took out his spiral-bound notebook and smiled. What he did for his art.

'Fire away.' Clay Wentworth sipped at his drink with the air of a man who has better things to do than be interviewed by the press. 'Which area d'you want to major on?'

'Your hobbies. Horseback riding, for example.' Gavin smiled as Clay looked pained.

'It's rather more than a hobby,' he said. 'And we call it racing.'

The man wasn't bright, Gavin decided as he asked a few routine questions, noting down Clay's highly predictable answers, and there was something oddly immature about the way he occasionally glanced at the old curmudgeon, his father, before he spoke. It was almost as if he were a schoolboy rather than a grown man approaching middle age and the chairman of a company.

'You've had a spot of luck with the opposition,' Gavin said, 'A racing friend of mine said the Kim Muir was going to be easier to win than many expected.'

'I'd prefer to win on the racecourse against the best opposition.'

'So you'll be hoping this – ' Gavin referred to his notes ' – this Tanglewood doesn't suffer any untoward accidents?'

For a moment, Clay looked up sharply, as if he were about to depart from a carefully prepared script, but then the look of urbane boredom settled back on his face. 'Ron Charlesworth looks after his horses,' he said, 'I'm sure there will be no problem.'

The bar was empty now, and the barman was making enough noise as he washed up the glasses to suggest that he was planning to close up soon.

'Why d'you do it, Clay?' Gavin asked easily. 'I mean you've got everything – you run a company, you're not a teenager any more. It's *dangerous* riding those things, isn't it?'

Clay Wentworth looked out at the racecourse on which darkness was now falling.

'In a way, it's like business,' he said. 'You have to have the right product, your horse, if possible with a unique selling point that will cut it in the market-place. Speed, stamina, courage. Then you've got to gather the right team about you – from Ginnie Matthews, who I see as a sort of Technical Director, down to Joe, the lad who does my two horses. Without the right executive team – the "boardroom mix", I call it – the product has no position in the market-place.'

With a thoughtful frown, Gavin made a note in his notebook. It read 'Bollocks'.

'Then there's the personal challenge. The preparation for the launch of your product, the race. You have to be ready, fit. You have to know about the opposition. And on the day, it's all about concentration, skill – and, of course, keeping your nerve.' Clay looked pleased with his little speech. 'Then it's all down to luck.'

Gavin smiled. 'And there was I thinking you rode horses for fun,' he said.

'There's that as well, of course,' Clay said coldly.

More out of politeness than through some journalistic hunch, Gavin turned to Clay's father, who was sipping impassively at his champagne. 'What about you, Sir Denis?' he asked, raising his voice slightly. 'What do you think of your son's love of racing?'

The old man turned to look at Gavin with cool distaste. 'Whatever gives my son pleasure, gives me pleasure,' he said.

'Right.' Gavin made another careful note on his pad.

'Daddy?' he wrote. 'Check out Daddy.'

Although the walls in the Victorian row of houses were solid, Peter Zametsky could hear the thud of reggae music from the people next door. It was still early evening; by two in the morning the wall would shake.

Not that Peter minded. At least he could still hear things. The sound of other people's partying reminded him that he was alive.

He could feel, too. Right now, he felt the weight of two inprints on the bed, only one of which was familiar.

'He's asleep,' Klima said. She seemed to be fussing around with a blanket. 'He loves to sleep on your bed.'

He felt her touch the other weight, which was much lighter than the baby, and heard a rustle of paper. Money. Klima was counting the money again.

'It seems too easy, *moje kochanie*. I'm frightened. I think we should tell the police.'

Peter made a sound in his throat which a stranger might have taken for a cough.

'Don't laugh, Peter,' said his wife. 'There's something wrong. If this man was dealing with Mrs Markwick, why did he come to you? And whoever heard of a Czech paying out £5,000? Not even in vouchers – in cash.'

Peter extended a hand and ran it through the notes as if they were a pool of warm water. Of course, Klima was right. The deal stunk. But what more could be done to him? The Italian who had taken away his face must know that he could give him no more information. As for the Markwick woman, her behaviour hardly merited loyalty. Not a single visit while he was in hospital and no mention of compensation above his salary.

'Someone's going to get hurt,' said Klima.

Peter made a sound, both anguished and angry. It meant, 'So long as it's not us, I don't care.'

'*Kochanie*.' Klima touched his hand. 'I hope you're right.'

Alcohol was brainfood for Gavin. The same substances that would render another man comatose – indeed, rendered Gavin comatose when he wasn't working –

propelled him forward when he was working on a story. Admittedly, the propulsion often took him by a strange, indirect route, full of odd and inexplicable stopins, but that was good. Booze made him an instinctive reporter, who relied on an unsteady sixth sense that took him to destinations that mere logic would never find.

After the ordeal of passing twenty minutes with the Wentworth father and son team, feigning interest in Clay's banal, non-committal replies, he had needed a top-up before he went home.

'Give us a real drink, my friend,' he muttered to the barman, after saying his goodbyes to Clay and Sir Denis.

'We're closed, sir.'

Gavin held up a £10 note. 'If you've cashed up, no need to give me the change.'

The barman took the money and, with remarkably little grace for a man who had just received a tip, said, 'I'm locking up in two minutes.'

There was something odd about Clay Wentworth. Gavin had met a few sportsmen, professional and amateur, in his time; invariably, they came alive when talking about their sport. With Clay, it seemed forced, almost rehearsed. If riding nags at speed over bits of wood gave him no pleasure, then why did he do it? And the father seemed utterly uninterested in racing. Gavin gave a little shudder of satisfaction as the cognac burnt its way down his throat.

Maybe it was social. Yet the jokey questions Gavin had posed about the high-profile entourage of spectators Clay brought to watch him race – Lol Calloway, Alice Markwick, the late Digby Welcome – had been received with glazed indifference. 'They're friends,' he had said. 'They like a day at the races.'

It didn't wash. Gavin thought of Alice Markwick and of what he had heard or read about Welcome and Calloway. None of them were the types to spend afternoons at chilly racecourses for the sake of friendship. Money – that was what interested them all. Yet there seemed to be no gambling factor at work here.

Draining his glass under the hostile glare of the barman, Gavin slipped off the barstool and swayed palely for a moment. He extended a queasy hand to the bar to steady himself.

'Think I night have overdone it.' He smiled apologetically at the barman.

'You've had a heavy afternoon.'

'Too right, mate.' Gavin buttoned his bomber jacket.

'I trust you're not driving.' The barman polished a glass self-righteously. 'Drink and drive, you know.'

'It's not the drink that's the problem,' Gavin said. 'It's the fresh air. An afternoon of that's enough to make anyone feel woozy.' He shook his head like a man trying to shift some unpleasant thought from his mind, then made his way out of the bar, bumping against a couple of tables.

The racecourse was deserted now although there was the sound of voices coming from the Press Room, which was thoughtfully located close to the bar.

'Poor bastards,' Gavin muttered, thinking of the journalists urgently filing copy about how one nag ran faster than another. 'What a way to earn a living.'

At the bottom of the stairs, he looked onto the course where a tractor was already harrowing the turf between the fences. It took a moment of concentrated effort to remember where the car park was but then, seeing a couple of cameramen lugging their equipment behind the grandstand, he followed them. The car must be somewhere in that direction.

'Better call Raven,' Gavin said to himself. Paul had mentioned that Zena Wentworth had managed to get him an invitation to one of Wentworth's poker evenings. The boy was smart enough to extract information as effectively as the regulars would extract money from him.

Gavin was wondering vaguely at what price to Paul's innocence Zena's co-operation had been obtained as he tottered into the car park. There were only a few cars there and his car was near a van into which the two cameramen were already loading their equipment.

'And so we bid farewell to picturesque Lingfield Park,' he sang out softly as he fumbled in his jacket for his car keys. He wouldn't be going racing again in a hurry, that was for sure. Too many horses. Too much standing up. Above all too much fresh air.

'Mr Holmes?'

At first, Gavin thought that the words had sounded within the alcohol-drenched recesses of his brain. He hesitated by his car.

'Do you have a moment?'

He turned, swaying slightly. The two men by the van appeared to be filming him – one, a small man wearing jeans, was training a video on him, the other was raising a large stills camera to his eye.

'Hullo, what's this then?' Gavin straightened his tie in a humorous way. 'Profile of Gavin Holmes, investigative journalist at work? Fame at – '

The camera held by the second man made a sound like a toy car being started, high-pitched and comical. Gavin looked into the lens then he felt himself thrown back against his car.

'What? *What*?' he heard himself saying feebly. At first, he thought the blackness came from a blow on the back of the head, yet the force had come from the front, hurling him backwards. 'What?' His arms felt behind him for the roof of the car and he sagged, his head lolling forward, like a boxer on the ropes. It wasn't a pain in his eyes, it was an ache, an anaesthetic tingling. Gavin rubbed them, as if to take away the darkness. Then he felt the knife against his throat.

A voice said, 'Move.'

Gavin pressed back against the car, 'What d'you want from me?' he whispered.

'Get away from the car.'

In the blackness all around him, Gavin moved forward. 'I can't see,' he sobbed. 'What the fuck have you done?' He needed to get away. Perhaps back on the course there would be someone who could help him. Arms outstretched like a sleepwalker, he took what he thought was the direction of the car park.

The blade of the knife touched him on the base of the throat, more gently this time. 'Turn,' said the same voice, with its odd foreign accent, 'Go the other way.'

Gavin turned back towards the car but, in his blindness, he must have wandered to its left because his hands felt the high brick wall against which the car was parked. He felt his way along the wall to the left. Maybe he would reach the road. There were no more orders from the men. Gavin sobbed with relief as he heard the engine of the van being started somewhere behind him. They were leaving him, thank God – sightless but alive. He fell against another car. Turning, he made his way back along the wall. If he could reach his car, maybe he could let himself in and lock the door until help arrived.

The van was driving away, yet seemed to hesitate, as if it were manoeuvring itself out of the car park. 'Don't let them come back,' Gavin sobbed. To his right, the van revved louder.

For perhaps two seconds, he realized what was going to happen. The van was coming towards him, reversing, it sounded like. Gavin broke into a run but it was too late. His last scream was drowned by the sound of the engine and the crash of metal against human flesh and brick.

The photographer jumped out of the van and, without a glance at the body by the wall, wiped some traces of blood from the back of the van with the damp cloth he was carrying. There was no need to arouse unnecessary suspicion.

'Off we go,' he said as he jumped back into the passenger seat.

The van left the car park at speed.

Stroking the Opteeka B, the photographer found that it was still warm. Carefully, he put it back into its aluminium case and locked it, pocketing the key.

'That's some machine,' said the driver, turning down a side road. Within two minutes, the van would be dumped and he and the crazed professor here would be making their way back to London in separate cars.

'Video?' said the photographer.

'It's all there.' The driver nodded to a hold-all on the floor of the van. 'I think you'll find my camera work is more than adequate.'

The photographer didn't answer. He was not a sadist, and being a party to the loss of life gave him little pleasure but, right now, he was exulting.

He hadn't seen a thing, the poor bastard. Fi-Fi was good, but this was better. It had been the perfect experiment.

Chapter
12

It was the entrance of a loser, a lamb to the slaughter, a patsy – but that suited Paul fine.

'Mr Raven.' Clay Wentworth was the first to react as Paul stood at the door, having been shown in by a butler. He had been sitting in a deep armchair but got to his feet like a public schoolboy whose housemaster has just walked into the room. 'What a surprise.'

Paul smiled. 'I meant to ring,' he said. 'Poor old Digby Welcome invited me some weeks back. I meant to be here last week but I had an accident.'

The arm had only come out of its sling yesterday and a stab of pain darted through his shoulder as Clay shook his hand with a muttered, 'Never knew you played.'

'I have a lot of time on my hands.'

Clay glanced at Paul's walking-stick and, for a brief moment, seemed embarrassed. 'You know we have a no-railbird rule.'

'Sorry?'

'We don't allow railbirds – kibitzers.' The smile on Clay's face lost some of its friendliness. 'Non-playing spectators,' he explained.

Paul grinned goofily. He had been warned by Mary that he would be tried out with some recondite poker slang. Her advice had been to play the innocent. 'No, I'm here to play,' he said, patting the side of his jacket. 'I've got enough for the, er . . .'

'Pot?'

'Pot.'

'How exactly did you know where we were playing?'

'Zena,' said Paul significantly. 'We're friends.'

There was a tension in the room that was not entirely explained by his presence. As Paul was introduced to the four other guests, he noted that they seemed wary, like people forced together who have little in common but their habit. Alice Markwick he recognized. Then there was a stockbroker, a barrister with florid skin and a loud voice and a man called David who said he worked in a bank.

'A bank?' Paul acted surprised.

'Not that kind of bank,' said Clay coldly. 'Drink?'

Most of the gamblers seemed to have Perrier or wine. 'A whisky would be nice,' said Paul.

'We're just waiting for our last player,' Clay said, handing him an over-generous whisky. Uneasy small talk had been resumed among the other guests.

'I was a friend of one of your regulars.' Paul lowered himself carefully into a hardback chair. 'Alex Drew.'

'Alex.' Clay shook his head. 'Terrible business.'

It was another five minutes, during which Paul sat, contributing only occasionally to the stilted conversation, before Lol Calloway appeared, complaining about the traffic into London.

'Lol, you know everyone except Paul,' said Clay. 'Paul Raven.'

The balding rock'n roller winked, clicked his tongue and made an oddly old-fashioned six-shooter gesture with both hands. 'How ya doing, man?' he said.

'I'm doing well,' said Paul.

With a palpable sense of relief, the party moved to a table in the corner, and ceased to be an ill-assorted social gathering. The Wentworth poker school was in progress.

'We normally play Texas Hold 'Em,' Clay said, pulling up an extra chair at the table for Paul. 'That all right with you?'

Paul furrowed his brow. 'Just run it through for me, will you?' he said.

'Standard seven card stud. Each player's dealt two cards – five communal cards are revealed. You bet after the deal, the flop, the turn and Fifth Street.'

'Flop? Fifth?' Paul allowed a look of panic to cross his face. 'I'm sure I'll pick it up as I go along.'

Let them think you haven't a clue, Crazy Mary had said. Every poker school needs a supply of pigeons, plump and clueless. Play two or three games like an amateur and they'll be falling over to get at you. Then you hit them.

Ignoring his instinct to take the early games slowly, fold early and get a sense of how the others played, Paul laid £50 on the first game, despite being dealt a phenomenally poor hand. The flop gave him a low pair – two sevens – and when Alice, unable to keep the sparkle of triumph from her eyes, turned over a triple queen, Paul gasped in astonishment, revealing his pathetic hand with a wimpish 'Whoops!'

After two more games like this, played with transparent ineptness, Paul sensed a stir of interest around the table. It had been some time since fresh money had been introduced to the school. Even if the new man lacked big funds, his participation in the game would help the pot. Even Lol Calloway had a chance to stay in play that much longer.

'Tonight doesn't seem to be my night,' Paul said, as Clay Wentworth won another hand in which Paul should have folded but had stupidly insisted on playing.

He had lost £350 of his £2,000 when, with the banker, he retired to the other side of the room to sit out a couple of hands. Feigning a mood of deep gloom, he managed to discourage conversation as they sat by the fire.

So this was what had set Alex on his way to destruction. It seemed inconceivable, absurd. Paul had read somewhere that the serious gambler, the addict, is acting on a deep psychological need to punish himself – that, however much he wins, he'll return to the table for the throw which will finish him. Certainly there was more to Alex than his loud and cheerful manner revealed. Yet he never gambled on horses. All Paul's sources – Jim Wilson, the valet, the other jockeys, Ginnie Matthews – had agreed that he had no contact with bookmakers. And in racing, there was no jockey who placed illegal bets regularly without at least some of his colleagues knowing.

'Seems to be my lucky night,' Clay Wentworth muttered from the table as, with a languid hand, he pulled in the pot for another game.

'You're not a regular then?' the banker interrupted Paul's thoughts.

'No. I'm having a bit of difficulty with this Texas Hold 'Em thing.'

'Goes in runs, like everything.' The man stared gloomily at the fire. 'How much are you in for?'

Paul resisted the bait. 'Enough,' he said.

'Are you lads in or out?' Lol Calloway called from the table. The banker threw his cigarette into the fire and wandered back to the game.

'Next one and I'm in,' Paul said.

Crazy Mary hardly lived up to her nickname when it came to poker tuition. No one could have been saner or cooler. She knew Clay – he was a regular at most of the gaming clubs and a better than adequate social player. He liked seven card stud, and Mary had guessed correctly that Texas Hold 'Em would be the favoured game at his poker evenings.

'It's one of the easiest games to play,' she had said. 'But to make money at it, you have to be good.'

Paul had learned the moves – how to make like a high roller while playing tight, how to watch for 'tells' in other players, the jargon and in-talk. Mary had laughed when he had told her that, unbeknownst to Clay, he would be playing against his own money. The fact that, win or lose, Wentworth would be out of pocket, thanks to his wife's contribution, gave Paul a confidence that the other players lacked.

'But play as if it was your money,' Mary had advised. 'Too much confidence and you can go on tilt.'

It was almost one before Paul began to play seriously, by which time he was down to £700. The few games he had won, he made seem like fluke victories and celebrated them with excessive good spirits. By now, the banker had lost interest and, muttering something about throwing good money after bad, he pocketed his remaining cash and bid the school farewell. Clay's look of disapproval at this early departure suggested that he wouldn't be invited in the future. Calloway had lost more heavily than Paul and seemed to be what Mary had called 'steaming' – playing with wild lack of judgement. The barrister was making money but Miles, the stockbroker, had descended into something of a sulk.

Paul glanced across the table. Alice Markwick had seemed distracted and was marginally down on the evening. The biggest winner, of course, was Clay.

'I hope those aren't your life savings you're blowing there,' he said amiably to Paul as Miles dealt them in for another round.

Paul thought of Wentworth's wife and her long, prying fingers. 'No, but I earned it the hard way,' he said.

'Let's hope you don't lose it the easy way.'

It was strange. Clay must have been £2,000 up on the evening, yet there was something restless and unhappy about him. Paul sensed that it had something to do with his presence.

Clay glanced at his cards and, without a moment's hesitation, pushed out £700.

Alice, Lol and the barrister folded but Paul, following his instinct, called, matching Clay's bet. To his left, Miles glanced at him with some surprise before folding.

The man made an unconvincing bully, Paul thought as, for a moment, he held Clay's stare. All his life he had been surrounded by solid, strong men – his father, his business rivals. He had seen the look on their faces as they closed the deal, turned the knife on some poor sap. But when he had to tough it out, like now, the merest hint of uncertainty, of a deep inner weakness in his soul, betrayed him and spoilt it all. As he went all-in, trying to break Paul, he was like a bad actor playing Macbeth.

Paul held two eights in the hole. The flop had brought an ace of diamonds, a jack of spades and an eight of spades.

Somewhere, in the poker textbooks, Clay must have read that once you've earned the respect of your opponents, you can frighten them into folding even if your hand is weak. The other players had reacted according to the book. Paul hadn't.

Impassively, Clay turned over his cards, revealing that he was holding an ace, jack, queen and king, inferior to Paul's trip of three eights. Abandoning the dewy-eyed amateur act, Paul pulled in the pot with the smallest of smiles. To his surprise, Clay left the table, as did Alice Markwick.

The idea had never been to make his fortune and Paul played the next two games tightly, folding early as he tried to catch the conversation from where Clay and Alice sat by the fire, but they were talking too quietly.

It was almost three in the morning before Paul was able to take his moment, by which time Lol Calloway had bowed out with his normal string of obscenities. Miles was playing well, but Alice had lost interest, limping in late and low in those games where she didn't fold. Clay was down by a few hundred but appeared to have unlimited funds backing him.

The buck was with Paul, and by chance, he dealt himself the sweetest hand imaginable – two kings, followed by a flop of a king, a five and a four. After Alice and Miles had folded, Clay chewed his bottom lip in a pathetic attempt at a bluff, then pushed £1,000 into the centre of the table.

Paul hesitated for a minute or so. Then he raised with all the money he had before him, confident that, even if Clay had aces wired in the hole – two aces – he was on a loser. The last two cards to be turned, a nine and a queen, sealed his fate.

Clay went for the full bluff, raising Paul by another £2,000 with a triumphant little smile. 'We work on the basis of IOUs in this school,' he said. 'Two weeks to pay.'

For a moment, there was silence in the room. Lol ambled over from the fire where he was sitting. 'You are one hard bastard, Clay,' he said quietly.

Paul looked at the two kings in his hand like a man reading his own death sentence. 'IOU?' he said. 'I hadn't realized I could run up debts.' Suddenly he found himself thinking of Alex. It was this easy to be caught in the gin-trap of indebtedness. The harder you pulled, the tighter you were held.

'You're with the big boys now, Paul,' Clay said. 'This isn't a social event.'

At poker, as in racing, there are amateurs and there are professionals. Paul swallowed, playing for time, allowing the tension around the table to build up. And professionalism was more than a question of skill and knowledge; it was a state of mind. Although Paul's experience of poker was limited to a few light-hearted games with the other jockeys and a two-hour lesson with Crazy Mary, he thought like a winner. Clay Wentworth was an amateur to the marrow of his bones.

'Perhaps,' Paul said, reaching into the inside pocket of his jacket, 'I could bring this into play.' He threw a scuffed and faded piece of paper onto the pile of money. 'It's worth £2,000 of anybody's money.'

Clay leaned forward and picked up the piece of paper, a list of horses' names, most of which had been deleted. At last, there was panic. 'Where did you get this?' he asked, quietly.

'Win the hand and it's yours.'

Paul glanced around the table. Alice had looked away but seemed disturbed by the turn of events.

'What on earth's going on?' Miles asked. 'Is that an IOU?'

'Of a sort,' Paul said. He stared hard at Clay. 'Accepted?'

Clay nodded. 'Tricky little bastard, aren't you?' he said, turning over his two cards to reveal two jacks.

Paul flipped over the two kings. As he reached out for the pot, taking the piece of paper first of all and returning it to his inside pocket, he said, 'It's been copied, Clay – and two people know I'm here.'

'We need to talk about this – privately,' Clay said. 'The game's over.'

'That game's over,' said Paul. 'The other is just beginning.'

They should have stopped shooting. Alice Markwick stood on the steps of Clay's house in the early hours of the morning, and felt lost. The night had passed in a dream of poker hands, low birds and bantering conversation. Had she lost money? Did Paul Raven know about Opteeka B? Was Clay at this very moment revealing secrets that could destroy him and her? She didn't care.

They should have stopped shooting.

Alice wasn't aware of the whine of a milk float, approaching her from down the road. It stopped ten yards away and, with quite unnecessary jauntiness, a young man in his early twenties jumped out of the cab, took two pints from a crate and, whistling, walked towards the entrance to Clay's house. ''Ullo,' he appraised the dark, slender woman standing on the doorstep with a cheeky up-and-down look. 'Heavy night, darlin'?'

Alice looked at him slowly. 'They should have stopped shooting,' she said.

There was a roar in her ears. Alice wasn't drunk, although she had tried during the evening to dull the pain with the occasional vodka tonic. With a huge effort of concentration, she remembered where she had parked the car and, as the milk float moved away, she walked slowly down the street, feeling for the car keys in her handbag as she went.

Sometimes it felt lonely on the small, deserted island that she had chosen to inhabit. She wasn't made for relationships, for confidences, for the ghastly domestic messiness of cohabitation, so after the death of Eric, she had kept the world away from her little island. At times like this, she regretted it. She wanted to talk to someone. There were girlfriends, of course, but they belonged to another world

– a world of music, laughter and easy gratification. If she rang them, they would misunderstand what she wanted.

Alice unlocked the door of her Aston Martin and drove carefully back to the flat in Islington.

She knew what she had to do when she arrived. Without even checking her answering machine, she walked into the sitting-room in which all the lights had been left blazing. Behind a mediocre nineteenth-century landscape painting there was a safe which, tapping out a number on its security board, she opened. The videotape lay there, like an unexploded bomb.

She had to see it just once more.

Alice poured herself another vodka tonic from a cocktail tray in the corner. Her television and video were designed into a bookcase and, having inserted the tape, she sat on the sofa and, curling her legs unde rneath her, watched the recorded last moments of Gavin Holmes one more time.

Despite inept camera-work, it was clear that Opteeka B had passed this, its most important test, with full marks. One moment he was standing there, unsteady but in control, in front of his car, the next he was as blind and helpless as a newborn kitten.

Alice gripped the glass. This was what she wanted, she told herself. It would provide a future free of the insecurity which had haunted her since she was a little girl in Prague. She would never have to suffer in the way that her mother had suffered. Freedom came with a price-tag attached.

On the screen, Gavin was feeling his way towards the exit of the car park. Then, with the knife at his throat, he was turned back to the wall.

The violence she didn't like. Even while Opteeka B was being developed, she would sometimes wake at night, ambushed by visions of how her brain-child would be used. If she could have won a lifetime of security with a device to save a child's eyesight, or assist in major operations, nothing would have made her happier, but of course that was impossible. Life paid badly; it was with death that you made a killing.

Tears filled Alice's eyes. She wiped them away angrily, forced herself to watch the screen.

Like a rabbit blinded by a searchlight, the man blundered along the wall, then turned back. The speeding van filled the screen, but the roar of its engine was not loud enough to obliterate entirely Gavin's last scream of terror. The experiment was proved, there was no need to keep filming. As the van moved forward, the camera trained on the journalist's twitching, bloodied body.

Dry-eyed now, Alice stared ahead of her. Petrin had his evidence. It would soon be over.

'They should have stopped shooting,' she said quietly.

'Perhaps I ought to tell you that my wife and I have no secrets.' Clay Wentworth sat at the mahogany desk in his small study and puffed at a large cigar he had just taken from a silver box. 'We tell each other everything.'

Paul looked up at him from a deep armchair. Clay had recovered his composure somewhat since the final game in the night's poker school. He had bid farewell to

the other guests with cool courtesy and before ushering Paul downstairs to his
small room with the weary disapproval of a schoolmaster.

'So it came as no surprise that you were in possession of that particular piece of
paper,' Clay continued.

'You accepted it as a bet. You must want it back.'

'What a pathetic thing to do.' A look of irritation crossed Clay's face. 'Your little moment of melodrama. Yes, of course I'd like it back.'

'You can have it.'

'But you've got a copy.'

'The photocopy of a scrap of paper is hardly going to serve as evidence.'

Clay leaned back in his absurd leather executive chair, like a bad actor in a soap
opera. He was probably an amateur at business too, Paul reflected. The layout of
his dark womb-like little study suggested a deep insecurity. The guest chair was
lower than Clay's so that Paul had to look up at him. The desk lamp was posi-
tioned to dazzle him. Doubtless a psychiatrist might say something about the big
cigar Clay was toying with as he spoke. Despite his position and his money – or
perhaps because of them – the man was a loser.

'You have a deal in mind, I suppose,' Clay said. 'Some sort of cheap blackmail.'

'You'll have the list back, once you've told me what happened to Alex Drew.'

'Alex?' Clay looked surprised, as if he had forgotten that the man had ever existed. 'I really didn't know him well.'

'He came to your little evenings.'

'Bloody awful gambler, your friend. Ran up debts of fifty big ones.'

'And committed suicide.'

'It's happened before.' Clay puffed at his cigar and waved away the smoke as
if, with it, he could make memories of Alex fade. 'You knew the boy, Paul,' he
said reasonably. 'He lived for racing, but he had his weaknesses – women, the
need to be seen in the right places. I liked him. He begged me to let him join us
on Thursday nights; I thought I was doing him a favour.'

It was almost four in the morning and, as he listened to Clay Wentworth trying
to lie his way out of trouble, Paul felt a profound weariness. 'I'm not interested in
this bullshit,' he said, 'Tell me – '

Clay held up a hand. 'I covered his debts, that's how much I liked him. He owed
me around thirty – the rest was to other members of the school. I asked him to go
to his parents but he was too proud. Tragic. I wish I'd been able to talk to him.'

Outside the window, a blackbird with a faulty body clock had started singing in
the darkness. For a brief moment, Paul thought of his friend – Alex, joking as
the string pulled out at Charlesworth's yard; Alex, talking to Jim Wilson in the
weighing-room; Alex, his face a mask of pale determination as they circled around
the starter before a race.

Misunderstanding his silence, Clay added, 'It was a terrible shock to all of us.'

With the clarity of vision that comes with the graveyard shift, Paul saw that it
wasn't greed for money or social acceptance that had led Alex to his death. It was
weakness – the weakness of Clay Wentworth that somehow infected all around
him.

'I'll tell you what I'm going to do,' Paul said softly. 'I'm washing my hands of this whole business. I'm going to hand this small piece of evidence – ' he patted his jacket pocket ' – to the Jockey Club. Just in case they reach an opinion that no respected amateur could possibly be guilty of driving a professional jockey to his death, I'll also tell the police everything I know. What happened to me. What happened to Alex. And what happened to the horses on the list. Then, just to make sure, I'll give the story to a journalist friend. Between them, they'll discover the truth about Mr Clay Wentworth and his friends.'

'Journalist?' Oddly, Clay seemed most alarmed by the least potent threat in Paul's armoury.

'Nobody you know,' Paul said. 'I've found out enough about Alex's death.'

'You know less than you think,' Clay muttered flatly.

There was a soft knock at the door. Before either man could react, it had been pushed open and a dishevelled figure in a white silk nightgown and a dressing-gown half hanging off a slender shoulder, stood at the entrance.

'Zena, what a nice surprise,' said Clay coldly.

'How did it go, Paul?' Zena asked woozily. 'Make lots of money, did you? Spend my investment wisely?'

'Yes.' The interruption was doubly annoying. Clay had seemed on the point of cracking. His wife's determination to reveal that he had been gambling against his own money was an unwelcome diversion. 'We were talking about Alex.'

'Oh, Alex.' Zena entered the room, running a hand through her hair. Whatever she was on, pills or booze, had done little for feminine allure, and the make-up around her eyes seemed to have smudged or run earlier in the night. 'One of our first victims, wasn't he, darling?' She smiled in the general direction of her husband as she sat on the edge of his desk, affording Paul an unavoidable view of her thighs.

'You're drunk. It's late. We're busy,' Clay said. There was a tightness in his voice that Paul had not heard before.

'I screw 'em, you kill 'em, isn't that right?'

'Alex committed suicide.' Clay glared at his wife but, behind the threat, there was something shifty and defensive. 'There's no need to bother Mr Raven with this.'

'I'm sure Mr Raven –' Zena smiled crookedly at Paul and waggled a bare foot in his direction ' – would love to know this.'

Paul waited.

'Did you know a man called Gavin Holmes, darling?' Zena said suddenly. 'Journalist on the *Guardian*, nice man, bit of a lush – ' she paused ' – good lover, though. Killed today. Accident at the races. On the news it was. They say he was pissed, but we know better than that, don't we, darling?'

'Is this a joke?' Paul asked. 'Is Holmes dead?'

'Crushed against a wall. Went to Lingfield Park. Weren't you at Lingfield today, darling?'

With a sudden movement, Clay stood up and, taking Zena roughly by the arm, propelled her, drunkenly protesting, out of the door. Paul heard snatches of angry conversation in the hall. Eventually, Clay returned, closing the door behind him.

'Sorry,' he said. 'She gets rather emotional sometimes.'

'Is she right?'

'I heard an item on the news about this man.' Clay returned to his desk. 'It's the first time I've even heard his name.' He smiled wearily. 'It's all history,' he said. 'I'll tell you about the list you have, and you can do what you like with it.'

'History?'

'Yes.' Clay seemed haggard, broken by the events of the evening. 'I wish I had never become involved.'

The tape on the answering-machine turned slowly. The voice of Clay Wentworth, weary but not defeated, sounded in Alice Markwick's flat.

'. . . an executive decision, no more or less. I've thrown him off the track. He has discovered why Drew died, which is all he really wanted to know. I managed to persuade him that the journalist's death was some sort of weird accident. He's finished his little quest. He'll leave us alone now . . .'

Alice sat on the sofa, an empty glass hanging loosely from her hand, the blank grey television screen before her.

'. . . the unfortunate fuss this evening about my shopping-list,' the voice from the tape continued. 'I even managed to persuade him to leave that with me so it's a question of hanging on until Wednesday. After that, we're free of . . .'

As if awakening from a dream, she put the glass on the floor, stood up and turned the television off. She pressed a button, removing the videotape and locking it once more in the safe.

Clay was still talking as Alice switched off the light and walked slowly to the bedroom.

Chapter
13

It wasn't like they show on the silver screen, the gathering of wrongdoers at a small terraced house in Perivale on the outskirts of London. The picture of the Virgin and child above the mantelpiece was good, so was the way one of the young men, the one with a moustache, cracked his knuckles occasionally, but the rest, three Italians sitting in cheap chairs by a gas fire, was too light, too domestic, too English – more *EastEnders* than the Godfather.

'So,' Tino, the older man, smiled with satisfaction. *'Il Cavallo di Troia* is doing his work.'

'Cavallo? Troia? What you talking about, papa?' The grey-haired man's son Salvatore looked mystified, as did Giorgio who, for a moment, was distracted from his knuckle work.

'Dio, do they teach you nothing in English schools. *Il Cavallo di Troia?* The Trojan Horse?'

'What's this, some kind of racehorse, is it?' Giorgio asked.

The older man laughed, but he felt sad. Even in Naples, where he had been raised, children understood the rudiments of classical education. Here, it seemed, school provided a foundation course in getting into girls' knickers and listening to loud music but little else. Occasionally he looked at Salvo and his friends and wondered whether the problem was not more with them than with the system but he quickly dispelled the thought. No, there was something rotten in the heart of this country. 'It's a reference to Greek mythology but it doesn't matter,' he said. 'I meant Calloway.'

'Ah, Johnny Geetar,' said Giorgio. 'He rang me. He does his work well.'

'It's impossible to get the *machina* from the factory, papa,' said Salvatore. 'Calloway says it's kept in some kind of bunker, guarded by the guy who uses it. Short of getting hold of the Markwick woman, there's no way we can find out where it is.'

'So?' Tino looked surprised. 'What's the problem? You get her.'

'That's just it,' said Giorgio. 'We don't have to. Our Trojan whatsit has told us where it's going to be used next.'

'Cheltenham, Tuesday,' Salvatore interrupted eagerly. 'There's a big race meeting and, in one of the races, a horse called Tanglewood's running. They're using the machine to stop it.'

'Where?' Tino sat still, waiting for the boys to understand.

'Cheltenham, papa. We told you.'

'Start, finish. First fence, last fence, bend. It could be anywhere.' Exasperation entered Tino's voice. 'We don't even know what the fucking thing looks like.'

For a moment, there was silence in the room, apart from the sound of Salvo's mother washing the dishes, humming to herself, from the kitchen across the hall.

Tino sighed. '*Cazzo*, you're useless, you two. You're not going to make it by knowing how to use a knife, how to make a man talk, how –' he glared at Salvatore ' – how to smash up guitars.' He tapped the side of his head. 'Think,' he said more quietly. 'If you want to survive outside the law, you have to use this, you know.'

Giorgio and Salvatore looked at the floor, resentful yet slightly afraid, like two errant schoolboys who know that a lecture is on the way but don't have the nerve to interrupt.

'This is our big break,' Tino continued. 'We can go on working our little patch in London, running the girls, pushing the dope, carrying out the occasional bank job. But England is small, you want to get away. *Dio*, I want to get away. West Coast of America, or Chicago, or maybe New Orleans. They understand there. And, with this, they respect us.'

'We've got large parts of London tied up,' Giorgio muttered sulkily. 'Isn't that enough?'

'Not for these guys. They are big time, the true brotherhood.' For a moment there was silence in the room, and the unspoken word 'Mafia' hung in the air. Apart from a few Sicilian connections, Tino's London network was no more than an unofficial mafia and mention of the word was regarded as boastful, or even bad form. After this, they would be able to embrace the name with pride. 'They need a passport, a ticket of entry,' Tino continued. 'If I can go to Signor Guiseppi Vercelloni in New York and present him with the perfect weapon – a camera which blinds temporarily – our links with America will be assured.'

'Where?' said Salvatore eventually. 'We need to know where the photographer will be.'

'I'll call Calloway,' said Salvatore. 'I'm sure he'll be pleased to hear from me again.'

'This Cheltenham thing – it's big?' Tino asked. 'Lots of people?'

Giorgio nodded. 'They say it's a big deal for English racing.'

'Excellent,' said Tino.

Occasionally Zena Wentworth suffered from serious regrets and right now, as she lay naked on pine boards while her back was massaged by a beautiful and muscular Turkish homosexual at an exclusive health club in Chelsea, she found there was no escaping them.

She regretted the abortions when she was a teenager that later prevented her having children. That was normal. She regretted her dependence on alcohol and recreational drugs. There was nothing new there. She regretted the day that she had met Clay Wentworth, and even more the day that she married him. That regret was with her at every waking moment. She regretted not telling Paul Raven everything she knew about Clay and Alice Markwick. This was new, a fresh psychic wound that had opened a few hours ago.

She winced. 'You're a sadist, Adnan,' she gasped as the fingers of the Paradise

Health Club's most popular masseur seemed almost to reach into her flesh and touch the backbone.

A light laugh. 'Mmm. You're close, Mrs Wentworth,' the Turk said coquettishly.

In her life, she had done so little that was good. She gave her mother and her father Christmas presents, she went to church on the occasions when it was expected of her but, apart from that, she and common decency had parted company years ago. No one asked Zena Wentworth to be a godmother to their children.

Now was her chance, the time for a single act of blazing charity that would signal a turning-point in her life.

She thought of the conversation between her husband and Paul Raven which she had listened to, sitting on the stairs, after Clay had told her to go to bed. By his standards, he had been almost honest. He had told Paul about the small clique of investors who had put money into Alice Markwick's firm. He had explained precisely why Opteeka B was such a valuable scientific breakthrough. He had even confessed to the on-site racecourse experiments. But that was where his honesty had ended.

'What about the future?' Paul had asked.

'It's finished. The Ministry of Defence took possession of it this week. Our little investment has paid off.'

Only fear and weariness had stopped her going back into the study and confronting Clay with his lie.

Paul had asked about Gavin Holmes.

We knew nothing of that, Clay had said. There are undesirable elements interested in Opteeka B. He very much feared that Holmes had become involved with them and had paid the price.

She hadn't been surprised when Paul appeared to believe the line that Clay had sold him. Alex's death was explained. He had his own life to think of. The world of secret weapons was nothing to him.

'Turn?' the masseur asked.

Her back and shoulders tingling, Zena rolled over. It was a moment that even she found slightly disconcerting as she lay naked, her flesh glowing with sweat, beneath the entirely indifferent gaze of an oriental god. 'Are you absolutely sure that you're 100% gay, Adnan?' she smiled.

The man's eyes flickered down her pale, slack body, as if to confirm the rightness of his sexual orientation. 'Correction,' he said, starting to work on her left calf and thigh. '110%.'

After she had left the Paradise Health Club, Zena drove at speed back to the house. Ever since she had been a teenager, she had driven fast through London but there was a precision and determination to the way she took the streets now. Adnan always had that effect on her, as if his powerful hands had the power to cleanse her of poisonous thoughts, to make her as fresh and clean as the skin of her body. The good resolutions rarely lasted longer than the effects of the massage but her few hours of virtue convinced Zena that she was not entirely lost.

She ran up the steps, the keys of the house in her hand. Letting herself in, she took the stairs to the bedroom and sat on the side of the bed. Breathlessly, she dialled Paul's number. He deserved better than to be deceived by her husband.

'Paul,' she said, leaning forward, her hand on her forehead like a Victorian moral-ity painting called The Ashamed Mistress or A Confession. 'It's Zena. No, wait, don't hang up – ' She hesitated. 'There are two things you should know,' she said. 'You should go to Cheltenham on Tuesday. Clay's little game isn't over yet. They're going to stop Tanglewood.'

At the other end, Paul asked a question but, before she could reply, a finger had broken the connection. Zena looked up to see her husband standing before her.

When he spoke, his voice was gentle, just like it was in the old days, although there was no tenderness there now. 'And the second thing?'

Clay replaced the telephone and lifted her face towards him like a man raising a pistol.

'The second thing, my sweet deceitful darling?'

The BBC was not generous with its offices. Producers, even tubby, self-important pro-ducers like Bernard Green, tended to be given a quality of work station which, in any other business, a junior secretary would find unacceptable.

Bernard was gazing at the wall-chart in front of his desk wondering, not for the first time that day, how he was going to bring in a programme on Northern Ireland on time, under budget and in a form that would not offend BBC governors, their wives or dinner-party friends, when the dull green phone beside him gave an uneven wheeze of a ring.

'BBC Psychiatric Intensive Care Unit,' he said laconically. It was one of his favourite jokes. 'Mr Joseph? For me?' Then, with a double-take that shook his ample frame in the tight off-white shirt he was wearing, he sat up straighter in his chair. 'Ah yes, Mr Joseph. Send him up.'

He put down the telephone with a muttered, 'Sodding hell.' Standing up, he reached for a corduroy jacket that had been left on top of an old grey cabinet. He put his head out of the office door and said, 'Be a love, Irene, and fetch us two cups of tea. Unexpected guest. Yugoslavian journalist called Joseph.'

A tall woman with glasses and the forbidding look of a senior librarian glanced unaffectionately in his direction, but, like the overweight ornament on a cuckoo clock, Bernard had ducked back into his office.

'Hot, steaming piles of shit,' he muttered to himself. 'How dare he come to see me here?'

As usual, Petrin seemed entirely at home when he was shown into the office, charming Irene and even accepting the grey, weak tea in a styrofoam cup with a modicum of grace. As the door closed, Petrin looked around the tiny office. 'How cosy,' he smiled.

'I frankly find your pitching up like this at my place of work, unannounced, beyond – '

'Shut up.' Petrin allowed his smile to disappear like the winter sun behind grey clouds. 'I have no problem with my security. If you're on some sort of list of sus-pects here, then you only have yourself to blame. Can we talk?'

Sulkily, Bernard said, 'We don't bug people at the BBC.'

'Next Tuesday, you will have a camera crew at Cheltenham. You will be obliged to attend yourself.'

Bernard shifted himself in his chair and gave a hopeless little laugh. 'My schedule's ridiculously tight but I just might be able to move a few things around.'

'How co-operative of you.'

'The camera crew's out of the question.'

Petrin looked at him coldly.

'We have such things as unions over here,' Bernard continued. 'I can't just send a crew off to some racecourse. There'd be questions. We're meant to be cutting back on – '

'I didn't expect this sort of attitude from you of all people, Bernard. Particularly given your years of service for us. Years – ' he paused significantly ' – of which I have extensive notes and tapes.'

'I deserve better than this,' Bernard said weakly. 'It could finish my career if it got out that I'd been working for you.'

'The alternative certainly will. The choice is yours.'

'What do you want these men for anyway? They're very difficult, technicians. Ask them to do something that's not in their contract and you've got a strike on your hands.'

'Men? What men?'

Bernard was paler than usual, and his face was greasy with sweat. The unpleasant smell of human stress filled the airless office.

'The camera crew.'

'Ah, I failed to make myself clear. I don't need your technicians. I want to borrow some equipment for the afternoon. And, of course, we'll need a pass.'

'We?'

'You and me, Bernard. We are the technicians.' The stink in the office was becoming really quite unbearable.

'It's not possible. There are all sorts of regulations to bear in mind.'

Pausing with his hand on the door-handle, Petrin said, 'Do it, Bernard, or the Director-General gets your personal file.' He opened the door and switched on a smile. 'Thanks so much for the restorative cuppa,' he said, winking suavely at Irene.

Sleep had never been easy since the attack in the laboratory but, ever since he had accepted money from the man called Josef, Peter had found himself waking in the middle of the night, drenched in sweat. He dreamed of himself alone in a barren snowscape but when he touched the snow, it burnt his flesh like battery acid, and Klima was before him melting, her mouth wide in a soundless scream, her eyes uncomprehending as she disappeared and he was unable, despite everything, to make a sound, while he cowered from a hand pressing him into the evil, death-dealing snow and a child was screaming, his son –

'Peter, Peter, calm.' His wife held him down on the bed and, as the sobbing subsided, Peter Zametsky knew with utter certainty that he had to act.

* * *

'Let's go to bed.'

Angie looked up from the floor where she had been sitting when the phone rang, bringing the news about Gavin Holmes' notes, and saw that Paul was lost to her.

'Mmm?' he frowned.

'Make love, remember? Act like a normal couple for a while.'

Paul leaned forward and ran a hand slowly over her fine blonde hair across her cheek, tracing the line of her lips. 'I've got to warn Bill Scott.'

'Who?'

'He's riding Tanglewood at Cheltenham. He must know that they're trying to stop him.'

Angie laughed briefly. 'You always were a romantic, Paul,' she said. 'I offer you my body and you prefer to go and chat to another jockey.'

'It's not a chat.' A flush of anger suffused Paul's cheeks. 'Christ, you should know what can happen to a jockey in a bad fall.'

She looked away. Every time she believed that she and Paul were going to be able to live a life of some normality, he was dragged back into the murky side of racing. 'It will never leave us, the ghost of Alex Drew, will it?' she said.

'This is no longer about Alex. He was weak. Some unscrupulous bastards put pressure on him to put me through the rails. He couldn't live with his guilt. But there are the other horses.'

'Why not just hand all the evidence over to the Jockey Club or whatever it's called?'

'What evidence? A bit of paper. A late-night conversation after a game of poker. And, remember, this is Mr Clay Wentworth we're talking about.' Paul smiled bitterly. 'The respected businessman.'

'It will never end,' Angie said bleakly. She thought of the day she had realized, back at the hospital, that this was the man she wanted. Since then she had given up her career for him. She had become involved in a sport she had once believed was inhuman. She had given him – a small thing but her own – her virginity.

'A few more days,' he said, as if reading her thoughts. 'Then it will end one way or another.'

Wearily, she nodded. 'So we collect Gavin Holmes' notes, then what?'

Paul looked at her almost impassively. 'You collect the notes, I go to see Bill. Time's against us now.'

Angie stood up and reached for a light green shoulder bag she had left on a chair nearby. 'This is how they do things up your way, is it?' she asked. She let her arms swing ape-like before her and said in a Neanderthal voice, 'Me macho man, you little woman run around for me, right?'

Paul looked into her angry, hurt eyes. 'This is important,' he said quietly but, as she turned away towards the door, it occurred to him that maybe nothing was as important as to hold her lithe and slender body close to his. 'There'll be time for love later,' he added.

But she was gone.

The photographer had been surprised to get a late commission only two days before the final experiment, and not entirely pleased. He was a professional; he needed to prepare himself for the pay-off, not run about the country doing last-minute errands for her ladyship.

'I wouldn't have asked you,' she had said. 'But I need someone I can trust.'

That was fair enough. When it came to tact, keeping schtum while all around him were shooting their mouths off or asking stupid questions, the photographer had few equals.

'You won't need any assistance, will you?' she had asked sweetly. 'After all, our man isn't exactly going to run away.'

So he had agreed to keep it simple, keep it in the family.

Mrs Markwick had been curiously distracted, confiding secrets which normally she would have kept to herself. There was a small hitch, she had said, Raven was taking an unhealthily close interest. He needed to be de-activated for a few days.

De-activated? What the hell did that mean?

Mrs Markwick had explained. He was to be brought back to the bunker beneath the office, and kept with Fi-Fi for a while. Mrs Markwick would find someone to guard him. The price of his freedom would be carefully explained to him – one word to the authorities and immobility would be the least of his problems.

A bit elaborate, wasn't it? Surely it would be simpler to –

But no. Something had happened to Mrs Markwick. Ever since the last, highly successful experiment, she had a look in her eyes the photographer had never seen before. Distant, almost wistful. She wanted no more killing. We fulfil our agreement with Wentworth, then it was farewell to Opteeka B and good riddance.

He didn't like it. Kidnapping was messy. It could go wrong.

The photographer sat in the driver's seat of an old, battered Citroen parked outside the Blue Boar Tavern, Leatherhead. This was G and T country and, although it was Monday, the pub car park was full of company cars whose occupants were doing business the English way over steak and chips and an agreeable glass of Chateau Plonk. It wasn't going to be easy, breezing off with an unwilling individual, even one with wonky legs.

He's a boy, Mrs Markwick had said, an innocent and, as if to prove it, she had given the photographer Raven's number and told him to ring him. He was to be a friend of Gavin Holmes, a fellow journalist. He had some of Gavin's notes which the *Guardian* refused to touch. He owed it to Gavin to get them into the right hands. Could we meet? Say, the Blue Boar, Leatherhead. The car park, for security reasons. One o'clock, Monday, fine.

Candy from a baby.

The photographer lit a cigarette. It was five past one, and he was beginning to worry. The only person in the car park was a young girl with short blonde hair, wearing jeans and a light blue jacket. She seemed lost.

Then she saw his car and started walking towards it.

Until today, Paul's acquaintance with the young amateur Bill Scott had been restricted to occasional weighing room banter, but now, as he talked to him in his cottage near Wantage, he found that Bill reminded him of Alex Drew a couple of years back – the same enthusiasm for racing, the same diamond-hard will to win behind his easy manner.

'Let me get this right,' Bill said, sitting in towelling dressing-gown outside his sauna. 'You're saying that if I hadn't tracked Skinflint onto stands side at Wincanton, I'd have been brought down by some weird weapon that blinded my horse?'

Paul smiled. Described in Bill's broad West Country accent, the idea sounded even more absurd than it was.

'That's why Drago's Pet fell on the inner. They got the wrong horse.'

'Not very competent, were they?'

Sweat was still running down Bill Scott's face, the result of a final wasting session of the day. Although his weight on Tanglewood in the Kim Muir posed no problem, he had another ride earlier in the afternoon for which he would have to do ten stone two. 'The only reason I was tracking Skinflint was that my horse doesn't like to be left alone. Drago's Pet was fading so it made sense to go with Wentworth, even if he was taking the longest way round.'

'Not that competent,' Paul said, 'but ruthless. Three other horses fancied for the Kim Muir have been taken out. They claim that they've proved what they needed to prove, and that nothing will happen at Cheltenham, but I don't trust them.'

'You think they'd try something? At the National Hunt Festival?'

'The bigger the crowd, the easier the job.' Paul shrugged. 'I hope I'm wrong but the fact is, with Tanglewood out of the way, Skinflint's a certainty.'

'So what do I do? Watch out for a missile-launcher by the second last and duck?'

'How d'you normally ride Tanglewood?'

'Hunt him along for the first couple of miles, then start improving. He's a clever sort so jumping's no problem – I can place him anywhere. As I say, the only problem is that he goes to sleep where he hits the front.'

'That's perfect. If you can keep him covered up as long as possible, they'll have to get at you over the last couple of fences. Stay in the middle of the course to make yourself a more difficult target.'

Bill looked doubtful. 'It's a three mile 'chase at Cheltenham. If Skinflint's ten lengths up at the third last, you're not going to get me holding him up to avoid getting zapped.'

'You're right.' Paul stood up. Like any serious jockey, Bill Scott understood that danger went with the territory. Missing the chance of a winner at the biggest race meeting of the year because of the obscure threat of some secret weapon was hardly likely to appeal to him. 'Do me one favour, though. Try to stay on the stands side coming up the straight. I'll cover the inner.'

'I'll try,' Bill said, although the look on his face suggested that he had more doubts about Paul's sanity than his own safety.

'You're going to beat Skinflint tomorrow,' Paul said, hesitating by the front door. 'Do it for Alex, okay?'

Bill smiled indulgently. 'You just watch me,' he said.

The man in the Citroen had long grey hair and there was a high colour to his big rounded features. He looked like a film director who had once been big in the sixties, or a moderately successful second-hand car dealer or – yes, or a journalist. He opened the window to the car as Angie approached.

'Mr Davison?' she asked.

The man seemed suspicious of her. 'I was expecting Paul Raven,' he said.

'I'm Paul's friend,' she said. 'He's had to go somewhere and asked me to collect the material.'

'Wasn't the arrangement. I told him I wanted to see him personally.' The man glanced towards the girl's car, a Mini. There was no one else with her.

'You can trust me,' she said, a hint of desperation in her voice.

The man hesitated. 'Get in,' he said reluctantly, nodding in the direction of the passenger seat on which there was an orange file.

'Can't you just give it to me?'

'Forget it.' He started the car.

'No.' Angie walked round, opened the door and, as she stepped in, the man picked up the file to make room for her.

With the engine still running, he said, 'I need to explain this stuff to you.' Opening the file, he took out a small pistol. 'Sorry,' he said. 'I wanted your boyfriend but you'll have to do.' Pointing the gun at her, he leaned across and, with his left hand, locked the passenger door. 'We've got to make a little trip,' he said. 'All right?'

Angie sat back in the seat and closed her eyes. 'Thanks, Paul,' she said quietly.

Before – long before – he heard from them, Paul knew something had gone wrong. He cursed himself for not checking the journalist who had called with the *Guardian*. Not only had he failed to see the trap, but he had sent Angie into danger instead of him. As darkness fell, he recalled their last conversation, her sad, defeated words. 'It will never end.'

And why had he exposed her to Christ knew what risk? In order to warn an amateur jockey that someone was going to stop him winning a horse-race – an amateur who, it turned out, suspected him of being deluded.

He called Angie's flat. There was no reply. Her friend in Putney hadn't seen her. Crazy Mary was working on the early evening shift. Finally, he contacted the manager of the Blue Boar. No, he had seen nothing strange, the man replied impatiently.

'A friend of mine was meeting someone in your car park,' Paul explained. 'She seems to have disappeared.'

'Oh yeah?'

'She was in a Mini, registration A663 BLB. Is the car there?'

Sighing, the man put down the telephone. 'It's here,' he said when he returned. 'But no sign of your friend.'

Paul put down the phone. He should call the police. And say what? My girlfriend was meeting a stranger and hasn't been seen for a couple of hours? The world was full of disappearing girlfriends.

He was reaching for the telephone when the doorbell rang. He hobbled across the room and flung open the door.

The first thing he noticed was that the man was wearing dark glasses despite the fact that night had fallen. Then the face – or what was left of it. The man made an eerie gurgling sound.

A woman stepped forward out of the shadows. 'My husband says we have to talk,' she said.

Chapter

14

Stress affected her in a strange way. She knew other people who became tetchy and ill-tempered, or who resorted to intense alcohol therapy, or who simply slept. Right now, Alice wished she was like them.

But she wasn't.

Her heart was beating like that of a teenager going out on her first date as she drove across London from the flat in Islington to the office. The chain of events over the last twenty-four hours had filled her with dread – to lose the deal at this late stage because of some interfering little jockey seemed absurd. Yet the word from Clay was unambiguous. His silly bitch of a wife had tipped Raven off. He had to be stopped.

The hitch, followed by the solution.

He wasn't that smart, falling easily for the lie about Gavin Holmes and his notes. She had no worries about sending the photographer. After all, Raven's legs were still weak. The photographer was strong. He was also armed.

The hitch, followed by the solution, followed by the fuck-up.

Alice gripped the steering-wheel with anger as she thought of the call summoning her to the office.

'She's here.'

'She?'

'Raven sent his girlfriend.'

She had cursed. Then it all became clear. So the jockey has sent his lover into the lion's den. Very heroic. Perhaps it wasn't so bad. In fact, perhaps it was better.

'What shall I do with her, Mrs Markwick?'

'I'm on my way,' she had said.

She parked the car in the forecourt, uneasily aware that tomorrow's last experiment was no longer uppermost in her mind, that her hands were clammy. She checked her face in the rearview mirror, then stepped out of the car and walked briskly towards the darkened offices.

May she be fat, she said to herself as she unlocked the door and ran up the steps towards her office. May she look like a horse. She walked into the executive bathroom and unlocked what appeared to be a cupboard. May she have cropped, greasy hair. She descended a dark spiral staircase and pushed open a heavy metal door. At first the bright strip lighting blinded her after the darkness, then she saw the photographer at his desk, the gun on the blotter before him. He glanced across the room. May she have unfortunate skin.

The girl was tied to a chair, her arms bound at the elbows, each of her feet tied to the legs of the chair. She was small and slender and, when Alice first looked at her, a curtain of fine blonde hair concealed her face. Then she looked up, fear and anger in her light blue eyes.

Damn. It was as Alice had feared. The girl was perfection.

She really wished that stress didn't affect her this way.

As soon as Angie saw the woman standing at the door, smiling at her in that peculiar way, she knew she was in trouble. At first, she hadn't understood. The man with the gun and killer's eyes, the trip to London, her legs tied together with rope, the brightly-lit room that smelt of rabbits – none of it made sense. But now she began to see it all.

'Mrs Markwick,' she said. 'Would you mind explaining what all this is about?'

Alice ambled forward, picked up the ugly, black pistol that was lying on the desk, ran a finger down the silencer that was on the barrel and put it back carefully as if it were a piece of antique china. She dressed well and expensively, Angie noticed, and the long dark curls which might have seemed ridiculous on a woman of her age gave her a sort of cold stylishness. 'How d'you know my name?' she asked in a low voice, in which a foreign accent was just detectable.

'I've seen you at the races with your friend Clay Wentworth.'

'He's not my friend.'

'You haven't answered,' said Angie. 'Why are you doing this?'

Alice pulled up a wooden chair which she placed in front of Angie. 'You're hardly in a position to be asking me questions,' she said, as she sat down. Angie shrunk back from her. There was something faintly alarming about this woman, the way she sat too close so that Angie could smell the expensive scent on her. There was a rustle of silk as she crossed her legs. 'You don't look very comfortable,' Alice said, a hint of mockery in her voice.

Angie's shoulders ached and the back of the chair was biting into the flesh of her upper arms, but she said nothing.

'As it happens, this matter can be easily resolved,' Alice said. 'I would like you to make one call to Mr Paul Raven. Then you can relax, we'll take off the rope and let you go – maybe tomorrow night.'

'What am I supposed to say?'

'I don't want him to go racing tomorrow. I have a little project which, I'm told, interests him. There will now be . . . an alternative attraction.' Alice lingered over the word then, as if returning to more practical matters, she said, 'At four o'clock, he will receive a call at his house. It will tell him where in London he will find you.' She smiled. 'That's all. No money. No information. He'll just have to miss the races.'

'He'll tell the police.'

'Not if he likes his little girl, he won't. If anything goes wrong at Cheltenham, your friend will not be getting you back in the condition he last saw you.' Alice hesitated. 'Personally, I had hoped Gavin Holmes would be our last casualty.'

Angie looked away. There was an unsettling intimacy in Alice Markwick's smile.

'One call?' Alice gave a girlish pout. Without taking her eyes off Angie, she added, 'Maybe you need a little encouragement. Maybe you'd like to see our performing rabbits.'

Behind her, the photographer reached for his camera. 'Fi-Fi?' he asked.

'Yes,' said Alice. 'Fi-Fi.'

It took a long time to get the truth out of Peter Zametsky. The strain of the past few months and the fact that he was unable to enunciate in a way that was comprehensible to anyone but his wife meant that his account of the development of Opteeka B, the deadly experiments demanded by the Markwick Instruments' main investor Clay Wentworth, and the deal with Czechoslovak Intelligence was halting and unclear. But gradually, through the translation of his wife Klima, the truth unfolded.

In the end, Paul knew everything except what he needed to know most. Who was holding Angie.

'My husband says he has not the address of Clay Wentworth,' Klima said.

Paul shook his head. 'They wouldn't keep her there. It's too obvious.'

They listened as, for almost a minute, Peter gasped and gurgled, what was left of his face showing increasing animation.

When at last he finished, there was silence, as if Klima was reluctant to convey what Peter had told her.

'The people who did this to my husband,' she said eventually, 'they too want Opteeka B. Is possible, he's thinking, that they find you as rivals. Perhaps they have your girlfriend.'

Paul reached for the telephone and dialled a number. 'Ginnie,' he said. 'Angie's disappeared. I think it's something to do with the race tomorrow. Give me Wentworth's number.' He jotted down the number on a pad, promising to keep her in touch with what was happening. When he dialled Wentworth, there was an answering machine.

'Wentworth, this is Paul Raven.' He spoke quietly and firmly. 'My girlfriend was meant to be meeting a journalist today. She's gone missing. If this has anything to do with you – *anything* – you should know that the police have been informed. You have my number. Ring me when you get in, whatever time it is.' He put down the telephone and pushed it away. 'We'd better wait,' he said. 'Maybe she's trying to contact me.'

It was the scream he heard first.

They must have been holding the telephone close to her mouth because, as Paul picked it up, the receiver reverberated in his hand. At first it seemed an alien, unrecognizable sound but as the scream subsided into sobs, he knew it was Angie.

'Mr Raven?' A man's voice came onto the line. 'We have your girlfriend. She will be released tomorrow afternoon if you do what we require.'

'Yes?'

'You should wait by your telephone tomorrow. At precisely four o'clock, you will receive a call from us which will tell you where you can find her. Go to Cheltenham or talk to the police and your friend will pay the price.'

'I'll do it,' Paul said quickly.

'Maybe you would like to talk to her – in case you think we're not serious.'

Angie seemed quieter now, almost sleepy. She whispered something which at first Paul couldn't catch. Then she repeated it. 'I . . . can't see,' she said. 'I . . . can't see.'

The phone went dead.

For a moment, Paul stood, the telephone in his hand. Then he put it down slowly. 'They've done something to her eyes,' he said.

With an odd croak of excitement, Peter Zametsky stood up, speaking quickly and incomprehensibly to his wife.

'We have to go,' Irina said finally. 'My husband knows where they are keeping her.'

It was like waking from a dream. Angie moved her legs slowly then gently touched her eyes. There was a distant roar within her head and an ache behind the eyes but, when she opened them, she was dazzled by the light. Someone was touching her wrist. A woman with a distant, soothing voice.

She assumed that she had fainted. Memories of the night's events seemed as though they had happened somewhere else, and to someone else. She remembered the gun, being tied to a chair, the sinister dark-haired woman with the Eastern European accent. Then there was the rabbit, at one moment able to avoid the vicious electric pole wielded by the man, the next unseeing and panic-stricken. Its body had seemed to shudder when it had run blindly into the prod before collapsing. What had the man said as it lay, twitching in its death throes. 'Fi-Fi's last experiment,' he had said, almost sadly.

The low moaning sound that Angie heard as her head cleared seemed close. Then she realised it came from her.

'It's all right,' the voice said. 'You're all right now.'

For some reason, she was afraid to open her eyes, as if the blinding machine, the fake camera, was still directed at her. It had been like a blow to the head and, after the shock had receded, the true horror had begun.

'Open your eyes, my sweet.' The voice was almost a whisper now. 'You're safe.'

Through half-closed eyelids, Angie saw a hand, its long index finger stroking the dark red weal on her left wrist where the ropes had been, as if to smooth away the pain. She raised her head slowly, and opened her eyes.

'All over.' Alice Markwick's face was close to hers. Her sight restored, Angie saw in cruel detail its every contour – the tributaries of wrinkles leading into her wide eyes, the flecks of dark on the cold grey of the irises, the covering of down on her upper lip, the maze of tiny red veins at the base of her nostrils, the dark red tongue moving between the thin, glistening, grooved lips as she spoke.

'He's gone now. I've sent him away, Angie. I've untied you now that the business part's over.' The cold hand tightened on Angie's wrist. 'It's just you and me now. The night is young.'

Angie leaned back, pressing against the chair, but was too weak to escape Alice's insistent grip. 'What do you want from me?' she asked.

'Company. Girl talk. The usual things.'

The woman was mad. That much was certain. Since her hit-man, the man who had captured her, had gone and Paul had been set up for the following day, she had changed beyond recognition from professional woman to husky-voiced vamp. 'I want to hear all about you,' Alice was saying. 'Every little thing.' Angie thought she preferred the professional woman.

Over Alice's shoulder, she saw a hypodermic needle lying on the desk.

'Yes,' Alice said, following her eyes. 'I gave you a little jab while you were unconscious. It's a relaxant, nothing alarming. Now – ' She walked behind Angie's chair ' – if you'll excuse me a moment.'

Closing her eyes wearily, Angie said nothing. Fear had given way to a desperate need to sleep. Her head fell forward. Somewhere distant, she thought she heard a rustle, like the sound of falling clothes.

'Angie.' A hand cupped her chin and raised her head. She must have lost consciousness again. 'How do I look?'

Alice Markwick turned girlishly in front of her. Instead of a business suit, she was wearing a sheer black velcro dress over black tights. Her dark make-up was absurdly over-dramatic.

'You look like a witch,' Angie sighed.

Alice laughed and opened a small black handbag that was hooked over her arm. 'A devil more like.' A pair of handcuffs dangled from her hand. 'And you're my disciple.'

'What are you talking about?'

Alice stepped forward and touched Angie's face with the handcuffs.

'It's party time, my little one,' she said. 'I'm going to take you out on the town. We're going to celebrate in style.'

Like her husband, Klima Zametsky was seeing nothing, but that was because, as Paul's Saab hurtled through the streets of London, her eyes were tight shut. The country roads at eighty and ninety miles an hour she could take; Paul's town driving was another matter. She had gone beyond fear and nausea into a state in which she merely waited for the sickening crunch of metal, the searing pain and blackness of the inevitable crash.

'We're approaching a large roundabout with signs to Wembley and Willesden,' Paul said urgently. 'Which way?'

Peter made a sound which he interpreted as 'Left'.

As the car took the corner with a squeal of tyres, Peter added another instruction.

'The turning right after the Blue Turk pub,' Klima said faintly. 'Second right into the industrial estate.'

When they arrived, driving slowly past the offices of Markwick Instruments plc, there were no cars parked outside and no lights from the inside of the building.

'Now what?' Paul stopped the car around the corner and hesitated for a moment. He was hardly in a position to climb in through a window, and, of his passengers, one was blind, the other frozen with fear. 'Is there a back entrance?' He turned to look at Peter who was in the back seat.

Before his hairless, unseeing face, Peter held two keys.

* * *

It was a version of hell, Angie thought, as she stood unsteadily at the entrance to a large, dark room whose strategically placed lighting revealed murals of spectacular obscenity. In the centre of the room was a small, brightly lit swimming-pool surrounded by fake pillars and marble steps. The place was noisy and crowded and occasionally wild laughter could be heard above the pulsating music.

'Welcome to Slaves,' Alice said to her. 'London's wildest club. You'll love this, little one.' She stepped forward, tugging the handcuffs which connected her left wrist with Angie's right.

Angie stumbled forward. Her head was clearing but this felt like a dream – the Greek, neo-classical decadence, the noise, the pungent smell of marijuana. A tall black woman with a shaven head wandered past them, trailing a dog lead at the end of which, held by a black leather studded collar around the neck, was a subdued, slightly plump woman in her thirties. Both mistress and slave glanced at Angie appraisingly.

They found a table near the swimming-pool and a young waitress in a revealing toga took their order.

'I don't see any men,' Angie said quietly.

'Butch, fem, mistress, slave – they're all here,' Alice said, her eyes sparkling with pleasure. 'This is the first time I've been able to come with a partner.'

Angie looked at a trim, short-haired couple, one in a leather shirt, the other in a denim suit, and wondered vaguely who was meant to be dominating whom.

'You're crazy,' she said.

Fleetingly, as the three of them stood in Alice Markwick's office, Paul wondered what kind of woman it was who developed a bizarre secret weapon, planning to sell it back to the country from which she had fled, and who, for inexplicable reasons of her own, had become involved with Clay Wentworth.

Then he heard a sound from the adjoining executive bathroom.

'My husband wants you to follow him,' whispered Klima.

Feeling his way along the wall, Peter led them through a hidden door and down a steep spiral wooden stairway. The three of them paused before a heavy metal door, beyond which no sound or light came. Paul took the key and silently turned it in the lock. He pushed open the door and stepped inside.

Behind him, Peter groped for a switch that turned on the harsh strip lighting.

The first thing that Paul saw was a dead white rabbit lying in a run on the far side of the room. Then, near the desk, two wooden chairs sat facing one another. Beside one of them, there lay two coils of rope.

Peter said something as his hands ran over the open door of a wall safe by the desk, then groped inside its dark interior.

'The Opteeka B camera is gone,' Klima translated.

Near the ropes a small pile of women's clothes lay in a heap on the floor. Paul picked up a dark blue jacket, then let it fall over the chair.

'Angie's?' asked Klima.

Paul shook his head.

A dreary monotone emanated from across the room where Peter stood. Klima seemed embarrassed, briefly lost for words.

'What's he saying?' Paul asked.

Klima blushed. 'This woman,' she said. 'My husband thinks that she likes girls.'

It was a strange paradox, to feel free at Slaves, but that was how it was with Alice. She had been here before but never with a partner and Slaves was not a place for meeting new friends. Most of the few loners there liked to watch and Alice had never been a watcher.

She noticed the covert glances in their direction, the way the other women looked at them. She smiled at Angie who was staring ahead of her. They made a good couple, one of them dark, tall and dominant, the other young, blonde and adorably submissive. 'Happy?' she asked.

'Take this absurd thing off my hand,' Angie said. 'I feel ridiculous.'

'Why should I trust you?' Alice asked, a flirtatious trill in the voice.

There was no alternative. For the first time that evening, Angie looked her full in the eye. 'You can trust me,' she said softly.

'You like it here?'

'Very much.'

Alice looked at her suspiciously. Was it possible that this sense of freedom had clouded her judgement – that the knowledge that, within twenty-four hours, her future would be secure had allowed her to relax her guard?

Angie seemed to have moved closer, so that her face was inches away from Alice's. Moments ago, she was pale and unsteady; now the colour had returned to her cheeks.

Slaves had that effect on a girl. 'Unlock me,' she said, 'and maybe we can get away from this noise.'

Alice ran a hand gently down Angie's forearm, toying briefly with the handcuff around her wrist. 'D'you like champagne breakfasts?' she asked.

'My favourite.'

'Then a quiet day at the flat, watching television?'

'The races?'

Alice laughed softly. 'Of course, the races. The Kim Muir Steeplechase. Then it's back to your little friend.'

'Please.' The girl's blonde hair was almost touching her face now. Alice imagined she could feel the warmth of her flesh. 'Unlock me.'

Alice looked at her sideways. 'I'm not sure about you.'

'I – ' Angie went through a pantomime of girlish embarrassment. 'I went to a girls' boarding-school, you know.'

'What happens there?'

'It makes this – ' Angie nodded confidingly in the direction of the throng of chain and leather gathered across the swimming-pool ' – seem like the fancy-dress at a church fete.'

Alice sipped her glass of wine thoughtfully. She had always prided herself on the erotic instinct that alerted her to girls who were broad-minded in every sense. As soon as she had seen Angie, tied so heartbreakingly to the chair in the office basement, she felt an affinity that was more than the mere tug of attraction. At first she had put it down to the stress of the moment but now, as she filled her glass yet again, she was sure she was right. 'How strange,' she said, looking deep into Angie's eyes, 'that something so bad could lead to something so good.'

'So bad?'

'I didn't want it, not all the nastiness and violence and lying. I just wanted to make enough from my husband's firm to retire, and live the life I was meant to lead. But – ' Alice waved the free hand which held her glass, spilling wine on the table ' – there's no money in lasers. You think there is, but there isn't. Not peaceful, friendly lasers. So when Zametsky, out of some weird scientific curiosity, began researching into optics, I encouraged him. It needed extra investment so I brought in Wentworth and Calloway.'

Angie listened patiently to the older woman's rambling account. Doubtless Paul would be expecting her to be taking notes but right now Angie had only one thought on her mind – to get away from this drunk, and very possibly insane, lesbian. 'What about Digby Welcome?' she asked, more from a need to keep the conversation going than out of genuine curiosity.

'That was something different, a sort of long-term blackmail. He introduced me to my husband when I first came to London. Welcome knew rather more about my past than was good for him.'

For a moment, the two of them sat in silence, Alice lost in the fog of memory, Angie deciding when best to raise once again the question of unlocking the handcuffs.

'All over tomorrow,' Alice said suddenly. 'One last obstacle – one last little death – before I hand over the whole thing to someone else. Or rather – ' she smiled crookedly ' – three last obstacles.'

'Maybe we could celebrate together?' Angie whispered.

'Would you?' Alice seemed almost tearful. 'You'd stay? After the race?'

Angie raised the wrist held by the hand-cuffs. Frowning, Alice reached for her bag and produced a small key. Fumbling drunkenly, she released the lock.

'Thank you,' said Angie, rubbing her wrist.

'Poor you.' Alice lowered her head to kiss the deep red mark, closing her eyes as if to shut out the noise and vulgarity all around them.

She never saw the wine bottle raised above her like an executioner's axe, catching the light as it fell, shattering with implacable fury on the back of her skull.

Angie ran through the dark streets of Islington. Freedom was a taxi-ride – a ten-minute drive to Mary's flat. Monday was an early night for her and, even if she were entertaining a man friend, she would normally be at home.

Her head was quite clear now but she was trembling from shock. If the need to escape from Slaves hadn't been so pressing, she might have fainted herself as Alice slumped forward, blood pouring from the back of her head. Luckily the regulars at the club regarded violence between partners as normal. By the time they had realised that this was rather more than an advanced love game, she had slipped away.

She turned onto a main street and, seeing three men walking on the far pavement, she slowed to a walk. In London vulnerability could attract the wrong kind of attention. Images from the evening crowded in on her. The death throes of a rabbit in a brightly lit basement. The impact of the camera, throwing her backwards. The slender finger, tracing the rope mark on her wrist. The crazed dark eyes, unfocused by desire and alcohol, staring at her longingly in the club. Snatches of conversation – nastiness and violence and lying, all over tomorrow, one little death, celebrate together –

As Angie shuddered with revulsion, a black taxi, its light shining like a beacon, turned a corner towards her. She held up her arm and it pulled up beside her. She gave the driver Mary's address and settled into the back seat, still breathing heavily.

One little death. Now what did that mean?

Chapter
15

Of the approximately forty thousand assembled at Cheltenham racecourse on the afternoon of Tuesday 12 March for the first day of the National Hunt Festival, slightly under half were there because of an abiding interest in racehorses. The rest were in attendance for professional, social or ritual reasons. For the pickpocket or the society hostess or the Irish clergyman, Cheltenham covered three red-letter days in the diary. To miss it would be unthinkable.

Tino Marchesi liked seeing the English at play – in fact, as he strutted across the grass in front of the grandstand in his green checked suit and trilby, a new pair of binoculars around his neck, he felt almost English himself. He wondered vaguely whether in America, where he was about to become a leading member of the brotherhood, such occasions as the National Hunt Festival existed. He hoped so. They reminded him of the good things in life – friends, sportsmanship, nice clothes, money.

Behind Tino, his son Giorgio slouched moodily with his friend Salvatore. The older man glanced back and smiled. Sometimes he despaired of the younger generation. Both wore bulky long leather coats and dark glasses and looked around them as if at any moment they could be jumped by some hit-man among Cheltenham's army of tweed and cavalry twill. If they had been wearing signs reading 'Hoodlum' and 'Gangster' around their necks, they could hardly have made their backgrounds more obvious.

'Relax,' said Tino. 'You're frightening the racegoers.'

The three men found a bar but, to Giorgio's disgust, they had to fight their way through a crowd of loud and happy middle-aged men and women before being served. It was a strange and unwelcome sensation to be one of a crowd. In London, they were given space at the bar and were served almost before they had ordered.

'So.' A glass of champagne in his hand at last, Tino looked at the racecard. 'Ours is the last race. Will our guitar-playing friend Mr Calloway be here?'

Salvatore smiled broadly, displaying a vulpine set of white teeth. 'He had to rehearse, he said. "Gonna give it, like, a miss, man." '

'But he's told us everything we need to know.'

'One of the last three fences. We take one each. After they make their move, we grab the machine and disappear,' said Tino. 'No macho stuff, okay? No violence.'

'Sure.' Salvatore nodded, while Giorgio looked disappointed.

Tino sighed. Today was not going to be easy.

'Ey!' Salvatore said angrily as a tall woman swathed in mink pushed past him, carrying two glasses before her like a mother in a parents' day egg and spoon race.

'Sorry, darling.' Zena Wentworth looked over her shoulder at the dark young man in a black leather coat.

'The noise, my dear,' she muttered to herself as she progressed through the crowd. 'The *people*.'

This was definitely the last race meeting she was ever going to attend. Apart from its few advantages – being able to wear mink without getting dirty looks and the chance to chat with friends from London, for example – Cheltenham was every bit as depressing as Plumpton or Wincanton.

With some difficulty, she fought her way through to a corner where Sir Denis Wentworth sat, staring at the throng around him with evident disapproval.

'Here we are,' she said, placing a whisky and soda before him and sitting down. 'Whoever said the middle classes knew how to behave in public had never been to Cheltenham on Champion Hurdle day.'

Sir Denis looked at her, his face a picture of apathy.

'It's like a rugger scrum back there,' Zena added, nodding in the direction of the bar.

The old man sighed, then raised his glass. 'Chin-chin,' he said quietly.

'Here's to Clay's last race,' Zena smiled.

'Hmm?' Momentarily Sir Denis seemed interested.

'He told me this morning. Win or lose, he's hanging up his boots. I don't think his heart is in it, to tell the truth.' She sipped at her drink, an orange juice, and grimaced. 'Clay gives up racing, I go on the wagon – it's quite a day.'

'You give up booze?' Sir Denis sniffed. 'Fat chance.'

'No booze, no substance abuse. I'll be a new woman.'

Zena smiled brightly but her father-in-law looked away as if to confirm that whatever she did, however she reformed, his view of her would remain the same. Christ, she needed a drink – an afternoon spent with Sir Denis Wentworth would have a methodist reaching for the vodka. Not for the first time she wished that Lol and Suzy Calloway were there – even Alice, who had behaved so oddly recently, would have broken the monotony. It was a puzzle why Clay's little fan club had deserted him at what could be his finest hour.

'There's something else I'm giving up,' she said.

Sir Denis glanced across the table with a weary *now*-what expression.

'Yes,' said Zena. 'I'm giving up Clay. I've decided to leave him.'

For a moment, there was silence between them. Sir Denis took another sip of his whisky, swilled it around his mouth, and swallowed it as if it were cough medicine. Then he smacked his lips and, for the first time that Zena could remember, he smiled, revealing yellow teeth and pale gums.

'Excellent,' he said.

'It's no good,' Angie said, as she walked slowly beside Paul up the slight incline towards the weighing-room. 'I've tried to like all this –' she looked at the racegoers hurrying past them to see the first three horses in the Champion Hurdle enter the winners' enclosure '– but I guess I'm just not a racing person.'

Paul laughed. 'You've hardly had the best introduction,' he said.

'I still feel sorry for the horses.'

She was paler than usual after last night, Paul decided, but otherwise she seemed to have survived her ordeal at the hands of Alice Markwick without ill effects. She had been tearful when she arrived at Crazy Mary's flat to find Paul was waiting there too. After visiting the Markwick offices, he had sent the Zametskys home and then, on a hunch, had rung Mary, who had suggested he should stay at her flat. After an hour or so, Angie had arrived at the door, upset but unharmed.

'There's only one horse I'm worried about today,' Paul said, 'and that's Tanglewood. I've got to have a word with Bill Scott in the weighing-room.' He squeezed her arm. 'Stay here. I'll be out in a minute.'

He felt bad leaving her alone after what she had been through, but it had been her decision to come to Cheltenham and it was important to reach Bill with the information Angie had gleaned from Alice last night. One last obstacle, she had said – rather, three last obstacles. It made sense.

Jim Wilson was the first to see him. 'Can't keep you away from this place, can they?' he said. 'How's the back coming on?'

Paul waved his walking-stick. 'I'll be throwing this away soon,' he said.

'Good on yer, Pauly.'

Bill Scott was chatting to Dave Smart, a cup of tea in his hand. His ride in the first race had finished well down the field, but most of the tipsters in the morning papers had suggested that, if Tanglewood could beat Skinflint, the Kim Muir would be his.

'Hullo, it's Hopalong Sherlock,' Bill said as Paul approached. 'Any news?'

Paul smiled. He didn't blame Bill for being sceptical – foul play was part of racing and, if you worried about who was trying to stop you winning, you'd never get into the saddle. Sensing that he wasn't wanted, Dave Smart wandered off, leaving Bill and Paul alone.

'It's happening,' Paul said. 'We know for sure.'

'So I keep him covered up as long as possible.'

'They're going for you at the third past, the downhill fence.'

'How d'you know?'

'It doesn't matter. Stay in the centre of the course, covered up if possible, and leave the rest to me.'

Bill shrugged. 'No problem,' he said. 'I wouldn't have hit the front by the third last anyway.'

Wishing him luck, Paul was about to return to Angie when he saw Clay sitting alone in a corner.

Never had the man looked less like a jockey. He was too big, the colour on his fleshy cheeks was too pale, the expression on his face suggested that he would rather be anywhere than riding one of the favourites at Cheltenham.

Paul was standing in front of him for a moment before Clay came out of his daydreams.

'Ah, the poker expert,' he said, aiming unsuccessfully for a jocular, patronizing tone. 'What a surprise to see you here.'

'You told me it was all over. I don't believe you,' Paul said quietly. 'If your people try to stop Tanglewood today, the world's going to know about it.'

'I told you after our little game of poker,' Clay said. 'I'm finished with all that.'

'Is your friend Alice Markwick here?' Paul asked very suddenly.

'I haven't seen her. I have better things to do than worry about who's here to see me.'

'Seems ungrateful under the circumstances.' Paul made as if to move away, then added, as an afterthought, 'I believe she had a small accident last night. You might pay her a visit – ' he smiled ' – after you've ridden your winner.'

Outside the jockeys' changing-room Paul saw Ginnie Matthews waiting near the scales for Clay to weigh out.

'Is that bloody jockey of mine in here?' she asked Paul.

'He seems to have a lot on his mind,' Paul said. He hesitated, wondering whether to tell Ginnie that he was convinced friends of her owners were out to ensure that Skinflint won, but then thought better of it. Either way, she wasn't involved.

'Paul,' she said. 'We need to talk.'

'About Clay?' Paul asked wearily.

'No, about you.' Ginnie frowned. 'I need an assistant trainer and was wondering whether you would be interested.'

Paul's first thought was of Angie. She was not exactly in love with racing and the idea of more chilly days waiting outside weighing-rooms was unlikely to appeal to her. 'I'd need to think about it,' he said.

'No hurry.' Ginnie saw Clay walking gloomily towards the scales with the saddle under his arm. 'Here we go,' she said.

'Good luck, Mrs Matthews,' Paul said, touching her lightly on the arm.

At first he didn't recognize the couple as they walked towards the entrance to the paddock – the old man seemed too old, the woman more elegant and calm than he remembered. Then, as if she sensed his presence, Zena Wentworth turned and stared at them for a moment. Her father-in-law tottered on, ignoring her.

'That's Zena Wentworth, isn't it?' Angie asked.

'Aye,' said Paul, remembering the cold knowing hand as it edged up his thigh. 'Let's get down to the racecourse.'

But it was too late. Hands sunk deep in the pockets of her mink coat, Zena walked slowly towards Paul and Angie. 'I wanted to tell you the second thing,' she said simply.

'Second thing?'

'What I was about to tell you the other day on the telephone before I was interrupted.'

'You told me enough.' Paul made to move away, but Angie caught his arm.

'No,' she said. 'It might be important.' She turned to Zena. 'Go on, Mrs Wentworth.'

'*Cherchez le père*,' said Zena. Then, as if regretting what she had said, she turned and walked quickly towards the paddock.

'What on earth was that about?' Paul asked.

'The father,' said Angie. 'She's telling us Sir Denis is involved too.'

The decision to make the hit at the third fence from home was not stupid, Paul

reflected as he made his way down the course with Angie. Although, as Bill Scott
had pointed out, there was the risk of Tanglewood still being covered up by other
horses, there was a good chance at the end of three miles that the field would be
strung out. It was a downhill fence that often caused grief as jockeys kicked on
for home, so that there would be few awkward questions in the event of a crashing fall. The fact that the crowd around the fence was thinner than at the last two
fences would make Tanglewood an easier target.

'Anyone you recognize?' Paul asked as they crossed the course to the inside rail
where a group of photographers had gathered. Angie scanned the men as they chatted easily to one another and shook her head.

'I hope Alice Markwick was right about it being the third last,' she said
quietly.

Across the course, the crowd were now hurrying away from the paddock to place
bets or to take up a favoured vantage point in the stands. As the field of fifteen
made its way down to parade in front of the grandstand, Paul glanced at his racecard.

Under normal conditions, it was a race of limited interest to him. Tanglewood
was no more than a good handicapper but had the advantage of being ridden by
one of the best amateurs around. Skinflint, the class horse of the race, was carrying two distinct drawbacks – top weight and Mr Clay Wentworth. Beyond them,
there was a young Irish horse called Fiddlers Three whose best form had been over
two and a half miles, a grey mare from the north called Busy Lizzie and, also in
with a chance of a place, a big plain six-year-old called The Killjoy who was trained
by a successful permit holder down in the West Country.

As he headed the parade, Skinflint looked about him like a horse for whom
Cheltenham, with all its excitement and drama, was his natural home. Ginnie had
him looking superb and, briefly, Paul felt a pang of envy for Clay, who had done
so little to deserve a horse of his calibre.

Angie laid her hand on his as he leaned on his walking-stick. 'You're out there,
aren't you?' she said quietly. 'Whatever happens, you've got racing in the blood.'

'Yes.' Paul thought of his brief conversation with Ginnie Matthews, and knew
that he wanted to accept her offer. 'I'd rather be up there than down here.'

Like any good professional, the photographer had walked the course. Now he stood
some hundred years away from the jockey and his girlfriend across the course on
the stands side, and made his final plans.

Something had gone wrong last night, as he had known it would. The moment
Mrs Markwick had looked at the girl, there was trouble in the air. That brisk, cruel
competence had softened to something almost vulnerable. The photographer had
protested when she had told him that she would guard Raven's girlfriend until the
following day, but it was no good – Mrs Markwick had that look in her eyes and,
as usual, she got her way.

He took the machine with him, though. There was no way that he was going to
risk leaving that with her.

When he had called in the morning, there was no reply, and here was the girl,
free and with her boyfriend. The photographer ran a hand tenderly over the heavy

black machine that hung around his neck. It didn't matter. They couldn't stop him now.

His instructions were laughably simple.

In a darkened flat in Islington, Alice Markwick watched the field for the Kim Muir Steeplechase at Cheltenham parading before the stands. Her head was bandaged. She hated herself for last night. But she was confident. Not even Raven or his vicious little bitch of a girlfriend could stop the photographer now.

Freedom, at last.

'Good luck, Clay,' she said, and laughed.

None of the photographers at the third last fence had the look of a killer, Paul decided. Several of them he recognized as regulars at race meetings, freelances and agency men. A few of the racegoers had small cameras but nothing that answered the description of Opteeka B that Peter Zametsky had given him.

'I think we may be on the wrong side of the fence,' said Paul, glancing up the hill to the bend some hundred yards before it. 'You get a clearer view of the field as it's approaching the third last from the stand side.'

'Shall I stay here?' Angie asked quietly. 'Just in case you're wrong.'

The field were turning in front of the stand to canter down to the start. 'No, this time we stick together.'

It was as they were crossing the course that Paul saw the dark young man in a long leather coat pushing his way through the crowd on the stands side. Although he was hardly the typical Cheltenham spectator, the man had no camera. Languidly, he walked on the course, staring straight ahead of him.

A racecourse official nearby shouted, 'Horses coming!' and the leather-coated man, abandoning his dignity, scurried over to Angie's side of the course.

Paul looked across and smiled. A small-time spiv. There was nothing to worry about there.

Cazzo, he hated horses. Salvatore looked around him in the hope that no one had seen his moment of panic. A slim blonde girl glanced at him briefly, then turned away. She was just his type. Salvatore sighed – the sooner this business was over and he could return to his life of minor crime and major pleasure, the happier he would be.

Looking up the racecourse, he could see Giorgio in place at the second last fence. Doubtless Tino was covering the last. The waiting was over.

The man in the black leather coat had seemed absurd as Clay had cantered past him, leaning against Skinflint, who seemed to be pulling harder than usual today. That was one of the few points in favour of riding in races; it gave you a chance to look down at the people, mere spectators, who had come to see you.

Yes, this would be his last race, whatever happened. Briefly, he envisaged himself at some future National Hunt Festival, a solid comfortable figure in the paddock watching as some wretched little jockey was given a leg-up onto one of his horses. By then everybody would be happy – Ginnie, because Skinflint could be

ridden by a professional; his father, because he was no longer obliged to come racing; and, above all, Clay himself because he was grounded, his feet on *terra firma*
for the entire afternoon.

He cantered past the starter's rostrum, turned and trotted back to the first fence.
'Clear round, eh?' he said quietly, patting Skinflint in front of the fence.

'Are you going on?' Bill Scott asked him.

'We'll be up there,' Clay said, smiling palely. Normally he disliked this habit
jockeys had of asking what kind of race you intended to ride – it was like a business rival casually asking for details of your development plans – but he had no
worries with Scott or Tanglewood.

Briefly he wondered why Bill Scott had bothered to ask him whether Skinflint
would be among the front-runners. He was the sort of jockey who did his homework and would know how Skinflint was ridden. Of course, when Clay hit the
front at the top of the hill, rather than making his run later, Scott would be surprised – but then Tanglewood would be pulled from the rest of the field like a
thread from a skein of wool, into the sights of Opteeka B. Clay was confident that
he could outstay the rest of the field up the Cheltenham hill.

The starter stepped forward and, as the field circled around him, began to call
out the names of the jockeys.

Petrin felt comfortable in his new Savile Row suit. Perhaps, when this little stunt
was over, he could consider staying in Britain. Across the course, the field was
lining up. No, better stick to his plan; America was better. 'They're off,' said the
racecourse commentator.

'For Christ's sake, pretend to shoot some film!' Petrin nudged the overweight
figure before him. With a resentful sigh, Bernard Green looked into the eyepiece.
'Who'd have thought, when I joined the Party at Cambridge, that I'd end up as a
fake cameraman at a race meeting?' he muttered.

'You do it beautifully,' said Petrin, raising an expensive pair of binoculars to his
eyes.

After the first mile, Clay found himself wondering whether the plan to stop
Tanglewood had been necessary. Skinflint loved Cheltenham and seemed to
respond to the atmosphere of a big crowd. At every fence, he outjumped the horses around him, gaining so much in the air that Clay had difficult preventing him
from hitting the front.

As the field passed the stands, he was going easily in third place behind the grey
Busy Lizzie who had set a good pace, and the Irish horse Fiddlers Three. Four or
five lengths behind the leading group, the rest of the field was bunched up and, as
they turned into the country, Clay looked over his shoulder. There was no sign of
Tanglewood.

The pace quickened down the back straight and, when Busy Lizzie made a mistake at the waterjump, Clay had no alternative but to move up on the outside of
Fiddlers Three, whose jockey was already niggling at him. Behind him, the leaders of the following group were moving closer but, from the sound of the cracking whips and jockeys' curses, none of them was going as easily as Skinflint.

'Give him a breather going up the little hill before the open ditch,' Ginnie had said. 'Stay with them until the third last, then make the best of your way home.' Clay kicked Skinflint into the open ditch. The horse stood off outside the wings and landed two lengths in front of Fiddlers Three.

'Here we go,' muttered Clay. This was where he disobeyed his trainer's instructions. Bill Scott was too experienced a jockey to allow himself to be given the slip. As he set off in pursuit, he would provide a perfect unimpeded target for Clay's unofficial helper among the photographers.

Clay was five lengths clear as he gathered Skinflint for the downhill fence. He glanced at the crowd on the far side and, as if some distinct, instinctive part of his brain were tuned into the fatal laser of Opteeka B, he sat up straight in the saddle.

'No,' he screamed.

But it was too late.

It took Paul the briefest of moments to realize two things. The first was that the man operating Opteeka B was not standing by the fence but some fifty yards back. The second was that his target wasn't Tanglewood at all.

Simultaneously with Clay's scream, Skinflint faltered, his gallop becoming an unstoppable, drunken stagger into the base of the fence. Almost balletically, the horse's hindquarters formed an arc over the fence while miraculously, and fatally, Clay stayed in the saddle, his eyes dilated with horror as the earth hurtled towards him.

There was an unmistakeable crack as horse and jockey hit the ground together.

Beside him, Angie gasped. She had looked away from Skinflint up the hill. 'Look!' she said suddenly. 'It's – ' but already she was running.

'Angie!'

The photographer glanced back and, sensing trouble, he put the heavy camera under his arm and jogged, casually at first, up the hill.

'Bastard!' Angie kicked viciously at his trailing leg and as the man sprawled on his face, sending Opteeka B flying, she fell on him. By the time he had recovered from the shock, Paul stood over them, his walking-stick raised.

'It's him,' Angie said, breathing heavily as she stood over him. 'He's the man who kidnapped me last night.'

Behind them, the field was streaming up the hill to the Cheltenham roar, but already a small crowd was gathering around Paul, Angie and the photographer.

'My camera,' the man said weakly.

'Fetch the police,' Paul said to a young man in a dark leather coat who had just run up. Briefly the man looked alarmed, then muttering 'Yeah, sure,' he walked off quickly towards the stands.

Paul looked back to the fence, where Skinflint still lay on his side. A few yards away, two ambulancemen were crouched over the inert form of Clay Wentworth.

'Why Wentworth?' he asked the man cowering on the floor.

The photographer muttered, 'Orders from the top. Give me back my camera and I'll explain everything to you.'

'Camera?' Paul glanced at Angie, who shook her head. 'What camera?'

* * *

It didn't feel like triumph, merely the satisfaction of a job done well. Tonight, when the photographer returned, she would contact Petrin for the exchange – Opteeka B for financial security and freedom. Alice looked at the silent television screen on which presenters of a children's television show were dancing about in mute inanity. Perhaps, if Clay's race had not been the last to be televised, she would have been treated to a few more shots of her business partner, prostrate on the ground where he belonged.

She imagined that he was not badly injured, simply shaken up enough to understand that no man exploited Alice Markwick and emerged a winner.

There was a price for everything.

The machine was still warm. That was odd. Josef Petrin ran a hand over the dark metal of Opteeka B which lay on the passenger seat of his hired car. It had been so simple, so painless, so casual a victory, that he felt almost tenderly towards this country in which crime was as easy as picking up an object from the ground and merging into the crowd. Bernard had squawked when Petrin had told him to take the train back to London, but that had been an easy decision. The fat Englishman belonged to the past, to the days of grim ideology and patriotic duty; he wouldn't understand that times were different now, that it was every man for himself. Doubtless, Petrin's motherland could use a device like Opteeka B, but he was going private. This time tomorrow he would be in New York. The CIA maybe? There was too much risk there. He had been told the Mafia paid well for the right product. He even had a contact, a man called Guiseppi Vercelloni.

Petrin smiled. A new suit. A new toy. A new future. It had been a useful trip.

They stood in a gloomy little group outside the Treatment Room, as the last few racegoers made their way home, their conversation desultory and weary.

'How's the horse?' Paul asked.

Ginnie shrugged. 'Tough little bugger. He'll be a bit sore in the morning but the vet says nothing's broken.'

Again, Paul saw Skinflint turning, as if in slow-motion, the look of paralysed fear on Clay's face, the crack which, he now knew, was of a human bone not a horse's.

'They say our friend is co-operating with the police,' he said. 'Alice Markwick will be receiving a call at any moment.'

'There's no evidence,' Angie said quietly. 'What can they do without the laser?'

'Apparently the whole thing is documented at Markwick Instruments. The police had received a tip-off from Lol Calloway and picked up three Italians after the last race. They didn't have the camera but seemed to know something about it.'

The moment they saw Zena standing at the doorway to the Treatment Room, it was clear that questions were unnecessary.

'He's dead,' she said flatly. 'Broken neck. Multiple head injuries. He never regained consciousness.'

Angie stepped forward and took Zena by the arm.

'It was Alice Markwick,' said Paul. 'She wanted him out of the way.'

'No.' Sir Denis Wentworth appeared at the doorway and stood, staring across the racecourse. He seemed older, a diminished and pathetic figure. 'No,' he said. 'It was me.'

'He always was Daddy's boy,' Zena said with a trace of bitterness in her voice.

Sir Denis spoke as if in a trance. 'You want to ride horses, I told him, you ride to win. Prove yourself like I proved myself. Get yourself the best horse and win the best race. Then I'll know you're man enough to take over from me.' Tears filled his eyes at last. 'Of course, he couldn't do it the straight way, he had to cheat.'

'You old fool,' Zena turned on him savagely. 'He may have been weak but he was braver than you'll ever be. And more honest.'

'He was giving that horse a good ride,' Paul said. 'If it hadn't been for the Markwick woman – '

But Sir Denis had turned and was walking with silent dignity towards the car park, as if he knew his son better than anyone and that, whatever had happened, he had been right, that he had done it the Wentworth way. They watched him as he made his way out of the racecourse without once looking back, an old man, alone.

Chapter 16

It was high summer and, although he received the occasional call from journalists raking over the ashes of what had become known as 'The Wentworth Scandal', Paul had allowed his life to slip into the routine of an assistant trainer.

Sometimes, when leading the string out on a quiet old 'chaser called Slavedriver, he found himself thinking about Alex, about Clay Wentworth and the nightmarish events of last season, but the moment would pass. He had an unspoken agreement with Ginnie Matthews that nothing from the past should distract them from planning for the forthcoming season. Once, when they were walking past the field in which Skinflint had been roughed off for the summer, Ginnie had muttered, 'If only he knew,' and Paul had smiled but said nothing.

In September, he would be required to appear in court as a witness in the case of the Crown vs Alice Markwick in which the principal charge was one of aggravated manslaughter. Although the prototype for Opteeka B had disappeared, the evidence of the photographer had been enough to build a substantial case against her. A number of further charges relating to the way she ran her business were said to be under active consideration.

Paul avoided taking breakfast with Ginnie, preferring to spend the time with Angie who had moved in with him, working as a freelance nurse in the Lambourn area.

So she was there when Paul received the letter from Sir Denis Wentworth and was leaning over his shoulder as she read it, with growing astonishment, at the breakfast table.

Dear Mr Raven

I write to you regarding the death of my son Mr Clay Wentworth.

It is now almost four months since the unfortunate events at Cheltenham and I have had much time in which to consider them. As you may be aware, I hold you in no way responsible for Clay's accident although I find it regrettable that you did not think fit to inform the police of your suspicions of Mrs Markwick.

The blame, I accept, is hers, for her financial greed, and mine, for the unreasonable expectations I had of my son. To demand that he should 'prove himself' in a way that was independent of my influence was, I now see, an impossible burden for him to have carried. I regret this.

I have spoken briefly to my former daughter-in-law Zena Wentworth who believes that some sort of compensation is due to you for the accident which ended your career. Although my legal advisers tell me that you have no case in law against me, I have decided to make a one-off gesture of goodwill towards you.

As you may be aware, my son left his racehorses to me. I have resolved to sell all of them except for Skinflint. That horse is now legally yours.

I trust this meets with your approval. A formal letter follows. Mrs Matthews has been informed of my decision.

Please note that this action is taken without prejudice and is in no sense an admission of guilt.

Confirmation of receipt of this letter would be appreciated.

Yours sincerely

Sir Denis Wentworth

For a moment, there was silence as Paul read the letter again.

'His normal charming self, I see,' Angie said.

'Poor old bastard,' Paul said. 'It's probably as near to being generous as he's ever been.'

'What will you do?' asked Angie. 'We can't afford training fees.'

'If Ginnie comes in as a partner, I can.' Paul smiled. 'You can come racing again – you know how you like that.'

Standing behind him, Angie put both arms around him and kissed his ear. 'The humane, politically correct thing to do would be to retire him.'

'All right. After he's won his third Gold Cup.'

Angie laughed. 'You're a cruel bastard, Paul Raven,' she said, allowing her hand to slip inside his shirt.

Deep in thought, Paul took the hand, kissed it and stood up. He walked slowly towards the bedroom, then turned, smiling at the door. 'How about a celebration?' he asked.

'What about your career? Your horse? What about racing?' There was a hint of mockery in Angie's voice as she walked slowly towards him.

Paul put his arm round her.

'Racing can wait,' he said.